BLOOD
AND MONEY

BLOOD AND MONEY

The Saga of California®
A Western Story

ROBERT EASTON

Five Star
Unity, Maine

Copyright © 1998 by Robert Easton

Five Star Western
Published in conjunction with Golden West Literary Agency.

August 1998

First Edition

Five Star Standard Print Western Series.

The text of this edition is unabridged.

Set in 11 pt. Plantin by Al Chase.

Printed in the United States on permanent paper.

Library of Congress Cataloging in Publication Data

Easton, Robert Olney.
  Blood and money : the saga of California : a western
story / by Robert Easton. — 1st. ed.
    p.   cm.   (Five Star standard print western series)
  ISBN 0-7862-1154-7
  (hc : alk. paper)
  I. Title.
PS3509.A7575B58   1998
  813'.52—dc21   98-22721

Again for Jane

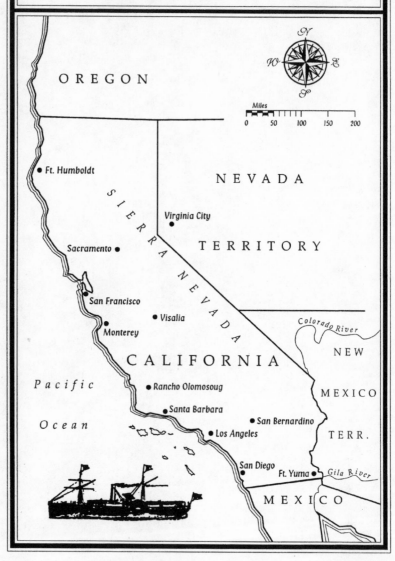

C·A·L·I·F·O·R·N·I·A
& ADJOINING REGIONS ◈ 1861

OREGON

N
W · E
S

Miles
0   50   100   150   200

● Ft. Humboldt

NEVADA

S I E R R A

● Virginia City

Sacramento ●

TERRITORY

N E V A D A

● San Francisco

● Visalia

● Monterey

Colorado River

NEW

CALIFORNIA

Pacific

● Rancho Olomosoug

MEXICO

● Santa Barbara

Ocean

● San Bernardino

TERR.

● Los Angeles

● San Diego

Ft. Yuma ●

Gila River

MEXICO

Chapter One

As she sat dozing on the verandah at her Rancho Olomosoug on the Central California coast, a hand fell on old Clara Boneu's shoulder, and she heard the voice of her beloved granddaughter-in-law Sally: "Wake up, *Mama Grande!* A war's broke out!" It was April, 1861.

Clara shook her head irritably. "War? Where?"

"Back East. Americans fightin' each other!"

"The *gringos?* Let them kill each other off and good riddance!" the old woman snorted, straightening herself in her cowhide chair and brushing her fiery red hair from her forehead. "Look what they've done to our valley! Look at that dust cloud!" But, when she turned to point to the great dark cloud that had been there so vividly for her a moment earlier, there was no cloud, only a few wisps of dust blowing up the valley from the newly plowed fields of the *gringo* squatters hardly a mile from where she sat.

"You must have been dreamin', Grandmama!"

Had it been a dream? Or a premonition? Clara shook her head again. "I must have fallen asleep." Yet, intuitively, she didn't doubt the truth of her vision of the dark cloud, for she had lived long enough to recognize the verities that speak to us in their own way.

Daughter of a Chumash chieftainness, widow of a Spanish *conquistador*, Clara had been a child of nine when she had first seen white men ride into what was now called the Santa Lucia Valley. She had been present at that fateful first contact between two races. She had helped welcome the strangers as gods and benefactors, had fallen in love with and had later married fair-haired Antonio Boneu, and with him had created this great

Rancho Olomosoug of which she, Clara, once known as Lospe the Flower, daughter of the People of the Land and the Sea, was now mistress. Her beloved Antonio lay buried there atop that dome-shaped hill across the valley — beyond those wisps of dust — beyond those fields of wheat and barley and pastures with cattle and horses which she'd thought of as his as well as hers — beyond the Indian Village by the river where, as she and he had once dreamed, her people would be free to live as they'd always lived, or otherwise if they chose. The dome-shaped hill looked down at her every day, and she imagined Antonio doing so, too.

Now she turned indignantly back to Sally. Her granddaughter-in-law was blonde, blue-eyed, freckle-faced. Sally was a squatter's daughter, a *gringa*. Yet, Sally embodied Clara's dream of a unity of races and of cultures. Like herself, Sally had married outside her own kind, yet had never turned her back on them. Clara saw the future in willowy, tough-minded Sally. If only she could have a son. If only Pacifico weren't inept in that way as in so many others. "Now, what's all this about a war?"

"Father O'Hara just came from town with the news. Here he is!"

Still youthful despite his forty-eight years, gray robe swirling around him as he stepped purposefully onto the verandah, Father Michael O'Hara had been momentarily detained by the many who came to greet him on his periodic visit to bless, baptize, marry, and, if need be, bury members of Clara's numerous household. "Ah, *Tía* Clara, there you are!" The Franciscan had first arrived in this valley years ago to restore, by zeal alone if necessary, the crumbling ruin that was Mission Santa Lucia and to renew its illustrious past which, he had discovered, included this old woman who had been baptized and educated there as a girl. To him, Clara was a mother figure, a rich resource of information and wisdom, so old yet so vital she was like time itself without apparent beginning or end. His hair was red like hers. A front tooth chipped in a school-yard fight and a black patch over his right eye indicated that his way might not have been easy. "Has Sally told you?"

"More than I wish to hear!" Clara held out her hand. He kissed it. To her, he was solace, support, confessor. She motioned to the chair beside her, and he dropped into it with the intimacy of long friendship. "More than I wish to hear!" she repeated with emphasis. "Haven't we had enough bloodshed already? You lack an eye because you were looking on during one of our many quarrels. Haven't we had enough bloodshed right here?" she stormed, having gotten her wind up. "Indian and Spaniard, Spaniard and Mexican, Mexican and American . . . and now the Americans have begun fighting each other? What's the matter with the human race?"

"You've been looking at it longer than I," O'Hara chuckled. "You tell me."

She searched his face. Then suddenly calm: "Sometimes I wonder if you're not right . . . there is no salvation without the shedding of blood. What's happening?"

He told of Fort Sumter having been fired on by South Carolina troops, of President Lincoln's call for seventy-five thousand volunteers, of Confederate President Jefferson Davis's counter-call for eighty thousand Southerners. "It means national war, civil war. North against South."

"And the West?"

"It may divide us, too." He motioned toward the squatters' cabins down the valley, meaning that the Jenkins family, Sally's family, were of Southern origin. "We may have here the nation in a nutshell."

"But I don't want the nation in a nutshell!" Clara cried. "I've had enough. I'm old. I'm sick of trouble, sick of the fools

9

who make it for themselves and the rest of us. Let them kill each other off, I say, and let us have our land back as it was before the Americans came and stole it from us and plowed it all up and caused all that dust. You saw that huge black cloud, didn't you?" she demanded sharply.

O'Hara nodded indulgently, though, like Sally, he'd seen no cloud. Catching the look they exchanged, Clara snorted: "Oh, I know you two think I'm losing my mind." And when they protested, she suddenly became serious: "What is this going to mean for us, Father?"

They were interrupted by the clatter of horses' hoofs on the stones of the interior courtyard and shouts of welcome, and after a moment her grandson, Pacifico, and his chum, Benito, appeared. They were dusty and sweat-stained and looked as if they'd ridden far and hard as they exchanged formal greetings with O'Hara and casual ones with Sally and bowed obediently to Clara.

"And where have you two been?" she demanded, as if they were wayward boys rather than married men.

"Chasing wild bulls, *Mama Grande*. Catching them, too!" Pacifico cried, looking toward Benito for corroboration. "Right, Benny?" Pacifico was tall and fair, Benito short and dark. Benito was usually the leader, Pacifico the follower. Clara's interest was roused.

"Bulls? Where?"

"In the clearing among the pines. Mine got away. Benito caught his. A black of the old Spanish strain."

"Yours would get away," she scoffed. And to Benito more charitably: "What did you do with yours?" Benito was the son of her friend, Santiago Ferrer, the storekeeper in town who supplied her with goods and advice. She'd known Benito all his twenty-two years and liked him and his wife, Anita.

"*Tia* Clara, I left my bull tied to a tree to calm him. I hope

10

that meets with your approval." He was fond of his Aunt Clara. Her tirades didn't bother him.

"Well, I wish you'd tell the rest of the country to calm down," she stormed on. "Listen to what Father O'Hara has to say!"

The priest told them about the war. Pacifico's reaction was so instantaneous it stabbed into Sally like a knife blade. "Let's go to it, Benny, what say?" It seemed proof he didn't love her.

"Why not?" Benito agreed, with a wink at Sally, and she wondered what Pacifico may have told him about their marriage, or what he had guessed.

"Don't speak such foolishness," Clara declared. "Why, you wouldn't even know which side to join!" A palpable falsehood. The secession of Southern states, occurring over the past five months, had been much discussed in the valley, and she well knew that Pacifico's and Benito's loyalties were like hers. Clara didn't side with the great plantation owners of the South. Slavery was not for her. Nevertheless, she continued to scold. "You'd run away and leave Sally and me, and leave Benito's beautiful Anita and those two adorable children, to fend for ourselves? I never heard such nonsense!"

"I was just joking." Pacifico tried to placate her, though the thought of escaping her displeasure and his increasingly loveless marriage suddenly began to appeal to him seriously.

"No, you're serious. I can tell!" And she rounded upon the grandson she secretly adored: "You, the man of this family! You who wear at your belly the belt with the silver buckle I stripped from your father and gave you as head of this household when he ran off to the wilderness to play wild Indian! With all the troubles I have" — waving one hand down the valley toward the squatters, the other toward the dark mountains of the interior — "your father a hunted renegade back there! The *gringos* overrunning our land! The price of beef falling, and my debts mounting! And now you want to run off and play soldier?"

Sally intervened anxiously. "Benito, you surely wouldn't leave Anita and the children?" Their marriage had proved happy and fruitful, hers troubled and barren. She suspected that Pacifico was seeing other women, and she waited for some affirmation of his love, but his eyes didn't meet hers, and she decided he might, indeed, use the war as a means of escape.

"Oh, it wouldn't be for long," Benito replied lightly. "We'd be home in three months. How can eleven Southern states stand against twenty-three Northern ones?"

Sally flared up. "If you're both serious, I say good riddance! If you want to go, go ahead!"

"Let's hear no more of this nonsense," Clara ordained.

Pacifico stood silent, embittered, hating her for so often opposing him, so often comparing him to the absent father he didn't love and who didn't love him. And he passionately wished his mother had lived to know and be known by him. He suddenly felt it might be very good to be free of this domineering old woman and the wife he no longer loved. "It may be my patriotic duty to go, Grandmama," he replied stubbornly.

"Mine, too," chimed in Benito. Sensing his friend's resolve hardening, his began to do likewise, though for a quite different reason. His marriage had been so happy it had become boring. He hunted wild cattle because it was a relief from the constraints of domestic bliss.

Clara turned imploringly to O'Hara. "Speak to them, Father. They're out of their minds. Besides," she scoffed, "the *gringos* won't accept them. They'll call them greasers and turn them away!"

O'Hara raised both hands with a deprecating smile. "I think they've been sufficiently spoken to." It saddened him to see

Clara making a fool of herself, driving out what she most longed to keep. Hoping to smooth matters, he took his silver snuffbox from the pocket of his robe and offered it to her. "Yes," he continued benignly, "though I should never wish to stand in another's way, I see we have much to do right here to keep the peace."

Clara declined the snuff, but drew a cigarette of native tobacco from the pocket of her Mother Hubbard and lit it with one of the new-style friction matches. O'Hara took a pinch of snuff, stuffed his nostrils, and sneezed. "How will this war affect my claim to my ranch?" she asked as if the others were not present. For years her claim had been in litigation under the new American law, requiring her to establish title to land where she'd lived all her life, and now her case was before the Supreme Court of the United States in far-off Washington City.

"It may make things harder."

"And more costly? Yes, there's always money." And that reminded her of her growing dependency on the San Francisco financier, Eliot Sedley. Sedley had loaned her money to pay her legal bills and other debts. He had taken as security a mortgage that could make her ranch his any time he chose to foreclose. "I'm afraid Eliot will be so busy making money in the war, he'll have no time for my affairs."

"Knowing him, I think he'll not forget you. I think he has your interests genuinely at heart."

"Sometimes I wonder."

So they talked on, engrossed in what they were saying, and, when they turned to look for them, the young people had disappeared.

"I'm afraid they've gone their own way," sighed Clara.

"Yes," agreed O'Hara, "as they must, and as we must realize."

"Was I too harsh? I had to speak my mind, didn't I? I had to make myself clear?"

"But perhaps not quite so clear, my dear. You can be rather overpowering, you know."

"Oh, Father, I hope I've not made a terrible mistake!"

Chapter Two

Three hundred miles northward in San Francisco, Eliot Sedley, the cool, sagacious financier who held the mortgage on Clara's ranch, was dining privately with his hot-headed Secessionist father-in-law, George Stanhope, in an elegant bordello on upper Washington Street. Sedley was thirty-seven, Stanhope ten years older. Stanhope was massive, imperious, with prow-like nose and short, pugnacious upper lip. Sedley was only of medium size, but even while sitting down he loomed large. His gray eyes and level tone emanated authority and good sense as well as a promise of ruthlessness if need be. They were discussing the war as they enjoyed the New Orleans style meal Madam St. Clair had personally prepared and served. But before bringing them their *café brûlot*, she eavesdropped discreetly at the kitchen door. Exotic Mary Louise Jackson, to use the name she went by in other company, was part black, part white, and could pass as either. Once Stanhope's slave, now Sedley's lover, she played a triple rôle tonight as hostess, mistress, and secret Union informant.

"Why isn't this the time for us to rise and seize California for the Confederacy?" she heard Stanhope ask impatiently. A native Louisianan temporarily transplanted to San Francisco, Stanhope fostered a network of Southern sympathizers throughout the state as part of a nationwide effort. Here, as elsewhere, they were known as the Knights of the Golden Circle. Buckingham Jenkins, Sally's uncle, whose family occupied the two squatter cabins on Clara Boneu's ranch, was an ardent member. "My boys are spoiling to get into this fight," Stanhope continued. "So am I."

"But the war's hardly begun," Sedley cautioned amiably.

Stanhope's zeal was beyond question. His judgment was another matter. And whichever side won this war, Sedley intended to be on it. He was one of the richest and most powerful men in California, and he never committed himself until he was sure what he was doing. "Would it be wise to rise now when the Federals are expecting it?"

But Stanhope persisted. "If we wait, we may be too late. Now, while people are making up their minds which flag to follow, they can be led either way."

"With the Unionists in firm control of the military?" Sedley raised his eyebrows persuasively. "You don't want another fiasco like Alcatraz, do you?"

Against Sedley's advice Stanhope and his firebrands had planned to seize Alcatraz, the island fortress in the bay, turn its huge guns on San Francisco, and demand the city's surrender. The commander of all U. S. Army forces in California, General Albert Sidney Johnston, himself a Southerner, had rebuffed their secret solicitations and had warned against "any such treason."

"That was before the war broke out," Stanhope objected, "before Johnston felt able to show his true colors." The famous general had resigned his commission and departed for Los Angeles on his way to join the Confederacy.

"Even so, will an uprising work now?" Sedley countered. "The Federals are rushing reinforcements from Washington Territory. Little Phil Sheridan arrived with a contingent this afternoon. They know what the stakes are. As California goes, so goes the West Coast. So goes the war, maybe. Besides, they've got their eye on you as they have on Johnston. No, I'd wait a bit if I were you."

Stanhope flared out. "You say *you*, not we. Sometimes I wonder which side you're really on!"

"Better for me to appear neutral, as in the past," Sedley

rejoined calmly. "That way I can be of more help. You heard what I said at lunch." They had met at noon with their Los Angeles henchman, Earl Newcomb. "I said . . . 'Earl, wait and see. We don't want to lose the state like we did Alcatraz, by moving before the time is ripe.'"

Stanhope subsided with a frown, sitting back in his red velvet chair, fingering his glass of champagne, then refilling and draining it, while Sedley took a sip from his. "You're probably right as usual, damn you, Eliot. You're a cool customer, too cool for my taste sometimes." But there was respect in Stanhope's tone. "We can't do it without you, that's sure."

A native of Boston, Sedley had dropped out of Harvard to sail around the Horn in one of his family's ships to trade along the California coast. That was how he had first met old Clara and fallen in love with Rancho Olomosoug. He had stayed on the coast and had seen the sleepy Mexican village of Yerba Buena on the shore of San Francisco Bay transformed by the Gold Rush of 1849 into a bustling seaport metropolis, now numbering sixty-thousand inhabitants from nearly every country on earth. Taking advantage of opportunities, Sedley had prospered mightily. The waterfront lots he had bought for fifteen dollars were now worth fifty thousand. His mines poured out gold. His mills poured our lumber. His bank fostered developments of many kinds. His ships brought in and carried out goods at enormous profit, while his farm and ranch lands with their wheat, grapes, cattle, and sheep yielded him perhaps the greatest richness of all: that sense of owning, of belonging, of being king of all you survey. But Sedley was a silent ruler, preferring to wield power quietly, to control unobtrusively from behind the scenes as in the case of Rancho Olomosoug and old Clara.

Stanhope, by contrast, relished the limelight as a Southern

17

leader. Like his old friend and fellow planter, Jefferson Davis, he was a political dreamer on a grand scale. They had served together in the war against Mexico. Long before this war broke out, they had been dreaming of moving California onto the Southern side in a struggle they saw as inevitable. "With California's gold," Davis had told Stanhope, "a confederacy of Southern states would be financially solvent and would reach from Atlantic to Pacific, with the possibility of extending its power into Mexico, Central America, and the Caribbean Islands."

"Suppose," Sedley continued calmly now, "you were to wait and see what happens to General Johnston? If the most sought-after man in the country escapes across the deserts of Southern California and the wilds of New Mexico Territory to Texas, then turns around and leads an army back this way, what a decisive moment *that* will be! The man Lincoln offered a major-general's commission, the man Lincoln hoped would head his Northern army, that man coming to California at the head of Southern troops? That could be the time to rise, George. You asked my opinion. There it is."

"I like the sound of what you say," conceded Stanhope a little tipsily, face flushed by the Dom Pérignon plus the wine taken earlier. "I wish more Yankees were like you. There'd be no war."

Sedley shrugged off the compliment. "What's the latest from our loved ones in New Orleans?" His marriage three years ago to Stanhope's desirable daughter, Victoria, had been hailed as a fortuitous union between North and South. He had seen it quite unromantically as a chance to align himself with a Southern aristocracy that dominated California and the nation. She had seen it as union with rising wealth and power. Now Victoria and her mother, Sarabelle, and brother, Beauford, back home on a visit, had been trapped in New

Orleans by the Union blockade of the port.

"Beau has enlisted in my old regiment."

"You must be very proud of him."

"Yes, I'd be there with him if it weren't for all I have in hand here. Damn, I'd like to take a crack at the Yankees myself, Eliot. They've forced this war on us. When I think of those New Englanders and New Yorkers getting rich off our cotton and trade, while piously decrying slavery, I get mad. Didn't they sell us the slaves in the first place?"

"My father sold them to your father. It's as simple as that, George."

"And don't they know we've got two hundred thousand free Negroes in the South prospering and not bellyaching one whit . . . and some of 'em has got slaves of their own?"

"No, I don't think they do know."

"And don't they realize we regard the Negro as our sacred trust," Stanhope ranted on, "to Christianize and elevate to the status of civilized human beings? As for that baboon, Lincoln," — Stanhope's face grew livid — "he escaped assassination in Baltimore three months ago on his way to Washington to be inaugurated, but he mayn't be so lucky next time."

"You don't wish Honest Abe harm, do you?"

"Do I! He's the most hated man in American history, Eliot. You know that as well as I. He didn't get one vote in our Southern states. Even in the North he'd never have won without that three-way split. He's a minority president, and he shouldn't be allowed to wreck our nation. Somebody's got to stop that maniac before he brings disaster on all of us. Why, he wants to Africanize this country. If he's not stopped, we'll be a nation of mulattos and quadroons!"

Mary Louise, quietly listening at the door, gritted her teeth. She'd like to see Stanhope dead, but far better, she reasoned, to have her arch enemy useful to her and the Union cause.

19

Through him the innermost secrets of the Confederacy might be revealed, and that could be sweet revenge for monstrous wrongs. At his Louisiana plantation Stanhope had raped her and had continued to molest her until she ran away to the North, leaving their young daughter, Hattie, in his hands. Years later, having married the wealthy white man, James Jackson, and having been widowed, Mary Louise had returned as operative on the Underground Railroad to rescue her daughter. She had dogged Stanhope and his family to San Francisco. Here, under the alias of Madam St. Clair, masked also by being Sedley's housekeeper and mistress, she had succeeded in freeing Hattie with the help of the city's underground. Now her powerful clients and her intelligence network of black porters, waiters, stewards, barbers, cooks, and maids provided valuable information to the Northern cause.

"Do you want me to go to New Orleans and fetch our womenfolk?" Sedley offered Stanhope soothingly. "There are blockade runners from Mexico."

"No, Vicky's mother's very ill. She wouldn't leave her. Besides, we've got property that needs looking after . . . the plantation as well as the house in town. Vicky can look after things. She's a capable girl, Eliot."

"That's one reason I married her." Sedley let a note of conclusion come into his voice. "I'm going to Sacramento City tomorrow to meet with Stanford and others about a railroad linking California with the East. Stanford's just back from Washington. He's talked to Lincoln, says the railroad will have the support of the President and Congress. I'll let you know what develops. Meanwhile, keep me informed. And if I were you, I'd tell your firebrands to keep cool. Wait and see what happens to General Johnston. As Earl Newcomb told us at lunch, Southern sympathy is strong in Los Angeles. It may be your best place to start an uprising, with or without Johnston, even if it does have only five thousand inhabitants, including dogs."

But Stanhope wasn't ready to terminate. Petulantly he complained: "You've never cut me in on your railroad scheme. What's the matter?"

"The matter is, my friend," said Sedley, with just a shade of testiness, "that Stanford, Huntington, Hopkins, the Crockers are all Abolitionists, all anti-slavery. They might ride a Southern Slave Democrat like you out of Sacramento on a fence rail, tarred and feathered."

"Damn their black Republican hearts!" Stanhope flared up again. "You know the day I'm waiting for? The day Jefferson Davis rides into Sacramento on their god-damned railroad and stands there as President of this state, too, having ridden to it on rails laid with their nigger-loving Yankee money! Let 'em build their railroad, Eliot. Let 'em build it. Then we'll take it over and use it, eh?"

"Right, George. That's a good one!" Inwardly weary, outwardly amiable as ever, Sedley raised his glass.

"You'd like Davis, Eliot. He's a fine gentleman. Little too moderate, that's all. I want you to meet him sometime."

"Let's drink to that! And to General Johnston!" And they did.

Mary Louise decided she could delay no longer. "Your coffee, gentlemen." She entered with two cups of *brûlot* on a tray. Each contained a strip of orange peel studded with cinnamon and cloves and cooked in brandy New Orleans style. She was wearing a simple black crinoline with wide white collar. Its simplicity set off her hourglass figure and the exotic beauty of her patrician features with their olive complexion. She moved with easy confidence, so changed by time and circumstances, such artful use of rice powder and straightened hair, that Stanhope no longer recognized her as his former slave and concubine. Sedley knew nothing of their earlier relationship. Thus she deceived both men for survival's sake and to liberate her people from slavery. She'd heard much tonight that could be useful when transferred to proper ears in her underground of Abolitionists and Northern sympathizers.

Stanhope made an unsteady attempt to put his arm around her as she set his cup before him, but she evaded him deftly.

"Don't be impatient, George," Sedley chaffed him, "that can be your great failing." And to her: "Where are you keeping Dolly?"

"Yeah, where's my Dolly?" Stanhope echoed with a lecherous wink.

"Dol-lee!" Mary Louise called commandingly. A moment later a gorgeous strawberry blonde entered by the other door. She's was wearing what looked like a pink negligee. Stanhope's face lit up. "By God, it's about time we got down to business!"

Later Sedley and Mary Louise laid talking together in her silk-canopied four-poster, the cool air of early morning blowing over them from the open window. Sedley seldom slept in his Rincon Hill mansion these nights. It was as though he were a bachelor again, and Mary Louise once more his housekeeper. Their relationship was open, unpossessive, no entanglements other than mutual self-interest. She never mentioned her Northern sympathies or Southern antipathies. Nor did he reveal all of himself to her. She said now: "I've a little money I might invest. What would you advise?" For years he'd helped her make money. It amused him to do this, tickled his sense of the bizarre which their relationship embodied.

"I might give you a tip, if you promise to be nice to me."

"You tip me first."

He chuckled at her shrewdness. "My Big Bonanza Mine at the Comstock Lode over in Nevada Territory has struck a new vein of high-grade silver. When the news gets out, its shares will skyrocket. Now what do I get in return?"

She gave herself to him with that yielding, yet withholding, that tantalized him, that increased her mystery and his desire. Sedley was the most sexually powerful man she'd ever known, and he satisfied her completely in that way as in many others, and she satisfied him likewise.

Chapter Three

Deep in the wilderness where they'd been hiding, Clara's outlaw son, Francisco, and his twelve-year-old son, Helek, of whose existence she'd never dreamed, were descending the slope of Iwihinmu, the sacred mountain. Naked except for waistnets, they wore flint knives thrust through the topknots of their dark hair. They were following the condor that seemed fixed in the sky ahead, its wings unmoving as it rode the air as if by magic, for it was Sacred Condor, their dream helper and that of their Chumash ancestors since immemorial time.

Francisco was showing his son the world. He and his second wife, Ta-ahi, had decided that, despite the risk, it must be done. Their Helek must be shown a larger reality in order to increase his chances for survival. Back in the family's hideaway in the lee of the great mountain, Ta-ahi waited with Letke, her fifteen-year-old daughter from her first mating, and prayed for the return of husband and son.

"How does Condor know where he's going?" Helek asked.

"Because he sees what cannot be seen by human eyes." Francisco reiterated words taught him in his youth by old Tilhini, the wise man, his mentor in the ways and beliefs of his mother's people. And as if it heard him speak, the great bird turned and came soaring back in a wide arc, and, as it passed close overhead, it cocked its bald red head down at them as if to see if they were following, if they were measuring up, as it surveyed them with its ages-old red eye, at the same time revealing in sharp outline the triangular patch of white feathers under each black wing. And then it turned again and glided on westward toward the lowlands and the sea.

Following it, they descended from the pines to the chaparral country and came at mid-afternoon to the Cave of the Condors as Francisco guessed they might, though he had made no mention of it, lest his son's expectations be unduly roused. This was the very place he had been brought as a boy by old Tilhini, guiding him on such a quest as he was guiding Helek now. Francisco felt the condor had led them truly as he looked up the hillside at the scallop-shaped opening in the rock that was the dark mouth of the cave and saw with amazement a human figure standing there.

Yes, it was old Tilhini, and, yes, Tilhini was painting the rock, and Francisco remembered this was the season of the summer solstice when such painting was traditionally done, and he thought that time had stood still and years counted as nothing.

Placing a cautionary hand on Helek's arm, he whispered that the astrologer-priest was keeping the forces of the universe in balance while communing with the Sky People. "As he paints, he prays, so that our middle world may be in harmony with those above and below. Come quietly."

As they drew closer, they followed the movement of Tilhini's yucca-fiber brush from the pigment containers in his waistnet to the rock and back again. The old man's back was toward them, and he was painting something upon something else. They saw it was a human figure, in deep sky blue outlined with red, superimposed upon the white outline of a spread-winged bird.

"Welcome," Tilhini suddenly said, his back still toward them, continuing to paint though evidently aware of them all along.

"Greetings, old father," cried Francisco joyfully. "I did not expect to find you here."

"Why not?" demanded Tilhini roughly, still painting, still not turning his head. "It is the season." Then abruptly he faced them. "Why should I not be here? Because you thought me dead, and the old ways forgotten? But they are not forgotten, and I am not dead, as you see. But who is this?" His eyes fell upon Helek so piercingly that the boy felt as if struck by them.

"This is my son, old father. Like me when I was young, he comes seeking. I'm showing him the world."

Tilhini nodded with approval. He seemed as old as time, but vigor shone from his eyes and joy at what they saw. He was naked except for his waistnet, and his skin was the color of earth and, therefore, like Helek's and Francisco's, but the hair that came down to his shoulders was white rather than black. To Francisco, he seemed part of that vanished past when he himself, the half-breed — only child of the Indian princess, Lospe, later known as Clara, and the famous *conquistador*, Antonio — first entered this world. They had wanted him to follow their illustrious footsteps and embody, as they had, a union of two peoples, two ways of life. But he had not followed. First a spendthrift and playboy in the white man's world, now an outlaw and resister, he had chosen his own way, and it had led him into an unhappy marriage with fashionable Constanza, then, after her death in childbirth, it had led him away from the son named Pacifico he didn't want and back into the wilderness to join a band of refugees from white encroachment. Among them he had found a happy marriage and from it emerged another son, this son whom he wanted as he wanted life itself. Above all, he had found a purpose. Their fellow refugees had been hunted down or driven by desperation to find safety on the reservation or at his mother's Indian village, but he and his family remained firm in their wild freedom.

All this crossed his mind as he looked at Tilhini, so ancient he couldn't last much longer, yet as enduring as the rock on which he painted, and Francisco's heart ached for all that Tilhini represented, all that he said without speaking.

"Old father," he continued, "we have come, my son and I, to find once more the ancient way and to know the world. Sacred Condor, our dream helper, such as you are over-painting there, has led us. It seems propitious that we find you here. But I cannot believe it is by chance."

Tilhini's naked belly glistened in the sun. Joy continued to well up in his eyes like spring water, sweet and cool yet self-contained and measured. "Something told me you would come, my son. Something was leading me, too. It is not easy," he continued with a sigh. "The breath grows short, the legs are heavy." The long journey into the wilderness from Clara's Indianada had been a challenge, Francisco could tell, as the old arms embraced him, and then Helek, and he felt their love and warmth, though Helek couldn't help shrinking a little under the touch of this desiccated old stranger.

Sensing this, Tilhini said kindly: "Come, and I shall show you wonders." And taking the boy by the hand, he led him inside the cave, Francisco following, while Tilhini explained the paintings on the walls, telling how great seers and artists of past times were inspired to do them — the red sun disk, the white moon crescent, the fiery comets with their streaming tails, the symbol like the head of a garden rake that represents rain.

At the far end of the cave, alone upon that entire wall, they came to a large, rather crude figure outlined in black. It resembled the scarecrow in Tilhini's corn patch back at the Indianada, and, thinking of this, Francisco marveled again at the old man's transformation from ranch worker into seer and painter, last of an ancient line.

"This is Sacred Condor," Tilhini told Helek. "You've seen an actual condor. Both are one and the same."

Awed but not intimidated Helek inquired: "How can that be?"

27

"It simply is. Only Kakunupmawa knows why."

Moving on, Tilhini pointed to the water skater who serves as messenger between Sky People and humans, and the fiery mandala that stands for the universe. "And now we come to what is most important of all." Tilhini paused before a small hole in the eastern wall through which daylight could be seen through the rock. "This is the eye of Kakunupmawa." And he explained how the rising sun at the winter solstice enters the hole and illumines the interior of the cave, as it illumines all the world. But the hole also constitutes the head of a complex humanoid figure in red and blue and green and yellow. Tilhini contemplated it silently.

"What is it, father?" Francisco prodded him.

"It is Kakunupmawa." Tilhini invoked the words and the thought behind them reverently. "God almighty."

"Why does he have that hole for his head?" Helek blurted out.

"Because," replied the old man gravely, "that hole *is* his head. He is the hole, the painting, and the world outside and the sky above. He is everywhere, everything. All is Kakunup-mawa. Through that hole we enter into him, and he enters into us."

Son and father fell silent before the old man's words and the significance of the painting.

"And now what is it you want of me?" Tilhini asked, resuming an everyday tone as he conducted them back to the outer world.

Francisco knew his moment had come. "Wisdom and truth, old mentor. My son seeks knowledge of the world and a true path into it."

"Nothing in the world is without a name. Does he have a name?"

"Only what his mother and sister and I call him. He lacks

a name such as only you can give, a true name, such as you once gave me."

Tilhini smiled enigmatically, yet with pleasure, too, and even benign amusement. "But does *he* want a true name? Let him speak."

"I do," Helek answered gravely, sensing the momentousness of this occasion.

Tilhini turned to Francisco. "He is too young to have lain with a woman. But has he eaten any fat or greasy foods lately?"

"Only the seed meal like yours that we carry in our waist-nets."

"He has never taken momoy?" — meaning the extract of the hallucinogenic datura plant.

"Never."

The old man turned to Helek. "My son, do you want to go on a vision quest?"

"Yes, old father." Helek had never heard of a vision quest, but it sounded inviting.

"Then let us begin." Taking a small wooden bowl from his waistnet, Tilhini poured a few drops of water into it from the basketry jug which stood against the rock nearby. Then, taking four flat white seeds from his deerskin pouch, he placed them in the water, macerated them with a small pestle of green stone, tasted the mixture, added three more drops, tasted again. "Now you will have a dream," he said invitingly, "in which your true name will be revealed, as your father's once was, here on this very spot. Drink, and it will taste both bitter and sweet," he added, "for momoy is like life itself. Drink, and remember everything you see in your dream. Do you hear? Everything!" Though feeling a little apprehensive Helek nodded obediently and drank. "Lie down and be still," Tilhini commanded kindly. Helek lay down on the dusty earth at the cave's entrance. "This is the beginning of your vision quest. It is a first step along the ancient path. Close your eyes."

Already the old man's words and image were receding into a darkness that quickly became as bright as day, and Helek found himself soaring like a bird, higher and higher, arms outspread and covered with feathers like a bird's wings, until he was so high he could see all the world below, and at the mouth of the cave, sitting beside his body, the tiny figures of Tilhini and his father. On and on he soared till he came to a golden valley. Down its center a sky-blue river ran and emptied into a body of blue water, endlessly vast, such as he had never seen before but which must be the sea his father had described and he had often imagined.

Filled with wonder, he soared on until he saw, directly below in the valley, a great house such as his father had described as having lived in as a boy, with smaller houses around it and strangely dressed people with white skins coming and going from it and strange four-legged animals standing nearby it. And also nearby, at the river's edge, was a village of thatched huts where people with skin like his own were coming and going and bathing in the stream. All of it glowed with a marvelous light as if with magic.

Suddenly Helek found himself down there among those strangers of differing skins, who turned gladly as one person and came to welcome him, an old woman at their head who must have been his famous grandmother; and, as she and the others opened their arms to embrace him, perversity seized him, and he slipped through their embraces and became a bird again — almost against his will, it seemed. Soaring high, he left them diminishing far below, arms uplifted toward him, while he returned and reëntered his body at the mouth of the cave.

Opening his eyes, he suddenly felt sick at his stomach. Tilhini and his father sat beside him. It was growing dark.

"What did you see?" Tilhini inquired gently. Before Helek could answer, he vomited. "That's all right." Tilhini spoke casually as if nothing unusual had happened. "Here, take a drink." He handed him the basketry bottle. Helek sat up, drank, felt better. "You have been with momoy, Mother Truth," Tilhini continued. "What has she shown you?"

Helek told what he had seen, but it now seemed so fantastic as to be unbelievable.

Tilhini nodded reassuringly. "All is as it should be."

"But what does it mean, father?" Francisco broke in.

"It means he, like you, is Helek . . . the Hawk . . . the far flyer, the lone hunter, the solitary seeker after truth."

Francisco was astounded. He had not told Tilhini the boy's name. "Is Helek his true name, then?"

"Helek is his true name." Tilhini pronounced the words solemnly like a benediction.

"But it's the name I gave him when he was born!"

"You gave truly. He will be a leader of his people."

Francisco was speechless. Helek listened in awe. "He, too, will soar far and wide, as you have," Tilhini continued, voice rising, "and he too. . . ." He stopped abruptly as if having seen something startling.

"Go on, old father!"

Tilhini shook his head. "I go no further. The rest is in Sacred Condor's hands. He will guide this boy, as he has guided you . . . and brought you safely back to me." The old man no longer sounded prophetic, but sentimental, even wistful. "He may be the last. I sha'n't come here many more times. And the young grow fewer and less interested, while the white man's whiskey and disease and bullets destroy them. No, I shall not return many more times. But *he* may. The rock will grow lonely, yes, but he may. . . ." Tilhini's voice broke and then resumed, addressing Helek: "I wish I had my cord of

31

sacred white down from the breast of condors and eagles to place around you at your naming, but time and the rats have destroyed it." And now his words grew strong again. "Yet may the ancient web hold!" He lifted his arms high and spread his fingers wide as if delineating some invisible net. "May the ancient web hold! May you become part of it! May it protect you and yours forever!" His voice trailed off wistfully into a dying fall that sent a shaft of sadness and foreboding through Francisco as through Helek.

"Well said, well done, old father, dearest friend!" Francisco declared heartily to hide his misgiving. "We are deeply in your debt. You are deeply in our hearts. Now, since night comes on, may we build a small fire and share our food and drink, secure that in the darkness the smoke will not reveal our whereabouts to the A-alowow, the White Ones, or other intruders, while we share news of those we love who are not with us?"

"Yes," Tilhini said resignedly, "yes, let us share. Let us strengthen the web!"

Chapter Four

It was night in the simple parlor of a modest redwood house on Montgomery Street where it began to climb Telegraph Hill a few blocks from Mary Louise Jackson's elegant Washington Street premises. The room's central feature was a round table of plain oak and eight matching chairs. For years room and table had served as secret meeting place, main station, on San Francisco's Underground Railroad which had helped fugitive slaves escape their masters. Though slavery had been prohibited in California since it became a state eleven years earlier, Southerners such as Stanhope had brought slaves here, such as Mary Louise's daughter, Hattie, who sat at the table. The occupants of the other chairs had helped Hattie, and many more, find safe havens in the city or in Canada.

"Let's hear what Mary Louise has to tell us," Charles Mornay was saying. This was Mornay's house. These were his friends. He wore a businessman's black broadcloth suit with white shirt and black stock. Mornay was a successful produce commission merchant, and his auburn hair and beard were neatly trimmed, and his backbone was ramrod-straight with conviction. Deeply religious, he had been a dedicated Abolitionist all his adult life.

Mary Louise, sitting beside her daughter, patted Hattie's arm from time to time as if to make sure she was there. She told what she had overheard Stanhope and Sedley say about the war and General Johnston. "We've got to prevent them from seizing California."

"We will," affirmed Mornay. "I'll speak to General Sumner at Army headquarters in the morning, and I'll send a wire to Baker in Washington City . . ." — meaning Edward D. Baker,

33

U. S. senator and President Lincoln's confidant, formerly a San Francisco attorney and their colleague. "Additional troops left for Los Angeles yesterday. It's evidently going to be a hot spot."

"If they let black men fight, I'll volunteer," Reuben Stapp declared. He, too, sat beside Hattie. A free-born black, Mary Louise's son-in-law had come West from Philadelphia in search of a better life, walking all the way with a party of white Quakers. Now he was Mornay's partner. "Hattie and I've talked it over," Reuben continued, "and she wants me to go." He turned to her for confirmation. She smiled back at him proudly. Hattie wasn't glamorous like her mother, but she radiated a goodness like Reuben's. Their two-year-old son, Charles, asleep on the couch nearby, was named for Mornay. "Hattie could help you at the market," Reuben concluded. "She'd be especially good with our female customers."

"Thoughtful of you both," Mornay replied gravely, "and gallant of you, Reuben. Before it's over, black men will be fighting for the Union, I predict."

"How long will the war last?" Hattie asked anxiously.

"It may last years. This is for the body and soul of our nation. It won't be settled easily or bloodlessly." Mornay thought painfully of young people like Reuben, like Hattie, like his daughter Martha and her fiancé David Venable, who was already in uniform. Young people were most likely to bear the brunt, suffer most.

Now it was Martha Mornay's turn to speak, as they went around the table in customary fashion. Brown-haired, brown-eyed, pert-nosed, reserved yet outspoken when she needed to be, Martha taught at the colored school and helped run the Temperance Rescue Mission down on the waterfront. Martha shared her father's moral concerns, yet with an unpredictable streak as evidenced now. "I just hope they catch Albert Sidney

34

Johnston and hang him as a traitor!" she broke out passionately. Her outburst surprised Mornay. It was difficult for him to think of her grown up with a mind and feelings of her own. It reminded him he was an aging widower and that her flesh and blood would endure beyond his, God willing, into the new world, the new nation that must emerge from this war.

"Daughter," he reproved her gently, "General Johnston's not a traitor in his own eyes. He's being loyal to what he believes. We must be fair, even in war, if we are to build the City of God on earth." Mornay saw the war not only as a struggle to end slavery, but as a new American Revolution in which the common people, the Shovelry, so called, would take power from the Chivalry represented by Johnston and Stanhope; and then a nation long dominated by Southern gentry and their friends like Sedley would at last be ruled with justice by ordinary people.

While sharing this vision, Martha viewed the war also as an almost insurmountable barrier between her and her absent David, between them and their happiness, between all young people and their happiness, and this had moved her to speak out so emotionally. "Papa," she added, "General Johnston was disloyal when he might have been loyal. For me he represents all those who did likewise and brought the war on us, put David in uniform, brought us here tonight to think about fighting and killing our fellow humans."

"Hear, hear!" cried Virgil Gillem from beside her. Wry, lanky, asthmatic Gillem owned and edited *The Daily Sentinel*. He was an old and close friend of Martha's and of her David who was once a member of this round table, though now he was in uniform among Iowa's volunteers. Gillem was the group's secret ally in public, their colleague in private. He was a flagrant womanizer but secretly adored the chaste, conventional, yet unpredictable Martha. So it was hard for him to disagree now. "Gadfly," he called her by the pet name he and David had given her years ago, "I respect your view, but I beg to differ. I beg you to include Johnston in your usual charity. I was there, remember, when he told Stanhope to go jump in the bay, after the estimable scoundrel suggested Johnston hand over Alcatraz to him and his Secessionist hotheads. I tell you Johnston's a man of honor caught in a tragic dilemma like the rest of us."

"That may be," she rejoined, "but, if he escapes and returns with an army and Stanhope's firebrands rise to join them, it will make a tragic dilemma that much worse."

Sensing an impasse, Mornay intervened. "Maybe he'll lead a rising without ever leaving the state. What then? Eve, what's on your mind? What does the new woman say? Doesn't all this play into your hands as Gillem's Los Angeles correspondent-to-be?"

Tall, awkward, Eve Radovich was Martha's closest friend. But unlike Martha, Eve was a fiery radical. Her father had been crushed to death in a stamp mill at Sedley's El Dorado Gold Mine. Her mother had brought her to San Francisco and had eked out a living as seamstress for them both until she died. Eve had been on her own since she was fifteen. First she had sewn overalls at the Levi Strauss factory while continuing her education at the Mechanics' Library. Then Gillem had given her a job as typesetter, one of the first of her kind, and then he had let her express her fiery social concern in a series of hard-hitting articles about the working girl, signed simply "Eve." For a time he had been her lover in that casual way that Martha couldn't approve yet found intriguing. For Martha love and chastity went hand in hand. Her David would be her only mate. Yet, Eve and Gillem remained her dear friends and on good terms with each other.

"Don't make fun of the new woman, Charles," Eve admonished Mornay as if his equal. "I'm going to show you and Virgil Gillem a thing or two. I'll report you the truth about Los Angeles as no man ever could, and, if Johnston is there, I'll find him."

Mornay chuckled. He liked Eve's outspokenness and courage and thought her a good friend for Martha despite her faults. In Los Angeles she'd be living with his old friends and fellow Abolitionists, Ambrose and Ethel Curtis, helping Ethel in a new kind of school for very young children called a kindergarten, while Eve concealed her true identity as investigative reporter for Gillem. "Speaking of watching people," Mornay continued as he went on around the table, "Wing Sing, what about you? What can you tell us?"

For years Wing had been Mornay's cook and housekeeper. Now he operated his own laundry with the help of one of his cousins. Other cousins brought him news from all over the city where they were employed in various capacities. Wing's cousin, Yee, was a servant in Stanhope's town house on Green Street in what was known as the Southern Enclave. "Yee tellee me Stanhope takee tlippee up-down statee, no say whelee."

"He wants to contact his Golden Knights," Mary Louise put in. "Dolly told me."

"When does he leave?" Mornay asked Wing.

"Tomollow."

"Tomollow and tomollow and tomollow cleeps in this petty pace flom day to day," teased the irrepressible, sometimes insensitive Eve. "How can you write a history of your life in California if you can't pronounce tomorrow, Wing?" They all knew Wing was writing his experience in California into a book called THE LAND OF THE GOLDEN MOUNTAIN. It would tell how he had panned for gold in the Sierra foothills, had been beaten and ejected by Indians who claimed the land was theirs, had been hounded by knife-wielding runners sent by the Chinese labor contractor who'd brought him from Canton and demanded payments he could not make, and how he had found refuge at last at Mornay's house.

"Tomollow I explain!" beamed Wing, undismayed. He sat there smiling, his black skullcap covering most of his hair and the rest of it hanging down the back of his chair in a pigtail. "Tomollow I enlistee like Reuben," he added surprisingly, "but they no takee China boy. No lettee ride bus, even!"

"But they will," broke in Mornay, "someday they will let you ride the bus, Wing, just as they will Reuben. That's also what this war is about. Now, would all of you like to hear David's letter?"

"I'm sure Martha's not interested," Gillem teased.

"Don't be silly, Virgil!" she retorted.

Her father winked at the others. "She don't have to listen." But she blushed as he read aloud: "Keokuk, Iowa, on the Mississippi River, June Second, Eighteen Sixty-One. Dear Comrades, Here I am beside the Father of Waters, drilling till I'm ready to drop, waiting for a steamboat to carry us downstream a few miles to invade Missouri on behalf of the United States. As some of you already know, following the outbreak of war, I resigned as pastor of St. Matthew's Episcopal Church in Philadelphia, where I was biding my time till I could get a pulpit in San Francisco. And following Lincoln's call for volunteers, I repaired me to my native Iowa and enlisted in its militia as a private soldier, believing this a people's war and best seen from the ranks. I've no ambitions to rise higher, but only to eat something better than hard biscuit and boiled-to-death coffee. Meanwhile, nobody knows I'm a minister, and I don't let on."

Seven years had passed since David sat at this table. He had helped Mary Louise and Reuben free Hattie from Stanhope, then had answered what he believed God's call to go

East and study for the ministry. Mornay regarded him as a son, Martha as a husband. She had fallen in love with him at the rail of the steamer, *Golden Age* — she twelve, he eighteen, she newly motherless, he all but penniless — as they had entered together through the Golden Gate into a fabulous new world.

"Our uniforms came today," he continued, now, while Martha's heart beat faster as her father read: "Trousers of dove-gray with a blue stripe down the seam. Blue frock coats with brass buttons. Also today we elected our first lieutenant. There were four candidates. Much electioneering. After three ballots we chose a fine fellow named Jim . . . not Jeff! . . . Davis. If Jim don't pan out, we'll dis-elect him. There's democracy for you! We ended the day with a prayer meeting and Bible discussion. There is surprisingly little support for Abolition. Repeatedly I hear . . . 'I'll fight to preserve the Union, not to free niggers.' Yet, I welcome this new comradeship. I believe it will grow, and grow better, like mine with you.

"Give my love to our beautiful city and to the glorious land where she is set. And let freedom ring everywhere! David."

"Sounds just like him," Gillem commented. The others agreed, though Mary Louise complained: "Seems to me he's encountering the same prejudice in the Army you find everywhere else."

Then, noticing tears in Martha's eyes, Mornay changed the subject. "Had a young visitor today, a Spanish Californian named Pedro Díaz. He's up here from Los Angeles to see what's going on. Ambrose Curtis sent him. He's a protégé of Ambrose's and a potential ally of ours, I gather. Said he wanted to see what a city was like and to observe the training camps at the racetrack and out at Hunter's Point. I gather he'd be volunteering, too, if he weren't the main support of a large family. He's a nice fellow, speaks good English. I tried to get him to come home with me, but he said he didn't want to impose. You may meet him on the boat, Eve. He's going south tomorrow, like you."

"But don't throw yourself at him as you have a habit of doing, or he may run away and never come back," Martha warned.

"If I like him, I'll run faster than he does," retorted the unabashable Eve.

"Oh, Eve, I'll miss you!" cried Martha.

"All of us will," her father agreed, "and now let's all join hands and pray for Eve's success, and our success, and David's safety," and in their customary fashion they all joined hands around the table, while Mornay called on God Almighty to bless their endeavors.

Chapter Five

In one of the two squatter cabins just down the valley from Clara's hacienda, Buckingham Jenkins was admonishing his older son, Goodly, and his nephew, Stubby Gatlin, in stormy tones. "You fellows hold your horses, and you'll get all the war you want right here in California! Stanhope gimme the word, didn't he? We're gonna wait for Gen'ral Johnston to come back from Texas at the head of a army. Then we'll rise!"

"Johnston, he ain't even left for Texas yet!" retorted Goodly sullenly. He chafed under his father's authority and the drudgery of the homestead. He wanted to see the world. "Me and Stubby, here, we want to join up now." Goodly was not a giant like Buck, but he was nearly as large.

"Yeah, Uncle Buck," little Stubby agreed, "we want action."

They sat on homemade wooden stools at a homemade puncheon table along with Buck's younger son, Elmer, and Buck's white-haired father, Abe, while his wife Iphygenia and Elmer's young wife Opal prepared to take up supper from the black-iron cook stove and serve them. The cabin door was open to the summer evening, as if to let out the heat of the argument as well as of the stove.

"You'll get action!" Buck stormed on. "Just be patient, you hear me? Then we'll rise and take over this state and this ranch," indicating it with a gesture.

It had been at a private meeting in the back room of the Buckhorn Saloon in Santa Lucia — population two hundred — that Stanhope had told Buck: "Hold yourself and your men in readiness. Prepare to rise when I give the word."

"Yes, sir," Buck had replied dutifully. Stanhope had been his colonel during the war with Mexico. "Though outnumbered bad, we whupped the greasers good," Buck liked to boast. "Together we brung what's now California and most of New Mexico and Utah and Nevada Territ'ries into these United States." Together they hoped to bring California into the Southern fold. "Meanwhile, let's be true to the great cause in which we're engaged and to the ideals of our sacred brotherhood," Stanhope had concluded. Those ideals included being anti-Catholic, anti-Jewish, anti-foreigners as well as anti-North. They had exchanged the secret handclasp of the Knights of the Golden Circle, first fingers extended, and Stanhope had continued his journey southward to spread his message.

Now Goodly shook his head and scoffed at his father. "Waitin' for you and your Knights to rise is like waitin' for Ma's biscuits. Maybe it ain't ever gonna happen."

"Hold your tongue, or you won't get no supper!" Iphygenia Jenkins threatened from the stove. Iphy was stooped and gaunt from much labor. Her hair was graying, but not her spirit. She had raised two sons and a beloved, motherless, fatherless niece, Sally, now up at what she called "the big house" thanks to having married Pacifico. Iphy gloried in Sally's step up, as she thought of it, though she was disturbed by the way Sally's marriage had been going lately and by the thought of Pacifico leaving for the war. Iphy had come across the plains and mountains from Missouri riding in a covered wagon with white-haired Abe and Buck leading the way on horseback. She still saw California as a promised land. Granted that promise had gotten a bit dim just before supper on this hot night, but that didn't dismay Iphy. "Right, Opal?" she continued to her daughter-in-law. "We don't take no sass from any man, do we?"

Opal nodded noncommittally. "Opal is plain as sin," Iphy had confided to relatives back in Missouri, "but she's a good girl." She and Elmer occupied the adjoining cabin, but took most of their meals with the others. Opal was grateful for Iphy's valiance. It shielded her from a world she found difficult to face. Goodly, for instance, had made clear he'd like to have her. "Oh, don't take him seriously!" Iphy always scoffed. Iphy at times seemed strangely indulgent toward her eldest.

"Wait!" Goodly echoed Buck sarcastically, with a wink at Opal. "Seems like all we do is wait, wait, wait!"

Like Clara at the hacienda they had waited for years for the courts to decide whether her claim to her ranch was valid. If it was, they would lose their squatter claims. If it wasn't, they'd own a piece of their promised land. Old Abe and old Clara, weary of turmoil, had arranged the uneasy truce between the two camps. But waiting grew tedious, and more and more it all seemed to Goodly like a sell-out that began with Sally's marriage to Pacifico. "Elmer'll still be here to help if I go," he grumbled on. "He don't want to go to war, do you, Elm?"

"You just want to duck out," Elmer retorted. Half-cowed, half-infuriated by his bullying elder brother, he deeply resented the way Goodly shirked work, claimed the center of attention, and made eyes at Opal.

"Well, whatever else happens," sighed Iphy loudly, as she stirred the huge cauldron of succotash, "we'll be here at the stove, eh, Opal?"

"I didn't say don't go, I said wait," Buck rejoined. "Stanhope's nobody's fool. He knows what's goin' on, him and Sedley. You think you're smarter than they are?" This silenced Goodly. Buck turned to Abe. "Granpa, what do you say?" The scar-faced old mountain man sat silently, puffing his corncob pipe as if pondering weighty matters. Actually he was biding his time while his fractious clan argued. Abe had buried his wife in Marion County, Missouri, long ago. He'd never owned slaves. He hoped Missouri would stay in the Union and so, too, California, but he kept such hopes pretty much to himself, especially at moments like this.

Goodly tried a new approach. "Dad, you went off to fight the greasers, didn't you?"

"You're damn' right I did, and I'd do it again."

"Then why shouldn't Stubby and me get our licks at the Yankees?"

"Yeah," put in Stubby, "what's wrong with that, Uncle Buck? Them two from the big house" — he lumped Pacifico and Benito together — "is a-gonna join the other side. Why shouldn't we join our'n?"

Like Goodly he despised Pacifico and Benito. The four had had it out at a brawl during a dance in Father O'Hara's disused warehouse, Goodly and Stubby getting the worst of it. That defeat had rankled. But dominating the antagonism was big-otry. Goodly and Stubby scorned Pacifico as a greaser and Benito as a Jew. Benito and Pacifico looked down upon them as poor white trash.

Iphy demanded wearily as she and Opal took out the biscuits from the oven and prepared to serve the chitterlings, collards, and succotash: "Why go lookin' for a war when you've got one here every day?"

"There!" Grandfather Abe exclaimed, as if he'd at last heard words of wisdom. He emphasized his comment with a solemn puff of smoke and a spit in the direction of the fireplace.

"Sure, there, now," Buck added, as if the matter was settled.

Losing all patience, Goodly lashed out derisively: "*There, now, what?* Waiting for you and your Knights to rise is like waiting for a dead Injun to shit!"

Buck hit him so hard he fell backward off his stool, struck his head against the cabin wall, lay stunned, blood pouring from his nose.

"Murderer!" Iphy flew at Buck and pummeled the back of his head and shoulders with both fists, screaming: "Kill your own flesh and blood, would you?" Elmer watched wide-eyed, but with secret satisfaction. Opal stared noncommittally. Stubby cried out in protest: "Uncle Buck, you shouldn't've done that!" Old Abe sat quietly, puffing his pipe, as if nothing unusual was occurring.

Goodly picked himself up slowly, then made a rush at his father.

Iphy thrust herself between them, shrieking: "Granpa, Granpa, you gonna sit there while your offspring exterminate each other?"

But Abe continued to preside over his cantankerous family with serene detachment. The scars of the grizzly's claws showed clearly in the sunset light as dark furrows down the left side of his face. The lobe of that ear was missing. He had met the grizzly as he had entered this valley for the first time many years ago, coming alone on foot down the river. He had killed the bear in a hand-to-hand fight. As a young mountain man he had deserted Lewis and Clark at the mouth of the Columbia and had made his way southward toward the fabled land of California, finding what he sought in this glorious valley of Santa Lucia, then years later leading his people back to it. They didn't think of themselves as squatters. They had fought for this land and had suffered great hardships to reach it. They felt it was rightfully theirs.

And now, in a moment of silence, the sweet sound of a guitar floated down to them mockingly, it seemed, from the big house where Pacifico, Benito, Sally, and Anita were having a painful last supper under the imperious supervision of old Clara. "Play your guitar!" she had ordered Pacifico in an attempt to cheer things up, and resentfully he played it, while the others on the verandah sat by in grim silence, waiting for food to be served that they did not wish to eat, while the night came down around them and an owl hooted from the hillside.

Iphy took command. Shoving husband and son apart with

a force that sent them staggering, she snatched the cleaver from its peg on the wall next to the stove and brandished it. "The first one makes a move ag'in' the other, I'll chop his block off!" Again there was silence. "Meantime, I want peace in this house and, by God, I'll have it." She continued to brandish the cleaver.

"*A*-men!" Abe suddenly pronounced, and began to sing in a high falsetto:

> **"Tis many years have passed away**
> **Since first I learned to watch and pray,**
> **But now I lead a sober life**
> **In a happy home with a lovin' wife!"**

"Sure, there, *now*," muttered Buck, wiping his right fist on his trouser leg, sitting down as if the matter was, indeed, settled. Goodly turned and stalked out the open door into the gathering darkness, wiping his face with his red bandanna, muttering curses under his breath. Stubby followed.

Chapter Six

Up in Sacramento, the state capital, often called Sacramento City though it was hardly more than a town, the six principal shareholders of the newly incorporated Central Pacific Railroad were meeting in the back room of Leland Stanford's grocery store on the bustling river front. Eliot Sedley was among the six men. Stanford as president presided. Clearing his throat, he began in his slow, rather ponderous way: "Judah has some bad news for us, I'm afraid. Judah, tell us what's on your mind."

Since his boyhood in Troy, New York, railroads had fascinated Theodore Judah. They were the new technology of the day. They gripped his imagination as airplanes and spacecraft would grip those of later generations. As a youth he had studied engineering at Rensselaer Polytechnic in hopes of someday building railroads. And he had helped build short ones in New York and California. Now at thirty-five, bearded, intense, he was passionately obsessed by the idea of building one like no other ever built — one that would scale the Sierra Nevada and cross the desert and plains beyond and link California with the rest of the nation. After hundreds of hours in the field afoot and in the saddle Judah had discovered a route he believed better than any other. It ran northward and eastward from Sacramento over the Sierra at Donner Pass and on down into Nevada Territory. But the re-survey he had just completed showed that to build along this route would cost eighty-eight thousand dollars a mile, or fifty percent more than the original estimate and several times more than the anticipated Federal subsidy. Thus Judah concluded his painful explanation. "I offer no excuse. I simply underestimated the difficulty of the terrain."

"Then why not choose another route?" Sedley suggested with his usual amiability. He knew Judah was the driving force behind the project, knew Judah had tried in vain to persuade financiers in New York and San Francisco to back him, and had, at last, interested these four Sacramento merchants who, along with himself, had just listened to Judah's candid statement.

"Because," Judah went on passionately, "this route is best. It's the shortest. Yes, it's steep. Yes, there'll be three miles of tunnels through solid granite. But any other route will require even greater cost."

"Best or not, if we can't pay for it, what good is it?" grumbled Collis P. Huntington, a large man with a square jaw and a shrewd brain. Huntington had begun his business career at fourteen in Connecticut as a peddler of dry goods, then had operated a hardware store in upstate New York before moving it here. "Eighty-eight thousand a mile!" he echoed Judah sardonically. Then he brusquely added: "I'm wondering if the time hasn't come to call the whole thing off?"

Huntington's partner, tall, skinny Mark Hopkins — Uncle Mark, they called him because at forty-eight he was much older than most of them — said nothing as customary. He was a natural follower, their expert bookkeeper and treasurer.

But Charles Crocker, a two-hundred and fifty pounder like Huntington, flared up. "Don't back out on us now, Collis, you old pinchpenny. Nothing ventured, nothing gained, I say." Crocker was a dry goods merchant, but he was also a man of action. He had begun life like Judah in Troy, New York, then had emigrated to California to engage unsuccessfully in mining, then successfully in dry goods. "Let's get on with it. I've laid my money on the line like the rest of you, and I'm ready to back it up, on one condition . . . that Eliot stays with us."

All of the "big four," as they would someday be called, were prosperous, but not wealthy. Nor were they fashionable men. All were bearded in the style of the Shovelry. All were strongly anti-slavery, as Sedley had pointed out to Stanhope. They were among the handful who, just six years ago, had founded the Republican Party of California, had gone all out for John C. Frémont, their fellow Californian, as President of the United States and lost, then, less than a year ago, had campaigned for Lincoln and won. Their railroad linking California with the East could enormously strengthen the Northern cause and, they hoped, make them much money. With Sedley's help they had accumulated the one hundred and fifteen thousand dollars in stock subscriptions legally required to incorporate their company. But without further help toward launching a venture that could cost tens of millions, they could not proceed.

"Nevertheless, our prospects are not as dark as might appear," Stanford resumed in his deliberate way, thus giving everyone, including himself, time to think at this crucial moment. Like Crocker and Huntington, Stanford weighed well over two-hundred pounds. Like them he had come from upstate New York where he had once practiced law. Unlike them, he was an active politician. "During my recent visit in Washington City," he continued, weighing each word, "I received assurances from the President and Congressional leaders that a railroad bill will pass, and that we are the leading contenders to receive its subsidies. Of course," he lowered his voice modestly, "if I'm elected governor in September, it may help matters. I'll be in a good position to secure subsidies from the state legislature and from county governments along the route of our line."

"You don't say!" Huntington mocked him crudely. Stanford's pontificating irritated Huntington, although, like the others, he recognized the advantage of having Stanford as governor. He himself had no political ambitions, indeed no

49

ambitions of any kind but to make money. Sedley, biding his time, evaluating all factors at play in this unfolding drama, thought Huntington the shrewdest player of the lot. Judah might have the dream. Huntington had the money sense.

Hopkins, in a rare show of independence, voiced his approval of Stanford's statements. Crocker and Judah added theirs. Though still not ready to commit himself, Sedley decided to add his. "Leland, your leadership is essential. We all know that. I personally will do my utmost to see that you're elected."

"That's very gratifying! I thank all of you!" Stanford beamed and nodded in his earnest, if sometimes maddening, way, ignoring Huntington and thus isolating his adversary. "I especially appreciate your support, Eliot, always have, always will."

Sedley decided to make his move. He was in this because he believed the railroad could be the best thing for California since the Gold Rush. It could bring undreamed of prosperity to the state and to him, regardless of who won the war. And Stanford as governor could be very useful.

"Leland," he chuckled amiably, "against my better judgment, I'm going to extend the credit you fellows need to keep you going. On one condition."

There was silence. There was bated breath. Then Stanford asked deferentially: "What is that condition?"

"That you give me a twelve and a half percent override on all profits." It was the way Sedley liked to do business — let others take most of the risk, do most of the work, let them be the focus of praise or blame while he remained in the background ready to share in their success. "Of course, my override will be a private matter, protected by confidential written agreement among us."

"Twelve and a half percent?" snorted Huntington. "Why that's outrageous! And what's the half percent for anyway?"

"That's to pay off Lady Luck," smiled Sedley. "We'll all need her help before we're through."

All but Huntington broke into answering smiles. Such light-heartedness, such geniality, such easy grace from a man so rich and powerful whose help they so desperately needed was, indeed, infectious. Forget the twelve and a half percent. There might never be any profit, or even any railroad. And there was no alternative, but failure.

Huntington grumbled with a scowl: "This is too serious for joking. I want to think about it." The others waited silently. But the more Huntington thought, the more he decided that he, too, had no better alternative than to accept Sedley's offer. "All right," he said finally, "in for a penny, in for a pound. I go along."

"Thank you, Collis," Sedley said modestly, as if they were all doing him a favor, as if they had traveled to his office, not he to theirs. Such practical humility was also part of his method. "I appreciate your confidence." Then he spoke disarmingly to all of them. "I believe in you fellows. You've stuck your necks out and taken a risk nobody else would take. I admire that. That's why I'm with you."

Now that the route was settled he could begin to buy up land along it, land sure to soar in value if the railroad was built. He would not tell Mary Louise what had transpired. It was one of those compartments of his life he didn't wish to share with her. But her intelligence network would keep her informed of his whereabouts, and she would guess the truth by what Sedley didn't tell her of his trip to Sacramento, and would inform Mornay and their round table group.

"Eliot, we're all in your debt," Stanford plodded earnestly on, deliberately making a pun while pretending not to. "I know I speak for all our colleagues when I say a heartfelt thank you!"

Chapter Seven

When Francisco and Helek woke, old Tilhini was gone. The cave mouth gaped behind them. The seer had vanished as if with the darkness, and Francisco knew it indicated that he and his son must continue their journey alone. Yet, now he felt more certain of their way.

An oriole's piping whistle summoned them. They rose and stood together, facing the breaking day, and gave thanks in the manner of their people:

> **Great dawn, breath of the Sun,**
> **Welcome to the world,**
> **Welcome to the world!**
> **All is Kakunupmawa,**
> **All is Kakunupmawa!**

Then they descended the hillside and bathed in the cool river that began as a spring gushing from the roots of a tall sugar pine on Iwihinmu, the sacred mountain, where they had begun their journey. They immersed themselves in its life-giving freshness, scrubbing their bodies with soaproot, then drying them with smooth sticks. Afterward, as they munched their seed meal, Helek asked: "What did Tilhini mean when he said we are the People of the Land and the Sea?"

"Come, let us find out," answered Francisco, knowing perfectly well, but it was among the things he wished the boy to learn as he showed him the world.

Leisurely they followed the river toward the valley Helek had seen in his dream vision. Francisco wished his son to absorb experience gradually during this journey of discovery

— this quest also for Helek's identity under the name Tilhini confirmed upon him at the mouth of the sacred cave: Helek, the Hawk, the far flyer, one day to be leader of his people as Francisco had been and was, one day to embody the resistance to white conquest. In the manner of their ancestors they carried their bone-handled flint knives thrust through the topknots of their hair. They would avoid established trails, two earth-brown people blending with the landscape, naked except for waistnets. When hungry they would eat the seed meal Ta-ahi and Letke had prepared them before they left the hidden valley. They would supplement their diet with fresh rose hips and blackberries, and the seeds of the chia sage, so nourishing that a handful could sustain them all day. And when thirsty they would drink from the river.

Francisco pointed to a mother quail slipping soundlessly away, almost invisible in the undergrowth, her furry brown chicks following her. "Like the quail we must learn to live silently and almost invisibly, finding safety in our surroundings."

Next he indicated the five-pointed leaves of a water maple. "See how they are like human hands opening to the sky and light? So let us reverence the trees that feel and speak in their own way, for they, too, are alive." And as he said such things, Francisco became as a boy again, once more full of wonder and belief. "All is Kakunupmawa," he reiterated. "All is Kakunupmawa."

He showed Helek how to hold a grass blade between his thumbs and blow upon it to make the shrill sound like that of a rabbit in distress which attracts foxes whose skins could prove useful or coyotes whose friendship is important. As they sat quietly under an elderberry bush laden with clusters of dark blue berries, a coyote, gray-brown, appeared from nowhere and approached so close they could see the yellow of its eyes before it faded back into the chaparral. Francisco said: "Perhaps he's a messenger from Sky Coyote, our benefactor who shines at night as the North Star, never changing, guiding us on our way, and that is why coyotes must never be harmed."

As they moved on, they suddenly heard, very close, the deadly buzz of a rattlesnake, and Francisco leaped aside with a warning cry. Where he had been about to plant his foot, the snake lay coiled, ready to strike, tongue darting in and out.

Trembling at the narrowness of his escape, Francisco explained how Katayin, Lord of the Dead, sends out rattlesnakes to bring in people who've been bad. By the narrowest of margins, perhaps because of some good deed he'd done, perhaps by pure chance, he'd escaped Katayin. "Death takes many forms, you must understand . . . as does life," and, then inspired by sudden thought, he bent down and picked up a handful of rich humus from under an oak by the stream. "This, too, is death, but it is also life." He pointed to the scarlet mimulus springing from the humus. And he did not kill the snake and admonished Helek never to do so.

At night they lighted no telltale fires that might betray them to the A-alowow, the White Ones, but Francisco played softly on his four-holed flute of elderberry wood — played traditional Chumash melodies in haunting, monadic key such as were played, he explained, at sacred dances among the People of the Land and the Sea and which now passed into the spirit and memory of Helek.

And then one day they came to a tall, white-trunked sycamore with earth disturbed around its base by the tracks of many large animals which Francisco recognized but did not at first explain, for his attention was fixed on the trunk at a level with his eyes where four small oval-shaped pieces of fresh skin were fastened by means of fresh willow pegs into a design that was like a sign. Francisco read the sign with anger and alarm.

"What is it?" Helek asked.

"It is the skin of the feet of Tuk-e-em, the spirit of our mountains. But more than that, much more, it is the work of the A-alowow who have killed Tuk-e-em, whom they call a mountain lion." And he continued soberly: "It was put here to frighten us by the White Ones who would like to kill us as they have killed Tuk-e-em."

Helek had never met a white person. "What are they like?"

"In due time you will learn."

"Are they always bad?"

"Not always, but quite often."

And then the question Francisco had been waiting for. "You and I have their blood, don't we?"

There it was, out in the open at last. Till now he had not thought the boy old enough to understand. Now he explained their ancestry. "I am half, you are, therefore, half of my half, or one fourth." In the silence the tree beside them seemed to bear witness.

"Then who truly are we, Father?" The boy's eyes were wide with wonder, and Francisco knew that he must answer wisely.

"Father and son! That is the foremost thing to remember! Another . . . because we carry their blood, the white men hate us more than if we carried none of it."

The boys eyes grew larger still. "Why is that?"

"I do not know why blood hates blood. It's all the same color. You'd think it could get along with itself. But it hates. And so we are doubly cursed in the eyes of the A-alowow because we have some of what they have."

Helek was silent a moment. Then he reached out and took his father's hand. "Nevertheless, I should like to see an A-alowow."

"You will, I promise."

They traveled on more warily than ever, and Francisco

thought with concern of wife and daughter behind in the hidden valley. He had warned them never to venture out. But he couldn't be sure what might happen to them even in such a secure hiding place. In the dozen years since the Gold Rush some fifty-thousand California Indians had been killed or had died of disease and despair in the greatest decimation of native peoples due to white encroachment yet on record, and, though Francisco had no way of knowing the exact number, he sensed the truth from what had happened to him and his people.

They came to what appeared a small blue lake, but was in reality a hollow covered with dark-blue lupine. It's beauty was breathtaking. "It's how our world looked before the white men came to it," Francisco explained, still speaking softly because of what had happened to Tuk-e-em. When he paused, he heard, as if by evil chance, human voices approaching, mingled with the thud of horse hoofs. He drew Helek back with him into the chaparral just a moment before he saw Buck Jenkins and five other white men, one after another, riding toward them across the blue-lupine lake, trampling its beauty underfoot, their gun butts protruding from their saddle scabbards.

"Who are they, Father?" whispered Helek, though he had guessed.

"They are the A-alowow."

"But they have four legs!" He thought horses and riders were one.

Francisco whispered the truth. Helek stared, for this was a great wonder.

Buck was saying loud enough for them to hear: "The damn' rascal don't leave no tracks. But you can bet he's somewhere hereabouts."

What, above all, Buck couldn't forget or forgive was the

California sleigh ride that Francisco had given him up the main street of Santa Lucia, arms pinioned to his sides by Francisco's reata. Everybody had watched, everybody had laughed as he had struggled to keep his feet behind the galloping horse, but he had fallen and was dragged in the dust. Nor could Francisco forgive or forget that humiliation suffered at Buck's hands when the squatters had first encroached on Rancho Olomosoug, even into the sacred oak grove belonging to his mother's people since immemorial time, and ordered him out of it at pistol point.

"Homer," Buck addressed the rider behind him, "if he's got a woman with him, it likely means kids by now."

"So we take 'em and sell 'em like we done the others?" queried Homer.

"Not this lot. I'd as soon sell a passel of young skunks. No, we exterminate this lot."

While awaiting further word from Stanhope, Buck and his Santa Lucia Rangers, as they had styled themselves, were augmenting their meager incomes by capturing "wild" Indians and selling them to white settlers. A good house girl, useful also in bed, could bring as much as sixty dollars.

"I'd think twice before I threw away that kind of money," Homer objected. He was Stubby Gatlin's father. Stubby and Goodly used to go along on these hunts.

"Well, maybe we ought to keep the women," Buck conceded.

Francisco's grip on Helek's arm tightened. They crouched silently in the chaparral until the riders disappeared, and even then the repellent smells of strange men, strange horses, strange leather, strange gun metal drifted back to them along with Buck's and Homer's words, defiling the air, it seemed, filling the two fugitives with disgust, anger, fear. They had seen the lion skin wrapped in a tawny bundle behind Buck's saddle.

"He would like to take our skins home with him as he is taking Tuk-e-em's," Francisco whispered. "Do you understand what you have seen?"

"I understand," answered Helek grimly.

Chapter Eight

No matter what happens I shall love you for all eternity, Martha Mornay had written him, and her letter warmed his heart as the *River Queen*, carrying Sergeant David Venable and his fellow Union volunteers down the Mississippi, approached Hannibal, Missouri. He heard someone say: "There it is . . . slave soil!" His comrades had chosen small, spry, golden-haired, naturally likable, naturally leader-like David as their sergeant, and he had reluctantly accepted. **I do not seek authority, but when it seeks me out I feel I must accept it,** he told Martha and Mornay. Now the words "slave soil" filled him with aversion, yet strengthened his resolve, as he stared at the little town nestled in green trees at the foot of a wooded bluff. If the Rebels were going to resist their landing, perhaps it would be with cannon from the top of that bluff.

But the Rebels apparently had no such ideas, for they disembarked without opposition, and, as they advanced into the town, the people of Hannibal greeted them, some with scowls, others with smiles, especially the Negroes. Yet, the blacks seemed reluctant to talk, apparently having been warned by their owners.

Even so, David, at the head of his reconnaissance detachment, found one old man, barefoot, wearing a ragged pair of trousers held up by one frayed suspender, who volunteered the information that a young white fellow named Sam Clemens had organized a band to resist the invaders "but dey skedaddled when dey heered de steamboats was a-comin' down de ribber."

"Where are they now?"

Jim waved a hand westward toward invisible regions beyond the high bluff. "Yonder somewheres, I reckon."

"Where did Sam Clemens live?"

Jim pointed to a white cottage a few yards up the unpaved street. "Dat de widder Clemens's place."

Moments later David was knocking at the door of the house that would be immortalized in TOM SAWYER. When it opened, he was confronted by a slight, middle-aged woman with sharp, disapproving eyes, spectacles halfway down her nose, and a determined chin. A light brown shawl covered the shoulders of her faded lavender dress. Evidently she had just been sewing, for a gold thimble gleamed on the middle finger of her right hand.

"Beg pardon, ma'am," David began politely, "may I ask some questions?"

"You may ask, but I may not answer!" Jane Lampton Clemens, the original of Tom Sawyer's Aunt Polly, replied haughtily. Jane came from a long line of Kentucky and Virginia landowners and slave owners and liked to trace her lineage back to the English gentry. She despised Yankees as social inferiors.

"Do you know a young fellow named Sam Clemens?" David resumed.

"Why do you ask?"

"I'm told he's formed a company of militia with himself as leader."

"Nigger Jim tell you?"

"I'm not at liberty to answer that, ma'am."

"Then I'm not at liberty to answer you."

"Is Sam your son?"

"Young man, if you think you're gonna bully me into answerin' impertinent questions, you got another guess comin'. That's what you Yankees are, anyway, bullies!"

"Missus Clemens," he replied gravely, "we're not bullying anybody. We're here to keep Missouri in the Union."

60

"That's like sayin' you want to arrest a man to keep him from commitin' a crime!" She brandished her thimble. "Who appointed you our nation's policemen, I'd like to know!" With that she turned and slammed the door in his face, and thus David got very little from Aunt Polly.

He wrote Martha that night: **Outwardly these people resemble the rest of us. Inwardly I wonder how they feel about owning human flesh.**

Jane Clemens and her husband had owned slaves, and their son, Sam, had been largely brought up by their black girl, Jennie. Jennie had adored Sam. Sam had adored her. From her he had learned wonderfully entertaining stories about ghosts and goblins, black people and white people, that he never forgot and later used in his stories and books along with Jennie's characteristic speech patterns. Jennie had been no ordinary slave girl. One day when Jane Clemens had been about to whip her for disobedience, she had wrested the leather strap from Jane's hand. Sam's father had been called. He had whipped Jennie severely and warned her never to misbehave again. But John Clemens had soon run into financial difficulties and had sold Jennie "down the river" in the original meaning of that term so fraught with horror for so many, because the plantations of the lower Mississippi were notorious for their mistreatment of slaves. Thus Jennie had become the property of George Stanhope and a servant in his New Orleans town house. Young Sam had been broken-hearted when Jennie was sold. Years later he would tell how dear she had been to him.

Inquiring further around town David learned that Sam and his band had gone inland to join a Rebel force planning to recapture Hannibal. When he reported this to Lieutenant Davis, additional pickets were posted along the bluff above town, and excitement ran high among the soldiers below as they prepared to advance and engage the enemy. **It will be**

our first fight, David wrote Martha. **We're like a bunch of schoolboys getting ready for our first day of class. I think of you night and day. I wish I were there with you and the others, helping save California from Stanhope and Sedley, but I'll try to do my share here.** And he added fervently: **If God lets me survive, we'll build a life together that will express all the love, all the gratitude, I shall feel, of which you'll be the precious centerpiece.**

Meanwhile, Sam Clemens and his band were being sworn into the Confederate Army at Colonel Ralls's farm twenty-five miles distant. The venerable colonel was exhorting them to "defend our sacred soil against all invaders under whatever flags," which they promised to do. After lamenting their lack of uniforms, Ralls ceremoniously belted to the side of Lieutenant Clemens a sword nearly four feet long which Ralls had carried in triumph from Vera Cruz to Mexico City during the Mexican War. "May you always unsheathe it with honor!" he admonished Sam, then shook his hand and wished him and his men God's speed.

Sam had spent the past three years as a steamboat pilot on the Mississippi. He had been making good money and having a good time. But the war had closed the river to commercial traffic, thus putting him out of a job. So he had taken up soldiering in defense of the Southern cause. Sam was twenty-six, medium height, slenderly built, had curly auburn hair, a quick wit, and a natural talent for leadership.

With him at their head, the Marion County Rangers moved gingerly toward Hannibal, growing more reluctant the nearer they got, while David's regiment advanced to meet them. One night, while on guard duty, Sam saw the figure of a lone horseman approaching through the moonlight and shot him, only to find, as he bent over the man and watched him die, that he had killed an unarmed civilian. **I was down on him in a moment,** Sam wrote later, helplessly stroking his forehead; **and I would have given anything then — my own life freely — to make him what he had been five minutes before.**

David, not far away, quite unaware of what was happening, had no animosity toward Sam Clemens, only a mounting curiosity. Yet sometimes he wondered if he would kill Sam, or if Sam will kill him.

When Sam and the Marion County Rangers reached Bill Splawn's farm, it was after dark. No lights shown. **Thinking it better not to disturb our involuntary hosts,** Sam explained later, **we went to roost hungry in the hayloft of the barn.** He had just fallen asleep when someone shouted: "Fire!" Sam woke to see hay ablaze all around him. A ranger's cigarette had ignited it. Rolling hastily away, Sam inadvertently rolled out the loft window onto the yard below, severely spraining his right ankle. Thus he became the Confederate Army's first casualty of the war in northern Missouri.

Next morning after a whopping breakfast of bacon, eggs, and pancakes had been served by Mrs. Splawn and her house slave, Emma, the rangers continued in the general direction of Hannibal. Sam's ankle pained him badly, so that by midafternoon, when they reached Nuck Matson's place, he had pulled off his boot and was riding his mule with stockinged foot in the stirrup, ankle swollen to nearly twice normal size. When Nuck's wife, Birdie, saw it, she exclaimed: "Sam Clemens, you couldn't run two steps if the whole Yankee Army was after you. Get down and come in. Let the others go on. I'll take care of that ankle. You can catch up."

Sam was secretly glad of an excuse to interrupt his soldiering. It had become more irksome than he cared to admit. He hadn't been paid a penny. Except for breakfast that morning, he hadn't eaten for two days, and his ankle hurt like fury. Showing him her spare room, Birdie commanded: "Now, peel off those clothes and get into that bed while I fetch some liniment. Here's one of Nuck's nightgowns. Nuck'll be back soon. I'll post my pickaninny as lookout, 'case the Yankees come!"

She ordered little black Horace to watch at the front gate while she worked on Sam's ankle. Birdie was second cousin to Iphygenia Jenkins who from time to time wrote wistfully, heading her letters rather grandly "Rancho Olomosoug," saying she missed her Marion County folks, but praising to the skies the fertile soil and wonderful climate of golden California. **Goodly got into an awful scrap with his dad,** she had added in her last letter, **and went off to war along with his cousin Stubby and we ain't heard a word of 'em since.**

Sam's ankle kept him in bed all next day, fretting lest the Yankees arrive. Meantime, reports reached the rest of his Marion County Rangers that a large Union force was approaching, and they found discretion to be the better part of valor and melted away into the countryside. Nobody thought to go back and tell Sam.

Thus David Venable and his scouting party reached the Matson farm unopposed.

"Dey's come!" cried little Horace, running in from the gate. "Dey's here, Mis' Matson!"

Birdie darted into Sam's room. "Sam, hide quick. And for heaven's sake get that sword out of sight!"

Sam scrambled under the bed, clutching his four-foot sword. Birdie hastily spread up the bedclothes. She flung a patchwork quilt over them and hurried out, as David knocked at the front door while his men deployed to either side.

"Evenin', ma'am," he said politely, although it was only afternoon. He had fallen back easily into the speech of his Iowa childhood on the Missouri border a day's travel from where they stood. Yet, he didn't like the idea of searching other people's homes. It made him unpleasantly aware of the invasionary brutality that lay at the heart of war. "Mind if we take a look around your premises?"

"Why, not at all," replied Birdie cheerily. She sensed his reluctance to intrude and liked him for it. She also liked his curly yellow hair and aura of boyish innocence. "Come right in."

He said apologetically: "All of us won't traipse through your house, ma'am." Turning to his corporal, Mutt Howell, he suggested: "Mutt, you and the others could fan out around the house and search the barn and sheds. Perkins and I'll meet you back there. Come on, Perk. If you please, ma'am?"

As they reached Sam's room, Birdie warbled in her best notes: "This here's our guest room, Sergeant. You can see for yourself it ain't occupied." By this time they were standing beside the bed, and Sam's nose was a foot from David's shoes. Years later in San Francisco Sam and David would laugh about it, Sam declaring: "I was literally at your feet, and you never knew it." But now it was serious business for both.

"That's a mighty pretty quilt, ma'am. You make it yourself?" David reached down and touched one of its red patches, while Sam quaked below.

"Every stitch." Birdie managed what she hoped was a smile of proprietary pride.

After looking through the house, David and Perkins emerged into the yard, rejoined the others, and talked with Nuck Matson and his two older slaves, just coming in from the corn field. Except for a suspicion he couldn't quite explain, David decided that his information was wrong, and no Confederates were hiding at Nuck Matson's farm, or perhaps they had left before he arrived.

Sam left a few days later. Traveling alone, following back roads, he headed north for the Iowa border. It wasn't exactly healthy being a deserter from the Confederate Army, and at the same time wanted by the Union one.

When he reached Keokuk on free soil, Sam went to the house of his older brother, Orion, an Abolitionist lawyer. Orion had good connections in the Republican hierarchy and had just been appointed secretary to the governor of Nevada Territory and was about to leave for the West. Sam made arrangements to go with him. Sam saw it as a chance to leave the war and the rest of his past behind him and strike out for a new life, and maybe strike it rich in Nevada's mining boom.

David wrote Martha: **We're winning without firing a shot so far. At this rate the war may soon be over.**

Chapter Nine

Eve Radovich was standing at the rail of the *Senator,* hoping the morning fog would lift and give her a first view of Southern California. The voyage down the coast from San Francisco had been rough till last evening when the steamer entered the Santa Barbara Channel. Since then the sea had been smooth as glass, and that seemed to promise well. Eve felt excited at the prospect of being Gillem's anonymous correspondent in turbulent, Secessionist-minded Los Angeles, while helping Ethel Curtis run that new kind of school for very young children called a kindergarten.

Suddenly she became aware of the good-looking young man at her elbow. Judging from his dark features and homespun clothes, he could have been a Spanish Californian of the poorer class, though his black derby was in the latest style. Lifting it, he inquired shyly, yet with daring disregard of formality: "Excuse me, but are you Miss Radovich?"

She was almost too astonished to answer. "I am, and who are you?"

"I'm Pedro Díaz. I've been watching you, getting up my courage." He smiled engagingly. "Charles Mornay said you might be on the boat. I decided you must be you!"

Eve couldn't help liking him as she recalled Mornay's mention of the young man from Los Angeles — "one of us" — who visited him at his market stall as part of a get-acquainted trip to the city. She recalled, too, Martha's admonition not to throw herself at the first man she met. "How did you guess I was I?" she laughed, feeling fate intervening in her life.

Pedro Díaz looked a bit embarrassed. "He said you were tall, and beautiful."

"Well, I am tall, as you see. I'm a good two inches taller than you" — Eve wheeled into her uninhibited style — "but that needn't stand between us. How did you like San Francisco?"

"You really want to know?"

"Yes, tell me."

"It's too big, too busy."

"But," she protested, both surprised and intrigued, "from what Charles said, I thought you'd be in favor of progress?"

"Not progress of that kind." Pedro became serious. His large brown eyes regarded her gravely. "Los Angeles may be a sleepy little town. But people take time to stop and talk. Nearly everyone I met in San Francisco struck me as in a hurry to get rich. Progress seems to me more a matter of social justice than accumulation of wealth."

They became so engrossed in their conversation that Eve hardly noticed that the ship was approaching shore. A cluster of buildings on a low bluff loomed out of the fog.

"That's San Pedro," Pedro explained, "named for my namesake. We take the stagecoach there for Los Angeles. It's about twenty miles. Maybe we'd better get our luggage ready."

At that moment a big man with the face of a jovial bulldog came bustling toward them through the crowd, calling out heartily right and left: "Take the red stage, folks! It'll get you to the City of the Angels faster and cheaper!" When he saw Pedro and Eve, his face lit up even further. "Pedro, that goes for you and this handsome young lady. Won't you introduce me?"

Pedro obliged dryly. "Miss Radovich, Mister Newcomb."

"Welcome to God's country, Miss Radovich!" Newcomb rejoined, sweeping off his derby, bowing and beaming at her fondly. "See you on shore! Don't bother about Pedro. I'll be looking forward to serving you myself!" And he hustled on, promoting more business.

"Who on earth is that?" Eve asked in some disgust.

"That's Earl Newcomb."

"Not *the* Earl Newcomb?"

"Yes, *the* Earl Newcomb, Eliot Sedley's man in Los Angeles. I guess you've heard of Sedley?"

"Indeed, I have."

"Well, Earl's been up to see him, and I guess he's got his marching orders."

"To march us onto his stagecoach?"

"Not only that. He'd like to march us into the Confederacy, too."

Newcomb was, in fact, returning from that definitive meeting with Sedley and Stanhope in which Sedley recommended he wait and see what developed before committing himself and their joint interests to the Southern cause. A North Carolinian, Newcomb was typical of hundreds of Southerners who'd settled in Southern California in the past few years, attracted by its climate and cheap land — also because, geographically, it seemed a natural extension of the South and because its great *ranchos* served by Indians seemed like Southern plantations. Ambitious, hard driving, Newcomb had bought up land with Sedley's backing. He had established stagecoach and freight lines between San Pedro and Los Angeles and between Los Angeles and the interior, and, partly to advance his fortunes, he had married the only daughter of a prominent *ranchero*. Gregarious, jovial, Newcomb liked to joke and tease. Secretly he regarded Pedro and all other *californianos* as members of an inferior race. As for exotic Eve with her height and impassioned good looks, she struck him as something he might like to conquer and add to his growing empire.

Ashore, two Concord stagecoaches, one red, one yellow,

stood waiting to receive passengers for the trip to Los Angeles. But before the tout for the yellow line reached them, Newcomb took Eve and Pedro under his vociferous wing. "I'm saving seats! You'll ride free as my guest, Miss Radovich. Here, Pedro, let me take her bag." He also took her arm and hurried her — Pedro following toward the red coach — helped her in, jumped in behind, slammed the door, and shouted up to the driver: "Ike, all full, let's go!" and to Pedro with a laugh: "Sorry, old man! Better luck next time!" The big Concord dashed off, leaving Pedro in its dust. Angrily Pedro turned toward the other stage. It too was dashing away, leaving him standing, bag in hand, in the cold fog.

Eve turned furiously on Newcomb. "Why, you've kidnapped me! Let me out!" The other passengers, all male, looked on with amusement.

"Why, my dear girl," he protested with an uproarious laugh, "I can't stop now. I've bet my competitor ten bucks I'll beat him to town. Pedro'll find a way there, if I know Pedro."

Eve sprang to the open window, screamed up at the driver to stop, but her voice was lost in the uproar as driver and passengers cheered on the six galloping horses, and the careening coach threw her backward into Newcomb's lap. He put his arms around her. "Say, I like this!" When she turned to slap his face, he caught her hand. "Now, Miss Radovich, that won't get you anywhere. You're my guest here. You might as well relax and enjoy the ride. Look there! The sun's coming out. Look at that scenery. Ever see anything like that?"

An hour later a frustrated and silent Eve was watching golden pasture lands give way to lush green vineyards, then to an unpaved street lined with one-story flat-roofed adobe houses. And then the red coach, still traveling at breakneck speed with its yellow competitor a few yards behind, dashed up that dusty street — scattering dogs, chickens, pigs, pedestrians, ox-carts out of its way — and came to a halt in front of a rather seedy-looking two-story hotel, amid triumphant shouts of driver and passengers and the cheers of bystanders. The bystanders included, she noticed, Mexicans, an Indian, and a black man as well as Anglos.

"Here we are!" cried Newcomb jovially. He flung open the door, jumped out, doffed his brown derby, and, with an elaborate bow, offered her his arm. "Welcome to our City of the Angels!"

Head high, Eve swept past him without a word, eyes fixed on the benign-looking middle-aged couple coming toward her from the verandah of the Bella Union. They had to be Ethel and Ambrose Curtis. They were. And they welcomed her warmly while Newcomb stood by, hat in hand, beaming triumphantly as if he'd just delivered something precious into their hands. "If I'd known she was coming to see you two Republicans," he joshed, "I'd have kept her for myself. She's got Dixie spirit!"

"Oh, nonsense, Earl! Hush, or I'll tell Carmen on you!" Ethel Curtis reproved him.

"She won't believe a word you say," he retorted. "She knows I'm a good boy!" And to Eve: "Miss Radovich, it's been a pleasure!"

"No, it hasn't!" she snapped. "You kidnapped me, Mister Newcomb, and I intend to get even!"

"Kidnapped? Why, I rescued you from the arms of a low-life *californiano*." He burst into an uproarious laugh, winked at Ethel and Ambrose. Since Newcomb was married to Carmen de la Vega, only child of the wealthy and influential Don Porfirio de la Vega and his socially prominent wife, Hortensia, he felt he could afford to joke about *californianos*. It was a rôle he liked to play: both ends against the middle. "And this is how you thank me?" he teased Eve. And with another wink at Ambrose and Ethel and another profound bow to Eve he went off to collect his ten-dollar bet from the driver of the yellow stage that had just pulled up behind them.

Hardly had he gone ten steps and hardly had Eve exchanged ten words with her new friends, when angry voices broke out from inside the hotel, followed by the sound of a shot. They all turned and saw a man stagger backward onto the verandah and fall, while a second man, pistol in hand, emerged and stood over him, glaring down, then glaring at the crowd and brandishing his weapon defiantly. "That's what nigger-loving Yankees deserve. Anyone else want a taste of my medicine?" No one stirred.

Then frail-looking Ambrose Curtis stepped forward and said with quiet authority: "Ben Trott, you bully, you ought to be ashamed of yourself. Jed Bryant's your neighbor. Now get out of my way." He bent over the fallen man, who lay unconscious on the boardwalk, blood pouring from a wound at the side of his head. "He's not dead, lucky for you," Curtis added in a moment. And turning to Newcomb, who came hurrying up, he said: "Earl, give me a hand." Together they carried Jed Bryant into the hotel, while Ben Trott looked on defiantly, grumbling: "He started it."

"Welcome to Los Angeles!" Ethel Curtis murmured to Eve as they watched in horror and dismay.

The Curtises' adorable cottage had adobe walls, a red-tile roof, a front garden lush with flowers, and an orange and a lemon tree. "Casa Adorada, we call it. Ambrose designed it," Ethel said. "He's an amateur architect. He calls it our Southern California house." Eve thought it charming. Jasmine and honeysuckle climbed over it. The interior was cool and inviting.

A spacious living room looked out through a sun porch to patio and rear garden. "That sun porch is where we'll teach our kiddies," Ethel said. Eve noted that it already contained building blocks and miniature chairs. "And out there in the garden each child will have his or her own plot to cultivate. We don't have children of our own, but, when Ambrose and I were in Germany, we visited one of their newfangled kindergartens and were so favorably impressed, we decided we'd establish one some day."

Eve felt Ethel with her warm heart should have had a dozen children of her own. Ethel showed her to her room. It, too, gave onto the rear garden through large, glassed doors such as she'd never seen. They stood open and took her right outside into that gentle sunlight and balmy air that seemed the essence of her new surroundings. Ethel was telling how she and Ambrose knew Mornay and Mary Louise back East in New Bedford where all were active Abolitionists in the Underground Railroad. "But the doctors warned Ambrose if he didn't leave that Massachusetts climate, he'd be dead of consumption in a year. We hated the idea of leaving. Ambrose had a good law practice. But since coming here, he's never felt better. You saw him in action just now."

"Does that sort of thing happen often?"

"Not every day. There were only twenty-five shootings last month. But I don't want to discourage you, my dear. This town is full of many wonderful people of many kinds."

They had hardly settled down in the comfortable living room with its Brussels carpet and leather-covered armchairs and sofa when Ambrose walked in. There was blood on his hands and sleeves, but he looked relieved. "Jed will live. It's just a scalp wound. The sheriff has jailed Ben Trott on a charge of assault with intent to kill. Of course, no jury will convict him, given the politics of this town. Now let me wash

73

and change, and I'll join you. Eve, I want to apologize for such a violent welcome."

"Don't apologize. It's what I came for. Real life!" She smiled from the heart. She liked both Curtises, and they evidently liked her.

Later over a lunch of spicy tamales served by Ethel's middle-aged Indian helper, Mary, Ambrose explained: "The war has heightened tensions to the breaking point. They raised the Confederate flag over city hall the other night, probably with Ben Trott's help. And Stanhope and his Golden Knights are ready to ride into town from their stronghold out in El Monte and take over things. If it weren't for the presence of Union troops, there might be fighting in the streets. There may be, anyway, if General Johnston says the word."

Eve pricked up her ears. "Is General Johnston still in town? I promised Virgil Gillem I'd interview him."

Ambrose looked at her with amusement. "But I wonder if he would like to be interviewed?"

"Why not? I'll give him a fair hearing," retorted Eve brashly.

Ambrose and Ethel exchanged glances. They had never encountered such temerity in a young woman. "Well," resumed Ambrose gravely, "if you're set on it, Johnston's been staying with his brother-in-law, Doctor Griffin, over on Main Street between First and Second. The Union authorities have him under surveillance. No telling where he is now."

"Then I shall see for myself first thing tomorrow," Eve announced with such assurance that they had to believe her.

"Let's not talk about war forever," Ethel suggested. "Eve, I want to tell you more about my new school and your rôle in it. But first tell us how Earl Newcomb kidnapped you, and what happened to poor Pedro Díaz. Pedro's like a son to us." She explained how the promising and ambitious Pedro clerked

74

by day at their friend Simon Koenig's wholesale grocery and studied law by night in Ambrose's law office, and how Ambrose and Simon paid his way to San Francisco as a reward for hard work and to give him a chance to see the sights of the city. "They think he'll be a civic leader someday. He comes from a good but very poor family, bless his heart. He's almost their sole support. We think the world of him."

Angry and resentful, carpetbag in hand, Pedro started walking after the disappearing stagecoaches, hoping to be given a lift by some wagon headed for Los Angeles, wondering how he would get even with Earl Newcomb.

He hadn't gone far when he saw three horsemen approaching at a lope, one a little in advance of the others, and he recognized the commanding figure of Don Porfirio de la Vega, Newcomb's father-in-law, owner of the unfenced grazing land through which he was walking, indeed of much of the countryside between him and the City of the Angels. Behind Don Porfirio were his *mayordomo* and his head *vaquero*. All three had been attracted, no doubt, by the sight of someone on foot in the open range, something virtually unknown in their pastoral world where everyone, except the lowest members of society, thought of himself as a cavalier and rode a horse.

"Pedro Díaz, what are you doing, walking like an Indian?" Don Porfirio demanded as he drew rein and looked down with disapproval. With his imperious disdain and great wealth and power, he was like something out of a feudal past. He sat a silver-mounted saddle. He wore a costly green velvet jacket and a broad-brimmed black hat and silver-mounted spurs with huge rowels.

"Because, like an Indian, I have no horse, Don Porfirio," Pedro replied mildly, though he despised the old don and the unscrupulous alliance he represented between powerful *cali-fornianos* and newly arrived Anglos like Newcomb.

"A very foolish thing to do," Porfirio scolded. "You will frighten my cattle. They are not accustomed to seeing a man on foot, and they may attack you out of their viciousness, which is very great. In every way this is foolish of you."

"Are you telling me not to walk upon this public road?"

"No, I'm telling you what is good for you in this matter as in others I think of. Very foolishly, you are a Republican when you should be a Democrat, a Unionist when you should be a supporter of the South and union with *it!* Thus you side with the wrong people against your own kind. Ambrose Curtis and Simon Koenig sent you to San Francisco, as everyone knows, to find out there how to stir up trouble here, just as now you are stirring up trouble for yourself. Look!" A band of longhorn cattle led by a ferocious-looking black bull was approaching. "This time I shall drive them off. Next time you may not be so fortunate." And so saying, he galloped away with his two retainers behind him. They cast back derisive glances, while Pedro stood there, furious with them and Don Porfirio and Earl Newcomb and with himself.

Gloomier than ever, he trudged on, bag in one hand, jacket hooked over his shoulder by one finger of the other, discouraged, perspiring, feeling he'd failed in every way, wondering if he'd ever see Eve again, when he heard a cheerful shout behind. He turned and saw Wing Fat, the fish peddler, driving his decrepit white-hooded wagon behind his decrepit old white horse. Pedro stopped and waited. As Fat caught up, Pedro felt it was perhaps just in time, for more of Don Porfirio's cattle were coming to have a look at him. Fat, who was not fat but very lean, exclaimed cheerily as he drew rein: "No walkee! Getee sole footee! Climb up heal!" He indicated the seat beside him.

"Thanks, Fat, I will!" Pedro grinned back and handed up his bag and climbed after it.

Fat was a cousin of Wing Sing who sat at Mornay's round table. Fat peddled fresh fish in Los Angeles every Friday, and regularly stopped at Pedro's house. Pedro had known Fat for years without really having gotten acquainted with him. "Fat, what are you doing on the road so late in the morning?" Fat usually started his trips to town before dawn, but this time he'd been delayed by the sickness of his old horse who had developed sweats during the night and was still shaky, as Pedro could see. Although he'd never found a great deal to say to Fat before, had, in fact, looked down upon him as a member of an inferior race, under the present circumstances he saw him in new light, and, as the old horse plodded slowly along, he asked Fat about his fisherman's life. "Velly fine life!" Fat replied. He then told Pedro how he had sailed from China in the very junk from which he had caught the fish that were behind them under the white canvas hood, cooled by wet burlap sacking; sailed from Canton northward past Japan and westward to the coast of Alaska, and southward to San Francisco, all with the help of the same cousins, actually members of his clan, who had helped him catch these fish. From San Francisco they had extended their operations southward until they had reached San Pedro where there was almost no competition, and fish and shellfish were plentiful along the neighboring coast and offshore islands.

Pedro began to see that there were remarkable things about Fat that he had never taken time to find out before. "So you like it here, Fat?"

"Thisee home now."

"Mine, too, Fat."

Pedro told of having been a fisherman himself as a boy when the river that ran by the Pueblo de la Reina de Los

Angeles, or Town of the Queen of Angels, teemed with trout, trout such as even now were picked up and sent wriggling along the open ditches that ran everywhere through it by the huge waterwheel that served the town. "But, then, my father was wounded fighting the Americans, and I had to go to work. My father helped besiege them on Fort Hill that overlooks the Plaza where you deliver us your fish, Fat, and then he helped drive them out of town, but he was hit by a bullet in the spine, and he's never recovered."

Fat nodded sympathetically, not catching all the details, but getting the gist. In fact, Pedro's father, Pasqual, had inherited their modest adobe on the plaza from his father Blas, who in 1781 was among the forty-four first settlers of the pueblo "including some with Negro or Indian or perhaps Asiatic blood like yours, Fat, so we've always been a mixture, and I guess we always will be."

Fat dropped him off in front of his house on the dusty plaza, a stone's throw from today's Union Station — the plaza that still exists at the heart of Los Angeles' Old Town, but did not then have tourist shops around its perimeters but, instead, the town houses of *grandees* such as Don Porfirio de la Vega and the dwellings of humbler folk such as the Díaz family, plus saloons and gambling dens and houses of prostitution, and the Church of Our Lady of the Angels that still stands today.

After Fat handed down his bag, Pedro took a silver dollar from his pocket and held it up, but Fat waved it away with a smile, jumped down, and, in business-like manner, took two large mackerel from under their wet sacking and handed them to him. "Two fishee, two bitee!" he insisted, until Pedro handed him back a silver quarter, thanked him warmly, and walked toward the doorway of his house, feeling exhilarated, then terribly let down as he realized he was home

78

again and that all the family problems he'd escaped during his trip were now back upon him, along with those generated by this day.

The next morning Eve knocked on the door of the vine-covered brick house on Main Street where General Johnston had been staying. A dark-haired, smiling, gracious woman in early middle-age opened it.

"If you please, may I speak to the general?"

"I'm sorry my husband is not here." Eliza Johnston was on the point of closing the door, but something about Eve made her hesitate. There was something of the hard-striving successor-in-favor about Eve that touched Eliza. Eliza was a second wife. Johnston's first had died after bearing him a son. Eliza had borne him three more. "Why did you wish to see the general?"

"I'm from *The Sentinel*."

"Virgil Gillem's newspaper? Oh, we knew Virgil in San Francisco. He's a dear. He's from Kentucky, as we are. Won't you come in?" Eve entered a conventional Victorian parlor, dark with lace curtains drawn, white lace antimacassars on dark chairs. "Please sit down," Eliza continued. "Tell me what Virgil wants from us?"

"He's asked me to interview your husband."

"I'm afraid you can't do that. My husband's whereabouts are unknown even to me."

"Then may I interview you?" Eve seized the opening.

"Why . . . ," Eliza hesitated.

"You can speak to me as wife, mother, woman," Eve urged.

Eliza surveyed her. She liked her. Here could be the chance to place her beloved Sidney before the world in true light. "Yes," she decided, "I will. If you'll promise me one thing. Virgil always seemed to present the news fairly. Will you

79

promise to be fair this time?"

"I promise."

Eliza ranged back over her life as stepmother and mother of Johnston's children. "After Sidney first resigned from the Army as a young man, we struggled to make a living on a farm in Texas. The enterprise failed. Sidney assumed our partner's debts. He reëntered the service and rose to fame, while he slowly paid off what we owed. Sidney is a man of absolute integrity." Then Eliza waxed flowery. "He is the beau ideal of a chivalric leader, without fear and without reproach. That's why North and South both want him to lead their armies."

"Is it true that he's planning to lead an uprising and seize California?"

"No, he only asks to be allowed to go his own way in peace, which is what all our Confederate states ask. I would like the public to know our true feelings. We love this country, North or South. We love California. We love our children. We have freed our slaves. We have malice toward no one. My husband agonized over his decision to side with the South. It was the most heart-breaking moment of his life. We are not wealthy. We have no home save this, my generous brother's house."

For over an hour they talked, heart to heart. Then Eve asked: "You've trusted me. May I trust you?"

"Yes, what with?"

"With my identity. I want to remain an anonymous reporter while I write the truth. Will you help me by keeping my secret?"

Eliza reached out a hand impulsively and seized Eve's. "Of course!"

Thus they entrusted each other. And thus Eve's first letter to Gillem's *Sentinel* appeared on its front page under the banner headline:

AN EXCLUSIVE INTERVIEW
WITH MRS. ALBERT SIDNEY JOHNSTON
BY OUR LOS ANGELES CORRESPONDENT.

It was unsigned except by the confidence Eliza and Eve had placed in each other.

Chapter Ten

A few nights later Goodly Jenkins and Stubby Gatlin, on their way to join the Confederate Army in Texas, reached Bill Traven's Dixieland Saloon on the plaza not far from Pedro Díaz's house. They hoped to find kindred spirits in these surroundings as they stood watching the monte table where a dazzling *señorita* dealt. Her red dress set off her dusky charms as did the red rose in her dark hair.

"Rosita, damn you, deal me an honest hand for a change, will you?" one player protested half seriously, half jokingly. He had a harelip that made him lisp.

Rosita gave him a scornful laugh. "Watch your words, *señor*."

Across the room, behind the bar, Big Bill Traven noted all this while serving up drinks impassively, as if doing his customers a favor by letting them drink his whiskey and play at his gaming tables, and this had the wonderful effect of making them think so, too. Behind Bill, on the wall above the row of bottles, a new Confederate flag with its stars and bars was draped over a portrait of clean-shaven, aquiline-faced Jefferson Davis, and at the bar there was a general consensus that Lincoln and his Yankees were going to get the shit kicked out of them in the days ahead.

Out of this consensus stepped a figure who'd been eyeing Goodly and Stubby, then exchanged a look with Big Bill Traven. He was a wizened little fellow with one squint eye and one popped wide, and, as he stepped up to the two observers at the monte table, he drawled in friendly tone: "You boys care to join me in a drink to Jeff Davis?" And when they gladly did, and gladly had another, he confided flatteringly: "I judge you two hail from somewheres south of Maine?" And when they admitted their Missouri origins, the wizened little man inquired further: "I reckon you know how to use these?" He touched the butt of the pistol he wore at his belt, as they wore theirs. They nodded, wondering where all this was leading. "Name's Copus," the little man continued. "Copus is looking for a couple of good men to drive a couple of light wagons acrosst the desert. You be game?"

"Sure, we be game."

"Clear acrosst New Mexico Territ'ry to Texas?"

"Sure thing, mister. That's just where we're headed." Lubricated by the whiskey, Goodly affirmed their desire to enlist in the Army of the Confederate States of America. "But might there be something in your proposal besides exercise?" he added.

Copus took a shiny gold double eagle from his pocket, flipped it flashing into the light of the lamp that hung from the ceiling, and caught it deftly. "Five of these at the end of the trip. Meantime, you look after our mules. We look after you."

"We?"

"You'll see."

He was interrupted by turmoil at the monte table. The hare-lipped man had accused Rosita Díaz of dealing off the bottom of the deck, and she'd slapped his face, and he'd grabbed her. Big Bill Traven was emerging impassively from behind his bar. Bill took the offending customer by the scruff of the neck, lifted him completely clear of the floor, carried him to the door, and threw him out into the dusty plaza. Wiping his hands on his apron, he returned impassively behind the bar, letting the lesson speak for itself, while the room that had fallen silent broke out into sound again, though at a reduced level.

★ ★ ★ ★ ★

At dusk two days later, Goodly and Stubby rendezvoused with Copus in a grove of live oaks at Warner's Ranch, sixty-five miles southeast of Los Angeles on the road to Texas. With Copus were thirty stern-faced, well-armed men who looked ready for any eventuality. Outstanding among them was a magnificently proportioned figure of commanding presence whom Copus referred to as the general.

"General?" Goodly asked.

"General Albert Sidney Johnston."

Goodly's eyes opened wide, as did Stubby's.

"He don't wear no uniform," Copus went on. "None of us does. Captain Hancock's blue dragoons is after us. You get the point?"

The point brought the war close. It made Goodly's skin prickle, and Stubby ask: "Who's the nigger with him?"

"That's his servant, Ran. Ran's a free nigger. Johnston freed 'im when they come to this here so-called free state of California, hah! Be careful how you treat Ran," Copus cautioned. Ran would be driving the general's ambulance, or light wagon, while Johnston rode horseback, along with other former United States Army officers who, like him, had resigned their commissions and comprised most of the company. "C'mon, I'll introduce you. Johnston don't bite."

The most sought after man in the country, the man both sides wanted at the head of their armies, stood well over six feet. He had broad shoulders, a large, square-jawed head, flowing brown hair and mustache that were graying slightly, for Johnston was in his sixtieth year. His gray-blue eyes glowed with a strange, almost other worldly, light most people found magnetic. Yet, his manner was modest and courteous. A West Pointer, like Davis who greatly admired him, Johnston had served, like Abraham Lincoln, in the Black Hawk War against

84

the Sauk Indians of Illinois, then had resigned his commission and tried farming in Texas, as Eliza had described to Eve. After failing, he had enlisted as a private in the army of the Texas Republic and had risen to become its Secretary of War. During the war between the United States and Mexico that soon followed, Johnston had served like Stanhope and Davis with distinction. Later he had successfully commanded an expedition against the Mormons of Utah Territory when they threatened to set up their own nation of Deseret. As secession fever swept the South, U. S. Secretary of War Floyd, a Southern sympathizer, had appointed Johnston commander of the strategic Department of the Pacific, hoping he would swing California to the Southern side. But Johnston had scorned Floyd's innuendoes and Stanhope's proposal that he connive at seizing Fortress Alcatraz. Yet, when his adopted state of Texas finally seceded, Johnston, also as Eliza had described, had painfully decided to resign his commission and offer his services to the South. With his family he had come to Los Angeles in route to the Confederacy. Hearing he was about to be arrested by Union authorities, he had slipped away from the house on Main Street, and here he stood, larger than life in Goodly's and Stubby's eyes.

"Glad to have you fellows with us," he said easily. He made them feel as if they had been here all along, were destined members of this special company under these oaks by these newly lit campfires, embarked, together with Johnston, on a great enterprise. "We'll need volunteers like you."

Later as Johnston lay on the ground wrapped in his blanket, watching the starry figure of Orion climb the sky, he thought of Eliza and their children behind him in Los Angeles. Beautiful, desirable Eliza was expecting another baby before long. A great surge of love welled up in Johnston for her and their youngsters and their shared dream. After the war he would retire to the ranch they hoped to buy. Located where the city of Pasadena would one day stand, it was a glorious expanse of grassland and green oaks that gleamed in his mind like paradise itself. Johnston realized the enormity of the commitment he had made, the dark days that must intervene before he would see the bright land of his dreams again.

Goodly was having thoughts, too, as he lay a few yards away. He looked up at the stars and wondered if he might be better off back at the cabin with Buck and Iphy, Elmer and Opal, and old Abe. For all their faults, they suddenly looked pretty good, as an unknown future opened perilously before him. He heard the horses and mules stirring in the darkness at the ends of their tethers. It gave him an idea. Might it be better to slip away and inform Captain Hancock as to Johnston's whereabouts and collect the two hundred and fifty dollar reward for information leading to the arrest of the famous general? Wouldn't that be better than facing what might otherwise lie ahead? But then he heard a step and saw the figure of the sentry outlined against the sky. A sentry's eyes are always peeled for a newcomer to turncoat and try to slip away. No, he was stuck where he was. Stubby, too. And then he recalled with pride their feelings when Johnston welcomed them. They were actually members of Johnston's party, embarked with him on a great enterprise that could bring them fame and fortune. He thought how envious Buck would be, if he knew this, how his father would look at him with new eyes, as would Iphy and Abe and the others. And this thought, above all others, separated Goodly from his old life and sent him into an unknown future.

Chapter Eleven

Francisco and Helek crouched in a clump of purple sage at the crest of the bluff overlooking the hacienda of Rancho Olomosoug with its outbuildings and corrals, its fields of barley and wheat unfenced but protected by ditches, its pastures where horses and cattle grazed, and its Indian village of thatched huts down by the river.

"It's what I saw in my dream!" Helek whispered excitedly.

"That means our quest is a true one. It is, indeed, your grandmother's place, the place where I grew up, the place where she did, too, though long before there was a big house such as you see."

Beyond the river rose the dome-shaped hill that gleamed like gold in the rising sun. Francisco pointed out the solitary oak at its summit under which Helek's grandfather was buried. Helek pictured the old *conquistador* lying there in the ground, blue uniform much faded now, his sword rusty, his yellow hair faded or turned gray — Helek could not decide which might be nearer the truth — but his grandfather's significance gleamed brightly in his mind, nevertheless.

As they watched, old Clara emerged from the hacienda and stood undecided a moment in the courtyard. Oppressed by thoughts of Pacifico's departure for the war, of Francisco's existence as hunted outlaw somewhere in the wilderness, by the ever-present proximity of the squatters, and by the uncertain future of her ranch while her claim to it languished in the law courts at enormous expense, she had decided not to ride out this morning as usual with Sally to see how things were going. Instead, she would walk up and refresh her spirit at the ancient shrine atop the bluff overlooking the house, almost exactly where Francisco and Helek were hiding.

"Go on," encouraged Sally, who had followed her into the courtyard, "and enjoy yourself. Forget everything, *Mama Grande*. I'll see to it!"

"No, you'll wait till I get back!" Irascibly turning away, the old woman strode off. Her Mother Hubbard swishing about her ankles, she followed the path through the vegetable garden that led to the hillside and, in the lee of it, became invisible to the two observers directly above.

"That is your grandmother," Francisco explained softly.

"Where is she going?"

"Perhaps to gather herbs in her garden."

"Who was that with her?"

"That is Sally, your half-brother's wife."

"I should like to meet her and my brother." Sally was the first young woman other than his sister that Helek had ever seen, and he was instantly smitten.

"Someday you will meet them."

Helek turned his attention to the two cabins a short mile down the valley. "Who lives there?"

"Buck Jenkins and his family." Francisco explained what squatters were.

"If they aren't supposed to be there, why don't we drive them away?"

"Because it would simply lead to more bloodshed, and the A-alowow would win in the end, because there are more of them."

"Must we never kill white men?"

Francisco replied thoughtfully: "Perhaps sometimes we must, just as they must kill us."

As they spoke, Buck and Iphy emerged, arguing, from their cabin like two birds squabbling. "I don't want you to hunt or kill Injuns!" Iphy was berating him. "If you hunt and kill other

88

people, Buck, how can you expect them not to hunt and kill poor Goodly?"

"Poor Goodly!" Buck mocked her. "Leave poor Goodly out of this. If poor Goodly is man enough to go his own way, let 'im go it. And don't pester me. I know what I got to do. Any man does. That's something no woman can understand."

"Well, I'll never understand you, that's for sure, and I wish you'd take that damn' thing down" — indicating the lion skin pegged to the cabin wall to dry — "it stinks. Just like you do, when you talk and act so murderous. Ain't you got no God in you?"

"Leave God out of this. He's got more important things to do, and so have I!" Buck retorted, and strode off toward the outhouse to escape her.

They were too distant for Helek and Francisco to hear what they were saying, but there was no mistaking their disagreement. "I don't like the squatters," Helek commented.

"Neither do I," replied Francisco and told how this feud with Buck had begun.

Meanwhile, Clara's spirits rose steadily as she climbed the winding trail up the shady hillside under the live oaks and California holly, among the maidenhair fern and last farewells to spring. She stopped frequently to catch her breath and to remember that this was the path up which old Tilhini and his predecessors had led her people since immemorial time to the shrine at the crest, with its ring of stones. The ring signified the circle of life which has no beginning or end. At its center stood an upright black pole, with red tip representing the blood of life, and attached to the top of the pole was the tuft of condor feathers representing the great bird that guides the People of the Land and the Sea. And she felt that when she stepped inside that ring of stones, her burdens would drop away, and her spirit would be renewed.

Francisco had already explained the meaning of the shrine to Helek, and now they heard Clara's heavy breathing as she approached. Francisco put his hand on his son's forearm to hold him very still while they waited to see her. She emerged almost beside them, her old head bare, her lined and weathered face radiant with the light of hope and faith as she crested the summit one more time. Francisco's grip on his son tightened. All his life seemed to flood back over him as he saw once more, so close after so long, the mother who had brought him into the world to experience all that had happened to him and now this.

Clara stepped inside the sacred ring and stood beside the pole, faced the rising sun, lifted both arms as if to embrace it, and they heard her say softly their own prayer: "Great dawn, breath of the Sun, welcome to the world!"

As she uttered these words, arms high, feeling life enter her, she heard a familiar voice speak out of the sage beside her: "Mother!"

With a gasp she turned. Francisco rose, hand still grasping Helek, bringing the boy up with him. "Here is your son, and your grandson!"

For a long moment she stood speechless, looking from one to the other.

"It is I, Francisco!" He stepped closer. "And this is Helek, my young hawk."

She flung herself upon them with an exclamation. "It is a miracle. But how? Why?"

Francisco drew her with them into the shelter of the fragrant sage. "I'm showing your grandson the world."

"Aren't you cold without any clothes on?" she cried with a mother's concern.

"You forget what it is to live in the old way," he admonished her gently.

90

"Yes, I forget, I forget. But you wonderfully remind me!" And she hugged them both to her again and again. "Now tell me all!"

Francisco, speaking casually to calm her agitation, told where they had come from, of the condor that guided them, of Ta-ahi and Letke left behind in the secret valley, of Helek's dream at the Cave of the Condors. "Tilhini didn't tell you of meeting us?"

"He hasn't returned."

Intuition told Francisco that Tilhini never would return, that the old seer had simply gone off somewhere to die, sensing his time had come. He felt a deep pang of sorrow, but merely lifted his eyebrows as if in surprise. "Tilhini confirmed Helek's name upon him and sent him on his vision quest, which has brought us to you."

"But your wife and daughter?" exclaimed Clara in further concern.

"My adopted daughter," he corrected. "They can take care of themselves. But what of my other son, Pacifico? And his wife?"

"She can take care of herself, but he cannot!" she snorted. "You've heard of the *gringo* war?"

"Tilhini told me."

"Pacifico has gone to it."

"That is utter foolishness. Why?"

"Because he is foolish and unhappy with himself and with me."

"And is he unhappy with his wife, too, as I once was with mine?"

"Yes." She looked at him sharply. "How did you guess?"

"One thing usually leads to another."

"If only Sally could have a child!" she burst out. Then incongruously: "The squatters are hunting you. Buck Jenkins intends to kill you."

"We saw him. The wilderness protected us, *Mamacita*, the wilderness and your love."

Tears flowed from her. She looked at him through them with radiant joy and pride in her prodigal son returned at last, son who disagreed with her way of life but chose his own and followed it and had come back to her. Then she turned fondly to Helek. "So you are my wild grandson?" For a moment she surveyed him. Then, sharply, as if he was a man and there was to be no nonsense: "What do you want most, Grandson?"

With inspiration springing from the emotion of the moment, Helek answered: "I want to understand the world, Grandmother!"

"Bravely spoken!" Clara looked with approval at his dark eyes, dark hair, dark skin, the features of her people, and Helek felt her approval and love pass into him. "You want to be a leader of our people like me, like your father?"

"Yes, Grandmother."

She suddenly clasped him to her. "You will! You will! By the light of this blessed day I prophesy. Tilhini was right! You will! But you'll also be part of my flesh, my spirit. Will you remember that?"

"I will, Grandmother!"

Francisco broke in: "*Mamacita*, our old worlds are dying as we speak. His is rising like this day. By knowing ours, I want him to be prepared for his. And now I think he and I must continue our journey."

"No," she protested, "no!" — seizing them both to her, tears streaming down her wrinkled face.

"Yes," said Francisco firmly, feeling the old, familiar clash of their wills, "but we won't forget. We'll be taking you with us, my mother."

She released them. "You are right," she conceded in subdued tone. And to Helek: "My grandson, this, too, will be part

92

of your world, I prophesy." She gestured at the land around them. "This Rancho Olomosoug! Love it as I have. Fight for it. Cherish it. Believe that it knows and loves you in return. Do you hear me?" she added fiercely, gripping both his hands with hers, fixing both his eyes with hers, so that, again, he felt her transmitted into him.

"Yes, Grandmother!"

"Now kiss me, here on the cheek!" She pointed. He put his lips to her old flesh and found it surprisingly young and warm.

"Now I leave you," she announced firmly to both. "I came up here to escape my sorrow. I leave filled with joy I never expected, grateful to Kakunupmawa, to Almighty God. Bless you! May they both keep you!" Finally, fiercely again: "May you fight on! May you prevail!"

Francisco embraced her silently, tears in his eyes. So did Helek, with tears in his. Then she turned without further word and began to descend the hillside.

Chapter Twelve

The mule-drawn wagons driven by Goodly, Stubby, Copus, and Ran, Johnston's former slave, churned up dust that wrapped them in clouds of choking heat, while Johnston and the others rode horseback around them as they all pushed on as fast as possible across the scorching desert. They were following, generally, the routes taken by today's Highway S22 and 78 on what was then called the old Emigrant Road, part of the Southern Overland Route from Texas to California. Their thermometer read one hundred and twenty degrees in the shade.

Whenever Goodly thought he couldn't stand it any longer, he looked at Johnston, erect and cheerful as if discomfort was nothing, and felt a little ashamed. And when they finally reached Indian Wells and Johnston was the last to drink and then helped them water their mules, Goodly's admiration rose higher. Stubby agreed. "An' him a famous gen'ral, yet he acts like anybody!" They felt challenged to be more than they were.

That evening Johnston wrote Eliza back in Los Angeles: **We must not borrow trouble, dear wife, but nerve ourselves to face it should it come. I think happily of you and our children safe in the custody of your generous brother.** He made no mention of the heat, dust, thirst, flies, sleeplessness, fatigue, or the strain of always having to set an example, always striving to follow that code of honor to which he adhered. But he added: **We have two young teamsters so eager and willing they inspire me to be better than I otherwise might be.**

Vallecito and Indian Wells behind them, the party passed into the heart of the Colorado Desert. **Marching into the evening to escape the heat we were astonished,** Johnston wrote Eliza, **to see a huge comet as large as Venus lighting up all the sky. Its tail was one hundred degrees long and stretched far into the Milky Way.** It was the Tebbutt Comet, popularly known as the Great Comet. **Its brightness made our route visible even at midnight and also favored us with great additional light the following night, so that, while marching through this inhospitable desert, although we had only a cloud of dust by day, like the children of Israel escaping from Pharaoh we had a pillar of flaming light by night.**

No sign of pursuit thus far. Captain Winfield Scott Hancock and his blue dragoons, misled by false reports put out by Copus and others, were searching for Johnston in the vicinity of San Pedro where Johnston had been planning to embark for Panama until friends had warned him he was about to be arrested.

Now they crossed a final, blindingly hot stretch of sand and warily approached a cluster of unstockaded buildings on a bluff overlooking the Colorado River from the California side. No telegraph wires connected remote Fort Yuma with the outside world. Yet, perhaps, news of their coming had preceded them. The Union garrison could be preparing to intercept them. They had no idea that telegraph wires across North and South were carrying word of Johnston's "sensational disappearance into the desert," that millions were wondering as to his whereabouts, that the authorities in Washington City had reiterated their order for his arrest as a traitor to the Union cause. But they clearly saw puffs of smoke from the fort and heard cannon shots. For a moment, they thought the shots were aimed at them, but, then, realized it was the Fourth of July, and this was a customary salute to a national holiday.

Still wary, they pitched camp at the outskirts of the village that had sprung up at the river crossing near the fort. They badly needed rest and recuperation, time to shoe horses and mules, have new tires cut for their wagons, and to purchase additional supplies for the long march ahead. On the evening of their second night at Jaegersville, Stubby was one of two sentinels patrolling the camp's perimeter when he heard a friendly Southern voice say from the darkness: "Chum, you fellows need a recruit?"

Stubby replied in his Missouri drawl: "Let's have a look at you first."

As the speaker advanced, Shorty made out a figure no taller than himself, but in blue uniform. "You really a Reb?"

"Sure am. So are a bunch more, yonder." The stranger gestured back toward the fort.

Shorty regarded him suspiciously. "Can you prove it?"

"Gimme a chance."

"Well, come along. You can talk to the major."

Tall, lanky, former U. S. Army Major Lewis Armistead, a Virginian in route home to offer his services to his native state, was the other sentinel that night. He queried the would-be defector in courtly, but firm, style. "What's your name, soldier?"

"Milsaps, sir, Corporal Milsaps, may it please you." Milsaps added a salute, then told Armistead what he'd told Stubby.

Armistead led Milsaps to the campfire where Johnston and the others were gathered. Two years hence, almost to the day, Brigadier General Lew Armistead would lead his men up Cemetery Ridge in Pennsylvania on that fateful last day of the Battle of Gettysburg and would die at its crest, inside the Union line, as Major General Winfield Scott Hancock — once a captain in California searching for a party of Southern sympathizers — came galloping up to stem the tide at this high-water mark of the Confederacy and found an old friend dead.

Now Armistead said to Johnston and the others: "Here's a fellow claims he can deliver Fort Yuma into our hands."

They listened as Milsaps declared: "Even some of our officers favors the South. We'll rise and seize the place, if you'll lend us a hand."

"We'll need time to think this over," Johnson remarked, and the others agreed. "Come back tomorrow at this same hour with one of your officers," he told Milsaps, "and we'll give you our answer."

After Milsaps had gone, a debate ensued. "If we accept his proposal, we ally ourselves with a turncoat," Johnston began. "If we don't, he may arouse the garrison and bring a hornet's nest about our ears."

"If we seized the fort," Armistead weighed in, "it would give us a toehold on California soil, but could we hold it till reinforcements arrived?"

Colonel Ridley rejoined: "Stanhope and his people might rise and back us."

"Before Federal troops could get here?" objected Armistead.

"My dad and his Knights of the Golden Circle are itching for a scrap," Goodly contributed, enormously proud to be part of this council of war. "They'd back us, like Colonel Ridley says."

Finally Johnston said modestly, for he had no authority beyond what prestige and persuasion may give: "I see no justification for seizing the fort. It would be equivalent to an act of piracy on the high seas. We're civilians," he cautioned, "and have no standing as members of the Confederate Army, and, even if successful, such a venture would deter us from our goal, which is to reach Texas as soon as possible."

The majority agreed with Johnston. Early next morning they all pushed on, keeping a wary eye toward the fort, crossing the muddy Colorado, eleven hundred feet wide, on Diego Jaeger's rope ferry and entering New Mexico Territory, a vast and sparsely settled region that would eventually become the states of New Mexico and Arizona. They avoided the settlement variously called Arizona City or Yuma on the east bank and followed the wagon road eastward, up the similarly muddy but much narrower and shallower branch of the Colorado, the Gila.

Eighty miles later they were approaching the Pima Indian villages, near present Gila Bend, when they saw a withered corpse hanging from a cottonwood tree and asked Ammi White at his nearby grist mill what it was.

"It's an Apache," the laconic White told them. "Pimas hung 'im thar as a warning." The Apaches regularly raided the peaceful Pimas, who raised melons, corn, and cotton in their fertile fields near the river. And White added: "The Pimas regularly kills 'em and hangs 'em up or chases 'em off."

Ridley and Armistead negotiated with White for the purchase of flour and fresh melons for the entire party, and then they pushed on into the high desert along the route taken by today's Highway 10 toward the ancient settlement of Tucson, dating from Spanish times.

Tucson stood beside a clear river at the foot of barren mountains and consisted of several dozen adobes housing some nine hundred people. Two of its leading citizens, Ezekiel Gilpin, a store owner, and Hernando Cota, a blacksmith, rode out to welcome them. "You've got nothing to fear in Tucson," Gilpin assured them, and Cota echoed him. In retaliation for the town's outspoken Southern sympathies, Union soldiers from Fort Buchanan, fifty miles nearer the Mexican border, had burned Tucson's only grist mill and source of flour. "Anti-Northern feeling's sky high," Gilpin informed them, but then he added a *caveat*: "The Federals are evacuating Buchanan. They're withdrawing eastward to the Union forts along the Río Grande, to make a stand there against an invasion from Texas, and they plan to intercept you fellows if they can."

Johnston and his party were elated to hear of Confederates

advancing from Texas, but alarmed by the immediate Federal threat. "How many of them are there?" Johnston asked.

"Two companies of infantry and two of dragoons."

"We'll have to hurry to stay ahead of them," Ridley put in.

But Armistead cautioned: "We must rest first. Our livestock's tuckered out. And we need new tires and more groceries."

So they took a hurried rest in a green meadow by the bank of the Santa Cruz at the edge of town, while tires were cut in Cota's blacksmith shop and supplies purchased from Gilpin's general store. Stubby wrote home: **I've seed a cigaro** [saguaro] **cacktis. Looks jest like a pitchfork stickin' out of the ground headfirst,** and Goodly boasted **we're a-marching through New Mexico Territory with General Johnston,** and, added with double meaning: **I snatched a little pussy from a Tucson *señorita* and I'm keeping it as a pet. Ha!** After forty-eight hours they pushed on. They had to reach Dragoon Springs, where the road from Fort Buchanan joined the main road, before the Federals did.

So they marched thirty miles that day, forty the next, fifteen before breakfast the next morning, and reached Dragoon Springs a step ahead of the Federals and pressed forward toward Apache Pass in the rugged Chiricahua Mountains, scene of many a massacre of whites by Indians. "Hope them Pimas killed off all them Apaches," Stubby muttered glumly as they approached the infamous defile of blood and death. As darkness fell, they felt safer. Indians rarely attacked by night. But they were in a fix — Federals were certainly behind, Apaches maybe ahead.

Scouts out ahead and behind, they groped forward and reached the spring in Apache Pass at midnight, to find the only water for thirty miles in either direction preëmpted by a party of Texas Unionists in route to California. An argument ensued, but it stopped short of blows when Johnston intervened diplomatically: "Friends, I'm a Texan myself. For many years I owned a farm near Brazoria. I'll respect your right to go to California, if you'll respect the right of me and my friends to go to Texas. We've all of us got a right to disagree, I reckon. Yet, we've all got a right to drink, too, don't we?"

They were on their way eastward next morning at dawn, but, before the sun was high, Copus called out: "Something dead up yonder!" Buzzards were circling over a nearby bluff. Investigating, they found that an immigrant party, attacked by Indians, had taken refuge on this high ground, but it had become their graveyard. Eighteen men, women, children, and babies lay dead, their mutilated bodies partially devoured by coyotes and buzzards. There was no time for a burial. Heads were bared. Johnston led them in the Lord's Prayer.

That night at Cook's Springs, Copus took his two young protégés aside. "You boys listen to me. If we gets overtook by Federals, you, me, and the rest of us has got to keep them blue bellies amused while the general rides full tilt for the border. Once in Mexico he's safe, understand?"

Johnston had been reluctant to agree to this plan, but Ridley and Armistead had persuaded him.

From Cook's Spring, near present Deming, New Mexico, they traveled sixty miles without water and without stopping, for the Federals were close behind, and reached the Río Grande near the Mexican-American village of Picacho. Fort Fillmore, supposedly garrisoned by Federals, was a few miles downstream. *But were there Union troops in Picacho?* they all wondered.

Armistead and Ridley took Goodly, who spoke a fair amount of Spanish, and rode cautiously into the adobe village at ten o'clock of this hot July evening. They found most of the inhabitants standing on the flat roofs of their houses to cool

100

off and be out of harm's way. Goodly called out boldly: *"¿Amigos, qué pasó?"* And the excited answer came back *"¡Tejanos!"* Texans! They were astonished to learn that a handful of Texans had captured, almost without firing a shot, the entire Union garrison from nearby Fort Fillmore — two hundred and eighty men against six hundred. It was an incredible bit of good news, and they hurried back to inform the rest of the party.

Exuberantly, they all pushed on next morning to find the victorious Texans in nearby Mesilla. These Texas volunteers wore mainly red flannel shirts, blue denim trousers, black jackboots, black slouch hats, and they were so elated by their easy victory, they were ready to conquer the world. "C'mon and join us, fellows. We'll march to California for starters! You show us the way!"

Goodly and Stubby were ready to do it. Jefferson Davis's dream, Stanhope's dream, Mornay's and Martha's and David Venable's and Abraham Lincoln's nightmare seemed about to be realized. Here was the vanguard of a force that could reach the Pacific, could make the Confederacy a two-ocean nation, could bring California's gold to Richmond, Virginia, the Confederacy's new capital, not to Washington City.

Balding, bearded, fierce-eyed Colonel John Robert Baylor, the Texans' commander, a former Kentuckian like Johnston, urged the older man to take command of their combined forces "and lead us in the conquest of New Mexico and on to California!" Tempting as Baylor's offer was, Johnston felt impelled by destiny to continue toward Richmond. He knew Davis was likely to offer him command of all Southern armies in the field, as Lincoln had offered him command of all Northern ones. Besides, he was troubled by Baylor's impetuosity. Three hundred men were not an army. "Colonel, your invitation does me great honor, but I must continue my journey to our nation's capital and offer my services there first" — to my

101

old friend and West Point companion, Jefferson Davis, he could have added, but didn't.

Johnston's party had come to the end of its journey. He bid them an emotional farewell. "We did it together. We endured. We prevailed. That says it all. May God bless you wherever you may go from here." And Johnston boarded the stage for San Antonio, eight hundred miles farther east.

"I'd die for that man," declared Stubby wistfully.

"I'd fight for him," corrected Goodly.

"You may get a chance to do both," Copus pointed out dryly, "when he's general-in-chief."

Canny Copus, always with an eye to the main chance, now suggested they join him in prospecting for gold below the border. Rich strikes had been reported in Chihuahua. But in their present exuberant mood, they were more tempted by Colonel Baylor's heady proposal that they join him and his men in the conquest of New Mexico Territory. "We'll be the advance guard of thousands to follow," he promised. "The people of the territory will rise and join us. We'll push on to your golden state and wade our horses in the waters of your blue Pacific!"

Elated at the prospect of returning home at the head of a victorious army, Goodly and Stubby joined up with Baylor.

Chapter Thirteen

"Irresponsible!" his mother scolded him, as Pedro Díaz, bag in hand, entered the gloomy adobe on the old plaza that had been his family's home nearly since the founding of Los Angeles. "While you were away, the devil got into this house!"

"Mother, mine," he replied wearily, "you exaggerate my importance, if you think my presence can keep away the devil." Putting down his bag, he embraced her cold shoulders. María Santísima Díaz was pale and wan from constant worry, constant prayer, constant labor.

"Do not be impertinent to your mother," she retorted, drawing away. "We are in the midst of a great trouble! Had you stayed home, it might never have happened!" she almost wailed.

He had heard her tales of woe so often, they had become a wearisome litany, and it seemed he had never been away to San Francisco, never met Eve Radovich, never been humiliated by Earl Newcomb, and been picked up and delivered at his door by Wing Fat.

"What has happened?"

"I cannot bear to say. I do not think you care, anyway, or you would not have deserted us!" She pointed to his crippled father, who lay snoring on the earthen floor, flat on his back. Empty demijohn beside him, Pasqual Díaz was already dead drunk, although it was only midday. "What could he do? She would never listen to him or to Mariano" — meaning Pedro's fourteen-year-old brother — "but only to you, although, unlike you, Mariano does not prefer the company of *gringos* to that of his own people!"

"What nonsense! I work for the *gringos* to earn money to

support our family. You know that. Also so that I can do someday what I want to do."

"And what is this great thing that you want to do?"

"Someday I'll tell you, *Madrecita*. Today you are too much against me. What's happened? Is it Rosita?"

"And why shouldn't I be against you?" she continued to circumlocute, raising sorrowful eyes and gaunt hands toward heaven and glancing up at the crucifix over the door above his head. "You desert us when we need you. You listen to those lawyers like Mister Curtis. What is so interesting about the law, when there is the law of God? You ought to go to church more!"

"But *Madre*, all I want is justice for ordinary folk like ourselves against *grandees* like the de la Vegas who make you work for little or nothing, doing their washing and sewing. Desert you? I bring you money. I give you love. Yet you chide me unmercifully!"

His father snored through all of this, lost in futile dreams of vengeance against the Yankees for his old wound, thought Pedro bitterly, and resentment against all the burdens he carried swept over him. And then his sister, Raphaela, appeared like a ghostly apparition behind his mother. Thin, frail, four years older than he, she was already a spinster, worn and stooped like his mother from work and loss of hope. Raphaela fixed her mournful eyes on him, accusingly, and delivered the news his mother has been unable to utter. "Your adored Rosita has run away."

He could not believe it. Of all the family, joyous, spirited seventeen-year-old Rosita was dearest to him. "Run away? Where?"

His mother covered her ears with her hands and turned away as Raphaela uttered the dreadful words: "The Dixieland Saloon. She left the day after you did. She followed your example." Raphaela, jealous of his fondness for Rosita, stated these words with spiteful triumph.

Horror ran through Pedro. Yes, Rosita rebelled at the defeatism of this dreary household, at dutifully drudging for condescending *grandees*. Yes, like him she was hungry for better things. But he had never thought of this.

"We've told Father Sarria," Raphaela added with gloomy relish.

"What did he say?"

The bells of Our Lady the Queen of the Angels across the plaza pealed as if Father Sarria was listening.

"He said to pray."

"Well, did you?"

"Do not be blasphemous. He's praying, too."

"And after a week still no result? Put more money in his plate!" Pedro could not help exploding in his rage and exasperation as he turned and strode out of the house and across the plaza toward the Dixieland Saloon.

He found Rosita at the monte table, just as Goodly and Stubby had. She was wearing that red dress that revealed most of her shoulders. Glancing over those shoulders, as he came up behind her, Pedro saw she was dealing the three-card monte he had taught her, played with a Spanish deck like the one at home. Rings flashed from her fingers. A necklace sparkled at her throat. He took her by both shoulders. "Rosita!" His voice was hot with emotion, not cool as he had intended.

She whirled in anger as players and bystanders looked on with amusement. "Take your hands off me!"

"But I'm your brother," he pleaded, half choked.

"Does that give you the right to tell me what to do?" she flared out at him. "Let me alone. I've gone my way as you went yours." And she turned fiercely back to her cards, while those sitting at the table and those who had been standing by

105

smirked and chuckled and paid no further attention to Pedro. And Big Bill Traven at the bar looked on impassively, his expression saying to Pedro: "Challenge me if you like, but is this your business? Can you make her do what she doesn't want to do?"

Pedro turned away without another word.

Chapter Fourteen

When Stanhope heard of Baylor's victory and Johnston's escape, he burst into Sedley's office in the Sedley Building on Montgomery Street in San Francisco. "Eliot, you son-of-a-bitch, I can't thank you enough for persuading me to wait. Now we can prepare to receive victorious Confederate troops in California."

Coupled with the news of the Union rout at the battle of Bull Run near Washington City — fought almost simultaneously with the Confederate victory on the Río Grande — it did seem that one Confederate could perhaps lick ten Yankees and the South would win the war sooner than later.

But Sedley cautioned: "George, it ain't happened yet. It's a long way from the Río Grande to the Colorado." Nevertheless, the possibility of California becoming part of the Confederacy began to seem real to Sedley.

"I've come to ask you one question," Stanhope continued.

"What is it?"

"Are you with us?"

"When a Confederate Army crosses the Colorado, ask me that question again, George. Meanwhile, I'd watch my step if I were you. They'll be looking for somebody to arrest, now that they've missed Johnston."

Mornay and his underground group were downcast at the news of the Union defeats. **An Army is being assembled here,** he wrote David Venable gravely, **to counteract the Confederate thrust into New Mexico. This is a crucial moment. There is considerable excitement, I might almost say panic.**

Mary Louise and Dolly prepared to entertain Stanhope and Sedley at supper that night in celebration of the Confederate victories. It would be the New Orleans style repast Stanhope relished — mint julep with Spanish sherry, *bisque d'écrivesse* with brown roux and fine onions, braised duck, stuffed quail, sliced turkey, stuffed artichokes, all accompanied by a white burgundy and a red Bordeaux-Médoc, followed by vanilla ice cream with pecan sauce and fruit crêpes and Dom Pérignon. And not till it was over and she had heard what the euphoric, tipsy, gloating Stanhope had ill-advisedly said in front of her and Dolly and Sedley would Mary Louise know what she wanted and what would lead to Stanhope's undoing — that his next move would be to establish an assembly point in the mountains east of Los Angeles overlooking the desert, from where Southern sympathizers could sally forth and receive Southern troops entering California.

I worry about you down there with your beloved Pedro, Martha wrote Eve. **I hope you are both safe. Remember your passionate nature and do not throw yourself at him headlong. I've not heard from my David for four long weeks. One can only wonder and hope when such silences occur, but I take comfort from the fact that the mails are so uncertain in these wartime days. What a strange world we all live in. Where is it taking us? But I must trust in God, though I know that is foreign to your heretical nature, dear as you are to me in other ways. Sometimes when Papa is busy Virgil walks me home from the Rescue Mission. I can tell he's in love with me, though he makes no mention of it, nor does he try anything fresh with me as he did with you. He's a wonderful person, I agree. I hope he finds the right woman even-**

tually. **He tells me about each new one that comes along and asks my advice. I tell him only he can decide.**

Buck crowed to Iphy and the others: "I told you Stanhope was right. We'll rise when the Confed'rate Army gets here, and I'll bet Goodly and Stubby'll be with it," he declared proudly, "and then we'll take over this here state and this here ranch."

"Wait a minute, general," Iphy replied tartly. "You're gettin' mighty free with other people's blood, not to mention their property. And as for Goodly, you druv him off. Now you want him back? I wouldn't be surprised if he comes and swats you one, like you done him. It'd serve you right!"

When Sally drove up in the buckboard behind her two chestnut sorrels, Anita Ferrer, her husband's best friend's wife, left her two small children playing on the front porch and hurried to greet her dear friend. While Benito was away at the war, Anita lived with her parents. Their modern two-story whitewashed adobe with a balcony extending across its front was of the new style called Monterey and stood on a slight eminence overlooking vast pastures in which, like Clara's, cattle and horses grazed.

"Have you heard the news?" Sally asked as she set the brake and tied the reins to it and stepped down.

"No, tell me!"

"Our husbands tried to enlist at San Luis, but were refused. Benito's father told me when I stopped in town. I thought I'd come right over and tell you."

"What happened?"

"The *gringos* don't want them in their Army, just as Clara predicted."

Anita clapped hands with joy. "Oh, what good news!"

Sally went on: "They're not coming home yet. They've gone

south to try again in Santa Barbara. Benito's father is very angry about it. He says they've been insulted."

"I don't care what Santiago says, just so they come home!" Anita cried. Her little Benito, aged four, and tiny Anita, two and a half, had followed their mother and now stood clutching her skirt and looking up curiously at Aunt Sally. "Come to the house and tell me more," Anita insisted, and, as they moved toward the cool portico under the balcony, Sally continued. "You're too forgiving, my dear, as I've often said. I told Santiago it serves them right to be turned down, after all the misery they've put us through. He and Ruth are cross as ever about their going in the first place. Yet, he wants to help them now, says these Southern victories will make Union volunteers that much more in demand, and he wants to see them vindicated as regular Americans. But I said I hope they get refused everywhere and come home with their tails between their legs."

"Oh, Sally, how can you be so mean? Don't you want your Pacifico back?"

"No, I'm not sure that I do," Sally declared frankly. "I rather like life without him. Clara and I manage things just fine as it is." Yet, beneath, her heart ached for a husband she could love, and she confided this secret truth, along with others, to the ears of her dear friend.

Chapter Fifteen

Colonel James Henry Carleton lowered the letter of recommendation he had been reading and looked over it sternly at Benito and Pacifico who stood before his desk in his headquarters on Main Street in Los Angeles. "So you two tried to enlist and were turned down?"

Carleton was in command now. Captain Hancock and his dragoons had gone East along with other regular army troops to serve in the Army of the Potomac, defending Washington City, leaving the defense of California to local volunteers under command of a handful of regulars like Carleton. Carleton was now engaged in assembling a force intended to keep Southern California in the Union and to repel a Confederate invasion.

"Yes, sir!" Benito responded to his question with spirit. "We tried to enlist in San Luis Obispo and Santa Barbara, but were refused because they said we were *californianos*. They said they were accepting only regular Americans."

"Humph," Carleton grunted and looked down at the letter, looked up at them. *Californianos* had full rights of citizenship in theory, but in practice were discriminated against as inferior. "Which of you is Ferrer?"

"I, sir."

"You look regular enough, though your skin is a little dark. What kind of a name is Ferrer? Spanish?"

"No, Irish, sir," Benito replied with a twinkle. "Originally Ferry, like Kerry." There was a semblance of fact. Some said the Irish were one of the lost tribes of Israel, and who could say where Benito's Jewish ancestors came from before they landed in New Spain, as Mexico had been called three hundred years ago.

"And Boneu?" Carleton eyed big, blond Pacifico.

Pacifico took his cue from Benito. "French, sir." Not much of a lie. France once ruled Catalonia, Spain's northeastern province, where Pacifico's grandfather, Antonio, had been born.

Carleton's blue eyes began to twinkle. He admired creative mendacity. He was a Maine Yankee with down-East shrewdness, and his ruddy face was mostly covered by a neatly trimmed beard and mustache. Since graduating from West Point, he had seen duty in Europe and much of the United States and some of Mexico. He had corresponded with Charles Dickens, written and published the definitive account of the battle of Buena Vista where he had been breveted for gallantry during the Mexican War. And if these two were of questionable ethnicity, there were other considerations such as this letter from his friend and supplier, Simon Koenig. It asked: **Please give these two fine young Americans a hearing.** Benito's father had instigated the letter. Although Santiago Ferrer had disapproved of Benito's and Pacifico's enlisting, his ire at their being rebuffed had overcome his disapproval, and he had written Koenig from whom he bought much merchandise: **The Union Cause of Freedom must be supported, as you and I agree, and if our young men will not support it, who will?** — and Koenig, then, had written Carleton.

Even so, Carleton was dubious, and nothing might have resulted had not a uniformed figure passed outside the window at that moment. It gave Carleton an idea, and he called to his adjutant: "Show Captain McCleave in." When McCleave entered, Carleton said: "Captain, these two say they want to join us and fight the Seceshers. They say they don't want to be segregated into de la Guerra's native cavalry. Claim they're not a breed apart. You want 'em in your company?"

Carleton and McCleave had soldiered together for years.

Dark-haired, dark-mustached William McCleave had risen through the ranks to where he was, thanks largely to Carleton's help. Having been discriminated against as an Irish Catholic immigrant tended to make McCleave more tolerant than otherwise. He looked over the would-be recruits with a veteran's eye. "You fellows know anything about horses?"

"We're ranch raised," Benito told him.

"You ready for a long march and a hard fight?"

"Yes, sir," chimed in Pacifico.

"Then come along," said McCleave with a touch of brogue and a friendly nod. "I'll sign you up with my cavalry."

And that is how Benito and Pacifico avoided becoming members of the segregated California Lancers, volunteers like themselves but destined for supporting duties, and became, instead, members of Carleton's front-line force, then training at Camp Latham by Ballona Creek — near the present-day site of Culver City and Sony Pictures studios — to repel the approaching Confederates.

Hardly had Benito and Pacifico departed with McCleave when Carleton's adjutant interrupted him again. "A woman to see you, sir."

"Woman? Who is she?"

"Says she's a news reporter, sir."

"Tell her I'm busy."

"Excuse me, sir, but I think you'd better see her."

Carleton glowered. "Why do you say that?"

"There's something about her, sir."

Carleton remembered the importance of good public relations. "All right, show her in."

Chin up, high-laced black shoes tapping the floor boards with determination, Eve Radovich sailed into the room. She was wearing a red wig with long curls from Ethel Curtis's amateur theatrical props. Her spectacles of plain glass were from the same source. She wore a black straw bonnet low over her forehead. Irrepressible, fun-loving Eve was determined to have this interview, while still protecting her anonymity. Gillem had said there was potentially a big story. "Carleton," he had warned, "will try to hide behind conventional humbug, but corner him, make him say something sensational." It had meant absence from Ethel's kindergarten, but Ethel was all for it. She loved hoaxes. This promised to be a beauty.

"And you're a news reporter," inquired Carleton warily, "Miss . . . ?"

"Thalia, sir," replied Eve politely, using the name of the mythic muse of comedy as she and Gillem had agreed. "I understand you don't often give interviews. But I thought," Eve paused demurely, "I thought to a woman you might?"

"Well, we'll see," harrumphed Carleton. "We must be careful not to reveal information useful to the enemy, you know. What paper do you represent?"

"*The Sentinel.* It's published in San Francisco, but circulates all over the state."

"I'm familiar with it. It's a good paper. Please sit down. What do you want to know?"

Pencil in hand, notebook on lap, Eve attacked head on, using a lead Gillem gave her. "Is it true Jefferson Davis was your benefactor?"

Carleton was taken aback, but rallied. "When Secretary of War, Mister Davis sent me to Europe to study cavalry tactics, if that's what you mean."

"What was the reason for the study?"

"He deemed it advisable to improve that arm of our service. The United States had recently acquired much territory in the West where cavalry was needed to protect our national interests, especially in operations against hostile Indians."

She made a note. "Does such preferment influence your attitude toward Mister Davis now?"

Carleton reddened. "Of course not. Miss Thalia, are you suggesting I am under the influence of the President of the Confederacy?"

Sensing she was pushing too hard, Eve changed her approach. "What are your main problems, now, sir?"

Carleton reeled them off. Assembling an army of raw recruits. Shaping them into an effective fighting force. Supplying them for a march of nearly nine hundred miles from here to Texas across hostile terrain. "It will be one of the longest and hardest marches in our nation's military history. Over a million pounds of supplies will be needed, not counting beef to be driven on the hoof and eaten six days a week."

Eve was genuinely impressed. "How will your supplies be transported?"

"By ship from San Pedro or from San Francisco around the tip of lower California to the mouth of the Colorado River." Carleton pointed to a map on the wall. "It's a voyage of two thousand miles. At the mouth of the Colorado they'll be transferred to shallow-draft steamer for the run upstream to Fort Yuma, our main supply base. From there some will go by wagon as we move eastward to meet the Confederates. But some will be carried on the backs of our infantry. Each of my cavalrymen, as he leaves here to march across the desert, will be leading his horse with a hundred-pound sack of barley on his saddle. Does that answer your question?"

"Yes, it does." Eve softened her tone even more. "But won't you find it hard to leave your wife and children behind?"

"My, you're very well informed, Miss Thalia!" Carleton felt embarrassed by this personal thrust, but resolved to go along. "Yes, it's hard. But that's military life. We hope to make our home in Los Angeles eventually."

"You've fallen in love with it as I have?"

"Yes, we think it's a bit of earthly paradise."

Eve moved onto that sensitive ground she'd been heading for. "Colonel, where do you stand on women's rights?"

"Oh, they don't concern me. They're not a military question."

"Why not? Our women fought alongside our men in the Revolutionary War, didn't they?"

"Unofficially, yes," he conceded.

"They fought bravely by all accounts. Why shouldn't they be allowed to fight in this war?"

Carleton attempted to put her off. "Judging from the militancy of some of our new women," he teased, "I wouldn't rule it out. A regiment of them would be formidable!"

"May I quote you?"

"Oh, Miss Thalia," Carleton turned grave, "I wish you wouldn't!"

Eve nodded sympathetically but noncommittally. She had what she wanted. And Gillem would headline it, she felt sure.

Chapter Sixteen

"Sidney, is that you?" Jefferson Davis called as he heard Johnston's step on the stair. "Come right on up!" And when his friend appeared in the doorway, martially erect, smiling affectionately, but expressing hesitation at disturbing him on his sickbed, Davis rose and embraced Johnston. "Nothing could be better for my health than the sight of you. Sit down. I'm weary of reading about your miraculous escape. I want to hear of it from your own lips."

Johnston's journey from San Antonio to Richmond had grown into a triumphal progress. Surviving desert heat and thirst, evading capture by Union forces, bearing first-hand news of victory in the Far West, he seemed to many Southerners the embodiment of victory everywhere, and they lined the road to cheer his stagecoach and later the railroad track to cheer his train; and, when he presented himself at the new White House in Richmond, a white-columned former private residence in classic Southern style situated at the corner of Twelfth and Clay, he was welcomed warmly by Davis's young second wife, Varina. "Go right upstairs, Sidney. He's expecting you."

Davis had had these neuralgic headaches before reluctantly accepting the Presidency of the Confederacy, but they had become more frequent since, sometimes prostrating him as now, yet his feelings toward Johnston remained as warm as ever. Johnston, four years older, was Davis's youthful idol. They had been together at college in Kentucky and then at West Point, and later in the Black Hawk and Mexican Wars. While Davis had gone on to become the South's leading citizen — soldier, United States Senator, Secretary of War — Johnston had followed his own distinguished career, and Davis still

117

admired him more than any other man he knew.

"New Mexico Territory may be ours," Johnston concluded his account, "if we can support Colonel Baylor promptly. With victorious troops poised on its border, California, too, could become ours, especially its southern portion which is strongly sympathetic to our cause."

"That's splendid news. We need California. With her gold and strategic location on the Pacific, we would have a two-ocean nation second to none in resources and importance. But what of George Stanhope and his people?"

"He may have as many as twenty thousand Golden Knights, ready to rise when he gives the word," Johnston continued. "Their potential for helping is great and should be encouraged, though I deliberately avoided involving myself with them while commanding the department, believing it inconsistent with my honor as an officer of the United States Army."

"That was like you, Sidney. But Stanhope's scheme for seizing Fortress Alcatraz was harebrained."

"George can be overly zealous. That's his fault. But he makes up for it in energy and determination. And he's in touch with key people, Eliot Sedley among others."

"Isn't his daughter married to Sedley?"

"Yes, but she's in New Orleans now. I saw her when I passed through. She and her mother and brother were there on a visit when war broke out. Beau, her brother, has enlisted."

"I remember him. Promising lad. Their plantation on the Louisiana side is not far down the Mississippi from my own. But can we count on Sedley's help?"

Johnston grew thoughtful. "He's a fence sitter. But if we were to approach with a victorious army, I think he'd topple over to our side. And bring a preponderance of power with him. We must move quickly, however. The Unionists are sending troops to the southern part of the state where our best hope lies. Is there anything to the report that France and England are preparing to land troops in Mexico to collect their debts there? Might they help us?"

"Yes, they'll be landing in Mexico and will almost certainly aid us from there and from other directions if we continue to win on the battlefield. The Union blockade of our ports has cut off their supplies of our cotton. Their mills stand idle. But first we must show that we can win. Then recognition of our independence will surely follow, along with military and financial aid. And once we've achieved final victory, Sidney, we can turn our attention southward to Cuba, Mexico, Central America which are naturally suited to our plantation system."

"A grand design," Johnston agreed. "It has my full support, and I feel sure it will inspire others." Johnston wasn't as sure as he sounded about his friend's expansionary vision but was too loyal to indicate otherwise, and, besides, he did not wish to dampen Davis's spirits at their moment of reunion. Davis's gaunt face and figure and nervous manner worried Johnston. Far from a firebrand like Stanhope, Davis, like Johnston, had opposed Secession but had championed the rights of states to choose their own institutions, including slavery. Davis had never sought the Presidency of the Confederacy, Johnston knew, but had accepted it out of a sense of duty, a quality Johnston admired.

Varina put in anxiously from the doorway: "Jefferson, I hope you're not overdoing?" She was fearful lest too much talk exhaust her frail husband.

"Varina, let us alone and tell the others to," Davis snapped peevishly, touchy about his physical weakness. After she had gone, he turned to Johnston with new purpose.

"Sidney, I hope you'll accept command in the West. We've got them on the run here in the East. Our victory at Manassas" — Davis used the Southern name for the battle of Bull Run

— "has put the fear of God in 'em. It's the West that worries me now. If we can't hold the lower Mississippi, we'll be cut in two. And if we can't hold the border states like your and my Kentucky, we'll be seriously weakened."

Johnston agreed. "What we do must be done swiftly, before they bring their full strength to bear."

"Will they stand the cold steel, Sidney? After their route at Manassas, I wonder."

"They'll stand it," Johnston predicted gravely, "and the longer we fight, the harder they'll be to defeat. We Americans are a proud people, Jeff."

For the better part of three days the two friends talked strategy and tactics and gossip and recollections of shared experience. Then Johnston accepted command in the Western Department as the Confederacy's highest ranking field general anywhere, with seniority over even Robert E. Lee, who would soon have supreme command in the East.

"Can you give us a western Manassas, Sidney?" was Davis's final, urgent question.

"If you give me the arms and the men, I've no doubt I can defeat them," responded Johnston soberly, yet confidently. He knew how difficult his task would be, how woefully unprepared for war the new Confederacy was, how hard it would be to beat an army of Western men from frontier states. And that was why he urged again that Colonel Baylor's victorious Texans be strongly reinforced before they attempted to push on toward California. Davis assured him they would be.

"What about Eliza and the children?" Varina asked. "Will you leave them in Los Angeles until after the war?"

"Yes." And Johnston told of his and Eliza's dream of a home there.

Chapter Seventeen

Eve was sitting with the Curtises and Pedro Díaz at Simon and Deborah Koenig's supper table. She sensed, as she looked across at Pedro, that her feeling for him was reciprocated. There had been no opportunity for them to be alone. Yet, her heart told her the moment would come, perhaps tonight, as she heard Simon Koenig saying to Ethel Curtis: "Well, Eve is a wonder. She's taken Carleton into camp. And now she tells us Stanhope's been locked up. What do you think about that?"

"I say good riddance of bad rubbish! I hope they keep him under lock and key for the duration of the war!"

"Now, my dear," Ambrose Curtis reproved his wife gently, "just because George Stanhope is a Rebel doesn't mean he's not entitled to a fair trial under the law."

Made euphoric at the prospect of a Confederate takeover, Stanhope had been arrested in the act of raising the Stars and Bars over the town hall at Belleville, in the mountains above San Bernardino fifty miles eastward from where they sat. Belleville, population ten thousand, twice that of Los Angeles, was the scene of a sensational new gold strike. Men of the most venturesome stripe, many of Southern sympathy, had rushed to it. Along with neighboring San Bernardino, whose mainly Mormon inhabitants tended to regard the federal government with antipathy, Belleville formed a kind of Confederate stronghold, as Stanhope had foreseen, at the gateway to the desert over which Southern troops could soon advance. Keenly aware of this, tipped off by Mary Louise and Mornay, Carleton had scouted Belleville and San Bernardino disguised in civilian clothes, then had had Stanhope arrested and sent north on the *Senator* to the Army prison on Alcatraz Island in

San Francisco Bay. There he had been held without trial, as a political prisoner, Lincoln having suspended the right of *habeas corpus* for the first time in the nation's history. Stanhope's arrest and imprisonment had created a controversy that had pushed Eve's sensational interview with Carleton far from the front page.

"Well spoken, Ambrose," Koenig rejoined affably. "No offense to you, Ethel. Merely a tribute to your husband's sense of fairness."

"Fairness," scoffed Ethel. "If we can't protect ourselves against our enemies, what will happen to fairness?"

Eve was bursting to interrupt, but felt it prudent to hold her tongue, while Deborah Koenig said from her end of the gracious table with its lace cloth, fine silver, and Dresden china and two silver candlesticks: "I side with Ethel. If we let Stanhope go free, no telling how much more harm he'll do." Like Simon, Deborah had grown up under despotism in their native Prussia. Simon had made his way first to freedom and success in America, then had returned and married her. Simon had a graying goatee and wore spectacles. Deborah was plump and eight years younger. Like the Curtises they were childless and regarded Pedro almost like a son. Now Simon turned to him.

"Pedro, you've been reading Blackstone's COMMENTAR-IES and the U. S. Constitution in preparation for your bar examination. What do you say on the subject of *habeas corpus?*"

Pedro answered with conviction. "I say it's an inalienable part of common law and of our Constitution. If one man can suspend it under the excuse of war or national unity or whatever, then where are we? In despotism, I say." His eloquence thrilled Eve, and her eyes told him so.

"You'd free Stanhope, then?" Koenig continued.

"Free him for trial, yes." Pedro had thought hard about this issue. It seemed to him that Spanish and Mexican and

Indian and Chinese Californians had been denied their rights by the conquering *gringos*, and that here was a similar instance of oppression. "It seems to me Lincoln is using ends to justify means. That can never be good in the long run."

"Spoken like a judge!" Ambrose put in proudly. "I agree with you, Pedro."

Simon turned to Eve. "Seems we've got women against men here, Eve. Two of your sex have sided with Stanhope against Lincoln. Where do you stand?"

"I stand with Stanhope," Eve broke out passionately, her dark eyes flaming with emotion as they did when she was deeply aroused. "Much as I hate what Stanhope represents, no one should be imprisoned without trial, in this country or any country!"

Pedro thought her perfectly beautiful and utterly desirable, and he, too, felt their union to be destined, even though she was a *gringa*.

"Spoken like Portia herself," rejoined Koenig approvingly. "Perhaps you should be studying Blackstone, too," he teased Eve. "Someday we'll have women lawyers, eh, Ambrose? Nevertheless, I must agree with Ethel and Deborah. If the Confederates win, where will *habeas corpus* be then? Let's face the facts. They're assembling an army in Texas to support Baylor and push this way. Will the right of *habeas corpus* stop them?" Koenig paused and raised his hands with a persuasive smile. "But now let's forget about war for a moment. Deborah and I invite all of you to adjourn with us to Don Porfirio de la Vega's fandango. It's a grand affair. He's asked us to bring anyone we like. Eve, it'll be a great chance for Thalia to write an intimate story of high society life in Los Angeles."

Eve's heart leaped at this proposal. Here could be her chance to be alone with Pedro at last. So she was dismayed to hear him declare firmly: "I beg to be excused. I don't get

123

along with Don Porfirio or he with me."

"I was afraid you'd say that," Koenig chided him good-naturedly. "Much as you may disagree with him, isn't he rather like Stanhope? Isn't he entitled to his day in court?"

"Yes, do come!" Eve burst out.

Pedro's dark eyes rested on hers tenderly. "I would like to accompany you," he replied gravely, wishing he could take her in his arms and make love to her, "but not tonight." And he smiled so meaningfully that Eve's heart melted as her disappointment rose.

Chapter Eighteen

Father and son moved as though outside of time, two naked humans alone together between earth and sky, as Francisco continued to show Helek the world. They crouched at dawn this morning in a waist-high clump of grass overlooking the village of Santa Lucia, and Francisco said: "That is where the A-alowow live."

"All of them?"

"No, just a few. Many others live in towns much larger than this." And he described cities such as San Francisco and faraway countries such as England and Spain, so that the boy's eyes fixed on his with amazement.

"The A-alowow are everywhere?"

"Everywhere."

"Why did they come here and take our land, if they already have so much?"

"Because they are greedy and very numerous."

"Will they ever go away?"

"I don't think so."

Helek fell silent. "What can we do, Father?"

"Resist. That is what I am teaching you. How not to be swallowed up. It is why I show you the world."

The growing light revealed greater detail below, and Francisco pointed out the unpaved main street of the ramshackle little town where he had dragged Buck Jenkins in the dust at the end of his reata. He pointed out the store of Santiago Ferrer "where food, clothing, and other valuables may be obtained in trade," and he pointed out the surrounding adobes of the older settlers and the newer wooden houses "of the North Americans." And finally he indicated the ancient mission on its crest where the street disappeared toward the river and the grassy hills beyond. "It's a shrine where they worship. The street in front of it is a very important trail. When I was a boy, it was called the King's Highway in honor of the great chief of Spain, though it was even less of a road than you see now."

"Where does it go?"

"Northward to that place called San Francisco."

"Named for you?"

Francisco chuckled. "No, I for it, or rather both of us for a very great man." And he told Helek about St. Francis.

"He was like Tilhini?"

"Indeed, yes." Francisco was delighted by his son's perception. "Quite like Tilhini. You see, the A-alowow have sky people, too. Among them is the great chief they call God. Like Kakunupmawa he, too, is revered because of his great power."

The mission bell began to ring. "What is the sound?" Helek had never heard a bell before.

Francisco explained and pointed out the gray-robed figure of O'Hara, minute in the distance, standing beside the half-ruined belfry, bending and straightening as he pulled the bell rope. "He is our friend," Francisco continued. "He, too, is like Tilhini. And that old mission behind him is like our Cave of the Condors, a sacred place. So you see, we have things in common with the A-alowow, important things."

They watched people coming and going on the main street, some horseback, some afoot, heard their distant voices, while at a greater distance to their left, where the river emptied into the sea as if being deposited there by the hills on either side of the valley, the fog began to lift and reveal the blue curve of Portola Bay, edged by dunes that shined like gold in the rising sun. As they watched this magnificent panorama unveil before them, Francisco said: "There is where it all began. There is where our people first met the white men, there, by those sand dunes. And you have heard what followed."

But now, coming toward them along the coastal road where it bordered the bay, they saw a cloud of dust, and from the dust emerged a stagecoach drawn by six galloping horses. While Francisco was explaining what a stagecoach was, it dipped from sight at the river crossing and then reappeared at the crest by the mission where O'Hara was just ceasing to toll the bell. There it came slowly to a halt in the small plaza where the main street widened. A figure stepped from it, and, even at this distance, Francisco recognized Eliot Sedley. Sedley was traveling alone as usual. He traveled not as a king in a royal carriage, but by ordinary stagecoach or hired hack. And he liked to arrive unannounced. That way he found things as they truly were, not as they might be arranged to please him. And thus he was returning to a valley that held some of his most precious memories and a place he regarded as his dearest possession, Rancho Olomosoug.

"Who is that?" Helek asked.

"An old friend of mine."

They watched as Sedley crossed the little plaza toward O'Hara, who advanced to greet him while the stage proceeded slowly down Main Street to Ferrer's General Store and came to a halt there. "Welcome, stranger," O'Hara called out to Sedley. "What good chance brings you here?"

"I'm on my way to see Clara, but I wanted to see you first. How are you?" Sedley embraced him. Though not of his faith, O'Hara embodied much that Sedley found admirable as well as memories that were precious.

"I'm as well as you look," replied the priest. "Come inside, and join me in a cup of chocolate? You must need refreshment after your journey."

So they went into O'Hara's living quarters in the long, porticoed, south wing of the mission adjoining the crumbling

127

church and bell tower, and there, in cool shadows, seated at the hearth, they were accompanied only by O'Hara's old black cat, Satan.

"I see Satan is still with you?" Sedley observed with a chuckle.

"Yes, I keep him near me as a reminder," laughed O'Hara in reply.

"And how is Aunt Clara?"

"Fit as can be expected at her age." And believing that at heart Sedley cherished the old woman as he did, O'Hara told of her latest tribulation, the departure of her beloved grandson for the Union Army.

"Pacifico has enlisted?"

"Yes, and Benito Ferrer with him."

"Ah!" From Sedley's noncommittal response O'Hara couldn't be sure which side he favored and decided not to ask. "And what of Francisco?" Sedley resumed.

"He is her greatest sorrow. No one has seen or heard of him. I'm afraid he is dead, though maybe he is, indeed, alive somewhere back there in the wilderness," — gesturing toward the head of the valley — "keeping up resistance to American rule. But if so, what a fantastic undertaking . . . trying to reverse the tide of history single-handed!"

"Yet rather like him," chuckled Sedley. Sedley liked the bizarre, the incongruous. It contained a creative force that appealed to him. "Francisco may be watching us at this moment, who knows? And what about the squatters?"

"Since you warned them, they've let her alone. They know she can count on you for help. She's very fond of you, Eliot."

"And I of her. And now I should be going. I'm hoping Santiago Ferrer or his man will drive me out there in his buggy as usual."

"I'm afraid the buggy is on its way to Rancho San Marcos.

Santiago and Ruth go there regularly to see Anita and their grandchildren since Benito left."

"And who minds the store?"

"Young Mark and his sister."

"Then shall I walk?" joked Sedley, deftly negotiating for what had suddenly come to mind, something that also appealed to his liking for the bizarre.

"Why not take my mule?" O'Hara offered. "She knows the way well."

Thus an hour later Sedley was riding up the valley on O'Hara's white mule, Faith, causing astonishment in those who recognized the great man astride such a humble animal; but it also was the kind of thing that amused Sedley, the kind of rôle he could play almost nowhere else but here, where he could become another self. And as Faith trudged along, he recalled those days when, as youthful supercargo aboard the *Enterprise,* he had gone ashore and ridden ahead to negotiate with ranch owners like Clara for their hides and tallow, the ship following. And so again in his mind the sturdy brig, two years out from Boston around the Horn, lay in the bay, while a long line of ox carts piled high with folded hides and bags of tallow came creaking down the valley along this very route — he and Francisco accompanying them, the drivers cracking their whips, the carts squeaking. And all of it hardly a dozen years ago. Yet, it might as well have happened in another world.

And so remembering as Faith bore him slowly along between earth and sky and the sun shone upon him, Sedley felt the change and renewal that his visits to the valley always brought. It seemed a good time to be absent from his office. There was a lull in the war while both sides prepared for major campaigns. Stanhope was locked up in Fortress Alcatraz where he could neither help nor hinder while becoming a *cause célèbre.* The price of gold was rising steadily because of the war.

Stanford's election as governor promised well for their railroad venture. And Vicky's continuing absence gave him the freedom he liked, including more time with Mary Louise, for, though Sedley never took her on his travels, she was never far from his mind.

From time to time he passed the cabins of legitimate home-steaders as well as squatters, and then as the valley narrowed and its embracing hills seemed to receive him home, he saw the Jenkins' twin cabins ahead and the hacienda on its low promontory beyond, and a horseman coming toward him. It was Buck.

At first sight of the white mule, Buck had thought Sedley to be O'Hara, bringing the mail as he often did when visiting Rancho Olomosoug, but now, as they drew closer and he recognized the great man, he was astonished and awed. Buck was not used to the caprices of the sophisticated, and the sight of Sedley upon Faith opened vistas so strange and wonderful that he took off his hat and held it up in homage as well as greeting. Sedley with perfect equanimity did likewise. His attitude toward the squatters was one of practical tolerance. They had their rights. Clara had hers. And as her mortgagor and friend, he had his, while they all waited the court's decision.

"Yes," Buck was saying, "I thought maybe you carried a letter from my boy, Goodly. He's gone off and enlisted." He didn't bother to say on which side, assuming Sedley's loyalties were the same as Stanhope's, for Stanhope had led him to believe so, but Sedley was quick to correct him. "I hope he comes back to you safely, sir, whichever side he joined." And having inquired as to the health of Iphy, and of old Abe whom he particularly admired for helping him and Clara maintain that uneasy peace between cabins and hacienda, he rode on.

"Eliot, you fraud," Clara hailed him affectionately, as he entered her courtyard amid the barking of dogs and the smiles and stares of her retainers, "what is a sinner like you doing riding upon a creature called Faith?"

"Why, Aunt Clara," he retorted jovially, "it is a measure of God's mercy!"

A few moments later they and Sally were sitting in that grim old parlor Clara had refused to prettify as a concession to a softer age. Its floors were still the original earth; its walls were earthen also. Its roof tiles were visible above its rafter poles, and its chairs were hard and upright as the old woman herself, Sedley thought, as he told what Buck had said and O'Hara had said, "and so Pacifico has gone off to war and left you two to run things?" He gave Sally a fond look. He had always been attracted to her while sensing her reserve toward him.

"Yes, Pacifico disobeyed me. I told him not to go. But he wouldn't listen."

"And what of Francisco?"

Clara's face feigned indifference. "I truly don't know where he is or what's become of him. He, also, is disobedient."

"Strange, but I had the feeling while in town that he was watching me. Could that possibly have been true?"

"Impossible. No one has seen him for years. Alas, I'm afraid he is dead." And her face assumed a mournful look that fooled even Sally to whom she had confided not one word of her encounter with Francisco and Helek. "And what about your Victoria?" she asked, trying to sound sincere, for Victoria Stanhope Sedley struck her as a condescending, spoiled darling of privilege, who regarded Rancho Olomosoug as a kind of toy with which to play and Clara as some kind of antiquated doll.

Sedley told how Vicky had been caught in New Orleans by the Union blockade.

"You must miss her." Clara knew the state of their marriage and disliked making this double talk, but, as with Sedley's entire relationship to her, she saw no way out of it, and yet she was fond of him.

"Indeed, I do miss Victoria, Aunt Clara, so I came here to be with you, and with Sally."

"What nonsense! What is it you want? Look, you've made Sally blush!"

Sally had reddened under his admiring look. She was grateful for his help, but resentful of his power over Clara and the ranch and thus over herself. "*Mama Grande* is the one to admire, Mister Sedley. She holds all things together, sets all of us an example."

"Indeed, she does. But what news of your husband?"

"Pacifico is about to march into New Mexico." She tried to sound proud and loving, but feared lest Sedley see through her pretense. "He says our forces are confident of victory." She wondered if Sedley guessed the truth about her marriage. There was something omniscient about him that always made her feel a bit uncomfortable.

"Please remember me to him." Sedley sounded faintly ironic. "We must all help in every way we can. *Tia* Clara" — turning back to her — "speaking of help, armies must have uniforms. Uniforms are made of wool. I'm stocking my ranches with sheep. What about you?"

"Sheep are like grasshoppers," she retorted scornfully. "They eat everything bare. And they stink. Furthermore, they have no dignity. They are not proud like my cattle. And besides," she added the clincher, "my Antonio never liked them, except for those needed to produce our wool. Turn these beautiful hills over to them? Never! Let the armies get their wool elsewhere. My land shall not clothe them."

"But at least you may feed them?" persisted Sedley genially, with a wink at Sally. Fencing with the old woman was part of his pleasure in these visits. "Beef, canned or dried, will be in great demand. Armies must eat. And they must wear shoes. Your hides, also, will become valuable as leather."

"Feed them and shoe them I am willing to do, if they pay the price. Are you ordering me to stock sheep?" she demanded.

"Aunt Clara," he protested amiably, "you know I never order you to do anything. How could I, after all your kindness to me over all these years? I'm simply suggesting what might make things easier for you . . ." — subtly reminding her of her debt to him, of his power over her.

"Well, I'll think about it."

Sally winced inwardly at this suggestion of submission on the part of her beloved benefactress. While aware of her faults, she adulated old Clara almost as a deity from another world, who had watched over her and guided her since those remote days of her first bliss with Pacifico.

"And now that we speak of money," Clara continued, "what about my debt to you? What of my lawsuit, or I should say what of the government's suit against me to take away my land from me while costing me a fortune?"

"That is one reason I came. As, of course, you know, your case is before the Supreme Court. But you have a new lawyer, Henry Wager Halleck. I've retained him because I wasn't satisfied with the way your case was progressing. Halleck will be serving you unofficially, because President Lincoln has just appointed him a major general and given him a high command, so he'll have many other duties to perform. But he is very well connected in Washington. And he was very prominent in the Army years ago before resigning his commission to become one of San Francisco's leading attorneys. Halleck knows more about land law than anyone else. Indeed, he's written a book about it."

"And I suppose his book and his prominence will cost me another fortune?"

"Don't worry. I'll continue to take care of such matters."

"While I continue to mortgage myself to the hilt and beyond? This is not my ranch." She came to the point bluntly as usual. "Any time you wish to foreclose on me, it is yours."

And, as usual, Sedley put her off amiably, but firmly: "Do not be hard on me, Aunt Clara. Without me you would have lost this ranch long ago to money-lenders because of the debts incurred by Francisco and his spendthrift ways as well as by you and your lawsuit. With me, Rancho Olomosoug is yours as long as you live."

"And after that?" she challenged unflinchingly.

"Let's not borrow trouble. Let's fix our minds on what is most pressing . . . to win your case, to clear your title to this land that we love."

"So that you can possess it?" she rejoined shrewdly.

"So that I may help you keep it as it is," he corrected her gently. To keep the ranch as it was would also be his purpose beyond her death, thus enshrining his special memories in its special beauty.

After a moment of silence, Clara cried out: "Well, I'm not dead yet!" and clapped her hands commandingly, and, when María Ignacia, her faithful housekeeper, appeared, she ordered: "Prepare a room for *Señor* Sedley. And tell Adriana we'll have roast kid for supper, since it is his favorite dish."

Sedley spent three days at Rancho Olomosoug, riding the hills with Clara and Sally amid surroundings more precious to him than any others, so unique they always refreshed him, and then he returned to San Francisco and Mary Louise and his rôle as king of California.

Mary Louise reported his return next day to Charles Mornay at his produce stall in the Great Pacific Market, and Mornay sent a coded telegram to Alan Pinkerton, head of the embryonic Secret Service in the War Department in Washington, Pinkerton functioning there under the pseudonym of Major E. J. Allen. **The King is back,** the telegram read.

After Sedley left them, Clara inquired of Sally: "What did you think?

"I admire him, but I don't quite trust him."

Clara sighed. "Neither do I. But what other choice have we?" Then she broke out: "Granddaughter, someday this ranch may be yours!"

Sally was amazed. "You mean if Pacifico is killed in the war?"

"No, but even if he isn't, you feel it, you love it, you care for it as he never has. And you care for me as he never has."

"*Mama Grande*, what are you saying?" she protested.

"I know very well what I'm saying, and so do you."

Chapter Nineteen

Eve Radovich found the de la Vegas' fandango fascinating despite Pedro's absence. It was held in their town house on the plaza not far from the Díaz's humble adobe. **As we approached, we encountered a dense crowd of common people,** she would write later in her letter to *The Sentinel*, **Indians, peons, the nobodies, the homeless, the curious, the envious, gathered outside in the darkness like moths around a flame. We made our way through these outsiders, and, as we reached the verandah, we found it crowded with *rancheros* and *vaqueros*, booted and spurred, some dismounted, some horseback, all drinking *aguardiente*, the fiery local brandy, and from time to time gazing admiringly through the windows at the pretty girls.**

Upon their arrival at the fandango Ethel Curtis turned to Eve and whispered — "Don't stand there staring. It's unladylike!" — and dragged her in motherly fashion after Ambrose and the Koenigs who had already entered the shining premises.

The room was packed wall to wall, with people, Eve's letter to her readers continued, **and a waltz was in progress to the accompaniment of violins, and a guitar, a harp, and a flageolet. Dark-eyed *señoritas* with pearly white skin wore dresses of bright colors that sparkled as they whirled under the chandeliers. The men wore traditional short velvet jackets and sky-blue pants with a gold stripe down the sides, or perhaps a business suit of black broadcloth.**

Courtly, austere Don Porfirio bowed over her hand. Eve

heard him murmur the traditional greeting — "My house is your house." — and she told her readers: **So naturally gracious was his manner it was hard to believe he's actually a rapacious old scoundrel who owns most of the land between here and the horizon and conspires, some say, with his son-in-law, Earl Newcomb, to control the destiny of the City of the Angels by delivering it into the hands of the Confederacy.**

Don Porfirio introduced her to his stately wife, and Eve described her to her readers: **Doña Hortensia bore herself like a queen, and wore gorgeous lavender silk and 'an** exquisite lace mantilla. She, too, greeted me as an honored guest, and I did, indeed, feel honored by their courtesy and hospitality. It speaks of a way of life fast vanishing before the crudities of our *gringo* civilization.

Beside Doña Hortensia stood her only child. **Heiress presumptive to all that her parents possess,** wrote Eve, **Carmen de la Vega y Newcomb is as plain as they are handsome. But she possessed the formidable self-assurance of a princess as she greeted me with a firm hand, sparkling with diamonds, and I remembered that these *californiano grandees* have escaped the fate of most of their kind, reduced to poverty by *gringo* money-lenders and land-shark lawyers.**

Next I come to Doña Carmen's husband, Earl Newcomb, our leading *gringo* magnate. He virtually kidnapped me the day I arrived here, as described in an earlier letter. Earl likes abduction. He's kidnapped virtually all this part of the state into his intricate web of business connections and family relationships. He wore the costume of the society he's married into and greeted me with a burst of jovial laughter: "Have you forgot our delightful stagecoach ride?" I assured him I'd not for-

gotten and was determined to have my revenge, and he assured me I never will, and I passed on in to the merry crowd.

Secretly Eve was terrified at the prospect of having to dance. This fear was her Achilles' heel. She thought of herself as too tall, too awkward to be graceful on the dance floor, yet dreaded being a wallflower. Sensing this, Ambrose Curtis made conversation. "See that old boy there with the kinky hair, kicking up his heels? That's Pío Pico, last Mexican governor of California. But don't call him a Mexican. That's a dirty word. Pico thinks of himself as Spanish, as do most *californianos*. It's much more prestigious."

"He looks as if he might have African blood."

"He does. He's the only governor of such blood California has ever had, or probably ever will, given the state of prejudice among us Americans, but he's an old rascal, too. In the days just before the American takeover, he distributed hundreds of thousands of acres to his friends, some of the forty who with him controlled the province of Alta California."

"Forty controlled the whole province?" Eve sensed another story for Gillem.

"Yes, and they're part of what we're up against now. They ruled their world like feudal lords before we *gringos* came along, and that's why some *californianos*, like our friend Pedro, think they're better off under American rule."

His mention of Pedro made her heart leap. Where was her loved one now? Why couldn't he have come with her? But she knew why. He was too proud to be patronized by the de la Vegas, and she was proud of him for feeling so.

The party was growing merrier. Emboldened by *aguardiente*, men were prowling gaily through the crowd with colored eggs in their hands. From time to time they crushed the eggs over the heads of unsuspecting females, showering their fair victims with scraps of perfumed paper. "What are they doing?" Eve asked, astonished.

"Oh, that's the *cascaróne*," chuckled Ambrose. "It's traditional. Just wait. Someone will crush one over you, and you'll have to dance with him."

A moment later she was startled by a gentle blow on the back of her head and heard the jovial laugh she loathed, as a shower of the perfumed scraps deluged her. Half flattered, half furious, she turned to see big Newcomb laughing at her, his powerful masculinity projecting itself over her like the perfumed paper. "May I have this dance, dear lady, all my sins forgiven?"

"I don't forgive sins, and I don't dance, thank you, Mister Newcomb, but I'll gladly talk."

"Then let's talk," he declared gallantly. "Truth or consequences?"

"Truth or consequences."

"Is it you who writes those shameless letters to *The Sentinel*?"

"No, that's Thalia. Now let me ask you," and she quickly formulated a question. "Were Confederate troops to enter Los Angeles would you welcome them?"

"I know you're hoping for a statement that will embarrass me, so I'll tell you God's truth." He eyed her teasingly. "I'd say let people decide. I'd put it to a vote. That would be what you Progressives advocate, wouldn't it? That would be democracy, wouldn't it? Wouldn't it be better than locking George Stanhope up in jail for expressing his opinions?"

"And it would be a humbug since Los Angeles, as you know, voted heavily against Lincoln and likewise against Stanford. It would be a humbug, Mister Newcomb, and quite like you. Therefore, it's my turn for another question."

Ethel Curtis and Deborah Koenig came up just then, engulfing Newcomb in talk while Eve turned away in relief to

139

Simon Koenig, who joshed: "I see you've made a conquest of your old adversary."

"I'd rather it were Pedro Díaz," she replied frankly. "I wish he hadn't been too proud to come."

"So do I, but he'll get over it. He'll go far, that Pedro. He's the best clerk I've ever had. I've known him to sleep on the counter, when necessary, with a pistol handy to protect our merchandise. I gather he thinks the world of you."

"Oh, I wish he did! Will he be admitted to the bar? Ambrose says no *californiano* ever has been?"

"I predict that he'll set a precedent."

Long after midnight, Eve concluded her letter to her readers, **we took leave of that imposing yet gracious quartet, Don Porfirio and Doña Hortensia, Doña Carmen, and Earl Newcomb, who stand like colossi at the center of society here, but not before I'd got even with Newcomb by crushing an egg over his arrogant head and making him the butt of much laughter. Then we made our way outdoors into that crowd of curious onlookers, the outsiders still gathered before the great house, still hungry for the wealth and power it represents. Among them I saw the giant figure of Polonio, the blind Indian, a familiar sight on our streets. Polonio's eye sockets are gaping apertures. His own people blinded him because in drunken rages he maimed and killed them as he lashed out heedlessly at the frustrations surrounding them all. They are the untouchables, these Indians. Outside the outsiders.**

Standing beside Polonio was patient Mary, the Indian who cooked and served for the Curtises, and Eve put Mary into her letter, too. **Mary was guiding Polonio through the darkness of this night. Once their people owned all this land as far as you can see, farther than Don Porfirio**

owns. Now they are outcasts who serve or beg from its new possessors.

Standing beside Mary in her coarse smock and Polonio in his rags, Eve was startled to see her own Pedro, and her heart leaped as their eyes met, as she heard Deborah exclaim: "Why, there's Pedro!" And Ethel added: "And there's our Mary with poor Polonio."

Ambrose waved a greeting. Pedro waved back but made no move to join them, apparently wishing to keep his distance.

"Astute politician," chuckled Koenig to Eve. "You know his secret ambition?"

"No, tell me."

"He wants to be county attorney someday, and he's evidently got his eye on the popular vote tonight."

"Oh, you don't do him justice!" cried Eve, outraged. "He's proud to be among the outsiders!" Clearly the Koenigs and the Curtises didn't appreciate Pedro's noble soul. Impulse seized her. "Don't wait. I'll catch up." And darting away through the crowd, a moment later she was at Pedro's side, eyes shining.

The earth under their coupled bodies was warm. The moonlight bathed them and the orange trees around them in milky light as they pledged themselves to each other again and again, and, after they finished making love, Pedro asked breathlessly: "Will you marry me?"

"Certainly not."

"Don't you love me?" he cried, astonished, aghast. He had had no time for girls. He took this one very seriously, the more so because she was a *gringa*, a member of the ruling class he was aspiring to join as well as to oppose.

"Of course, I love you. Come here to me." And again she

demonstrated that she did love him.

"Why won't you marry me?" he asked at last.

"Because I don't believe in marriage."

Chapter Twenty

The moment had come for Goodly and Stubby. This was real war at last, and they were laying their lives on the line, leading the Confederate advance toward California.

"You know the route," Captain Hunter had put it bluntly. "We'll follow you."

And now, through midwinter cold, Hunter and his rather scruffy looking un-uniformed volunteers known as Company A, Arizona Rangers, were riding off across the desert from the Río Grande, following the two Californians. It was a mission of the highest importance, and they all felt its significance.

Colonel John R. Baylor, hero of that first sensational Confederate victory on the Río Grande last July, had proclaimed the southern half of New Mexico Territory to be the new Territory of Arizona with himself as governor of this vast region extending to the Colorado River. Meanwhile, Brigadier General Henry Hopkins Sibley had arrived with an army of four thousand Texans to mop up Union forces remaining in the upper Río Grande Valley, and Sibley had ordered Captain Sherod Hunter to take a hundred volunteers and advance westward as far and fast as possible. "I'll follow as soon as I can," Sibley had told Hunter. "Raise the flag over Tucson. Rally people everywhere. Push on toward California. Keep me apprised of developments."

Goodly and Stubby at their head, Hunter's party reached Tucson in late February of 1862 in the midst of a snowstorm. Nevertheless, they were warmly welcomed and raised the Stars and Bars over the plaza to the cheers of the populace. Confidence high, they pushed on to Ammi White's grist mill on the Gila near the Pima villages where the withered corpses of

143

Apaches still hung as warning, as Goodly and Stubby had seen them last summer. White was now a known Union sympathizer said to be amassing flour for sale to federal forces should they advance from California, and they arrested him and placed him under guard in the back room of his own cabin and helped themselves to his flour and whiskey.

Just before dawn next morning Goodly, who had been on guard outside but had come inside to keep warm, heard a knock at the front door. He opened it and found himself face to face with a man in a blue uniform and dark mustache with a saber at his belt. It was the first confrontation between Federals and Confederates in the Far West. "I'm Captain McCleave," the man said. "Are you Ammi White?"

Just a few minutes ago Captain McCleave had told Sergeant Benito Ferrer: "I don't expect any trouble at White's place, but you wait here by this cottonwood and see what happens." And McCleave had ridden on ahead with the six enlisted men of their scout toward the cabin taking shape out of the dawn twilight. Discovering his capacity for leadership, McCleave had promoted Benito, while Pacifico, who seemed unable to handle responsibility, remained a private. Benito thought the world of McCleave — McCleave had accepted him and Pacifico against prevailing prejudice and had treated them squarely since. McCleave had become Benito's father figure, and the six men with McCleave were his trusted comrades. They were the spearhead of Brigadier General Carleton's new army of volunteers, two thousand four hundred strong, pushing rapidly eastward up the Gila from Fort Yuma. They had heard of no Confederates nearer than the Río Grande, and McCleave had seen no sign of them as he had approached White's silent cabin and knocked at the door, and Goodly had opened it.

Now Goodly thought quickly. "No, I'm not Mister White, but wait there a minute and I'll get him."

Leaving the door ajar, he woke Captain Hunter who was asleep on White's bed in the adjoining room.

The next McCleave knew, a man in red flannel shirt and blue denim trousers who looked like a frontiersman was pointing a pistol at his head and saying — "Surrender, sir, or I'll blow your brains out. I'm Captain Hunter of the Southern Army." — while Goodly and others of Hunter's party quietly took McCleave's unsuspecting men into custody.

It was light enough for Sergeant Ferrer, watching from down the road, to see much of this and guess the rest. Turning his bald-faced sorrel, Benito slipped away undetected, then alternately galloped and trotted until, by mid-morning, he approached the advancing Union column, the California Column as it was called. This was the kind of adventure Benito had been hoping for. It was in his blood. His adventuresome Sephardic ancestors had fled persecution in Spain for freedom in Mexico. But some had been burned at the stake for their stubborn adherence to Judaism. Others had boldly emigrated for freedom to the frontier province of Alta California, his paternal grandfather leading the way as *conquistador*-companion of Clara's Antonio Boneu who lay buried atop the hill at Rancho Olomosoug. Benito believed he was fighting for freedom now. That was the main reason he was here, that and the desire to be considered a regular American, that and the desire for a respite from marital bliss. He loved Anita and their children but loved more this commitment to something that seemed larger than himself or domestic bliss.

When Lieutenant James Barrett, riding at the head of the advancing column, saw him coming at a gallop, he drew rein. When he heard what Benito had to say, he replied tersely — "Sergeant, get yourself a fresh horse." — and then Barrett turned in his saddle and addressed the men behind him — "Captain McCleave and the others have been captured by the

145

Rebels. We're going to rescue 'em. Dismount and cinch up. Pacifico Boneu and Bill Semilrogge, I want you to go with Benito and scout the way. Keep your eyes peeled. We don't want another ambush." He didn't know whether they were up against a guerrilla band or an army.

Tense with over-eagerness, wondering if he could measure up now that the crucial moment had come, Pacifico over-tightened the girths of his saddle. His cinch-bound piebald whirled and kicked. Pacifico let out a scream of agony. A flying hoof had smashed his right hand. It was as if he had been destined for this, he thought, in his pain and self-reproach, almost as if he were back under Clara's and Sally's disapproving eyes. At the crucial moment he had failed to perform. He thought he had escaped his nemesis but seemed to have carried it with him. Crestfallen, humiliated, he went back to the medical ambulance, while Benito, Semilrogge, and Hank Thompson led the way forward.

Meanwhile, at Ammi White's cabin Hunter couldn't be sure how strong the advancing Federals were. McCleave wouldn't say, and his men gave conflicting accounts. Hunter decided to find out for himself. Leaving his prisoners under guard, he took ten of his best men, including Goodly and Stubby, and rode cautiously down the road toward California. In the dust they saw the fresh tracks of Benito's galloping horse and surmised that someone had given warning of their coming.

Cautiously they came to an apparently deserted adobe with adjoining corral, investigated warily, but found no sign of life around the old stage station. Then they concealed themselves nearby in a *barranca* Goodly remembered from last summer, where they could see half a mile ahead, and await developments.

Moments later three mounted figures appeared in the distance. "Let 'em come close," Hunter ordered. "Hold your

146

horses' noses so they don't neigh."

The three figures came close enough for Goodly and Stubby to recognize Benito. "By God," Goodly burst out under his breath, "I know one of 'em. He's from the place I live."

"Shut up!" Hunter warned.

But hatred for Benito welled up in Goodly, and he let go his horse's nose and shifted his short-barreled musketoon forward in eagerness. The horse neighed. Benito drew rein. Then his eye caught the glint of sunlight on Goodly's gun barrel. With a warning cry Benito whirled, and the bullet intended for him struck Bill Semilrogge in the left shoulder, and Bill called out — "I'm hit." — as he and Thompson and Benito raced away, lead whizzing around them.

"Surrender or we'll kill you!" Hunter yelled as he and the others burst from the *barranca* in pursuit.

Benito's answer was to turn and fire his dragoon's Colt, and, in doing so, he saw that Goodly and Stubby were among his pursuers. Amazed, incredulous, he couldn't believe war had come so close to home and to him.

Hunter pursued till the column of blue cavalry appeared in the distance. Then he broke off what became known as the fight at Stanwick's Station and turned back. It was just forty-six miles to California, and Bill Semilrogge and Pacifico were the first casualties of the war in the far Far West.

Benito's letter to Anita said: **I miss you and the children terribly but wish you to be proud of me where I am. We've had a scrap and Capt. McCleave and six men were captured, but we've got the Rebels on the run, now, and will get our people back.** In the interests of peace between ranchers and squatters of the Santa Lucia Valley, as well as his wife's peace of mind, he made no mention of the fact that Goodly and Stubby had tried to kill him and could try again, but said merely: **Pacifico got kicked by his horse and hurt bad. Tell Sally it's his right hand so he probably can't write much for a while.**

Chapter Twenty-One

On that lonely rock in San Francisco Bay called Alcatraz Island, Captain John Dewey escorted Eliot Sedley down out of the incessant wind and screaming seagulls to the prison cell in the basement of the citadel. George Stanhope thrust his hand through the bars and seized Sedley's. "God, Eliot, am I glad to see you!" Stanhope looked well, though pale and thin. "Have you come to get me out of this dungeon?"

"I've come to predict you'll be released soon and to bring you the latest news," Sedley responded amiably, holding up the folded copy of *The Sentinel* he carried in his other hand. "Am I permitted to say that much, Captain?" With a persuasive smile he turned to Dewey who was there to see that nothing more than a few words and a newspaper passed between visitor and prisoner. Dewey nodded, unsmiling, and Sedley turned back to Stanhope. "George, I've spoken to Governor Stanford. He's spoken to President Lincoln. . . ."

"Lincoln put me here, damn him," Stanhope interrupted in a rage, "but I'll get even! Look at this cell! Look at this bed!" His solitary cubicle contained a pallet for sleeping, a bucket for a toilet. "Is this any way for a human being to be treated?"

"Tut, tut," Sedley remonstrated. "Watch what you say. It was you who put yourself here, George, not the President." Sedley was speaking for Dewey's benefit, for the public record. "If you'd watched what you did, if you'd shown a little more respect for the Stars and Stripes, you wouldn't be here. No, it wasn't Lincoln put you here. Or even General Carleton. It was George Stanhope."

"Did you come here to lecture me?"

"I've come to say you have the honor of being one of America's first political prisoners. You've become a *cause célèbre*. Even your old adversaries like Gillem side with you, as you'll read here in today's paper."

"I don't want sympathy. I want out!" grumbled Stanhope, subsiding a little.

Sedley had waited until the controversy heightened, and he had seen how he could gain credit from both sides by intervening. Protests over Stanhope's arrest and imprisonment without trial had erupted across state and nation. Just as the issue had split the discussion at Simon Koenig's dinner table, it had split the discussion at Mornay's round table. Mornay and Gillem and Wing Sing had sided with Stanhope. Mary Louise, Reuben, and Hattie had disagreed with them. Martha had remained neutral. "I don't think it's worth arguing over," she had said, "when there's so much else to think about," meaning primarily her David, whereabouts unknown, even the fact of his existence unknown to her, day to day, night to night.

Sedley continued amiably: "Many people, including backers of the President like myself, feel as I do, George, that he made a mistake in suspending the right of *habeas corpus*. It's hurting the Northern cause. So you're helping the South, George, just by being here behind bars."

"That's cold comfort," growled Stanhope, "though I'm glad to hear you say it, and I appreciate what you and others are doing for me. Tell me what's happening in the war."

Sedley glanced at Dewey. "All I know of the war is what I read in the newspapers. I'll let you read for yourself after I go." He noted Dewey's signal that the time for their interview was up. "Be patient," Sedley cautioned, "and you'll be free. Here's today's *Sentinel*."

Accepting the paper with one hand, with the other grasping

Sedley's, Stanhope groaned: "I wish I were out of this place. What's the latest from our women in New Orleans?"

"Sarabelle's mother has died. Sarabelle has had a paralytic seizure."

"Too bad." Stanhope impatiently brushed aside this news of his wife's misfortunes. "What about Vicky and Beau?"

"She's with her mother. Beau is with Johnston."

"With Johnston? That's splendid news. I wish I were."

As Sedley emerged from the citadel, he noted the battery of huge Columbiads pointed straight at Golden Gate, ready to blast any Confederate vessel that might try to enter. But what impressed him even more — as a wedge of the pelicans that gave Alcatraz its name passed overhead — was his view of his city from this vantage point. Beyond the masts and funnels of the vessels at its wharves or at anchor near them rose his El Dorado Bank Building, and beyond it the city climbed its seven hills like a living entity, like a young Rome already a seat of empire, and he saw a vision of it a hundred years from now with commercial buildings and grand hotels scraping the sky, here at the gateway to the Orient, here at the edge of one continent and facing another, the commerce of all nations pouring through it, people of all nations inhabiting it. Commanding land and sea, it would be a monument to his vision, his faith, his money.

Sitting on the end of his pallet, Stanhope was reading about the battle of Stanwick's Station, as Gillem described it under a banner headline: **ONLY FORTY-SIX MILES FROM OUR BORDER IS TOO CLOSE FOR COMFORT!** Gillem expressed an anxiety sweeping the state: **Can General Carleton's men repel this daring thrust? Or are we to be treated to the spectacle of another Union débâcle, this time at our very doorstep?**

Gillem's editorial advocating Stanhope's release was a tribute to Gillem's sense of fair play at a dark moment.

Stanhope read it with relish. But it was those blazing head-lines that made his hopes rise high.

Chapter Twenty-Two

Hopes high, too, David Venable and his fellow Unionists, who had chased Sam Clemens out of Missouri and then advanced nearly to Nebraska, had gone back to Hannibal and boarded the steamboats that would take them to the great battle both sides had been preparing, a battle that would dwarf any in the nation's history. David had written Martha: **The good *Iatan* carried us on down the Mississippi, then up the Ohio, then up the Tennessee, and, while proceeding up the Tennessee, we were continually overtaking, or being overtaken by, other boats loaded with troops, until presently the river was alive with transports carrying us into the heart of the Confederacy.** Bands had played. Flags had flown. **It was the "pomp and circumstance of glorious war," as Shakespeare puts it, and made us feel like heroes.**

The heroes disembarked in the rain at an otherwise deserted spot called Pittsburg Landing, slithered their way up a steep bluff, and joined an immense throng painfully wading its way through mud to make camps in scattered woods. **We're part of the new Army of the Tennessee commanded by a new general named Ulysses S. Grant,** David continued. **Forty-thousand Confederates under Albert Sidney Johnston are twenty miles down the road at Corinth, Mississippi. We're waiting for the arrival of our Army of the Ohio and then, sixty thousand strong, we'll advance and crush Johnston.**

It was Sunday, April 6, 1862, and outside the conical-shaped white tent day was breaking. Inside David was hurriedly pulling on his shoes. The Tennessee quickstep, as they called the diarrhea that had plagued them since their arrival, had him in its grip again. "Where you going?" his corporal and friend since childhood days, Mutt Howell, whispered, raising a tousled head from his blanket while the others went on sleeping. David made an expressive face and hurried out to straddle the latrine trench before it was too late. That trench was the only one they had dug. Why entrench when you're about to advance and crush the Rebel army just twenty miles down the road?

After quieting the quickstep, David decided to go farther into the woods and enjoy this glorious morning, so clear after so much rain. Overhead the trees were leafing out. Around him redbud and stars of Bethlehem were in bloom. Death seemed an impossibility on such a morning, life eternal. The huge encampment, extending over a mile, was waking around him, and he smelled the smoke of breakfast fires and frying bacon and heard a lone voice raised in their new song:

Mine eyes have seen the glory
Of the coming of the Lord;
He is trampling out the vintage
Where the grapes of wrath are stored. . . .

Julia Ward Howe's poem, which he had first read in the *Atlantic Monthly* Martha had sent him along with the wool socks she had knit, was being sung to the tune of the soldiers' favorite, "John Brown Song," as it still is today — Brown, its inspiration, having been hung for trying to instigate an uprising of slaves.

The words moved David deeply. Surely the cause of freedom was righteous. Surely God was on their side. Like Mornay he saw the war as a second American Revolution aimed at overthrowing the power of the Slavocracy and making America truly free. He thought of his loved ones out there by the Golden

Gate where this day had not yet arrived. Martha's latest letter, which he carried in his pocket, told how she wished her love could protect him like a suit of armor but, **no, it cannot and you must do what you have decided to do, whatever the risk.** Also in that pocket over his heart he carried her daguerreotype inside a silver locket. Every time he opened the locket she looked out at him with those level no-nonsense eyes that he loved.

"You in Sherman's division?" a young boy asked, coming up from the nearby creek with a bucket of water in each hand. He couldn't be more than fifteen. "Creek's flooded," he added.

"No, Hurlbut's."

"They say there's Rebs out front, close." The youngster's eyes were wide, his voice tense with excitement.

"Oh, they've been saying that for a week," David reassured him in fatherly fashion and moved on, feeling a bit hypocritical. Why hadn't he been honest? Why hadn't he said — "You may die today, and I may die, too." — and asked God's mercy on them both? He silently did so now. And thinking who may live or die whenever the battle comes, he wondered if his chum from San Francisco days, Beauford Stanhope, brother of the glamorous Victoria with whom he was once in love, was perhaps down the road with Johnston's army. Strange if he and Beau should meet in battle. Yet no stranger than war itself. Martha's letter had said Beau had enlisted and that Victoria and her mother were still trapped in New Orleans by the blockade. Martha and Victoria had vied for his affections in those far-off days by the Golden Gate which glowed so brightly in his memory. Much as he loved Martha, he couldn't get enchanting Victoria out of his mind.

He came to a clearing in the woods. It was full of tents like his own, and in the middle of them stood, incongruously, a one-story log-cabin meeting house, Shiloh Church. Stark and elemental, it brought back a childhood memory: attending a log-cabin church like this, hearing Preacher Williams — a frontier homesteader like his father, dressed like his father in homespun but who'd felt "the call" — speak to them in rough-hewn words of God, of life, of death. By contrast fashionable St. Matthew's in Philadelphia where he himself had last preached seemed insufferably grandiose and pretentious, and once again he was glad he had resigned his comfortable pastorate to serve in the ranks and risk himself totally and let God decide what happened to him. He had said nothing to his comrades about his ministry and did not intend to. The rough-hewn meeting house represented the religion he had resolved to preach if he survived: elemental, popular, direct.

Just then he heard shots in the distance, then shouts coming rapidly nearer.

A blue-uniformed soldier broke out of the trees nearby, holding his bloody right arm with his left. Seeing David, he shouted as if announcing it to all the world: "The Rebs is coming! Hundreds of 'em!" And he rushed on toward the rear, while in the woods behind him David saw gray-clad figures everywhere, and throughout the Union camp he heard drummers beating the long roll of alarm.

Half-dressed men came pouring from the tents around the church, guns in hand. Their deep-throated shouts of defiance mingled with the high-pitched yells of the advancing Rebels.

And as he turned to run toward his own tent, those triumphant yells sent a cold shaft of dismay through David as he realized the ineptitude of his side and the superior boldness and skill of the Rebels who had achieved this humiliating surprise.

Four hours earlier in the darkness of that April morning General Albert Sidney Johnston and Lieutenant Beauford Stanhope had been sitting on a log beside a muddy road two miles from David's tent, gazing into the embers of a dying fire. To take their minds off the coming battle they had been talking of their favorite places in California. "Mine's Rancho San Pasqual a few miles east of Los Angeles," Johnston had said. "Eliza and I plan to make our home there." Johnston had known Beau for years and was very fond of him, though not of his father.

"I incline to Marin County, myself," Beau had rejoined. "It's across Golden Gate from the city, as you may remember. General Halleck had a ranch there. I visited it with Dad and my chum, David Venable. Davie and I dreamed of owning a ranch like it some day. You never knew Davie. He had a crush on my sister, but she married Eliot Sedley. He's joined an Iowa regiment, I hear. Maybe he's right up the road, yonder." Beau had gestured into the darkness.

Johnston had mused: "Speaking of coincidences, I wonder what coincidence brought us all here, after service or residence in California, to face each other in these muddy woods . . . you, me, your friend David, Ulysses Grant, and Cump Sherman, plus Old Brains Halleck over there in St. Louis running the whole Union show? We've all had a taste of California. We've all found her delicious. None of us wanted this war. Yet, here we are."

Johnston had not mentioned what had been uppermost in his mind. After weeks of falling back, drawing the Federals deeper toward their destruction, he hoped he had led his army up this muddy road through these soggy woods to whip them or perish in the attempt. Most of his men were like Beau, new recruits. They were so undisciplined, so unmanageable, it had taken them two days to advance eighteen miles. They had wandered off, gotten lost, and, despite orders to be quiet so as to achieve the surprise on which victory and their lives could depend, they had shouted and sung, had shot at rabbits and deer, had treated war as a lark while the fate of the Confederacy, the fate of Albert Sidney Johnston, hung in the balance.

Bitter criticism of Johnston had been rising across the South. It had surfaced here a few minutes earlier at the council of war by this fire. His second in command, Pierre Gustave Beauregard, had voiced it most sharply. "To attack now would be madness. We've lost all chance of surprise. They'll be entrenched up to their eyes and waiting for us."

Braxton Bragg, commanding the Second Corps, had agreed though less vociferously. Bragg was not volatile like Beauregard. But he had been equally opposed to Johnston's plan. "I, too, suggest a postponement." Leonidas Polk and John Breckinridge, commanding the First and the Reserve Corps, had emphatically supported Johnston. After patiently listening to all of them, he had said firmly: "Gentlemen, we shall attack at daybreak."

But Beauregard had persisted. He had been at Manassas. He had been at the siege of Fort Sumter. He thought he knew better than Johnston. "Buell's Army of the Ohio may have joined 'em. That'll bring their strength to sixty-thousand or more."

"I'd fight 'em if they were a million!" Johnston had replied curtly. "And now let's get some rest."

And then Beau had asked: "Will they run, sir, as they did at Manassas?"

Johnston had shaken his head. "These are Western men, Beau. They know how to fight. We'll have to break 'em." Johnston had glanced at his young aide and had wondered if they would both be alive at the end of this day.

Suddenly a huge figure had loomed out of darkness. It was Polk returning. "Leonidas!" Johnston had greeted him with pleasure. They had been roommates at West Point. Polk was as tall as Johnston, even broader chested, his presence almost as commanding. He was an Episcopal clergyman like David, a bishop in fact. Jefferson Davis had made Polk a major general soon after the outbreak of war. He had stood silently a moment, looking down at the glowing coals, then he had rumbled: "I just want to say one thing, Sidney. Back your judgment. There's only one way to go now. Forward." And having delivered himself of this brief homily, the bishop had extended his hand, not in blessing but in comradely encouragement.

"Thank you, Leonidas." Johnston had left the rest unsaid.

Beau had thought Johnston great in his understatement, his unflagging dignity, and courage. Polk had turned and disappeared into the darkness.

To some, Beau had seemed an empty-headed young Southern gallant, scion of the Chivalry, white plume rising jauntily from his broad-brimmed gray hat, long yellow hair flowing out from under it, and not much else there. Underlying, however, was an ironic yet thoughtful perception. It was much the opposite of David's earnest idealism, one reason they had hit it off so well. Easy-going, fun-loving Beau had opposed Secession and had infuriated his father by poking fun at the Knights of the Golden Circle, at what he had called "that nonsense of secret handshakes and dressing up in costume and marching around."

But when war had come, he had felt compelled to volunteer for his native South. And tonight he had been taking life very seriously, indeed.

Also awake into these early morning hours, Major General Henry Wager Halleck, pot-bellied, pedantic, commander of all Union forces in the Mississippi region as well as being Clara's lawyer, stood silent and alone in his St. Louis headquarters, rubbing his folded elbows with his hands as he contemplated the map on the wall before him. A blue pin marked the location of his Army of the Tennessee. Halleck was jealous of Ulysses Grant, its commander. Grant's recent capture of Forts Henry and Donelson had opened Tennessee to invasion and had catapulted Grant to fame. But Grant was only carrying out Halleck's grand strategy.

Balding, middle-aged, Halleck had never commanded troops in the field, yet he was the nation's leading military thinker. His ELEMENTS OF MILITARY ART AND SCIENCE was considered a classic. He had once turned down a professorship of engineering at Harvard. After having served in California during the Mexican War, Halleck had left the Army to practice law and had become one of San Francisco's leading citizens, as Sedley had pointed out to Clara. Soon after this war had broken out, Lincoln had made him a major general.

"Halleck, we need California's talent as much as we need her gold," Lincoln had joked when Halleck had called at the White House to discuss his new appointment.

"Thank you, Mister President. California will try to serve you in every way, I'm sure."

"You're fresh from the coast. What's the political climate out there?" Lincoln had put his feet up on the desk to indicate he was inviting confidence in a way that had astounded Halleck. Halleck had decided to be frank.

"The climate is very favorable to you, Mister President, except for one thing."

"And what's that?"

"The imprisonment of George Stanhope without trial."

"That's Carleton's doing. I've given my commanding generals a free hand. They're authorized to suspend the privilege of the writ of *habeas corpus* whenever they deem it necessary

160

in the interests of national security."

"I know that, sir, but Stanhope's becoming a martyr in some eyes. His imprisonment lends credence to those who accuse you of assuming despotic power. I speak as a loyal supporter, sir, but I must be frank. He's doing more harm in prison than he did out of it. Under any circumstances the chance of his leading a successful uprising in California is minuscule."

"Halleck, I appreciate that. It's just what I thought you might say." And Lincoln had put his feet down and had shaken hands cordially, all in a way that had amazed Halleck who'd heard about the gawky president's eccentricity and folksy shrewdness but now had experienced them.

Before leaving grubby, crowded Washington City, jammed with office seekers like himself, Halleck had called on his old acquaintance, eighty-one-year-old, long-haired, long-faced Roger Taney, chief justice of the Supreme Court, in his residence on Capitol Hill. After deploring the suspension of *habeas corpus* which he knew Taney opposed as unconstitutional, Halleck had touched delicately on the appeal of his client, Clara Boneu, now before the court. "Of course, I know your backlog is heavy, Mister Chief Justice, but I wondered when her case might be heard?"

"In due course, in due course," Taney had sniffed. Taney was an ardent supporter of the South and, therefore, as Halleck had guessed, had no great desire to see the Lincoln administration acquire more public land in California, a state that could yet, in Taney's view, side with the South. "If she's not a fraud, as are so many claimants under those old land grants, she'll get her due."

"I appreciate your spirit of fairness," Halleck had responded solemnly. "Her claim is, indeed, an exception to a bad rule."

Now Halleck was rubbing his elbows with satisfaction as he stood before the map in his St. Louis headquarters. As soon as Buell's Army of the Ohio joined Grant's at Pittsburg Landing, Halleck would proceed there and take command of an overwhelming force of nearly one hundred thousand which he would lead triumphantly, he hoped, into the Confederacy's vitals and sever the enemy in two and perhaps bring the war to an early end.

As he had written earlier in the evening to his beloved Elizabeth: **I get so homesick for you and our boy that I could turn my back with pleasure on all this, in exchange for a few days of us three together in the city or at the ranch in beautiful Marin.**

Like nearly everyone else on the Union side, Halleck didn't dream that Johnston would be so foolish as to attack a force so much larger than his own.

At dawn Johnston woke Beau with a fatherly hand on his shoulder. Beau scrambled to his feet, ashamed he had slept while Johnston evidently had not. Black Ran, who had accompanied Johnston across the desert and earlier during his campaigns in Utah and Mexico, was handing the general his coffee and crackers, and Beau saw his own Cyrus coming from the fire with his hot cup. Cyrus embodied the ambivalence Beau felt toward slavery. He disliked it but couldn't bring himself to do anything about it. Cyrus had been his property since boyhood. Cyrus, his same age, embodied the painful dilemma Beau would rather forget. So did Jennie Clemens, as she proudly called herself despite her mistreatment at the hands of her former owners, and now of Beau. Some black females accompanied the Army of the Mississippi as laundresses and prostitutes. But back at the New Orleans house, Jennie was pregnant by Beau. Yes, she very much embodied the ambivalence he felt as faithful Cyrus handed him his coffee, and he chatted with Johnston and the other aides. Yet, his dream for the future was of the ranch in Marin County he and David might own some day and of the life they might lead there, far from bothersome problems such as slavery.

No moonlight and magnolias here, Sis, he had written Victoria. **Just rain, mud, confusion, inefficiency, dissension, delay — you name it, we have it, including dysentery. Nevertheless, we'll prevail. Johnston is magnificent. Hugs to Ma and Uncle Percy. My usual obeisances to Your Highness. I'm hoping for a furlough when this is over. I'll stop at the plantation on my way to you and see how things are going.**

A few minutes later as he and his staff swung to their saddles, Johnston called out confidently: "Tonight, gentlemen, we'll water our horses in the Tennessee River!"

His plan was simple. The Union position was an open V. Rain-swollen and impassable Owl and Lick Creeks formed the sides of the V. Its bottom was at Pittsburg Landing. He would attack the mile-and-half front between the creeks but strike hardest on his right, toward the landing. He hoped this would cut Grant's men off from their only avenue of retreat, roll up their line, and cram them down the throat of the V into the river.

As he rode forward, soldiers at the roadside, waiting orders to advance, recognized Johnston. They cheered and put hats on bayonet points and waved them high. Johnston nodded encouragingly. "This is our day, eh, boys?

Beau felt everything fade out of him but a glorious elation. The light was growing. The ground mist was clearing. Ahead they heard firing. And as the sun rose round and red through the bare trees, Johnston pointed to it. "See! The Sun of Austerlitz!" Before Napoleon's victory at Austerlitz over Austrian

163

and Russian armies, the sun had risen out of a mist, and Napoleon had pointed to it as a good omen. But to Beau, not steeped so deeply in Napoleonic lore, the sun looked bloody red.

Chapter Twenty-Three

Moving in their own time, oblivious to all war but the one they are waging for survival, Francisco and Helek came to the ocean beyond the dunes at the mouth of the valley. They waded out into the water. "This is Sxa-amin," Francisco explained. "You have seen him in your dream vision. I have told you how he beats upon the breast of the earth as though he would make love to her. Now taste him. Pour him over your head. Become one with him. Together with Hutash he makes up the world, and here is where they join." Helek obeyed, as the gulls screamed overhead and the rollers came foaming in around them. "Now you are truly one with the land and the sea, truly of our people."

And Francisco explained how their ancestors had gone out upon Sxa-amin "as they went out upon Hutash to find food and fortune and live their lives. They traveled in wondrous canoes made of planks cut from driftwood with stone tools and sewn together with milkweed fiber such as we use at home, and Sxa-amin yielded them fish and shellfish and valuable skins of animals for wearing and for trade."

Just then Helek cried out in alarm as he felt something coil like a snake about his ankle, but it was only a strand of seaweed. Untangling it and holding it up, his father explained: "Like Hutash, Sxa-amin produces plants that can be used and eaten, for he, too, is alive in a variety of ways." And as the sea pounded upon the land around them Francisco explained that Hutash and Sxa-amin are constantly striving against each other for dominance "as do all living things, for there is no life without striving."

Traversing the shore stealthily, subsisting on mussels and

crabs and seaweed pods as well as the seed meal they carried in their waistnets, they came, after two days, to a mighty promontory that extended like a huge finger far into the sea toward the setting sun. "That is Kumquaq, the Western Gate," Francisco told his son, "though white people call it Point Conception. Through it our spirits leave this world after we die and travel toward the Land of the Dead."

Desolate, windswept, it seemed to Helek an awesome place, articulate yet utterly silent.

Standing at its utmost tip on a bluff high above the water, they watched the descending sun spread a pathway toward them that seemed real enough to walk upon. "It is the path we all must follow when we go to meet Katayin, Lord of the Dead."

"Is that his country?" Helek pointed to an island in the distance, and Francisco explained what an island was. "Once that one was inhabited by our ancestors who lived there in numerous towns, ruled over by a powerful chieftainess whose name was Lihui. In her grand canoe painted bright red and spangled with sea shells and cushioned by soft skins, four strong paddlers sped her over the sea."

"Where is she now?"

"She has gone to the Land of the Dead."

"And her people?"

"They have gone there, too."

"Then who lives on the island?"

"The A-alowow. It's their kingdom now. Or they think it is." A shadow passed over Francisco's face. "There are visible and invisible worlds, as I think you are learning. Some are like your dream vision. Some are like that island. One may live in one or the other. Both are real. But come, let us do as the spirits do."

They retraced their steps, bending before the wind, until

they reached the base of the promontory and there, descending the bluff, they came to a pool of sweet water embedded in smooth gray rocks just above the beach, surrounded by ferns and flowers. Francisco said solemnly: "This is where the spirits stop for a last drink before departing on their journey to the Land of the Dead. This is their last taste of life on earth." He knelt and scooped up a handful of the clear, cool water. "We may do this without sacrilege, for water gives life to all." And he put it to his lips.

Helek did likewise and found the water sweet beyond believing.

"We do this in homage," his father continued gravely, "you understand?" Helek nodded but remained silent. He was imagining his spirit someday joining that procession winging toward the setting sun and finally meeting the dread Katayin.

"What does Katayin look like?"

"You must ask the dead. No living being knows."

As they crouched among golden sea dahlias and delicate lavender iris, looking seaward, a family of dolphins, father, mother, child, leaped suddenly out of the water and came toward them playfully, now submerged, now flashing into view. Francisco explained the origins of these remarkable creatures: "Many years ago when our ancestors lived on that island out there, they had no way to come to this mainland where we are now, so Kakunupmawa built them a bridge consisting of a rainbow. He told them they might pass safely over his rainbow bridge, but warned they must not look down or they might fall. Most passed over safely, but some made the mistake of looking down. They fell off and were transformed into dolphins such as you see now. That is why dolphins are the only wild creatures who come to greet us humans . . . because they, too, once were human."

Helek was incredulous yet wanted to believe. "Did that

rainbow bridge really exist?"

"Of course," Francisco answered solemnly, "and now it is time to remember our loved ones who remain behind, and who will want to hear all that is happening to us," and they began gathering small, shiny, oval-shaped olivella shells to string into necklaces to take back to Ta-ahi and Letke when they returned to the hidden valley on the shoulder of Mt. Iwihinmu.

Chapter Twenty-Four

The cannonball tore off Mutt Howell's head and left the bloody stump of his torso reeling against David as if Mutt were still alive.

"God, God!" David cried out in horror and grief.

All the Ten Commandments, all the Sermon on the Mount, everything else in the world, even Martha and Mornay, went out of him, and only this reality, this bloody remorseless truth remained.

He laid the body down and wept over it, his own body wet with its blood.

"Here they come again!" someone shouted.

For two hours the Union line had fought desperately and fallen back, fought desperately and fallen back, trying to preserve itself against the Confederates' surprise assault. But now it was on the point of breaking.

A vengeful fury seized David, a fierce desire to kill, kill, kill. He snatched up his musket and fired over the still quivering body of Mutt at the figures advancing through the trees.

As if in answer to his desperate resolve, cheers came rippling toward him along his own ragged line. An officer on horseback was approaching. "It's General Sherman!" voices shouted.

David would not otherwise have recognized the man he had once dined with in San Francisco. Sherman was hatless, reddish hair standing up on end like an angry rooster's comb. His face was blackened with powder. His left hand was wrapped in a bloody handkerchief. His horse was bleeding from a chest wound. Much had happened to Sherman that David could not see. Since his successful days as a San Francisco banker, Sherman had tried his luck unsuccessfully at banking in New York, at law and real estate in Kansas, at superintending a military academy in Louisiana, continually dogged by failure. Having reëntered the Army at the outbreak of the war, he had distinguished himself at the battle of Bull Run but had failed in Kentucky when given high command. Now, as a division commander under Grant, he was on trial in more ways than one. One more failure might ruin him, one more bullet end his career. Now that he was face to face with oblivion, Sherman was discovering new strength, new certainty in himself. And David heard that new confidence as Sherman called out: "Steady, boys! Aim low. Make 'em sorry they came!" Sherman sounded as if the enemy were no more than an irritating nuisance, as if the focus of reality, of entitlement, of victory was here with him, with them.

Cheers went up, but David silently blessed Sherman. Sherman was here in the crucible with them, to live or to die with them, perhaps to show them the way out.

He aimed low as Sherman had directed and fired at the gray figures coming through the woods.

Out in San Francisco the sun was rising, Martha and Mornay were breakfasting in the house on Telegraph Hill, and Martha was nervously reading aloud the front page of *The Sentinel* that told of the great battle about to take place in far-off Tennessee. Mornay tried to reassure her. "He may never get near it. Last we heard he was hundreds of miles away."

But Martha guessed David would get near it. She felt that their payment for their love, for the nation's woe, had hardly begun, might go on for years, would test their deepest resources of faith and endurance.

Later at St. Giles's Episcopal Church on Pine Street where David might someday be pastor, she prayed God to spare her beloved. Mornay, kneeling beside her, secretly sharing her worst fears, likewise prayed silently for the young man he loved as a son and as a son-in-law to be.

In their cottage on Pacific Street, Hattie put down the paper with its news of the impending battle and said to Reuben with sudden anxiety that contradicted her earlier feelings: "You wouldn't really volunteer and go off and leave us, would you?"

"I would if they'd accept me."

"But what if you got killed?" she cried out.

"I won't." And he rose and went around the table and put his arms around her and kissed her, while little Charles, jealous, protested and tried to squeeze in between them.

Sedley and Mary Louise were breakfasting late this Sunday morning in the alcove overlooking her rear garden with its oval plot of grass surrounded by blue and white hydrangeas. He was reading *The Tribune*, which he subsidized, while she poured their coffee and continued: "So you think the outcome of the war may hinge on this battle?"

"I do."

"What if the South wins?"

"A crushing defeat may bring the North to the peace table."

"Will it release Stanhope?" He still had not told her of his visit to Alcatraz, but her spies had informed her, and she had passed the information to Mornay.

"Lincoln will release Stanhope no matter how the battle turns out."

She was honestly surprised. "Why?"

"He's too shrewd not to. He'll cut his losses there, just as he will when he finds it expedient to change his mind and free the slaves. That's my prediction. Do I gather you miss dear old George?"

"Of course," she smiled, "I'm very fond of him. Yet, he's

such a firebrand, such a hothead. And now if there's a big battle, which side would you bet on?"

"What makes you think I'd bet on either?" He liked to fence with her as with old Clara. Their mutual mistrust was a kind of bond.

"I just have an idea you might."

He pretended surprise. "You'd have me bet on the outcome of a bloody battle?" Then he probed. "Would you?"

"Sure, if I thought I'd win."

"Why, you're more unscrupulous than I suspected," he teased. Then he became sharply serious. "Got five thousand you'd risk?"

"Yes." She felt for the first time on the verge of penetrating the secret of how he made his money. And deep in her consciousness was the thought that the blood spilled in this battle would be a kind of compensation for the blood of slaves spilled by whites over centuries of oppression, and that any profit she might make would go to the Abolitionist cause.

"Well, now that's settled," he continued lightly, "what about another slice of toast and two fingers more of that Chateau Lafitte?"

The sun was overhead, now, and David and the others were on their bellies in a cart track depressed a few inches below ground level at the edge of a woods. They faced a meadow. Beyond the meadow were more woods where Rebels were assembling for another attack. Nearby, on their left, a peach orchard was in bloom, its delicate pink blossoms incongruously beautiful amid all this carnage. **Just a moment ago,** as David would write, **the meadow was alive with as fine a body of men as I ever saw, advancing toward us rank on rank, bayonets gleaming. We waited till they were almost upon us, then we rose and let them have it in the face, buck**

and ball — two buckshot and one ball. They went down like grain cut by a scythe. And David concluded: **A few survivors ran back into the woods as a vast and terrible groaning and moaning rose from that meadow and it seemed to me it was the voice of war, and we were all together there, North and South, living and dead, our flesh and blood mingled for better for worse. It was a new reality for me, sacred in a terrible way.**

In the woods across the field the Rebels were gathering for another attack, but then a stocky man in a blue uniform with a dark beard and a weathered black hat came riding by calmly in front of the men in the sunken road. He sat his roan horse masterfully. His rumpled uniform looked like he had slept in it, but a major general's stars were visible on his shoulder straps, and the excited word ran along the line: "It's Grant!" And David with astonishment recognized the young captain of uncertain manner and defeated tone, whiskey on his breath, who one night in the middle of a San Francisco waterfront street had squatted with him and Gillem and had peered down a dark hole and had heard water lapping down there among the pilings in the darkness. "I invested all my savings in a merchandise store, and they went down a hole as dark as this," young Captain Grant had muttered despairingly.

With his Julia, Grant had dreamed of getting rich in California and having a home there. Like Sherman he had been through hell since — had left the Army, had been unable to support his well-born wife and numerous children, like Sherman had been obliged to accept charity from a wealthy father-in-law. While grubbing out a living on a farm belonging to Julia near St. Louis, Grant had chopped wood beside her slaves and had hauled it with their help into town for sale. Grant had just about hit bottom down a dark hole. But here he was. He had been at his headquarters five miles distant when he had heard the firing and hastened toward it. Sherman had saved the day until Grant arrived. Now the Rebels were shooting at Grant. David heard the balls whistle overhead, but Grant rode through them as calmly and confidently as if on parade, as if saying: "Look at me, fellows. I'm an ordinary guy like you. They caught me off guard as they caught you. But we're still here. This fight is between us plain folk and the gentry. Let's win it."

Sherman had kept them from losing. Grant was telling them they could win.

And this time David found himself cheering with the others.

It was mid-afternoon. Galloping to find Johnston, Beau Stanhope's Ivanhoe balked with a snort, and Beau glanced down and saw at Ivanhoe's feet a red stream six inches wide and an inch deep. It was human blood flowing from the inferno all around him. Beau had never imagined battle would be like this. A bullet had cut away the feather from his hat. Another had nicked his boot. Spurring Ivanhoe, he jumped the river of blood and found Johnston sitting Fire-eater at the edge of a wood, calmly gazing at a meadow that was covered with dead and wounded men. Beyond the meadow was a blossoming peach orchard, then more woods and the Union line.

The carnage in that meadow had appalled and dismayed Johnston as it now did Beau. Johnston had willed himself to take the carnage into himself and contain it lest it overcome him. To Beau it seemed that everything that was happening at this moment was contained in Johnston, was all part of his plan for victory. Johnston seemed, indeed, to have risen above the confusion of the battlefield and to be dominating it by his serene presence. Actually Johnston was as desperate as Sherman and Grant. Like them he had been faced with failure, defeat, disgrace. He sensed this to be a decisive moment. If he could break the stubborn enemy line here, he might sweep on to the river and cut off the Union Army from Pittsburg Landing, bottle it up, and destroy it.

Beau drew rein and saluted. "Sir, General Breckinridge says one of his regiments is balking. That's the reason for the delay."

Johnston decided he must take the future into his own hands. "Very well, I'll lead the charge myself." And he galloped off toward Breckinridge's men, who faced that deadly field with its peach orchard, and Beau followed, a bit breathless as he felt the turning point approach.

Since morning when they overran the Union camp, Johnston had carried a little tin cup in his right hand. As David's tent was being looted, Johnston had ridden up and, after reprimanding his men yet wishing to show solidarity with them, he had leaned down and, as a joke to relieve tensions, had picked out Mutt Howell's cup as his share of the loot. He had carried it since as a good luck piece. Men chuckled when they saw him with a tin cup in his hand instead of a sword.

The sun sparkled on the cup now as he raised it and looked along the line of reluctant men who had seen only death in the field in front of them. Now they saw Johnston and his tin cup. His voice was stern yet playful. "Men, they're being stubborn. We shall have to put the bayonet to 'em!" And then, riding along the front rank on magnificent Fire-eater, he touched their bayonets here and there with his cup, making a tinkling sound that drew grins and cheers. Beau watched with admiration. When Johnston reached mid-point in the long line of bayonets, he wheeled Fire-eater abruptly. Pointing with Mutt Howell's cup toward the Union line, minimizing it with his gesture, he called out: "Come, my boys, follow me!"

Gently spurring Fire-eater, he moved forward at a trot, cup upraised.

With eager yells the Tennesseans poured after him across the meadow toward where David lay in the sunken road by the peach orchard. Beau followed, carried away by excitement, all thought of death forgotten.

As the line of bayonets drew closer, David rose to his feet with the others and shot gaps in it. But this time, led by that grand, seemingly invincible officer on that blood-red horse with a tin cup in his hand, it kept coming, coming. And as David knelt to reload, he realized that the Union line on either side of him was giving way, and he was being left alone. Angry, frightened, as he, too, turned to run, he raised his musket, caught the figure of the gallant officer in his line of sight, squeezed the trigger. Johnston felt a blow like a hammer tap strike his left leg just below the knee. And at that same moment David felt something hard and painful strike his left side and knock him to the ground. But not before he saw Johnston shift his leg slightly in the stirrup, as Johnston, brandishing Mutt Howell's cup, urged his men on toward victory.

At last the Union line was broken. It reeled backward toward the river landing. Johnston saw a victory of truly glorious proportions taking shape, that "Manassas of the West" he had promised Davis. He saw the Union Army destroyed, the invaders driven out of Tennessee, back across the Ohio. Following such a triumph, a negotiated peace might end the war, and he might realize his dream of returning to Eliza and their children in Los Angeles and spending his remaining years there in the garden of the West, as he thought of it.

Faintness seized Johnston. He had felt the blood in his boot, but, buoyed by the prospect of victory, he thought his wound a trifle. Suddenly his vision blurred. Battlefield and dream blended in his consciousness, and he reeled in his saddle.

Beau spurred forward. But before he could reach Johnston, others helped his idol from his horse and laid him on the ground. Beau dismounted and forced his way through the group around the prone figure. Johnston lay with closed eyes, as serene in death as in life.

David's bullet had severed an artery, and Johnston had bled to death without realizing he had been seriously hurt.

Writhing on the ground in pain, David thought himself mortally wounded. Then Rebel yells penetrated his pain. Scrambling to his feet, he saw his comrades disappearing through the trees in full flight while the Tennesseans bore down on him with leveled bayonets. **Bullets zipped and hissed around me,** he wrote Mornay and Martha. **I felt one pass through my hair, one pluck my sleeve, heard everywhere the cruel *iz-iz* of the Minié balls — conical bullets that expand when fired.** Running like mad he overtook his comrades, began to wonder how anyone shot through the body could run so fast. **Never slackening my pace, with my right hand I felt my left side which ached so painfully and found a spent ball. It had struck the locket where I carry Martha's likeness and lodged between my blouse and shirt.** It had bruised him painfully but not seriously.

Hurrying on among others in the massive rout, he reached rising ground where the narrow road descended toward the river landing. On the high ground he saw a line of cannon being emplaced, wheel to wheel, facing the oncoming Confederates, and moving along this new line was the unperturbable figure of Grant on his roan horse, Grant as calm as if this was a final trap he had been preparing for an unsuspecting enemy. Officers afoot or horseback were rallying men to the new line, but, feeling weak and defeated, David hurried on by. **Physically, morally, I looked the other way,** he confessed to

Mornay and Martha. **I felt others should carry the load and I be excused.**

So he fled on among the hundreds jamming the narrow, muddy road that descended toward Pittsburg Landing and the broad river where Johnston had hoped to water his horse.

Numbed with grief, filled with increasing foreboding, Beau Stanhope found Johnston's second in command, General Pierre Gustave Toutant "Shorty" Beauregard, at his temporary headquarters at Shiloh Meeting House and saluted. "I bring you sad news, sir." Beau controlled his words with great effort. "General Johnston is dead." And he related the particulars.

Likened to Napoleon because of his short stature and great ego, the usually voluble Beauregard had nothing to say for a moment, as he smoothed his flowing mustache between thumb and forefinger, staring with large incredulous eyes. "You are in command, sir," Beau repeated.

"It's an irreplaceable loss," Beauregard muttered. In fact, he had a low opinion of Johnston and felt he himself should have been in command from the beginning.

"Shall I tell General Breckinridge to press the attack toward the landing, sir?" Beau asked hopefully. He didn't think much of Beauregard. Compared to Johnston he seemed a dwarf.

Beauregard held up a restraining hand. Johnston had placed him at this strategic spot to funnel men and supplies to the front, while information flowed back to him from across the battlefield. Beauregard was aware of the terrible bloodshed, the frightful confusion, aware that it was now past mid-afternoon and the army had been fighting since dawn and was nearly out of ammunition and nearly exhausted. "We must hold a council of war before we proceed." Beauregard's earlier opinion that the attack was hopeless had been proved wrong.

He wanted to be right this time. "Tell General Breckinridge to report to me here."

Beau felt something changing, the spirit of victory dying, Johnston's spirit dying. Beauregard would wait and see. By then Johnston's spirit of victory would be dead.

"Very well, sir!" Beau saluted glumly, and turned away.

In his office in the El Dorado Bank Building, Sedley opened the telegram from New York. **Buy,** it said. It was from his man on Wall Street, Williamson. It meant buy gold on the New York Exchange. It meant Williamson had word from the *New York Times* reporter he subsidized that the North was losing the great battle at Pittsburg Landing, and, therefore, the price of gold would rise at the prospect of a longer war and the government's need to finance it by issuing bonds secured by California's gold. Whichever side won, Sedley and California prospered. Their gold financed the bloodshed. The longer the war, the better for them.

Sedley turned to Gordon Forbes, his office manager and confidant, and silently handed him the telegram.

Forbes read it, massaged the middle of his sandy head with the middle finger of his right hand, and without a word or a change of his dour expression handed it back.

"What do you say?" Sedley asked ironically as usual.

"What do you?"

"What will the price be tomorrow?

Forbes shrugged. "It closed at one hundred and two and seven eighths dollars per ounce yesterday."

"Then I say buy."

"How much?"

"Fifty-five thousand."

Forbes blinked. "Williamson better be right!" he said gloomily.

"He usually is."

"What's the five thousand for?"

"A friend of mine."

Forbes didn't ask her name but, knowing Sedley as he did, guessed it was Mary Louise. Their gamble would succeed or fail as David and Beau and their comrades succeeded or failed in the hours immediately ahead.

As David hurried on down the road toward the landing, jostled in the rout, it was as if he was descending into a pit of shame, when suddenly he heard the "Battle Hymn of the Republic" rising confidently ahead and saw, coming up the road, a freshly uniformed column, marching in route step, muskets at right shoulder. It was the vanguard of Buell's Army of the Ohio arrived at last. As they strode confidently up the hill, their faces unsullied by defeat, the newcomers joshed David and his fellow fugitives. "Where you headed, boys? The enemy ain't that way, he's this way!" They pointed up the hill and laughed with a derision that seared David's soul.

All at once he turned and began marching upward beside them. One or two others of the defeated did likewise, but the rest continued down toward the river.

As he neared the high ground again, David heard furious firing, and, when he topped the bluff, he saw smoke rising above the hub-to-hub cannons and the blue line that had formed around them. Gray figures were withdrawing into the woods opposite, into the twilight gathering there. Grant had beaten off a last attack. Cheers broke from Buell's men as they rushed to join the fight, and, although David felt the day might yet be saved, there seemed no longer a place in it for him. Weak from hunger, parched by thirst, side aching, weakened, too, by disgrace, he felt left out and wandered aimlessly off into the trees and gathering dusk.

Soon he saw a light in a house in a clearing. As he approached, he heard groans and screams and realized this was an improvised hospital. All around it on the ground lay the wounded, most of them suffering in silence. More were being brought in by stretcher-bearers. He threaded his way carefully through the expanse of suffering bodies toward the open doorway from which the light came. Peering inside, he saw bloody tables on which lay bloody men, bloody surgeons working over them with bloody knives and bloody saws while piles of bloody limbs — arms, legs, feet, fingers — lay beside the tables. An appalling stench sickened him. "This is my body and blood," the words of the Communion service came gruesomely to his mind, "which was given for thee to preserve thy body and soul. . . ." He turned away, overwhelmed, and wandered blindly off into the darkness, stunned by this vision of a truth such as he had never known before, this horror that dwarfed any he had imagined.

How long he wandered he could not remember before he saw Grant, sitting alone under a tree in the rain that had begun to fall. Grant's black hat was pulled down over his face. He seemed asleep, and David didn't disturb him but walked on toward the line of wheel-to-wheel cannon, picking up on the way a discarded musket that lay in the rain as if waiting for him. At the cannon he found exhausted men, sleeping in the mud. "What division is this?" he asked a lanky fellow who turned over and looked up at him.

"Sherman's, what's left of it."

"Where's Hurlbut's?"

"God knows!" The man behind the voice chuckled grimly. "God only knows, but if yore lookin' for a scrap, soldier, you can join up here. We ain't quit yet!"

David lay down gratefully beside this man who had refused to give up.

★ ★ ★ ★ ★

"Well, Grant, we had the devil's own day of it, eh?" Sherman asked later that evening. He had found Grant standing under the tree where David had seen him. Four horses had been killed under Sherman. Blood was still oozing from his left hand. His left shoulder was bloody, too. He had come to ask Grant his plans for withdrawing in the morning. But something stopped him, something that came from Grant's stubborn manner. Like Sherman, Grant was fighting not only for his own survival but for survival as respected mate in Julia's eyes, just as Sherman was fighting for survival in Ellen's and David in Martha's. The lower half of Grant's sword and scabbard had been shot away by a cannonball. It symbolized how close things had been, how near he had come to oblivion. Sherman felt the brotherhood surge up in them of those who had faced death together.

"Yes," Grant replied laconically to his question, "they gave us the devil today. We'll lick 'em tomorrow, though."

We'll lick 'em tomorrow. Much more passed unsaid between the two. Sherman was grateful for Grant's faith in him that had made him a division commander and had given him a chance to redeem himself today. Grant was grateful to him for saving the day.

Neither knew that Johnston, who shared their dream of a happy home in golden California, was dead.

Grant's prediction came true. Next day after five hours of bitter fighting, David found himself back at Shiloh Church where he had been the previous morning. But now, instead of dismay and defeat, a fierce exultation filled him, and he remembered with irony that passage from the first Book of Samuel where Shiloh is named as a place of peace. And, as he stepped again into the clearing by the log church, this time pursuing a retreating enemy, he was turning his head to shout triumphantly to those behind, when a Minié ball struck him on the inner side of his right thigh, grazing his testicles, breaking his leg, and he fell to the ground with a scream of agony.

Out in San Francisco, Martha was in the damp basement that served the colored school as classroom, leading her pupils in morning prayer. At the Great Pacific Market on lower Washington Street, Mornay and Reuben were serving Mary Louise who had come, shopping basket hanging from one arm, ostensibly to buy vegetables but really to report on what Sedley was up to, and Sedley was receiving, too late, the frantic wire from Williamson in New York: **Sell, sell!**

And in Los Angeles, Eliza Johnston was reading in *The Morning Star* the news of her husband's death.

Chapter Twenty-Five

"We have seen the place of death. Now I shall show you the place of life," Francisco said, and father and son turned away from the sea and the awesome surroundings of the Western Gate and, still avoiding all settlement, traveled inland toward the House of the Sun, of Kakunupmawa, the Lord of Life. As they came again to the heart of the wilderness, they saw, springing up from amid parched sand and stones in the middle of a dry wash, a gorgeous golden flower, its petals open to the sun.

"What is it?" Helek asked, for it seemed miraculously beautiful and astonishingly out of place.

"It is Summer Sun," replied Francisco. "It is Kakunupmawa's signpost. White people call it Blazing Star. It shows us we are on the right path toward his house."

Finding a trail nearby that climbed upward through pale gray saltbrush and spiny yucca, invisible to any but a practiced eye, Francisco led the way. Before long they came to the petrified vertebra of a huge creature of long ago lying beside the trail, just as he remembered it. It was as big around as his body. Its telltale flanges were still intact, and Francisco said to Helek as Tilhini once said to him: "This is a piece of the first people who lived when animals were humans. It, too, shows us we are traveling in the right direction." Staring at the whitened stone which once was alive, Helek marveled and tried to imagine a world populated by such creatures. "They were turned to stone by Kakunupmawa," Francisco continued, "so they might endure as reminders of what has been, what is called the past."

Climbing on, they felt a gust of hot wind from the east, searing their skins like heat from a fire. "We are feeling the breath of Kakunupmawa," Francisco explained. Though it was not yet mid-morning, the heat suddenly increased as if the sun was directly overhead, bearing down with all its weight. Another gust almost took their breath away. Francisco drew Helek under the protection of a gray-barked oak, the only tree on that arid slope. Now the searing wind was coming at them in hurricane-like gusts. Helek saw the leaves of the oak beginning to wither. Small birds dropped from its branches and lay gasping at their feet. He, too, began to gasp.

"What is happening, Father?"

Francisco explained gravely that every day Kakunupmawa passes overhead with a huge torch in his hand "and by lowering his thumb from time to time he allows more of the torch to burn, thus causing more heat on earth."

"His thumb must have slipped!" Helek gasped.

"Possibly," Francisco chuckled, pleased by his son's precociousness.

"Or, perhaps, Kakunupmawa is angry with us for trying to find his house?"

"Or is he testing us, asking us to make a greater effort?"

After blowing for an hour like a hot hurricane, bringing super-heated air rushing from the desert toward the sea, the simoom subsided as suddenly as it had arose. Putting pebbles in their mouths to start the saliva flowing, they climbed on. By mid-afternoon tall white thunderheads towered above them, and soon they felt a breath of cool air and then the welcome raindrops. They lifted up faces and hands and opened their mouths and thankfully let the rain fall upon them.

"Does this mean Kakunupmawa likes us?" Helek asked.

Francisco nodded with approval, for it seemed the boy was reading the signs truly.

At evening the sky cleared, and they saw pines outlined against a crest far ahead. To their left the sun was setting, a disk of orange fire, and out of it a dark speck appeared and came toward them swiftly. Soon the speck became a giant condor approaching at great speed, flying low, never moving its wings, passing so close overhead they could see its red eye as, once again, it looked down as if to see how they were measuring up, how their quest was progressing. It was so near they could hear the air whistling through its wings, and then it was gone into the east and the gathering darkness.

"Where is it going?" Helek asked in awe.

"Perhaps to its nest in our secret valley."

"Then Mother and Sister will see it?"

"I hope so." And Francisco felt it a good omen that their dream helper should appear at this moment as if directing their steps.

"I wonder if Mother and Sister are safe?" Helek had voiced this anxiety before, and again Francisco, while sharing it, reassured him: "I think they are. I think Condor will protect them as it does us."

"They'll be pleased by the seashells we're bringing, won't they?"

"I think they'll be very pleased."

"We will have a celebration when we get home?"

"We will have a feast, a memorable feast."

They climbed on under the stars, slept briefly, at dawn emerged onto a high meadow of golden grass fringed with pines, and from the meadows rose, bursting from the earth like buried bones — just as Francisco remembered — giant outcroppings of rock that gleamed in the morning light as if newly created. "They are the First People transformed into stone," he whispered. "They are Bear, Eagle, Coyote, and many more!"

Helek gazed with wonder at the majestic display and felt the power that emanated from it. "Where is the House of the Sun?"

"Come, we shall see."

Threading their way carefully through this strange pantheon, they came to a central outcropping, a huge rock with a sheer face pockmarked by time and weather with holes like eyes, and midway up that face was a gaping mouth, a cave into which the rising sun was shining.

"Is that the House of the Sun?" Helek whispered in awe.

"Yes. Now follow me."

Francisco led the way around one side of the huge rock, climbed its sloping back, and descended by faint steps chipped into it long ago that seemed to lead off into thin air but brought them suddenly to a narrow ledge along which they crawled, a sheer drop below, until they reached a hole, a side entrance through which the dim light of the cave's interior showed. "Look inside," Francisco whispered, drawing back so Helek could look.

The interior was a huge room, much larger than the Cave of the Condors, and its walls and ceiling were alive with paintings of many designs and colors, all dominated by a giant one that occupied the rear wall. "Who is that?" Helek asked breathlessly, for the figure looked almost human.

"That is Kakunupmawa. He has been waiting there for us all these years. Come."

Francisco crawled through the hole. Tense with excitement Helek followed. The floor of the cave under their hands and knees was covered with powdery gray dust unmarked by any feet, except those of mice and birds, and some very faint human imprints that might have been left by an old Tilhini and a young Francisco. Once inside, they stood upright and approached the sacred figure.

Kakunupmawa was depicted holding a fiery sunwheel in his left hand and in his right the torch of the Sun. Kakunupmawa's thumb was raised high up its handle toward its flame. His huge

187

rectangular torso was outlined in red, as were neck and head, but from the top of his skull ominous black rays reached outward and downward toward either hand, where sunwheel and torch blazed brightly in yellow limonite rimmed with fiery red ochre. It was awesome, sublime. "Who did it, Father?" Helek whispered.

"No one but Kakunupmawa knows."

The boy gazed for a long moment. "I would like to be a great man and paint rocks."

"Perhaps you will be." A shaft of sorrow went through Francisco, for he felt with increasing certainty that the time of the rock painters, the time of the astrologer-priests, the time of such profound beliefs was passing. Ahead lay a new world of which he and his son could, as he told old Clara, foresee very little. All he could do was prepare Helek as best he might. Taking a handful of seed meal from his waistnet, he scattered it in front of the painting as tribute.

"Is that actually Kakunupmawa?" Helek whispered, still breathless.

"No, it is just the idea of him. He himself is invisible."

"Yet, this is truly where he lives?" Helek sounded incredulous.

"Yes, but in the way I am explaining. Let me show you one more thing."

Though the huge painting seemed to mark the end of the cave, there was more, as Tilhini once had shown young Francisco, and this was a niche behind Kakunupmawa, imperceptible unless you knew where to look. It was just large enough for two people to squeeze into, and here absolute darkness reigned as if it prevailed upon the great figure of Kakunupmawa from behind. "Here is the final refuge," Francisco explained as he and Helek crouched there in a midnight blackness, "the place nobody knows. Not even Kakunupmawa reaches here, as you see. Someday you may need to come here. That is why I show it to you."

For the rest of this day they explored the golden meadow, wandering in wonder among its giant multi-shaped outcroppings that represented the First People of that time when animals were humans. They marveled at the clear, invigorating air, the radiant light, the many springs that watered the meadow — frequented by birds of various kinds and deer and other animals. Toward sunset they returned to the great rock and watched the last rays resting in the mouth of the cave far above their heads. "It's situated so that all day long the sun shines in it," Francisco explained, "and thus Kakunupmawa makes his home there. Out beyond where Kakunupmawa seems to disappear each night," he pointed westward, "lives Katayin, Lord of the Dead, as we saw from the bluff above the water at Kumquaq. But up here lives the Lord of Life. We are the people of both, you understand?"

And Helek nodded, though puzzled as to how the sun could be in two places at once. "How can it be?"

"It simply is," Francisco declared solemnly. Then speaking with words that seemed to come from the earth itself like the outcroppings around them, he said: "We are in this world but a short time. Then we pass on through the Western Gate. But Katayin and Kakunupmawa are here forever. And so is the darkness I showed you in that place behind Kakunupmawa," he added with sudden afterthought, remembering the darkness in his own life, wondering if it was immortal, too, hoping the boy would never have to experience it, yet knowing he would.

Later, as they prepared to sleep at the foot of the great rock, Francisco said: "Put your hand on it."

Helek did so and felt the heat still there though the sun had long gone down.

189

Much later, when he rose and went to pee, he touched the rock again in the darkness. It was still warm.

Then he realized this was truly the House of the Sun, truly a special place of great power and meaning, and he wondered what rôle it might play in his life.

Down at Rancho San Marcos, Anita Ferrer put aside the letter from Benito and began to scratch where the flea had bitten her ankle. Fleas were the bane of California. Climate and soil had united to produce them by the millions. Even at the most fashionable gatherings in San Francisco and Los Angeles, even in Sedley's drawing room atop Rincon Hill, it was quite acceptable to scratch yourself publicly, so ubiquitous and voracious was the flea. Thus, when Anita saw her beagle bring a dying squirrel onto the porch and the children gather around to watch it expire, she thought of nothing alarming when the dog suddenly began to scratch itself and, a moment later, young Benito and little Anita did likewise, and then she herself felt the sting of the flea.

She ordered her Indian, Mary, to remove the carcass, but by then the harm had been done, although she did not know it.

Chapter Twenty-Six

Wearing a black veil, Victoria Stanhope Sedley stood watching the pallbearers — her brother among them — carry Albert Sidney Johnston's body to its grave.

Many beside Vicky at this sad ceremony at New Orleans's old St. Louis Cemetery wept openly at thought of the South's model soldier, embodiment of its chivalric ideal, killed when on the verge of a decisive victory.

Being buried with Johnston were rosy visions of quick and easy triumphs. Gone was the boast that one Southerner can lick ten Northerners. Gone with Johnston were twelve thousand casualties from the Army of the Mississippi, representing more than a quarter of its total strength engaged in those two bloody days at Shiloh. The war was evidently going to be terribly long and costly.

All this went through Vicky's mind as she watched Beau and the others lower the magnolia-covered casket into the grave. She didn't weep. The sight strengthened her resolve to fight harder for the Southern cause. The once frivolous, once party-loving Vicky had become a clear-eyed, if passionate, Rebel.

She had just rebuffed another of Sedley's *pro forma* suggestions she rejoin him in San Francisco. **My place is here, yours is there,** she wrote back. **If you are as devoted to our Cause as I hope, you can do more good where you are, just as I can do more good here.**

She had no illusions about their marriage. It was a calculated merger of power and money, flesh and blood. She knew of his relationship with Mary Louise. He knew of hers with other men. Both followed the rule: anything goes as long as it doesn't cause scandal.

At the heart of Vicky's feeling for the South was the house where she was born on fashionable St. Charles Street in New Orleans. So was the plantation up the Mississippi at Stanhope's Bend where she had spent some of her happiest days. Its moss-draped oaks, fertile bottomlands of corn and cotton, deferential slaves singing happily while they worked, its stable of fine horses, the wild woods adjoining where she loved to ride, the great river embracing it, the great house at the heart of it, were as much part of her as her blood.

Back home now in the town house, after the funeral, she complained bitterly to Beau: "If I were a man, I'd put on a uniform and fight until every last damnyankee was dead."

"We had 'em on the run, Sis. If Johnston had lived, we'd have whipped 'em." And turning to their uncle who shared the house with them and their mother, he said: "I suppose you don't believe that, Uncle Percy, but I was there."

Courtly Percy Stanhope replied tolerantly: "I believe you, Nephew. What's more I respect your convictions about this war, although I may not agree with them. Nevertheless," he added benignly, "I hope we can continue to converse."

Vicky made a disapproving face. She adored her handsome, dashing brother, despised their mild-mannered uncle with whose views on the war and slavery she fiercely disagreed. In many respects the antithesis of her father, Percy Stanhope was professor of botany at the Military Academy of Louisiana until the war had closed that institution and put him out of a job. Like many in New Orleans and throughout the South his sympathies were with the North, and they had been the cause of explosive scenes between him and Vicky, and between him and her father. "And I suppose you're just delighted," she flared now, "that a Yankee fleet is on its way to attack our city?"

"No, my dear, not delighted, but confirmed in my predictions. We've sown the wind. Now we must reap the whirlwind. That it should fall so heavily on you young people breaks my heart but doesn't change my convictions."

In an effort to keep peace, Beau interposed: "If General Lovell is forced to evacuate the city, you can all go to the plantation."

Victoria stamped her foot. "I won't leave this house! I won't run! Besides," she rolled her eyes wearily toward the ceiling, "there's Mother." Upstairs Sarabelle Stanhope lay bedridden, her left side partially paralyzed, her once great beauty only a memory. Vicky found her almost intolerable. They had never gotten along, less so now that her mother was such a burden.

Beau shrugged. "All right, Sis, I hope you can have it your way. But I've got to get back to the fight. We've got to keep the Yanks from capturing Corinth. I'll just run up and say good bye to Mama first." He took up his battle-stained hat with its half-shot-away feather and started up the winding stairs. Part way up he paused and looked back. "Sis, I heard that an Iowa division was opposite us during the battle. Gave us a devil of a scrap. I had a hunch David Venable was in it."

"Well, you can keep him and your hunch, both," she snapped.

"Oh, come on, Sis. He can't help if he was once your ardent admirer."

"But I wasn't *his* ardent admirer!"

"Yes, you were. Just a bit. Come, now, don't fib!" He winked at Percy and went on up to say a few words to his mother for what he feared might be the last time.

Sarabelle Stanhope, propped by three pillows, looked up at him lovingly from the four-poster with its white silk canopy. Jennie Clemens also looked at Beau with love from her chair on the far side of the bed. Jennie was Sarabelle's constant companion now.

"Son," the mother's voice quavered with tenderness and despair. She feared this might be the last time she would see him. "You're not leaving me?"

"Yes, Mama, I must get back. We've got to hold Corinth."

Tears came into her eyes. "Don't go, Beau," she pleaded. "Don't leave me." Rejected by her philandering husband, then by her daughter, Sarabelle had been borne up by Beau's loving kindness and Jennie's. "All I have left will be Jennie!" And she squeezed the black hand she held in her own.

"Mama, I've got to. Jennie'll take care of you. Won't you, Jen? So will Percy."

"I sure will, God help me!" Jennie's eyes shined back at him. She hadn't told him of her pregnancy. She wanted their child. She feared Beau might make her abort it. A similar mixture of love and fear fed her loyalty to Sarabelle. Sarabelle had given her a home when she had none, when almost anything seemed better than another betrayal such as she suffered at the hands of John Clemens when he had sold her down the river. She didn't blame Beau for making love to her. She knew such things were customary. And she was truly in love with him.

As for Beau, he was genuinely fond of her, genuinely saddened by her plight as a slave, but still quite unable to do anything about it except be kind to her. He was also genuinely grateful for all she had done for his mother.

"Yes, Jennie will take care of you," he repeated, sending Jennie a private message of affection with that look.

Sarabelle glanced from one to the other. Sudden intuition told her what was between them. At first it was almost a final blow. She had accepted her husband's infidelities with his slaves as traditional. Somehow she couldn't reconcile those of her beloved son. Then in a moment of sublimation she did reconcile this one. Impulsively she clutched Beau's hand with her free one, held onto Jennie's with the other, thus uniting the three of them. "Don't forget your mother, will you?" she pleaded pathetically. "And promise you'll be kind to Jennie?"

"I will," he promised gravely, aware she had guessed the truth, deeply moved by her intuition of it, moved deeply, too, by Jennie's adoring look and by his mother's linking of them through herself.

Bending, he kissed Sarabelle's hand. Through it he kissed Jennie, too, and, Jennie sensed that he did.

Then, still holding her hand, he touched Sarabelle's lips gently with his. She wrenched both hands free and threw her arms around his neck. "Oh, Beau, Beau!" For a loving moment they embraced while Jennie watched, and it seemed to him Jennie blessed them, forgave him, by her look. He held out a hand to her. She clasped it in both hers. "Good bye, Jen!" Then, gently disengaging himself from his mother, he strode wordlessly from the room.

Chapter Twenty-Seven

"Now let's look at your wound," Lettie said briskly, using her nurse's voice, putting aside her pen and the letter to Mornay and Martha she had been writing for David.

In the big ward-room around them, formerly the hotel's ballroom, people were passing and repassing, visitors, orderlies, nobody paying them any attention. St. Louis was filled with wounded soldiers and their families. So was this room.

Lettie couldn't remember when she fell in love with him. Perhaps it was when she saw him being carried in on a stretcher, delirious. Her heart had gone out to the angelic, boyish face and yellow curls, the boy in man's form, the child she longed for, the man she hoped would touch her. No man had ever touched her as lover, nor had she ever touched any man in that way. Sometimes her spirit sank into darkness when she thought of it. Was she to spend her whole life alone and unloved? The thought nearly destroyed her will to live.

David lay dreaming of California. If he lived, there would be a new world to create out there, and he and Martha would have a hand in it. He thought of her and Mornay in a Far West paradise of light and hope, beyond war and death. The knowledge that he had submitted himself totally and had survived the battle sustained him, made him feel he would live beyond this war. Still he prayed for mercy for his own shortcomings and the world's, sometimes inwardly, sometimes aloud as at Shiloh, but to a new kind of God, larger, more unknowable, yet, at the same time, more all-embracing than before.

Lettie adored his dreaminess, his radiant goodness, his blue eyes, and hair the color of ripe corn. He made her think of summer fields and the sky.

Glancing at her, he thought again how homely she was, yet how decent and deserving, how starved for affection. "Oh, my leg's all right!" he protested as usual.

There had been that embarrassing, yet revealing, moment between them after he had wet his sheets during his dream. In the dream a female figure, resembling Vicky Sedley, had come to him naked, yielding herself shyly at first, then voluptuously, passionately. He had been unable to hide the consequences. Lettie had seen the stained sheets next day, had recognized instantly what had happened from having seen it in her brothers's beds. But she had said nothing, though it had set her pulse throbbing, her face burning with thought of what she longed for but might be forever denied. He had said nothing, either, but, watching her color, had found her momentarily desirable as his need for a woman had swept keenly over him. He had known it could and should lead nowhere, that he didn't love her, would never in his right mind dream of touching her intimately. Still he had felt a wave of compassionate pity for her which seemed beyond right or wrong, seemed a part of his new understanding of God.

"You do as I say, or I sha'n't mail this letter!" she scolded him, smiling now. She knew where his heart lay. She accepted her secondary position, relegated to the background, ever the helpful, the admiring onlooker. But still she hoped. "Come now!" she ordered.

Rising from her chair almost with desperation, assuming an authority she didn't truly feel, she bent over him. "Doctor Somers will be here soon. He'll think you're not being properly cared for!" She heard herself speaking with what seemed unnecessary loudness and rapidity as her trembling fingers fussed with his blanket.

With a hot flash he felt those fingers touch his leg, withdraw quickly, return and slide upward along his thigh as if inadvertently, as she rearranged his bedclothes. He felt an erection coming despite his efforts. Miraculously the bullet, penetrating so near, hadn't struck fully there. Supposing it had? Supposing he had been rendered impotent, incapable of love-making, of procreating? He had been very lucky. He knew it. God knew it. He had vowed repeatedly over the past days that he would show his gratitude all the rest of his life. But here he was, lusting after this pathetic creature, thirty-five years old if she was a day, obviously so love starved she had taken up nursing just to be near a man. And inevitably, it seemed, his heart filled with compassion for her, for himself, both caught in the implacable jaws of war, and he wanted to take her and enfold her against all the years of her sorrow and make love to her physically and spiritually, make her well.

She masked what she was doing with mocking chatter about his recalcitrance. She didn't know where the words came from. They seemed to flow into her and out spontaneously as if required. He felt with an embarrassing surge of delight her hand brush his erection, heard her sharply drawn breath, knew it was no accident, was dimly aware of voices around them, people coming and going as if at a great distance, Emmett in the next bed, coughing his lungs out, while they remained encapsulated in this private moment of shared magic, shared wrongdoing. But it didn't seem wrong, though he knew that it was, in a way.

She withdrew her hand, straightened the blanket, not looking at him, suddenly appalled by what she had done, what had happened, yet profoundly grateful. "I think I'll let the doctor change the dressing." Her voice rippled with subdued gaiety, with a new note of authority and of intimate understanding which he shared.

So engrossed were they in each other that they did not notice the approach of a distinguished looking middle-aged

198

man and a lovely young woman, until David heard Martha cry out his name and Mornay add in his deep voice: "My son!"

Father and daughter had left San Francisco as soon as David's first letter, written for him by Lettie, arrived. They had traveled by river steamer to Sacramento, thence by stagecoach over the Sierras and Rockies and down to St. Louis, reversing much of the route taken by Sam Clemens less than a year before. Martha instantly sensed the situation between David and Lettie, and the joy went out of her. Mornay saw only his dearly beloved son-in-law-to-be, still alive. "David" — pressing his hand in both of his own devoutly — "we came as fast as we could. Thank God we've found you in the land of the living!"

Martha held herself aloof as she gave him her hand. He sensed her intuitive perception of his relationship with Lettie, yet with all his heart and soul he wanted to embrace her, too, show her his new magnanimity of spirit, embrace and love her but in quite a different way from Lettie, not only with compassion but passionate joy.

He saw she was wearing simple brown gingham with matching bonnet and light brown traveling shawl that, all together, set forth her directness, her no-nonsense quality of getting straight to the point with those steady eyes. Her reproachful look gave him pain, made him color, yet also said — "I love you, nevertheless!" — as she took his hand in hers with a patient smile which she hoped cloaked her wounded heart. Her hurt was bitter. She realized how little she knew him, how much must be taken on faith. Yet, she forgave and loved him, guessing that perhaps it would always be this way.

As he saw her forgiveness, thankfulness surged up in him, and he knew that nothing else really mattered but their love.

Raising her hand to his lips, he kissed it, never taking his eyes from hers. She fixed hers on his tenderly, and in that look they plighted their troth.

Lettie, silently watching, was filled with vicarious joy, for them, for herself, knowing that down all the years ahead a part of him, a part of them, would be secretly hers.

Mornay said reverently: "Now let us bow our heads in prayer before Almighty God."

Chapter Twenty-Eight

"What if you get pregnant?" Pedro asked.

"I won't," Eve assured him.

"But what if you do?"

"Then I'll have the baby."

"Without marrying me?" He was appalled. It seemed she had no serious feeling for him.

"I've told you I don't believe in marriage."

"But that would mean . . . ?"

"Yes, that would mean. But think how much worse if you, as candidate for county attorney, someday were married to a big, gawky *gringa* who was suspected of writing scandalous things about everybody in town?"

He was dumbfounded. Then an ugly suspicion rose, and he retorted angrily: "You don't want to marry me because I'm Spanish, because deep down you think I'm a greaser!"

A thousand miles eastward, morning had come again, and Benito Ferrer and his scouting party were leading the way into Texas. The terrain here beside the Río Grande was barren and arid and shimmered with heat haze, but it felt good under foot. A moment ago it was enemy soil, slave soil, but now it was friendly soil, free soil, as their horses stepped firmly upon it.

To get here the Californians had traveled far, endured much. After the ambush at Stanwick's Station, after Bill Semilrogge was wounded, after Pacifico had had his hand smashed by his horse's kick and was sent back with Semilrogge to Fort Yuma, they advanced and took Ammi White's grist mill without a fight and then Tucson, too, as Captain Hunter, Goodly, Stubby, and the Arizona Rangers fell back before them, back clear to the Río Grande. There the Rangers merged with General Sibley's retreating Army of New Mexico that was then fleeing before the Californians. Sibley's dream, Jefferson Davis's dream, of conquering New Mexico and advancing westward died in the rocky confines of Glorietta Pass near the old Spanish settlement of Santa Fé. There, Colorado as well as New Mexico volunteers joined Federal troops and fell upon the Texans, fought them to a standstill, then burned their supply train. Without food or ammunition though not out-fought, Sibley's men were obliged to retreat and the bearded, sybaritic Sibley earned no respect by leading the way in his carriage filled with officers' wives while his men struggled and starved and thirsted on foot.

Yes, the hinge of fate had turned decisively, and it had brought Sergeant Ferrer and Corporal Pat Michaels and their scouts here to lead this first invasion of Confederate soil from the West, as they advanced along the old Emigrant Road beside the Río Grande, keeping eyes peeled for possible counterattacks and stragglers.

"There's a couple looks like Rebs!" Michaels pointed to the figures of two horsemen appearing hazily ahead out of the mirage, being overtaken by their steady trot.

Goodly and Stubby had deliberately straggled. They had had enough war. They had been looking for a chance to desert and, just when it came, they looked behind and saw a party of Union cavalry. "We better makes tracks for the river," Goodly muttered.

"*Pronto!*" Stubby agreed, and they turned their jaded mounts, thin and hungry as themselves, and spurred toward the muddy Río Grande. Across it they would be in Mexico while they made their way back to California beyond reach of Union or Confederate authorities.

Benito and Michaels galloped in pursuit of the fugitives,

their men following, Michaels drawing his carbine from its boot in eagerness.

"Not yet," Benito cautioned, "we want 'em alive!" And then recognition came. "By God, I know those two. They're from my home valley. They laid that ambush at Stanwick's Station!"

By now Goodly and Stubby were plunging their horses into the river. They slipped from their saddles and swam alongside, grasping their horses' manes with one hand, holding pistols high and dry in the other. A bullet could still reach them, and Michaels wanted to send one, but again Benito stopped him. "No, Pat, let 'em go. Good riddance. And look who's waiting for 'em!"

A band of armed horsemen in white clothes and big hats was riding forward to intercept Goodly and Stubby when they came ashore. "Maybe they'll wish they stayed on this side!" Michaels chuckled grimly.

"That's what I'm thinking. Let's push on."

Four days later they reached Fort Davis in the Davis Mountains, named for the Confederate President, and found its scattered wood and stone buildings occupied by mice and birds and the scalped body of a gray-clad soldier, apparently killed by marauding Indians. There on its parade ground, two hundred miles into what had been Confederate territory, the Californians raised the flag and took possession for the United States.

For Benito, remembering his recent bereavement, it was both triumph and heartache. If he had stayed home, had never enlisted, he would have missed all this. But his wife and children might still be alive. Perhaps they were, still in that heaven he couldn't quite accept. As the emotion surged up, he felt their closeness, their love, his love for them, his pain at their tragic death. The black death, the bubonic plague, carried by those fleas from that dying squirrel swept them away, as periodically the plague did other residents of Santa Lucia Valley and, indeed, of frontier Western places generally, often undiagnosed, simply accepted as a hand of fate. First came the sudden chills and fever, then headache and body pain, then the spots of blood that turn black under the skin, then delirium and sudden death. Sally, who was at Anita's bedside when she had died, had written to him: **Her last thoughts were of you, Benito. She loved you truly. More than you'll ever know, I think. We buried the two little ones beside her in the graveyard by the mission.** Benito could have gone home on furlough after receiving the news, but he had decided to go forward and try to forget.

Chapter Twenty-Nine

At the White House in Richmond, Virginia, George Stanhope was telling his old friend and fellow planter, Jefferson Davis: "Had we moved quickly after the outbreak of war, we might have succeeded in seizing the state, but Sedley advised me to wait. Now it may be too late. Shiloh has hurt our chances, and Sibley's débâcle in New Mexico makes matters doubly worse."

Lincoln had delayed his order for Stanhope's release from Fortress Alcatraz until the threat of a Confederate invasion of California had passed and Stanhope's leaderless network of Southern sympathizers were dying on the vine of deferred hopes. But, once free in San Francisco, Stanhope evaded surveillance, was smuggled with Sedley's help aboard his mail steamer for Panama, left it secretly at Acapulco, crossed Mexico to Vera Cruz, caught a blockade runner to Texas, and here he was. Mary Louise and Mornay could only guess at his whereabouts, thanks to information provided by one of the black stewards of her network when the *Panama City* returned to San Francisco.

"Don't blame yourself, George," Davis cautioned sympathetically. "You did all anyone could. Now let me ask . . . do you want to go back?"

"I'd rather not. After my imprisonment, my usefulness will be impaired."

"That's what I thought you might say." Davis had already decided that Stanhope's usefulness in California was over but wished to continue to employ his great zeal, wealth, and influence elsewhere. "Now let me propose something new that will keep you near the center of things, where we need you, and closer to your New Orleans home and your plantation, too. Your unjust imprisonment has given you great prestige and increased your support in many quarters."

Stanhope felt flattered. He had sometimes chafed at being compelled by circumstances to demonstrate his talents at the perimeter rather than nearer the center of action. His ego had been painfully wounded by his imprisonment. Now he felt himself being recognized by Davis in an appropriate way. "What is it?"

"Our Confederacy can't survive being cut in two by a Mississippi Valley in Union hands, yet that's what's facing us. We want you to help us by working clandestinely with our friends in Illinois, Indiana, Ohio where discontent with the war is rising and support for our cause has always been considerable. Those states provide most of the troops for the Union armies in the Mississippi region. If we can weaken Lincoln there, it will help enormously. It could mean as much or more than a victory on the battlefield. Our representatives in Canada will be lending a helping hand. What do you say?"

Stanhope felt more than flattered. "I appreciate your confidence in me, Jefferson. I'll do everything in my power to stir up trouble in Yankeedom. Just give me a free hand," he added savagely, thinking of his months of imprisonment, his other months of being restrained by Sedley, "and watch me go. We've got to win this war by every means possible."

"I don't rule out California," Davis continued. "You should keep in touch with Sedley and your friends there. This simply means a larger theater for your performance. What about Sedley? Where does he stand?"

"Squarely in the middle."

"But he helped you escape?"

"Yes, his man, Forbes, made all the arrangements. Smuggled me aboard from a rowboat after the mail steamer left the wharf. But Sedley's hedging his bets. He intends to be on the winning side. Even if he is my son-in-law, I say it."

"We need him and his gold. We're having difficulty buying armaments in England and France because of our precarious finances."

"He's selling it at market price in New York. I don't think he'll sell to you unless you can beat the New York figure."

At that moment they were interrupted by Davis's aide, Colonel William Preston Johnston, Albert Sidney's son by his first marriage, who entered and said gravely: "Excuse me, Mister President, Colonel Stanhope, but we've just received word that New Orleans has been captured by the Union fleet." Admiral Farragut's ships had run daringly by the forts at the entrance to the Mississippi, had destroyed the Confederate river fleet, then had sailed on up the river "and had trained their guns on the undefended city which General Lovell had evacuated," Johnston concluded.

Davis was silent under the heavy weight of this blow, but Stanhope burst out incredulously: "New Orleans captured without a shot fired?"

"That's the report, sir," Johnston replied coolly.

"Treason and cowardice! I can't believe it!" Stanhope grew livid.

Davis held up a restraining hand. "I've been in touch with General Lovell. He evacuated the city to save it from bloodshed and destruction."

"I say he did wrong!" Stanhope stormed on. "Without a shot? The miserable poltroon! Why, I just visited my wife and daughter there. If anything's happened to them, I'll lay it at Lovell's doorstep. He should be court-martialed and shot!" Davis's moderation had long irritated Stanhope and other fire-eaters, and now he turned on Davis. "We can't win this war without bloodshed, Jefferson. Outnumbered as we are, we've got to take risks, big risks. Sack Lovell. Put a fighting man in charge."

"We'll see about that in due course," replied Davis distantly. "But before you go, let's confirm what we just discussed."

"First let me speak to you confidentially." Stanhope controlled his rage with great difficulty.

Stanhope seemed to Davis almost beside himself. Davis, though irritated, signed to Johnston to leave the room and then asked calmly: "What is in your mind, George?"

"Authorize me to kill Lincoln." Stanhope's voice was hoarse with passion. "Lincoln's at the heart of our troubles. He ought to be made to pay. He's the most hated man in American history. North and South, they hate him. Why not? He's plunged all of us into this war. If my people had got him in Baltimore last year, none of this would be happening now. Sidney Johnston would still be alive. New Orleans would still be ours. Let me kill Lincoln."

Flabbergasted, Davis shook his head. "I can't condone anything like that. You want to kill the man who let you out of prison?" He couldn't quite believe Stanhope was serious.

"Lincoln didn't let me out of prison. Public opinion let me out. That's what got me out of my solitary cell with its rats and stink! Not Lincoln. He's an evil man, Jefferson . . . clever, unscrupulous, bloodthirsty. He's got to go, and I'm ready to send him on his way."

Davis realized Stanhope was in deadly earnest and should be talked out of his fixation. "You want to make him a martyr in return for his making you one?"

"It's not a question of martyrdom. It's a question of survival. If they win, they'll hang you, just as they'll hang me. With Lincoln gone, there'll be a negotiated peace. England and France will recognize us. So will other great powers. Aid will pour in. We'll have a great nation. France has an army in

Mexico already. She'll help us as she did our forefathers during the Revolution."

Davis replied firmly: "I'll never countenance the murder of Abraham Lincoln."

"Would you be sorry to see it happen?" Stanhope demanded, glaring at him.

Davis was silent for a fleeting moment. Then: "To be honest with you, I would be sorry." But Stanhope had seen his brief hesitation, read it as assent, while Davis continued in business-like tone: "Now let me hear you say you'll help us in Illinois, Indiana, Ohio, and other states where our Knights of the Golden Circle are already strong."

"I'm with you!" And Stanhope thrust out his hand, his mind made up in more ways than Davis guessed, as Davis returned his clasp.

Chapter Thirty

Sitting cross-legged at the mouth of the cave, Ta-ahi held the heavy stone pestle with both hands as she raised and lowered it in the mortar Francisco had hollowed out for her in the living rock at the threshold of their home. She was grinding acorns into meal. She put the meal in a basket to leach away its bitterness by pouring water over it, then would dry it in the sun until it would be ready to eat, alone or mixed with seeds or with berries fresh or dried.

From time to time Ta-ahi looked out over the valley that was her family's home. Shaped like a giant amphitheater, hidden deep in the heart of the wilderness, it was known as Masitumunumu-u A-almiyi or the Nesting Place of the Condor. At its head rose the waterfall cliff where the great birds nested. Around its sides rocky outcroppings — such as this one containing her cave — emerged like giant ribs from pine and chaparral, while the valley's floor was a grassy meadow, dotted with live oaks. The stream that plunged over the cliff and ran through the meadow was fringed with willows and alders; and the only way the valley could be approached by humans was from below, up the rushing stream which, as it left the meadow, descended over another, less precipitous, cliff down which it formed a kind of natural stairway, a stairway of water splashing over rocks and through beds of ferns, and up which Tilhini had led Francisco as a boy and where Francisco, seeking refuge, led her and her daughter.

Ta-ahi paused at her work to watch the mother condor feed her chick in her nest in the hole on the face of the waterfall cliff, and thought of herself and her own chick, Letke, out there now, gathering bulbs in the meadow, as they waited for

Francisco and Helek to return.

It had to be, she knew, that departure of husband and son. Yet, it was a painful wrench, a giving up of something in order to reach for something new. Helek had been born here in this hideaway. She remembered the day — husband and daughter had gone to the head of the valley to watch the waterfall, she had been alone, out there in the meadow, when she felt the pangs. She had swiftly scooped a hollow in the earth and had lined it with grass blades. Born out of the earth, born to the wild, was Helek, her young hawk.

Having experienced the world herself, she feared for him doubly now. She had had nightmares in which he was hunted from place to place as she had been. She had no idea of this present war between the states. The war she knew had been raging almost since Columbus discovered America. It was the war between native peoples and the European invaders. It was a war she knew well. Reared and first married among the Miwok to the north, Ta-ahi had seen white men, hungry for the gold of her Sierran foothills, shoot and kill her defenseless husband, while she and Letke had watched in horror from the undergrowth.

With no man to protect her, with her tribe dispersed and all but obliterated, Ta-ahi had fled south with her little daughter toward a rumored place of safety, traveling by night, hiding by day, refusing to become subservient to whites or Indians, sustaining herself and Letke by pride and not much else, until she had found that rumored Village of Refugees, high on the slope of Iwihinmu, the sacred mountain at the heart of Francisco's people's world.

There he, too, was seeking refuge and a new life after painful years in the white world. They had been married by a simple exchange of words and touch, and he had become a loving stepfather to Letke and a leader of the resistance. But Buck

Jenkins's Rangers had discovered the village. Flight and dispersal had followed. Some had taken refuge on the reservation. Some had gone to Clara's village. Some, like herself and Francisco, had chosen solitary resistance in the wilderness.

As Ta-ahi watched, the father condor came soaring in and relieved his mate at the nest so she could rest and seek food. It gave Ta-ahi a feeling of being profoundly connected, deeply at home, and filled her with hope that all would go well with Francisco and Helek, and they would return to her safely, here, where the great birds lived that were their dream helpers.

Then the distant scolding of Shosho, the tree squirrel, told her that out there in the meadow Shosho was probably disputing the foraging ground with Letke.

Like her mother, the young girl went naked except for deerskin flaps, before and behind, that served as skirt. Her black hair was worn with bangs combed forward, and the rest fell loosely upon her neck and shoulders. She carried a forked stick for unearthing bulbs. Strapped to her back was a conical basket for carrying them. She wondered why Shosho was scolding so shrilly up there in the branches ahead of her, but, remembering that Shosho often scolded his own kind, sometimes even himself, she continued digging the bulbs of the golden mariposa lilies, breathing a silent prayer of thanks to Kakunupmawa as she did so, for they were the cups from which he drank.

Then she saw the monstrous track almost under her nose. It was an oval depression, far larger than a human foot, freshly made in the duff under an oak. What could have made it? Then she saw another like it, and then another. The huge creature had gone striding ahead of her. Fleeing from her? Lying in wait? Shosho was scolding more shrilly now. Letke's heart began to pound. Should she run back and tell her mother?

No, that seemed childish as well as cowardly.

Laying down her stick, setting aside her basket, she wiped both perspiring hands on her skirt — and then for some unaccountable reason rearranged her dark bangs and bone earrings before stepping cautiously forward.

The next moment, in moist earth near the stream, she saw the footprint clearly. It took her breath away. It was nearly twice as long as her own foot and twice as wide, each toe and claw sharply defined. "Khus!" she murmured. She had seen bear tracks but never one like this and never here in this valley. *How did the huge creature get here?* A shudder ran through her. She felt an almost overwhelming desire to turn and run, but curiosity and fear itself held her still as, right before her eyes, something rose slowly out of the blackberry bushes, something furry, reddish brown, up and up till it towered nearly ten feet above her. She had seen bears but never one like this, standing on hind legs just like a human. She smelled his fetid odor. She quaked with terror as beady eyes on either side of a broad snout peered down at her, while the near-sighted grizzly strove to make her out.

As the two looked at each other, something passed between them. Letke could not have said what it was. But impelled by an impulse such as she had never felt before, she found herself speaking to the bear as if they knew each other. "Great Khus, I won't hurt you. Let us be friends, Khus. Let us share this place, Great Khus. I won't hurt you! Don't you hurt me!" — as step by step she backed away, never taking her eyes from his, wanting desperately to turn and run, making herself not turn and run, until out of sight behind a tree; then she turned and ran as never before, forgetting digging stick, carrying basket, everything but the great bear and her terror.

When Ta-ahi saw the frightened girl running toward her, she put down her pestle and stood up in alarm, wondering

213

what could be the matter. But when she heard what Letke had to say, she replied soothingly: "You did the right thing. You showed courage. Maybe Khus will not harm us, if we don't harm him."

"But he's so big, so fierce-looking!" Letke was breathless, trembling all over.

"I know. Yet, if we let him alone, he may not bother us."

"How do you suppose he found his way here?"

"I have no idea."

"I wish Father and Brother were here!"

"So do I."

Toward evening the bear came slowly up the slope toward them. Their cave was situated some six feet above ground level, accessed by steps Francisco had cut in the rock below it. Just when it seemed he was going to walk right up those steps, the bear stopped and looked at them, sniffed the air to scent them better, stared a while, then turned, as if satisfied, and lumbered slowly away, while the two inside the cave clutched each other with relief.

"You see, he may just be curious." Ta-ahi spoke boldly to hide her fear. "He may not harm us. He may be seeking refuge as we are."

But that night they lit a fire at the mouth of the cave and stayed awake behind it till dawn came.

Yet, during the days and weeks that followed, Ta-ahi proved right, and the two humans and one bear shared the valley peaceably. Whenever they saw Khus in the meadow while gathering there, they stayed at a respectful distance, and though he came, from time to time, to look at them in their cave, he never attempted to molest them.

Sometimes he disappeared. Wondering where, they followed his tracks to the point where the little stream descended that natural stairway of rock and water up which the bear had originally climbed, just as they had originally done. A few days later he reappeared, and they realized he was using the valley as a place of hiding just as they were.

Where the little stream from the valley flowed unobtrusively into the river far below, Buck and his Rangers, combing the back country for Francisco, had come across the track of a huge grizzly in the damp earth. "Funny, I never noticed that little creek before," exclaimed Buck, drawing rein. "Wonder where it comes from?"

"Don't reckon it falls from the sky," allowed Homer Gatlin. "Maybe that bear, it knows."

The huge tracks led them through tangled undergrowth along the little stream until they come to the foot of the natural stairway of rock and water up which the bear had clambered.

"By God, I think we've found his hiding place!" Buck exulted. "You fellows game?"

"If that critter can scale a place like that, I reckon a man can," Homer agreed, and the others concurred.

They tied their horses to trees and took their rifles in hand and began to clamber up through the ferns and vines and falling water.

Chapter Thirty-One

As he convalesced, Martha was constantly by David's side. She brought him delicacies to eat and drink, such as apple dumplings and the lemonade that he loved. She read aloud to him from Hawthorne's new novel, the gloomy, moralistic MARBLE FAUN, and Dickens's latest, the cheerful and entertaining GREAT EXPECTATIONS, and from the Bible and Book of Common Prayer. She made pencil sketches of David lying in bed in the ward of the hotel become hospital, its ballroom chandeliers hanging incongruously above the rows of cots with their maimed bodies.

Lettie hovered in the background, ostensibly busy with her nursing duties while sharing vicariously these loving moments of their reunion.

Through dream-like happiness David heard Mornay saying: "Your battle of Shiloh has changed the course of the war." His battle? No, his baptism into a life. Again he thought of that awesome passage from St. Paul's Epistle to the Hebrews: **There is no salvation without the shedding of blood,** and again the conviction surged over him that this war was a working out of God's salvation for him as for the nation. Only blood could wash away the sin of slavery. Only blood could usher him into a new life. "Corinth has fallen," Mornay continued in prophetic tone. "It's a triumph for General Halleck. California is very proud of Halleck. Admiral Farragut's fleet has captured New Orleans without firing a shot. The Slavocracy must be trembling in its boots, as it feels the righteous anger of the Lord being visited upon it!" Mornay sounded like Jeremiah, but his mention of New Orleans reminded David of something far from the prophet.

"Any news of Beau Stanhope and Vicky?"

"No, but their father's rumored to be in Richmond. He was released from prison partly on my urging. We must have justice as we go along, David, or we shall all end up in perdition. He's better off in Richmond than as a martyr in Fortress Alcatraz."

"And Sedley?" Still it seemed to David that he was asking after, hearing about, figures of a world remote from the new one he had entered, figures not baptized as he had been, figures who could never know the truth till they had been through what he had been through.

"The war has brought Sedley and California enormous prosperity, David. People are flocking to the West to escape the conflict or simply in search of better opportunities. And with the importation of goods from the East curtailed by the war, we've had to establish our own factories. Sedley's starting up a shoe factory and doubling the size of his iron foundry. Wealth beyond belief is being amassed and shamelessly displayed. In the Sunday parade along Montgomery Street I see women bedecked with diamonds, wearing powdered gold dust in their hair. While you boys shed your blood!" Mornay shook his head. "While we fight for greater equality, we seem to be creating greater inequality. And, yet, I must confess that my own business is prospering."

"And you left Reuben and Hattie in charge?"

"Yes, they can run things nearly as well as I can. But Reuben continues ready to enlist and to fight beside you, as soon as they accept black volunteers."

"You still think they will?"

"It's inevitable. Lincoln must broaden the purpose of this war. A war simply to hold the Union together isn't good enough. It doesn't move people deeply enough. The issue of slavery does move people deeply. And with the Negroes fighting on our side, think what a difference it would make in terms of national attitude as well as man power!"

While they talked, Martha sat quietly, holding his hand in hers. He could feel her unconditional love, encompassing all of him and his shortcomings, like the sun itself. She was more wonderful even than he imagined, more graceful, womanly, desirable, his wife to be, mother of their children. She seemed divine. Yet, in her smiling eyes lurked that impishness, that outspokenness, that years ago made him nickname her Gadfly.

As his leg healed, he started to walk again, first with crutches in the ward room, then in the little park near the hospital, Mornay and Martha steadying him at either side. Outdoors he felt truly reborn. Fresh air, sunlight, trees, flowers were like blessings beyond belief. Yes, he would be forever grateful, and he would live so as to express that gratitude.

"So you took pity on Lettie, did you?" Martha scolded as they sat on a bench beside a gravel path, Mornay tactfully gone for a solitary stroll.

David flushed. "How did you know?"

"Something told me."

"You read me like a book."

He tried to take her hand, but she drew it away with a frown. "No, I'm angry with you."

"And with good reason!" he conceded, mock-woefully, yet charmed by her playfulness.

All at once she became very serious. "Why did you do it?"

"Because," he groped for words, "because of her need."

"Her need!" Martha echoed sarcastically. "How noble of you! Her need! The illustrious minister, the man of God, the man of the world, condescending to take pity on a mousy little nurse. How magnanimous!"

"You're being unkind!"

"No, you weren't thinking of yourself," she went on. "No, it was just for the good of the world!"

"I don't like your barbed tongue."

"And I don't like your self-deception." Suddenly they, too, were at war. "Is that any way for a minister to think and act?" she upbraided him. "I think it's disgraceful!"

She made him feel so absurd that for a moment he almost hated her. "What on earth are you talking about? How did we get here?" he blurted out in frank dismay. Passers-by gave them amused looks.

"We got here because you make a fool of yourself with other women while thinking of yourself as the servant of the Lord. I bet you're still in love with Victoria Sedley."

"Martha, I'm shocked!"

"No, you're not. You know I'm right."

"I'm not in love with Victoria. Never was. Infatuated, yes. Not in love. I love only you. I know Virgil Gillem's infatuated with you. But I don't let it bother me. I love only you."

"Why should I believe that?"

"Because it's true. I've never loved anyone else."

She fell silent, her eyes searching his face. "Let's forget about Virgil. I wonder if you, if we, are ready for love. I wonder if this war hasn't distorted everything all out of reality."

"What are you saying? You don't love me?"

"I don't know. Sometimes I think you don't need a wife, only your work, your idealism, your God. I think you'll always put your ministry first and me second."

"You'll have your work, too. I'm not going to stand in the way of whatever you want to do, if that's what's bothering you."

She suddenly turned to him. "Are you going to be true to me from now on?"

"I swear it, so help me God."

"Suppose God doesn't help you? Will you still be true?"

He couldn't but chuckle at her shrewd irreverence. "Yes, I'll be true. With or without God's help. But won't we exchange vows of faithfulness as we're married?" he teased.

"I don't know if I can trust you till then. Miss Temptation might come along. So promise me now!"

He did, and she leaned forward and kissed him on the lips, her eyes suddenly filled with tears.

Mornay, returning, stopped at some distance so as not to interrupt these proceedings, and nodded approvingly.

Thus the days went by. This morning Mornay had gone out to buy the engagement ring in secret, as David had requested, and Martha was sitting by his rocking chair reading aloud to him. This was their last day together. Tomorrow she and her father would leave for home. But now she and David looked up in startled surprise as General Halleck, accompanied by aides and news reporters, entered the hospital ward.

Pop-eyed pot-bellied Old Brains had come to bid farewell publicly to his wounded men. Lincoln had summoned him to Washington to become General-in-Chief of the Army. As he moved rather awkwardly through the room, hat in hand, stopping to talk here and there, his baldness partially covered by wisps of graying hair, he looked more like a visiting professor in rumpled clothes than a famous general. Halleck, more intellectual than man of action, found it difficult to relate to people in the flesh, yet knew he must, especially these who had implemented his strategies and helped make him famous. When he came to David and Martha, he stopped and fixed David with those large unblinking eyes. "Aren't you David Venable?"

And when David, astonished, admitted that he was, Halleck demanded gruffly: "Didn't I last see you with Beauford Stanhope and his father at my Rancho Nicasio in Marin County across Golden Gate from San Francisco?"

"You are right, sir!" David, amazed, recalled vividly that brilliant day when they had all stood together at the crest of the hill and looked seaward toward the Pacific on one hand and inland to the bay and its islands on the other, and he had felt as an explorer might have felt gazing on new worlds for the first time.

"And how did you get here?" Halleck demanded further, and, when David told him, Halleck nodded with approval and turned to an aide. "Keep track of this young soldier." And to David: "When you're discharged from the hospital, report to my headquarters."

"Thank you, sir."

Halleck seemed about to depart, but hesitated. "What's the book this handsome young lady is reading to you?"

"LEAVES OF GRASS, sir."

"Isn't that a rather scandalous book?" Halleck intended a joke, but it fell rather flat.

"Walt Whitman is the great American poet in my opinion, sir," David replied firmly.

Halleck gave him an owlish stare. "Whitman's an obscene windbag, in my opinion. No young lady should be reading such trash. Is she your sister, your wife?"

"Wife to be!" David exclaimed proudly, and introduced Martha, and told where she came from, as she rose serenely and extended her hand to the general.

"Martha Mornay?" exclaimed Halleck, surprised in his turn, "Charles Mornay's daughter? All the way here to see your fiancé?"

"Yes," and Martha told him that she and her father were about to go home, now that David was about to be discharged.

Halleck suddenly relaxed into warm intimacy. "Well, happiness to the two of you! I'll expect to see you in San Francisco when the war's over. Remember me to your father, Miss Mornay. Though I may disagree with him on other matters, I agree with his choice of son-in-law."

As Halleck moved away, the news reporters clustered around the two young people to elicit further particulars for stories that would appear in papers across the country.

Chapter Thirty-Two

On this morning the old rodeo ground in the green hills of Rancho Olomosoug was alive with milling, bawling cattle. The two women rode among them, parting out cows with un-branded calves and also strays belonging to other owners — Clara on her dove-white mare, Paloma, Sally on her blood-red Cinderella. They rode astride in the manner long followed by some California women. Under divided leather skirts they wore gray woolen trousers. Their blouses were of bright blue cotton, their hats of black felt with low crowns and broad brims, and, beneath the hats, fitting snugly over their hair to protect it from dust, were red bandannas similar to those worn by the men who followed close behind. Those males included neighboring *rancheros*, but closest came Isidro, their *majordomo*, and Pacifico, their shared problem.

After being discharged at Fort Yuma as unfit for military duty because of his crippled right hand, Pacifico had come home, claiming to be a casualty of the "battle of Stanwick's Station that turned back the Rebels and saved California from invasion." At first people had believed him and had welcomed him as a returning hero, and Sally and Clara had felt that their hopes for him might have come true; but then reality had slowly emerged, and Pacifico had resumed his old inept ways, and now he was regarded as a joke. Nevertheless, he wore the silver buckle designating him head of the family. Clara was torn between her love for him and her scorn for him, Sally by her aversion and her pity. The two women shared the burden of his presence as they shared their fondness for each other and for their work.

"That roan cow with the droop horn is the mother of that

spotted calf with the bald face," Clara called out, pointing. In this milling mass, including steers, bulls, yearling heifers, and barren cows, it was not easy to distinguish which child belonged to which parent, but Clara's eye was unfailing. She and Sally nudged cow and calf together and started them moving out of the herd. Then Isidro and Pacifico took over and conducted them to its edge where they trotted off to join a second herd of mothers and children being held apart by *vaqueros* from Rancho Olomosoug and from neighboring ranches participating in the rodeo.

Clara wished Francisco and Helek were watching. Her encounter with her wild son and grandson atop the bluff remained something she dared not share with anyone, but it glowed as a bright spot in her memory. Where are they now? Would she ever see them again? How can they escape the harm arrayed against them? She fondly imagined them looking down at her at this moment from some hiding place and heard Francisco say to his handsome, promising son: "That's your grandmother down there on that white horse."

"What is she doing?"

"She is making rodeo."

"What is a rodeo?"

"Watch, and you will see."

So went the imaginary dialogue in Clara's mind. She could not help hoping that someday Helek might inherit her ranch and her dreams.

"Who is that young woman beside my grandmother?" she heard him ask.

"That is your half-brother's wife."

"Isn't she beautiful!"

"Yes, and very skillful, too. See how she rides?"

"I should like to meet her and my half-brother. Which is he?"

But as she undertook to describe Pacifico, Clara's imagination failed. He was such a disappointment, such a burden, she felt crushed. But the work of the day must go on, and, when nearly all the cows, calves, and strays had been parted out, she called to Isidro: "Time to heat the irons!"

While the others finished the parting, Isidro broke away and made a fire of fallen wood collected from under a nearby oak and put three branding irons into it. So well had Clara calculated that, by the time the irons were hot, the parting was finished and all except the *vaqueros* holding the waiting herd turned to the new task, the heart and soul of the rodeo.

As customary Clara, the *patrona*, lassoed the first calf. "Come, girl!" she summoned Sally to help.

"Ah, look, what a sight!" the men called out banteringly, patronizingly, as the two women became the focus of attention. Only these two moved as equals among the men. Back at the hacienda the others were gossiping and helping prepare the feast that would end the day.

Clara's loop sang and settled unerringly around the neck of a red bull-calf. She swiftly took her wraps around her saddle horn as she reined Paloma backward. Sally snared the calf's hind feet, and it lay stretched between them. The men cheered. "Well done, ladies!" But their tone implied that this female prowess was some sort of picturesque aberration.

As man of the household Pacifico wielded the knife that cut the Rancho Olomosoug earmarks — under-bit in left ear, swallow-fork in right. He bent and notched the ears deftly enough with his left hand and lay the under-bit piece to one side so that afterwards there could be accurate count of the calves marked today.

Then he cut open the calf's scrotum and extracted the glistening white testicles and cut the white spermatic cord that attached them to the calf as it bawled in pain. He lay the testicles on the grass beside him to be eaten later, while Isidro applied the branding iron to the calf's left hip, stamping it indelibly with the famous ⅋ , the initials of Clara's illustrious husband, Antonio Boneu, and the calf bawled again as smoke rose from its seared hide and flesh.

The other men called out bawdily as Pacifico removed the testicles: "After you eat them, man, you'll make Sally happy!" And he would eat them, they would all eat them, after they had been roasted over the coals of this fire at the ends of green twigs, but this customary ritual would not make Sally happy or him happy. Pacifico felt embittered and trapped, even as he wielded the knife of authority as Clara had ordered. Sally couldn't help reddening as the men called out in this bawdy way and eyed her to see what her reaction would be. But she laughed gaily in response, while Clara thought grimly that another pair of testicles was exactly what Pacifico needed, and Sally remembered how last night in bed, in a moment of compassionate yearning, she had reached out for him, but he had turned his back on her. She turned away, too, saddened, feeling bitterness rising, wishing for a mate who could love her and cherish her and give her the children she wanted.

Clara imagined Francisco and Helek looking down upon all this, having no idea what was truly going on, and Helek asking his father — "What is it called?" — and he replying — "A rodeo."

"Cut carefully!" she cautioned Pacifico now, as he rose from castrating the calf and kicked dirt into the wound to clot the bleeding. "We don't want them to bleed to death because of your clumsiness!"

"Yes, *Mama Grande!*" he replied dutifully, feeling her scorn, embarrassed by it in front of everyone, and, out of resentment and hatred, he began to think how he might get even with her and with Sally — laughing, popular, skillful Sally who was such a contrast to his own gloomy, inept self.

Chapter Thirty-Three

Standing before Pedro Díaz in his and Ambrose Curtis's law office on Main Street was, of all people he least expected to see this day, Wing Fat, lean and smiling as ever. After Fat had picked him up and given him that lift into town, Pedro had told him to come and see him if he ever needed help. He had seen Fat from time to time, driving his fish wagon around town, but never to talk to till now.

Now — the two of them alone in the one-room office furnished with two tables, four chairs, and a shelf of books — Fat explained his need. *Señora* Hortensia de la Vega whose household he had supplied with fish every Friday morning for years had decided he had taken advantage of her generosity and good nature and overcharged her, and had declared that she owed him only five and a half dollars instead of six and a half. When Fat had disagreed politely, she had lost her temper and burst out: "You *chino,* don't you dare speak to me like that!" and declared further that she would not pay him one cent and would have nothing more to do with him.

Pedro was about to advise Fat to dismiss the matter as best forgotten and to write off Hortensia and her debt as part of the cost of doing business, but then something stopped him in mid-thought, something very close to his heart. Hadn't he committed himself to helping underdogs obtain their rights and wasn't this underdog attempting to do just that?

Pedro had been admitted to practice law at the California bar on Wednesday, November 5, 1862, at a brief ceremony presided over by Judge Hackett in the old adobe city hall at the corner of Spring Street and Franklin Alley, not far from today's city hall. Several days earlier Ambrose Curtis had mentioned to Hackett that his protégé was ready to be admitted to the bar, and Hackett had asked dubiously: "He's a *californiano*, isn't he?"

"What's that got to do with it?" Ambrose had demanded, having foreseen such a question. "He's a white male of good character and over twenty-one years of age as the statute requires?"

"Let me think about it," Hackett had temporized, as Ambrose had guessed he might. Afterward Hackett had gone privately, as Ambrose also had guessed, to see Earl Newcomb and Porfirio de la Vega, to whom he owed his office, and ask their views.

"Pedro Díaz is not a white man," Porfirio had sniffed. "He has Aztec blood on his mother's side. Anyone who knew her family in Mexico before they ever thought of coming here will tell you that. No, Pedro is not a white man. He's a *mestizo* and does not qualify under the statute. Besides, as a legitimate lawyer he will only cause trouble for us."

"But Don Porfirio," Newcomb had soothed, "Pedro is a *californiano* just as you are. Are you prepared to go to court and say that he isn't a white man? After all, his skin is as light as yours."

Porfirio had turned on Hackett: "You can fail him when he appears before you for his oral examination, can't you?"

"I can," Hackett had admitted hesitantly.

"Porfirio, don't stir up trouble," Newcomb had advised his father-in-law. "Pedro is a bright boy and has studied for years to be admitted, as everyone knows, and as Curtis and Koenig will point out, and they will rally public opinion behind him and make him a martyr as our enemies did Stanhope and thus increase his popularity, and they will encourage him to try and try again if he fails now, thus creating a constant issue. No, Don Porfirio, I say let him pass if he can. It will serve our interests best not to make a fuss. And it will save you appearing in court against him."

Finally Porfirio had been persuaded by these cogent arguments, and thus Pedro had passed his oral examination and afterward had raised his right hand and had sworn to uphold the Constitution of the United States and the laws of the State of California and had been admitted to the bar with the hypocritically smiling approval of Judge Hackett, who played his assigned rôle so well as to exclaim: "Pedro, I've known you since you were a little shaver in knee britches. I'm mighty proud of you. So is this community mighty proud of you. You're a credit to yourself and your race," ending by a slip of the tongue on exactly the word he had intended to avoid, and thus speaking the truth despite himself.

Ambrose and Ethel Curtis, Simon and Deborah Koenig, and Eve Radovich had been proud witnesses of this historic, if farcical, event, but members of Pedro's family had been noticeably absent, except for Rosita, who had been proudly and admiringly there on behalf of her beloved brother, defiantly wearing her red dress and her jewels.

Much of this went through Pedro's mind while he mulled over what Wing Fat had told him about Hortensia de la Vega. "Fat, tell me more," he encouraged.

Fat gave a self-deprecating shrug. "She big lady. I Chinee."

"That don't matter, Fat. What matters is the justice of your case."

Fat said he had considered forgetting the whole thing, but, after his repeated requests for payment were ignored, he had decided that, if one customer could treat him this way, others might do likewise and he be demeaned and his business gravely injured. Besides, there was the personal affront. "Some no likee Chinee. Some sayee he lookee funnee." Fat laughed and pointed to his eyes and skin. "She big lady, I little Fat. But I no likee what she sayee."

Pedro did not laugh. "Fat, let me think about this. You have no right to testify in court against a white person because you're Chinese, but there may be other ways we can go." And then, anger rising in him, he added: "Yes, we may even go to court." Doña Hortensia embodied the formidable alliance of old *californiano* and new Anglo power they would be up against, but, perhaps, there was a way to breach that wall. "Let me think about it. I want to help you if I possibly can. Could you come again next week?"

When Ambrose Curtis returned a few minutes later and Pedro told him of Fat's visit, Ambrose shook his head dubiously. "Let's check the statute."

Reaching up, he took down from the bookshelf the relevant volume of CALIFORNIA STATUTES, thumbed through it to the page he wanted, then read aloud: " 'No Black or Mulatto person or Indian shall be allowed to give evidence in favor of, or against, a white man,' " and then wryly he added in his own words: "By decision of our State Supreme Court, Indians and Chinese are regarded as *of the same species*, I quote the court, and, therefore, a Chinese or Indian can't testify against a white person. That's the law. And it won't help Fat much in a case that boils down to his word against hers."

"But I want to help him. That's one of the main reasons I'm here."

"I know that very well. It's why I've helped you get here. But the question remains . . . where do we go from here in order to help Fat?"

They discussed it further that evening at supper with Ethel and Eve. Pedro often took supper with them rather than return earlier than need be to his own disapproving household. What particularly angered him there was the accusation that he was sweet on a *gringa* "instead of one of our own kind." And they still blamed him for Rosita's shame, as they called it, and she still refused to have anything to do with any of them, except for that surprising appearance in the courtroom on Pedro's behalf.

"I'd say take the case to court, and let Hackett throw it out, as he almost certainly will," Eve declared, eyeing her lover fondly. "That will bring the whole matter to public attention. I'll play it up in *The Sentinel*. Pedro can speak to Gonzales here at the *Amigo del Pueblo*. Together we'll raise a stench that will embarrass Doña Hortensia and Don Porfirio and may help change the law some day, though it probably won't get Fat the money he's owed."

"It would amount to a declaration of war on the powers that be," Ambrose cautioned. "Are we ready for open hostilities?"

"Why not? It's got to happen sometime. They'd still secede from the Union if they could and take us over. Why should we treat them with kid gloves?"

"It might help Pedro's future career," Ethel Curtis commented, "to be seen as a champion of underdogs," which is also what Pedro was thinking.

But he objected: "It could have an opposite effect. Plenty of people look down on the Chinese as I once did."

"The thoughtful will recognize your honesty in standing up for what you believe and your courage in challenging established authority," rejoined Ethel. "They'll see in it hope for themselves, plus a future in politics for you. If people feel you're honest, Pedro, they'll vote for you."

Eve added: "It will give you the support of some Negroes, too. True, they can't vote any more than Fat can, or than Ethel or I can, but after the war all that may change."

Finally Ambrose gave his considered opinion. "It's risky, but I think it might work . . . not at law . . . we'll lose the case . . . but perhaps in the long run politically. Let's think about it."

They did. And when Fat returned the following Friday, Pedro said: "Fat, we're going to take your case to court."

Fat beamed with pleasure, then asked solemnly: "How muchee costee?"

"Nothing."

Fat shook his head. "Then no takee!"

Pedro insisted, but Fat remained firm, and so it was finally settled that Fat would pay his own way toward possible justice.

Chapter Thirty-Four

On January 1, 1863, President Lincoln proclaimed an end to slavery "in all states in rebellion against the United States" and proclaimed further that the armed forces of the United States would accept black volunteers.

Lincoln came to these historic actions slowly and reluctantly. He did not want to alienate white public opinion. Yet, he felt a pressing need to take the moral high ground, to do what seemed right in God's eyes, and to increase the nation's military man power while giving blacks a chance to fight for their own freedom.

Actually the Emancipation Proclamation did not free a single slave, since it affected only areas under Confederate control. Thus it excluded slaves in the border states of Missouri, Kentucky, and Maryland that were still loyal to the Union. But it led eventually to the Thirteenth Amendment to the Constitution that ended slavery in all parts of the United States. And it implicitly enlarged the purpose of the war from one of holding the Union together to one of also ending slavery, and it brought blacks into the armed forces of the nation for the first time, as many blacks and many whites had been advocating.

As a leader of San Francisco's black community, Mary Louise had gone East to Rochester in upper New York State to confer with the eminent Negro leader, Frederick Douglass, her old friend from the Underground Railroad days in New Bedford, Massachusetts, and they had been among those urging Lincoln to accept blacks in the military. "I have two sons ready to enlist," Douglass informed the President, and Mary Louise said she had a son-in-law who was also ready. Reuben had written an impassioned letter to *The Pacific Appeal*, San Francisco's black newspaper that Mary Louise subsidized, asserting his willingness "and that of thousands of others of our brethren, free or slave, to take up arms against the Slavocracy."

Now Mornay wrote exuberantly to David Venable: **At last we have a nobler cause to fight for, and it comes at a crucial moment when Union fortunes are in decline almost everywhere but in the Far West.** After the capture of Corinth, the campaign in the Midwest had faltered. In the East, bloody defeats had roused public outcry and demands for peace. **The President's proclamation can reverse this unfortunate trend,** Mornay continued, **by uniting us all behind a greater purpose and bringing fresh blood and zeal to the fight.**

Reading Mornay's letter at Benton Barracks overlooking the Mississippi at St. Louis — where thanks to Halleck's intervention he'd been assigned as quartermaster clerk while completing his recovery from his wound — David wasn't so sure that Lincoln's words would translate immediately into greater unity. **I still hear grumbling over "fighting a war to free niggers," as they call it, and I wonder if such prejudice can ever be erased by proclamation; yet I, too, rejoice in the President's words and I rejoice at the prospect of Reuben and others like him joining me in uniform. Please tell him so. I hope he and I can fight side by side.**

Fate soon lent a hand. Secretary of War Stanton announced that, due to officer shortage, enlisted whites would be accepted as officers to serve with colored troops, providing they could qualify before an examining board. David made up his mind swiftly. **I shall volunteer to serve with the new black regiments,** he wrote Mornay and Martha, **and, despite my limp, hope to qualify before the examining board when it convenes here. It is the only way I can cast my lot fully**

with our black brothers.

Martha wrote back caustically: **My Dearest Limp, laudatory as your desire may be, I hope the board turns you down. Please think of your own safety just once. Why, the Confederates say they'll shoot any white officers captured while serving with colored troops! Must you risk yourself in every possible way? Is it an aspect of your desire for martyrdom?** Then she bore down: **I just want you to be a *little* self-protective for my sake, our sake, after you've risked and suffered so much!** And having spoken her mind, she added, to ease his: **Of course, I'll love you and be proud of you whatever you do.**

David went before the examining board, passed easily, and thus it was that, early in May of 1863, Captain David Venable, resplendent in new uniform, new sword at hip, found himself in New Orleans on furlough before joining his regiment farther up the Mississippi. On this sunny Saturday afternoon he was enjoying the sights of the city from a streetcar drawn by two gray mules, while he tried to forget the bad news he had just read in this day's *Picayune*. Union forces in the East had suffered another defeat, this time at Chancellorsville in Virginia. He wondered if the Eastern Army could ever win a battle. Yet even Grant and Sherman, whom he considered the ablest Union generals, had been stalemated in their siege of Vicksburg, the last Confederate stronghold on the Mississippi.

People boarded the car from time to time until every seat was filled. Some eyed him with a frown. Most paid him no attention. Most citizens of New Orleans were resigned to Union rule, now a year old. Then he suddenly saw Victoria Stanhope Sedley standing at the corner, waiting for the car, and realized he had been expecting her, subconsciously, knowing they would somehow meet, that their fates were intertwined. The sight of her after all these years took his breath away. She still bore herself like a queen, was still serenely, erotically beautiful with high cheekbones and seductive waist. She wore a form-fitting lavender dress with black dots, white cuffs and collar, and fetching black tie, and peeking out around the edges of her straw bonnet were those adorable dark ringlets he remembered so well. His mind raced back to rapturous moments in San Francisco before she had been transformed into Mrs. Eliot Sedley, and he to the Reverend David Venable, and they were still boy and girl, dancing the night away at the cotillion at the California House, carriage riding along the shore of the Pacific by the Cliff House, dreaming of immortal life and love. Almost before he realized, she was standing in front of him, and he was rising and offering her his seat, exclaiming — "Vicky!" — with all his old adoration.

She paled as she recognized him, and her eyes turned icy cold. "I wouldn't accept a seat from a damnyankee if I had both legs broke!" The passengers tittered.

It had been a painful year for Vicky. Living in a city under foreign occupation, as she put it, had changed her from Southern partisan into anti-Northern zealot. "I wish I could take up arms and fight like a man," she had told friends. Her mother had lingered on, thanks to Jennie Clemens's care. Lingering, too, another thorn in her side, was her uncle, Percy Stanhope. Percy shared a house divided like the nation. Like many of her friends Vicky kept a portrait of Lincoln at the bottom of her chamber pot.

She turned her back on David, leaving him staring at the nape of her delicate neck with its bundle of sausage curls, remembering how he had done likewise at St. Giles in San Francisco. He had been sitting in the pew directly behind her, Beau and Sedley at either side of him, she between her parents, she the proud daughter of the Chivalry, he the aspiring son of the Shovelry, he thinking her far above his reach, he abhorring her snobbery, vanity, prejudice yet still fascinated by her just as he was now.

"Vicky!" he implored.

But she was already ordering the driver to stop. "There's a smell here I can't stand. And it wears a blue uniform!"

Laughter broke out. David's face burned. Without a backward glance she stepped off the car and walked away under the magnolias. Nevertheless, she was remembering his initial attraction for her, his radiant goodness, his crown of golden curls that made him like some youthful deity of laughter and idealism. And she had to admit that his uniform set off his new handsomeness, his new maturity. But then she remembered what that uniform represented for her: humiliating loss of freedom, separation from beloved father and brother, loss of access to her beloved Bend plantation which remained outside the encircling Union lines. And so remembering she turned and deliberately spit, hoping those watching from the car could see that she was getting rid of a bad taste.

After a tour of the river front with its many vessels loading and unloading cargo, its warehouses guarded by Union sentries, its exotic aromas which seemed to speak for the French, Spanish, African cultures which helped create this colorful old city, David was walking along St. Charles Street in the fashionable residential section, still sightseeing, still unable to forget his painful encounter with his once adored Vicky. Dusk was falling, and the street was almost deserted as he noticed a well-dressed man sitting at the curb not far ahead, holding his head in both hands as if ill or injured. A top hat lay nearby. As David drew closer, he saw blood oozing from between the man's fingers. "Are you all right, sir?" he inquired with concern.

"No, but I soon may be, thanks to your arrival!" a genteel

voice responded. "The ruffians ran off when they saw you coming."

"Ruffians, sir? What ruffians?" David offered his handkerchief to help staunch the blood, and Percy Stanhope accepted it.

"Some of our Southern patriots, I imagine," Percy continued ruefully, "who, having surrendered their city, now vent their spleen on those who advised them to avoid war in the first place. Luckily, Captain, I wear a stiff hat" — indicating his battered beaver — "or they might have done me serious harm."

He had been returning from the apothecary's with laudanum for Sarabelle when he was set upon and caned "apparently by Confederate sympathizers since they went so far as to call me a Northern spy."

David helped him to his feet, and they walked on, side by side, David expressing surprise at finding a loyal Unionist in New Orleans, Percy responding: "There are more of us here than people up North imagine." He stopped before what seemed to David a very grand house, indeed, set amid lawns and gardens with white arches curving above a broad porch. "Captain, I'm Percy Stanhope. To whom am I indebted for such generous help?" And when David told him, Percy continued: "Won't you step inside and take a glass of sherry with me?"

"I'll be honored," David replied before quite realizing what his new friend's name might mean, but by then Percy was using the antique brass knocker, and the door was opening, and Vicky was facing David once more. This time he saw that her astonishment matched his, that perhaps she had been thinking about him as he had about her, though she feigned indifference.

"Uncle, you're bleeding!" She embraced Percy and examined his lacerated scalp. "What happened? Was it those detestable Yankees?"

"No, my dear, just two of our fellow citizens whose opinions happen to differ from mine. Thanks to this gentleman's timely appearance I was spared the full force of their convictions. Allow me to present Captain Venable. Captain, my niece, Victoria Sedley."

David bowed gravely. "Charmed, I'm sure!"

She swiftly seized her opening. "Though the captain may pretend otherwise," she snapped disdainfully, "we've met before," and, turning haughtily, she moved away a few steps across the parqueted hall, as if to give herself space in which to maneuver before she stopped and faced him again. Percy looked from her to David, perplexed.

David winked at him. "Yes, it was out in California years ago." He spoke with gentle irony. "I plead forgiveness. I didn't recognize Missus Sedley in these new surroundings."

"Ah!" A glimmer of the true state of affairs came to Percy, as did recollection of Beau teasing Vicky about David. "So much the better! A reunion after many years! Let's make it a joyous one!" Percy was not without irony himself. "Niece, we owe the captain a glass of sherry. Would you be so good as to ask Jennie to bring the decanter?"

Victoria turned back to them, her face a haughty mask. She was wearing a red blouse with flared sleeves, black bodice with fancy lace trim, as if there were no wartime shortage of materials, a hoop skirt bedecked with ruffles. It all seemed too dressy for an ordinary evening at home in a war-torn city. Coupled with her eager opening of the door, it made David wonder if she were expecting someone. But she ignored him and replied to Percy: "Jennie's upstairs with Mama. Did you get the laudanum?"

"Yes." Percy extracted the vial from his coat pocket. "I was

239

returning when I was interrupted so rudely. How is Sarabelle?"

Down the winding staircase came a sound of querulous complaining, followed by Jennie's soothing overtones. Jennie had remained loyally at Sarabelle's side. Who else would give her a home and feed her? Above all, she feared another cruel betrayal such as sold her down the river to the auction block here. Her baby, Sam, had died of croup at the age of two weeks, leaving her desolate. She had hoped he might grow up into a lovable boy like Sam Clemens. Beau had expressed sorrow over their baby's death, but she wondered how heartfelt that sorrow was. In any event, she might have a home here as long as Sarabelle lived, perhaps longer, for Percy was kind to her as Victoria was not.

Vicky was on the point of answering Percy that her mother's incessant complaining bored her nearly to death but, instead, simply reached for the vial of laudanum. She was not going to reveal her inner feelings to David, wasn't ever going to admit to herself again that she had once liked him. Still she couldn't help noticing his new handsomeness.

There was a soft double rap at the door. She moved quickly to open it before Percy could turn around. David heard her say too loudly, it seemed, too meaningfully: "We have an unexpected visitor, but come in!"

David saw an aristocratic-looking man about his own age, wearing rather dilapidated civilian clothes, step into the light of the chandelier. His proud bearing resembled Vicky's, and he, too, started perceptibly at sight of David but recovered quickly and produced a condescending smile, as Vicky with defiant sarcasm said: "Captain Venable, Major Taylor." Her tone said she didn't deign to add — "Army of the Confederate States of America" — after Taylor's name. David heard Percy's familiar: "Good evening, Dick." It added up to all he needed to know for the moment about Dick Taylor. He had heard of

240

Rebels slipping through the lines to visit loved ones in the city or spy on Union activities. The thought of Vicky in the loving embraces of this one swept over him, yet didn't trouble him greatly. It seemed part of the vast upheaval going on around them. He and Vicky were trapped in tragic affinity, tragic aversion, gripped and carried forward by forces beyond their control. Someday they would both be dust. But now he, too, would play at her game.

"Good evening, Major," he greeted Taylor coolly. "I see you're not in uniform?"

"Yes, I find it a welcome change, now and then."

"I do, myself, when civilian clothes are available but, just now, I'm on my way to a new post. And yourself?"

"I am, also, now that you mention it," replied Taylor with equal coolness.

Vicky eyed them with amused detachment. She suddenly seemed to David the primal female for whom two males were competing. He forged on. "May I ask what unit you're with?"

"General J. O. Shelby's brigade." With surprising frankness Taylor named the famous Rebel cavalry leader, clearly implying that his relationship with David was between officers and gentlemen if David wished it so. "And you, sir?"

"I'm about to take command of a company of United States Volunteer Infantry, Colored."

Taylor's face turned stony. Victoria's words dropped like rocks into the silence that followed. "There's no room in this house for nigger lovers."

Percy intervened. "Hush, Victoria, this is my house, too, you know. You refused to take the oath of allegiance. Had I not done so . . . more than willingly . . . you, I, your mother would have no roof over our heads. I'm glad to have someone under it who views things as I do."

"He'll be shot if captured commanding Negroes," Taylor

commented distantly, as if David was some third party not present.

"So will you be shot," David retorted with equal distance, "if you're arrested as a spy!" He had the power to arrest Taylor or to report him and Vicky to the authorities, but he didn't wish to prolong this painful charade. Turning to Percy, he said simply: "I must go. Thank you for your gracious hospitality." And to Vicky: "Please give my regards to your mother and brother. I remember them from happier days."

She flared back: "I'll do no such thing! And if my brother meets you at the head of your niggers, I hope he shoots you down like a dog!"

Turning his back on them without further word, David walked out into the night, surer than ever that only bloodshed was going to bring justice.

"I want to go to New Orleans and enlist there," Reuben told Hattie and Mary Louise. "You were both slaves there. I may as well start fighting from there."

"I said I'd never stand in your way. You go." Hattie was pregnant, but she didn't tell him, lest it keep him from going.

Chapter Thirty-Five

Francisco and Helek left the House of the Sun behind them and traveled to the far side of the wilderness, and there they looked down upon a desolate little valley hardly wider than a ravine but containing a narrow plot of open ground. Beside that plot was a forlorn adobe hut and beyond in the distance were two large unpainted, wooden buildings which were the reservation's headquarters and warehouse. "I want you to see some of our own people," Francisco had said.

Now, on the open ground, they saw a man guiding a plow behind a black mule, while a number of crows, cawing raucously, foraged for worms in the furrow behind them. The man was dressed in ragged white man's clothes, was bareheaded, and wore a red bandanna that held his white hair back from his face.

"Who is he, and what is he doing?" whispered Helek as they watched from the hillside, concealed in a thicket of wild cherry. Helek had never seen plowing.

"He is Halashu, once a leader of our people in their freedom but who came here with others years ago after the Great Dispersal, which I've described, when our people fled in all directions from the A-alowow. Some went to that village your grandmother maintains. Some went to the wilderness like ourselves. Some came here, and he is doing what white men call plowing, that is, ripping open Hutash to plant seeds in her."

"But why do they do that when she has already so many seeds?"

"Because that is the A-alowow's way. They're not satisfied with what Hutash provides but must cut her open to secure more."

This seemed to Helek a great wrong. "Doesn't Hutash object to such treatment?"

"Perhaps, but she acts with great deliberation, as I think you are learning. She may be waiting till the A-alowow, in their arrogance and greed, think they can wound her with impugnity, and then. . . ." Francisco snapped his fingers and shrugged.

"What will she do, Father?"

"Only Hutash knows. Meanwhile the A-alowow make Halashu and those like him, down there, dependent on the plow for food to eat."

"And is he confined to this little space forever?"

"That is his to decide."

The boy now felt rising anger. "But you told me all this land once was ours!" He swept his hand around the horizon. "What happened to it?"

Francisco told of the agreement signed by some whites and some Indians by which a million "of what white men call acres" were set aside and granted to the People of the Land and the Sea "though it was only a small portion of what rightfully belonged to them. Your grandmother, a wise leader, refused to sign the treaty, fearing what might happen. Yet others, trusting, signed in good faith and came down like Halashu and his family from their hiding places, believing the A-alowow promise that they would have a good life, their own homes, their own hunting and gathering grounds, and would be safe from oppression."

"And what happened then?"

"As usual the A-alowow broke their promise. Instead of a vast homeland where our people could roam freely, they were confined to this little space and were obliged to learn to plow in order to live."

"Why don't they run away and come back to the wilderness?"

"Two things keep them . . . the soldiers of the A-alowow who live down there in a place beyond those green trees called a fort, and their own laziness and fear. They know they've traded freedom for security. And they are too indolent or too fearful to strike out for freedom again, painful as their security is."

Down in the desolate valley beyond the trees they heard the sound of a bugle.

"What is that?"

"That is the A-alowow soldiers talking to one another."

Halashu had come to the end of his furrow where his wife, Alaquta-ay, wearing a gray woolen smock, was hoeing in the corn patch near their hut. Her head, too, was bare and white.

"What is she doing, and what is that in her hands?"

"It is a kind of little plow called a hoe, also used to disturb Hutash, and she has been using it among those green upright stalks that are called corn, which is very good to eat."

Alaquta-ay hobbled over to Halashu, and they talked, she leaning on her hoe, he on his plow handle. The two figures seemed to Helek tragically alone and forlorn. Francisco on his part wished he could speak to them, but that would be too dangerous, so, instead, he uttered the solitary, melancholy note of the mountain quail, the old rallying cry of the resistance, understood by all who knew the old free way.

Startled, Helek whispered: "Why did you do that, Father?"

"I want them to know we are still free, that the resistance continues. Look!"

It was as if life had reëntered the old pair. They stood erect and alert and looked about them.

Francisco gave the call again, so that there would be no mistake, and again a third time, feeling there was little risk because the A-alowow in their obtuseness would never know this was not the season for the nesting call of quail.

The two old people looked about them again to make sure no one was watching. Then they turned to the hillside, and each raised a right hand and waved — waved to freedom and the resistance.

Francisco asked his son with some excitement: "Do you understand what is happening?" Helek shook his head. Francisco continued: "We are the Freedom and the Resistance. Many years ago your Great Uncle Asuskwa, brother of your grandmother, led our people in a mighty uprising aimed at driving the A-alowow out of our land. But he was betrayed, and it failed. Then a great chief, Te-emi, led a fight for freedom. He marshaled forces, devised new tactics of entrenchment that nullified the advantages of the A-alowow horses and enabled men on foot armed only with bows and arrows to prevail. So you see, it can be done. We need not stay on a reservation like old Halashu and old Alaquta-ay who were once young and resolute but have submitted. Even now they would join us if they could."

"But what can we do to help them?"

"That is what we must decide. That is a main reason I show you the world. Like Chief Te-emi we must devise a new way of resistance."

"But can't we go home first?"

"Yes, we must go home first."

Chapter Thirty-Six

Don Porfirio de la Vega came storming into the office of Earl Newcomb on Spring Street just off Main and slapped down the copy of *The Sentinel* on the desk of his son-in-law, demanding furiously: "Have you read this?"

Despite Pedro's eloquent plea, Judge Hackett had dismissed Wing Fat's suit against Hortensia de la Vega for the six and a half dollars he claimed she owed him, and up in San Francisco Gillem had printed Eve's coverage of the matter on his front page, under the heading: **IS THERE NO JUSTICE IN LOS ANGELES?**

Newcomb broke into his usual jovial laugh. "Yes, I've read that ridiculous piece. What a joke, Don Porfirio!"

"Joke?" echoed the old don, more furious than ever. "Why is it a joke? My Hortensia is in tears. I am very angry. Who is this Thalia? He should be horsewhipped!"

"I think I know who *she* is. But I've no proof. So I can't horsewhip her."

As if he hadn't heard, Don Porfirio continued: "That upstart, Pedro Díaz, should be horsewhipped, too. He should never have been admitted to the bar. He's behind all this. And so is Ambrose Curtis. And Simon Koenig."

"And so is Wing Fat. And you can't horsewhip them all, Don Porfirio. And that is what I want to speak to you about. Please sit down." Newcomb stood up and proffered a chair. "It's time we had a serious talk."

Newcomb exuded confidence. He had pushed his freight wagons all the way to Salt Lake City and to Yuma City and to the gold mines of the southern Sierra Nevada. His stagecoach lines to San Pedro and to the interior were also spectacular successes. Meanwhile, drought and consequent hard times for cattle ranchers were creating problems for Don Profirio. No rain had fallen for nearly a year, and white bones rather than living animals populated his pastures, and the economy of his little town was depressed, as was his supply of money. Increasingly he was dependent on his son-in-law for financial help as well as advice. He sat down.

"The first thing to remember," Newcomb resumed, still jovially — Newcomb found life good and enjoyed the living of it — "is that very few people in this town read *The Sentinel*."

"But they are important people. And they are talking."

"Let 'em talk. Who cares? Laugh it off. That's what Judge Hackett did. The whole thing is ridiculous, Don Porfirio. Tell Hortensia not to let it get under her skin. What is important is to forget molehills such as this and not make mountains out of them but to pay attention to what truly matters. Let me give an example. When Fat's case against Doña Hortensia was filed, I went to Henry Hopkins over here at the *Star*. I didn't threaten to horsewhip him. I paid my advertising bill, a pretty good-sized bill, and I said . . . 'Henry, maybe you've heard of this little disagreement between Wing Fat and Doña Hortensia. Pedro Díaz is trying to make something of it. He's a natural troublemaker and a Republican. I don't think it's hardly worth mentioning, do you?' And he agreed with me, knowing where his bread comes from. Then I did the same thing with Gonzales at the *Clamor*. They were counting on Gonzales for support. But he knows who his real friends are. I didn't tell you because I didn't know how it would turn out."

"They're all black Republicans," grumbled Porfirio, though somewhat appeased, "and now they've got the niggers fighting on their side, they're even blacker."

"I agree. But we must be realistic, Don Porfirio. We must face the fact that the South may lose. The slaves you and I once imagined being brought here to turn rangelands into highly profitable cotton plantations may soon be slaves no longer."

"What are you driving at?" Don Porfirio was less than amused.

"Money," responded Newcomb, smiling broadly, "money, Don Porfirio. Though there may be no importation of slaves after this war, there certainly will be an in-pouring of white people such as we've scarcely imagined." Newcomb lifted a letter from his desk. "Sedley writes me urging us to acquire all the land we possibly can. He and his friends have received additional subsidies for their railroad. Think of it . . . they'll get twenty sections, twenty square miles, of public land for every mile of track laid, and the state legislature, thanks to Stanford's influence, will grant them millions of dollars in bonds and will allow local communities like ours to subscribe to their stock. Construction is now assured, and a branch down our way is the next step. We must prepare for the arrival of the railroad, Don Porfirio." Newcomb spoke with such assurance that the road already seemed built and people pouring in. "We must buy up this sleepy little town and all the land around it before it wakes to its destiny. Los Angeles will be a great metropolis some day, Porfirio."

But Porfirio remained dubious. "And where will the money come from to buy all this land you talk so glowingly about?"

"From Sedley. He'll hold fifty-one percent of the shares in our syndicate. You and I will own the rest. We'll be the operating partners. He wants to remain a silent one. He points out that now, while times are hard here and prices low, is the time to buy."

"Buy land now for a railroad that may not get here for years?"

"That's called foresight, Don Porfirio. You can subscribe

land instead of money, if you prefer."

"I'll think about it," Don Porfirio grumbled. "That Thalia should be horsewhipped, however. You say he's a woman?"

"I think she's the young lady who lives with Ethel and Ambrose Curtis. She came to your big party. Remember?"

"I remember I took rather a shine to her, confound her," admitted Porfirio, "and so did Hortensia and Carmen. They tell me she's thick with Pedro."

"That's a key connection. She came down here from San Francisco on the same boat with him. There's no doubt in my mind that Mornay and his crowd sent her. But let's laugh it off, Porfirio. They're like flies on a horse, these self-styled Progressives. They want to seize power under the guise of idealism. Let's keep our eyes on the horse, on the money. Just now your pastures are drying up because of the drought, and your cattle are dying. But rains will come. So will the railroad. So will more money than you've ever dreamed."

Don Porfirio relished this vision but pretended to brush it aside impatiently. "Our enemies are grooming Pedro Díaz to run for county attorney."

"Money, not horsewhipping, will defeat Pedro. With money we can buy more votes than they can. It's as simple as that. Even if the county fills up with Republicans, we can have the last laugh, Porfirio, if we have the money. Let them have their Chinamen, their barrio boys, and their other malcontents. We'll have the money. And the votes."

Chapter Thirty-Seven

As they crawled forward, side by side, on their bellies through the sweltering darkness toward the Confederate line, their men crawling likewise behind them, it was for Captain David Venable and First Sergeant Reuben Stapp a supreme moment.

It had come with unexpected suddenness. Receiving word that a Rebel force had occupied Stanhope's Bend plantation on its horseshoe curve of the Mississippi in a kind of no man's land between the opposing lines, David and Reuben and their men had advanced rapidly to help dislodge them. Leaving camp at Belle Meade, the regiment had marched through summer heat all afternoon and much of the night, guided by runaway slaves who informed them that the Rebels had driven off the plantation's women and children and old men but kept all able-bodied men to dig entrenchments and throw up breastworks.

Stanhope's Bend plantation. For David, as for Reuben, it loomed as a symbol of privilege and power and cruel injustice. Here Vicky and Beau had spent their carefree youth. Here Mary Louise and Hattie had been slaves. Now here it was at last, just beyond the breastworks they were approaching as they crawled through the sticky hot darkness, hoping they wouldn't be detected. Their mouths were dry with fear, their bowels loose with it. But their hearts were strong with something more powerful than fear. All of them were volunteers. Some like Reuben were free blacks. Most were runaway slaves who simply came into camp and offered themselves, **their flesh and blood, which was all they had to offer,** David had written Mornay and Martha, besides their courage and their desire for freedom.

Training with them had moved him deeply. **There's been much talk that Negroes won't make good soldiers. But I see no obstacle to prevent them. They take readily to drill. They don't object to discipline. They have quite as much average intelligence as whites and an even greater desire to fight.** Having served with both whites and blacks, David was in a good position to know what he was saying. **From experience in shooting wild turkey or deer,** he went on, **they have previous knowledge of firearms and, from evading their masters and overseers, they have become as stealthy as wild Indians when it comes to moving about in the woods.**

But it was their experiences during their strikes for freedom that most astonished him. **Damon and Pythias, our insepa-rable brothers,** he continued, **attribute their freedom to their grandmother, a grand old lady who often comes to camp to visit them. She and her husband tried to escape from Stanhope's plantation some distance upriver from our camp but were captured and taken back. The hus-band received five hundred lashes. While the overseer was viewing this punishment, she was collecting her chil-dren and grandchildren, twenty-four in all, including my daring brothers, in a neighboring marsh. There they found a broken-down raft which had been discarded as unusable. All got aboard after dark under the old lady's supervision and drifted down the river to our lines. One of my lieutenants, Bill Burnham, happened to be visiting aboard one of our gunboats when the raft touched its side. He saw the old woman stand erect and raise both arms to heaven and cry out: "My God, is we free at last?" Then she sent her grandsons to enlist.**

Such were the men crawling behind David and Reuben through the steamy June darkness, tangled among briars and tie vines, being stung by mosquitoes, and eaten alive by chiggers, scared but determined.

They jokingly call Reuben a "Buckra" or white Negro though not to his face, David concluded his letter, **because he was born free and is now their "overseer." He treats them in the same friendly yet dignified way he treats customers at the produce stall of Mornay & Stapp, and they do what he tells them because they know it is for their own good. They show no real jealousy toward him or toward us white officers, and I dare say that in no white regiment would you find less backbiting, swearing, or other misconduct, or more religious faith. When I lead them in prayers or hymn sings — not as a minister but as their captain — their fervor moves me to the depths of my soul.**

Over the objections of his lieutenants, David had insisted on leading this attack. "This one is peculiarly mine," he told them without further explanation.

Now he looked around for Reuben. There, almost invisible in the inky darkness, was his old friend at his right hand. *A good night for black men,* David thought, wishing his skin weren't quite so white. Had they moved stealthily enough to achieve surprise? Miraculously they had been undetected so far. Suddenly he smelled fresh earth. This must be the breastwork thrown up by the slave laborers. The thought infuriated him. And there silhouetted against the sky, hardly the height of a man above him, he saw a human figure.

When he first learned their objective was Stanhope's plantation, David again had the feeling that fate was drawing him and Vicky and Beau inexorably together, that it was their lot as creatures of their time to be inextricably united yet disunited. Now he felt it strongly again, a connection so powerful it seemed the ground under his belly was moving him forward and that the figure up there was Beau.

He turned to Reuben and pointed to the silhouette. Reuben nodded and shifted his musket forward. Like those of the men behind them its bayonet was fixed. At this crucial moment Reuben felt totally focused, totally without fear. **David makes us a good captain,** he had written Hattie. **He eats, drinks, sweats same as we do and sleeps on the same hard ground. When he gives an order, he sounds like he's talking, not ordering. Serving with him and these brave fellows, I feel I myself am an instrument of God's will. May He keep you safe, my dearest Sugar Plum, and may He bless you and little Charlie and little baby-to-be whose name will be Hattie, I bet you.**

David had drawn his sword. He and Reuben rose together. The men immediately behind them did likewise and so on back with ripple effect till the entire column was on its feet. By then David and Reuben were scrambling up the loose earth of the breastwork, hearts pounding, feet sinking, but hearing other feet pounding louder behind them. Black feet, white feet, the feet of a nation all moving together with one purpose.

The musket's blast almost struck David in the face, and his hat flew off, and he heard the fearsome Rebel yell as the crest to right and left of him erupted with flame and sound. Behind him rose the deep-throated Union shout. As he reached the crest, a shape lunged at him with a bayonet and an oath, but he side-stepped and thrust out, felt his blade sink home, wrenched it free, shouted in a wild excitement that overrode all other feeling.

Leaping into the trench beyond, he came face to face with a second figure, sword in hand, and rushed blindly at it, parrying a blow, slashing, parrying again, finally stabbing upward and home, under the rib cage from below, feeling his blade sink into the flesh, penetrate the life's blood, just as he realized the truth too late.

"Beau, Beau!" he cried, aghast, trying to support the slumping figure. "Beau, it's me! It's David!"

"Davie!" came the gasping response, as blood gushed up with Beau's words. "Davie. . . ." He faded away, but rallied one more time. "Davie, give me your hand!" And in a consummate effort, Beau smiled, smiled as the bright vision of his life died into pain and oblivion, smiled so that David could see the familiar, happy-go-lucky, well-intentioned, lovable Beau and all their California days together come to life one final time before sinking into darkness forever.

Half blinded by tears, David laid the body down and, in a kind of trance of horror and excitement, hurried to catch up with Reuben and the others in what had become a swirling hand to hand mêlée. All at once he found himself before a white-columned mansion. It stood serenely as if in the calm at the heart of a hurricane, its door opened as if to receive him. Light shone from inside as if to welcome him. As if borne forward, he mounted the broad steps, passed between two tall columns, entered the open door, and found himself in a great hall illumined by the light of the blazing slave cabins nearby and by flames that licked toward him from the interior of the house. He had often imagined Victoria in such a hallway, descending those regal stairs, sparkling with youth and beauty and heedless privilege, to meet her suitors. Ah, what would she say to this suitor in blue, sword in hand, the blood of her brother on its blade? There on the wall, framed in gold like so many kings, were her male ancestors. All had George Stanhope's imperious eye, prow-like nose, ruthless mouth and chin. It was the arrogant power in those faces that roused David's anger. He was here — it came to him like a revelation — to put down such power, to replace it with a more compassionate power such as may arise out of such horror as he had experienced this night.

Suddenly he was aware of a young Confederate officer descending the stairs toward him out of the wreathing smoke and flame, smiling as if to welcome him, hands behind his back as if to conceal a gift he intended to present. David stood transfixed as the young officer descended and walked up to him, eyes fixed on his, and then he saw that those blue eyes were filled with hatred, not welcome, and that they belonged to Victoria Stanhope Sedley, and that she, dark ringlets tucked under her fawn-colored hat, breast concealed under that gray uniform, was the young officer, a captain like himself, like her brother, Beau. He stood dumbfounded as he heard her ferocious words: "How dare you enter this house?"

He wanted to ask why she was here, why she was wearing that uniform, but, before he can formulate his questions, she saw the blood on his sword and on his arms and breast where he had clasped Beau. Intuitively she guessed, and demanded even more fiercely: "You've killed him? He's dead?"

"Yes, he's dead," David replied somberly, as the smoke and flame licked toward them, seeming to embrace them in a kind of hell.

"You'll regret it!"

"I already do."

Then she raised the pistol from behind her back and pointed it straight into his face. As he looked into its dark muzzle, he saw death, felt breath stop, life end, as she slowly squeezed the trigger. With incredulous relief he heard the click of the misfire, saw the savage hatred in her face change to rage and chagrin, as she stamped one booted foot and glanced down in disgust at the weapon that had failed her. It had been her father's .50 caliber single-shot dueling pistol, used by Stanhope with deadly effect on more than one occasion. With a curse she flung it at David, but it flew wide. "Damn you to hell!" Her words rang with hate. "May you burn there as this house is burning!" Then she turned her back and strode away toward the side door.

David followed, as if compelled, and saw Dick Taylor standing under the port cochere, holding a black horse and a bay, both saddled and bridled. Taylor wore his major's uniform and a holstered pistol. Taylor had brought Vicky through the lines in disguise, and Beau had loaned her his spare uniform so she could fight like a man in defense of her home. Taylor's eyes locked challengingly onto David's, but he made no move to draw his pistol as he waited to see what David would do. Sword still in hand, David stopped in the doorway and watched as Taylor coolly helped Vicky mount her spirited black horse. She didn't look back. It was as though she had erased David Venable from her life with that curse. All around the three of them the battle raged, but, here at the heart of it was still that eerie calm. She controlled her black masterfully while Taylor mounted his bay. David watched with a grudging admiration as they galloped fearlessly off into the inferno of flame and death.

Suddenly he realized the house was ablaze all around him. The Stanhope mansion had become a funeral pyre. He and Reuben and their men had done it. A new nation would rise out of these flames, reborn and dedicated to the proposition that all men are created equal, and he breathed a prayer and hurried out to join the fight.

At the slave cabins Reuben led the struggle. His wounded left arm hung useless. He brandished his bayonet with his right, urging on his men as the liberated slave laborers burst from the blazing cabins and joined the mêlée with shouts of triumph, some seizing weapons from fallen soldiers, others charging in bare-handed. David joined them, once again a soldier in the ranks, ranks he felt extending far beyond this moment to encircle the earth.

The battle of Stanhope's Bend, as it came to be called, lasted till mid-afternoon of that blazing June day. It was bayonet to bayonet, gun butt to gun butt, hand to hand. No quarter was asked; none was given. Finally Matlock's Texans and Couvier's Louisianans, and Dalton's California volunteers, fighting gallantly for their cause, gave way before the dogged determination of the blacks and their white officers fighting for theirs. As Colonel Matlock said later: "It exceeded in fury anything I previously experienced including Shiloh."

When the correspondent for Gillem's *Sentinel* reached the scene next day he found the victors burying the dead **including young Captain Beauford Stanhope, son of the noted Confederate agent, both former Californians,** and Noah Benson reported further that **Reuben Stapp, a black San Franciscan, was one of the heroes of the engagement. His wounded arm hangs in a sling, but he declares himself ready to fight on, while giving main credit for this remarkable victory to his men. "Their actions, their blood, speak louder than I could say."** Benson then interviewed Captain David Venable, **also from San Francisco, also one of the heroes of the battle,** and quoted David: **"There are no finer troops in the entire Army than my black volunteers. I've served with both blacks and whites and I know."**

But later, when he stood beside Beau's grave, David wept. Beau's former slaves had dug his grave in more ways than one, and a groan rose in David at the wonder and terror and pity of it all. Still he couldn't help thinking of Vicky. Though she had tried to kill him, he still found her fascinating. *Am I out of my mind?* he asked himself. He had made no mention to Benson or anyone of her being present at the battle. The fact that Mrs. Eliot Sedley was fighting on the Rebel side disguised as a man would make sensational news, but he wished no part of it.

Standing beside David at the grave was Reuben, a Reuben without malice now. **My hatred is gone, washed away in blood, mine and Beauford Stanhope's and my boys',** he would write Hattie, **but I'm glad that retribution has been made for your and Mama Louise's suffering here and for what my boys Damon and Pythias suffered.** The inseparable brothers had died fighting beside Reuben at the slave cabins. Another casualty had been David's lieutenant, Bill Burnham. **Burnham was captured and executed in cold blood by the Confederates,** Benson grimly reported to his readers, **by a bullet through his heart.**

National attention focused on the battle of Stanhope's Bend. It was the first in which blacks had fought whites on equal terms and had won. It helped change forever the view that blacks couldn't be good soldiers, couldn't fight as well as whites, weren't in other ways as good as whites. It brought Reuben and David to prominence; and in Washington City, a jubilant Lincoln told his general-in-chief: "Halleck, this battle is the Negroes' own emancipation proclamation."

Out in San Francisco, Mary Louise and Martha had been acting as midwives to Hattie, and, after eight hours of labor, Hattie had delivered a squalling baby girl into their hands. As they give the child back to a radiant Hattie to hold, they added the good news that Reuben and David had helped win a great battle and must both be alive since they've been quoted in the newspapers. "Let me hear what they say!" cried Hattie as she cuddled her newborn to her breast, so happy she felt she might burst with joy and pride. While Mary Louise held Hattie's hand, Martha read aloud what Noah Benson had written and the Associated Press picked up and delivered by wire across the nation. "Why, they're heroes!" cried Hattie.

Ambrose Curtis told Pedro Díaz: "This proves our point that a man's skin color don't matter, it's what's inside that counts." Ambrose tied news of the battle to Pedro's eloquent plea for Wing Fat before Judge Hackett. "It's going to help break down barriers among all races and help you when you run for office."

When news of the death of his son and the destruction of his mansion and the disappearance of his daughter reached Stanhope, he groaned aloud and redoubled his efforts to undermine support for the war in the key heartland states of Illinois, Indiana, Ohio. Feeling against the Lincoln administration was already strong in this region, especially its southern portion which before the war had many close ties to the South through personal relations and trade. Lincoln's Emancipation Proclamation had played into Stanhope's hands in unexpected ways. "See, it's now a war to free niggers," he and his agents argued, and many people agreed. "It's a war to Africanize America. You want your son to die fighting to free a nigger? You want niggers to flock up here from the South and take over your jobs? Live next door to you?" In Detroit free blacks had been beaten and lynched, and three dozen homes burned. Elsewhere Union soldiers, on furlough, had been ambushed and murdered. Armed bands opposing the war roamed at will in some sections. There was even a move on foot to create a new nation of heartland states with Abolition-minded New England left out.

Stanhope's latest scheme, in which he placed high hopes, was to set diversionary fires in Chicago while Confederate prisoners held in nearby Camp Douglas broke out and spearheaded a general uprising against the war. Yes, things had been going well until now. And, now, in his rage and agony of spirit at news of the death of Beau and the burning of his house and the disappearance of his beloved daughter who some said was fighting on the Confederate side disguised as a man, Stanhope initiated efforts to ascertain Vicky's whereabouts and to find suitable agents to help him kill Lincoln, whom he held accountable for Beau's death.

Chapter Thirty-Eight

Francisco and Helek came again to the spring that gushed from between the roots of the tall sugar pine high on the shoulder of Mt. Iwihinmu near where they had begun their journey, and Francisco said: "Let us drink and remember Sacred Condor who has guided us, for we have made a circle and will soon be home. But do not think that you have learned everything that the world has to offer. What I've shown you is only a beginning."

To Helek, it seemed a very large beginning. Evidently the world was a place of ever increasing wonder, continually bringing the unexpected. And when he said so, his father agreed, proud of the way his boy had grown in understanding.

"Now let us go home and surprise our loved ones who've waited so long."

Ta-ahi and Letke were moving slowly beside the stream that ran through the heart of their hidden valley. They were gathering juncus stems with which to weave baskets. They took care to pick only enough from the plant to serve their needs, and, after pulling the green stalk from the rhizome, they carefully cleared away the dried stalks that had accumulated from the previous season, thus encouraging future growth. They had continued on respectful terms with the great bear, and he likewise with them. Then, with one eye on the nearest tree in case he came to investigate them, they saw him out there in the meadow feeding on seeds of the mountain brome grass. "Something tells me something important will happen today," Ta-ahi said, smiling as they worked side by side, one eye on the bear.

"Perhaps Father and Brother will come home?"

"Perhaps."

Climbing silently toward them up the natural stairway of rock and water, following the bear's tracks, Buck and his Rangers came at last to the secret valley. As it unfolded before their astonished eyes, they stood for a moment in wonder at its grandeur, solitude, beauty.

Then, out in the meadow, sitting upright in tall grass, calmly pulling stems toward him with both paws and stripping them of their seeds with his teeth, they saw the great red-brown grizzly.

"By *God*," Buck whispered and the spell of wonder was broken. He raised his new Henry repeater, took careful aim, and fired, and the bear slumped over as if suddenly weary.

Then they saw the two women begin to run. Ta-ahi and Letke fled toward their cave, not knowing where else to go, but knowing the horror they had dreaded so long had come upon them at last.

"Don't shoot," Buck cried. "Come on, let's catch 'em!" And they ran to take alive the two that could be sold into captivity as indentured servants for as much as sixty dollars each.

Ta-ahi reached the cave first. She had made up her mind. She had discussed it with Francisco when he had given her his double-edged knife of blackest, sharpest obsidian that Tilhini had given him when he was a boy, saying it had belonged to the First People long before there were steel knives. It was so sharp it could cut a grass blade cleanly. "Keep it, in case," Francisco had said to her significantly. She had well known what he had meant. She snatched it from the niche in the cave wall where she kept her most precious possessions. But now would she have the courage to use it? The thought was appalling. Her spirit had to hold true till it reached the Western Gate and drank there at the spring at the foot of the bluff and then passed out over the sea like a musical sound. *My husband, I love you*, she thought with desperate, tearful longing. *I love you and our son. Give me strength! Now give me strength! I love you, my Letke*, she added tenderly, yet with terrible earnestness, turning to her daughter as Letke came panting into the cave behind her, and the shouts of their pursuers rose from the valley below. Tears almost blinded Ta-ahi as she plunged the knife into Letke's throat.

Then as the blood gushed out into the stone, with a prayer to the Sky People for courage and forgiveness, Ta-ahi shut her eyes and turned the knife upon herself. With a powerful slash she severed her throat from ear to ear and fell in a bloody swoon of death beside her daughter.

"Well, I'll be damned!" exclaimed Buck, scrambling into the cave a few moments later. "Look what's here, fellows!"

They stood silent at sight of the two bodies and the blood.

"Mother and daughter, eh?" Buck resumed. "He must be somewheres around. This must be their home." He pointed to the storage baskets lining the walls, the rolled-up sleeping mats, the ring of blackened stones at the center of the cave with its dead embers, dead as Ta-ahi and Letke lay now. "Reckon there was more than one kid?"

"Could be," Homer Gatlin surmised, "no telling. These here was too quick for us, that's for sure," he commented gravely as he looked down at the bodies. Homer was a lay preacher in his spare time. "What a shame. Pretty, ain't they?"

"Yeah, and worth good money," grumbled Buck. "But, say, look at that knife they done it with! That's worth having!" He was reaching down for the bloody knife when Homer warned: "Buck, that's sacrilegious. It might put a curse on all of us.

264

I'd leave it where it lays, if I was you. I'd leave them lay, too."

And so they did, though Buck complained about it afterward. He wanted to stay and set an ambush for Francisco, but the others convinced him it would be idle. "He'll see our horses, our tracks. He'll give this place a wide berth for days, weeks."

So they looted the rest of the cave, taking Francisco's finely-wrought bow of toughest elderberry reinforced with sinew, and his arrows in their quiver made from the skin of a mountain lion's tail, and the carefully-wrought ornamental baskets made by Ta-ahi and Letke, and departed.

And so Francisco and Helek found the two just as they had fallen, the knife between them, their blood soaked into the stone of the cave floor, their bodies cold.

Cold but free, thought Francisco with a sob in his heart, *free like their spirits.*

Helek was speechless with horror.

"I have shown you the world," Francisco said aloud grimly, "and here it is!" A great sob broke out of him as he knelt over the bodies and cried out for vengeance, for justice.

"But how could this happen?" Helek cried in dismay. "Is this Kakunupmawa's will?"

"It may be."

"Is this what Sacred Condor has guided us to?"

"It may be. Who knows?" sobbed Francisco.

"Have they gone to the Western Gate that we saw?"

"They have gone to the Western Gate."

Francisco looked up, but no condors were visible in the air above or on the cliff face by the waterfall. Buck's rifle shot had frightened them away. And the sun, though bright, seemed dim.

"Come, we must do what must be done."

Sorrowfully they made a funeral pyre of dry branches and

265

laid the two bodies upon it. Defying all caution in his agony of spirit, Francisco set it afire, and, when the flames were high, they threw into it the olivella shells they had brought from Point Conception and the piñon nuts they had gathered from the sacred precinct near the House of the Sun, and the knife Ta-ahi used to deliver herself and her daughter from bondage into what seemed everlasting life. Then they slipped away into the wilderness to continue their resistance and to face the darkness they felt surrounding them. "It is part of that darkness that lies behind the figure of Kakunupmawa in the cave that I showed you," Francisco said, "and we must try to penetrate it."

Chapter Thirty-Nine

"Reuben, I ought to refuse it unless they offer you one." David had been awarded the Congressional Medal of Honor for his gallantry at Stanhope's Bend. The nation's highest military award was being given much less sparingly than today, and several hundred would receive it before the war was over, but it had never been given to a black man. Nevertheless, Reuben insisted generously: "No, you take it, take it and raise a fuss about the unequal pay black soldiers get. That would be more to the point that hurts. I'd rather have twenty a month than seven and a medal, and my men would rather have the thirteen dollars a white private makes than the seven they get."

And that was one reason David stood one morning in the office of Secretary of War Stanton in the old War Department building across the street from the White House, while Stanton barked at him: "Captain, I'm promoting you to major. You'll be my special observer with General Sherman with regard to his treatment of freedmen, former slaves, whether as refugees or laborers, or as soldiers should he decide to employ them as such when he invades Georgia. I've selected you because you are known as the hero of Stanhope's Bend, and because General Halleck, here" — he nodded toward Halleck — "has recommended you. Your service with colored troops speaks for itself as does your record at Shiloh. Do you have any questions?"

"Yes, sir." The official reason for his being in Washington was suddenly clear to David. Stanton's ardent Abolitionism was well known. So was his antipathy toward Sherman whose attitude toward blacks was far less ardent. David suddenly saw himself in the middle of a ticklish situation. But he persisted with the matter foremost in his mind as the stocky, bearded, abrasive Stanton gazed at him impatiently, eyes magnified behind thick-lens spectacles. "I feel honored by your confidence, sir, and by General Halleck's. But I should hate to leave my men. I'm committed to serving with black troops."

"This way you'll be able to serve them even more, help the entire Negro cause which, I gather, is dear to your heart."

"It is, sir, and that leads me to something I should very much like to say."

"Then say it," barked Stanhope impatiently.

"It's about the unequal pay my men receive. They should be paid the same as their white counterparts."

"Ah," Stanton grunted with approval. His zeal for Negro rights had become almost a personal crusade. "That's just the sort of thing I hoped you might say. Come along. I want the President to hear you say it."

Halleck interjected: "I'll say good bye and wish you well, Major." Owlish-eyed Old Brains held out his hand stiffly. "You're fulfilling the promise I saw in you in the hospital in St. Louis." Halleck looked tired and subdued. In fact, he had been demoted to chief of staff while his former subordinate, Grant, victorious at Vicksburg, the last Confederate stronghold on the Mississippi, and at Chattanooga, the battle that opened the way for Sherman to invade Georgia, had been called to Washington and made General-in-Chief of the Armies of the United States. The tide was turning against the Confederacy, and Halleck's strategies had helped it turn, but his preference for the desk rather than the field and his lack of social grace had worked against him. "Remember me to your charming Martha," Halleck concluded with somewhat more warmth. "I hope to see you both in San Francisco when this war is over."

Then David and Stanton went across the street to the White House.

They found Lincoln in his office on the second floor, sitting at a desk littered with papers, busily signing some of them, using a steel-pointed pen with a wooden handle. As he looked up, he seemed to David incredibly care-worn, yet determined to be cheerful. David wondered if he'd remember their earlier meetings.

"Hullo, Mars," Lincoln greeted Stanton humorously, as he laid down his pen. "What's up now?"

"What you and I discussed recently, Mister President." Stanton was all gravity, all business. "Here is Captain, soon to be Major, Venable, recipient of the Medal of Honor, hero of Stanhope's Bend, who has something to say that I want you to hear."

Lincoln's care-worn face lightened further as he stood and held out his hand. "David Venable, it's good to see you again. You remind me of dear Ned Baker." A shadow crossed his face at thought of their mutual friend, David's colleague in the San Francisco Underground, later U. S. Senator, killed while gallantly leading his regiment in the Union débâcle at Ball's Bluff near Washington. "And it reminds me of that train ride in secret with you and Pinkerton through Baltimore on my way here to be inaugurated. It was shameful for me to arrive in our national capital secretly. I did it against my better judgment and was justly criticized for it. Stanhope's plot to assassinate me in Baltimore might never have materialized. But how are you? We're mighty proud of what you and your men did at Stanhope's Bend." Lincoln still spoke in that high-pitched voice that seemed to David out of keeping with his masculinity and rough-hewn frame. "Sit down. Tell me about that battle which did such credit to our brave Negro troops."

"They were the real heroes of that conflict. What troubles them now, sir, and me, too, if I may say so, is the inequity of their pay. They say they would rather have none at all than

269

accept less than a white soldier of comparable rank." And having let this sink in, David continued: "Reluctant as I am to leave them for my new assignment, I hope that by calling this problem to your attention, and to Mister Stanton's, I can play a rôle in solving it."

"We're well aware of the problem, aren't we, Stanton?" Lincoln replied soberly. "But it is Congress who must vote the money to redress this wrong. It seems to me we ought to be able to pay our valiant Negroes the same as we pay our valiant white boys. But until a majority in Congress sees it that way, it won't happen."

"It's a damnable outrage," Stanton burst out. "Before God and man it smells to high heaven, and I'll do all in my power to rectify it. This is a war for justice, Major. I thought you believed so. Now that I hear what you have to say, I know it."

"I'll return my Medal of Honor rather than see this injustice continue."

"You keep your medal," Lincoln intervened gently, "and let us deal with the injustice. Meanwhile, we want you to observe and to take counsel with General Sherman in matters concerning former slaves and their families who may come into his lines. It will be a delicate assignment. We think you're qualified for it because of your war record and because Halleck tells me how you knew Sherman in California. I don't want you to do anything to upset a good general," Lincoln cautioned, "but I want you and Sherman to do all in your power to safeguard the well being of Negroes as they seek protection under our flag, which is now their flag, too."

The words came slow and measured, carrying quiet but intense feeling. David had been among those quick to see that Lincoln's address on the battlefield at Gettysburg, following the crucial Union victory there, would become immortal. Now he felt the weight of Lincoln's words strike home upon himself.

He felt under fire but in a different way. Lincoln was shooting at him, shooting words of palpable weight and meaning.

"I understand, sir," David responded and saw, with a flash of insight, that Lincoln, too, understood what had passed between them. "There is one thing more," he added impetuously. "I should like to recommend my first sergeant, Reuben Stapp, for the Medal of Honor. He deserves it as much, or more, than I."

"We will take it under advisement," Stanton interrupted with genuine ardor. "It is what must come, must come, and, though Congress may balk, Congress will come to it eventually, Major. Let me have the particulars in writing. If white men can receive medals, so can black ones."

Lincoln nodded agreement. "Well said, Mars."

Stanton cleared his throat impatiently. He was a busy man, the administrator *par excellence*, the doer, the practical idealist. This day must proceed on schedule with its eighteen crowded hours of meetings, instructions, questions, answers, reports, decisions. Impeccably honest, incredibly hardworking, Stanton might miss the subtleties. But he would do his job with ferocious, selfless devotion. "Thank you, Mister President. That's all I had in mind," he grunted, almost boorishly, and rose, as a signal to David.

Lincoln rose and extended his hand again. As David gripped it, he felt its warmth, felt the President's heart, it seemed, beating for all the country, beating for a great national purpose now in its hour of severest trial. "I'll do all I can to justify your faith in me, sir!" He knew it was banal but could find nothing better, nothing truer.

Lincoln smiled understandingly. "I'll be counting on you. Remember, I, too, wish to retire to California some day." And David felt suddenly surrounded by a world of invisible realities much more important than visible ones.

★ ★ ★ ★ ★

After he took leave of Stanton in front of the White House, David paid a visit to his old friend from San Francisco days, Lafayette Baker, now head of the Secret Service, in his office in a two-story brick building at 217 Pennsylvania Avenue, a few blocks away. Baker had succeeded Alan Pinkerton as director of the newly established espionage and counter-espionage agency and had guided it brilliantly. Originally a Midwest farm boy like David, he, too, had gone to California to "see the elephant" of adventure and excitement. Together with young Gillem they had explored San Francisco's underworld, scuffled with its criminal element, gambled in Chinatown, visited the notorious White Boar Tavern on lower Pacific Street, and there witnessed the city's most unspeakable sight, a white boar copulating with a black woman. After David had left for the East to study for the ministry, the dark, keen-faced, fearless Baker had stayed on and had served with Mornay in the vigilance committee that had rid San Francisco of much of its criminal element. After the war broke out, Baker had come like thousands of others to Washington for a piece of the action and had won the confidence of Stanton and Lincoln by going in disguise to Richmond, being arrested there and questioned by Confederate authorities including Jefferson Davis, and so impressing them that they had sent him back to the North thinking he was *their* spy.

Now Baker was using skills developed in San Francisco and Richmond to track down Confederate spies and sympathizers as well as Northerners cheating on government contracts. On the wall behind him where others might display a **God Bless Our Home** motto, Baker displayed one saying **Death to Traitors.**

"I've got my sights on George Stanhope," he told David, after they had exchanged handshakes and recollections of old days. "Stanhope is behind much of the civil unrest in Ohio, Indiana, Illinois, that abortive attempt to set fire to Chicago, those riots in New York and elsewhere. He's trying desperately to encourage opposition to the war and bring about a negotiated peace, knowing he can't win on the battlefield." Confederate agents were active all over the country and also in Canada and Mexico. Arrayed against them Baker had some two thousand operatives, plus a regiment of cavalry stationed in Washington "which I command with rank of Colonel. We help guard the President and perform other special missions," Baker explained proudly, "but Stanhope is our main adversary just now. He's based in Canada and ranges up and down the border contacting his agents on our side. He hopes to see the President defeated for reëlection in November, but, if that don't happen, he's hatched a plot to kidnap Lincoln and hold him hostage until peace can be negotiated, or to kill him if it isn't."

David wondered where Stanhope's daughter was. He had not been able to put Vicky out of his mind or to find a proper place for her in it. She still seemed his dark angel as Martha did his bright one. And he still thought daily of Beau. Like the nation, he felt he was working out his salvation in blood, his own and Beau's and the others'. He still limped slightly from his wound, and Baker had commented on it. As if reading his thoughts, Baker asked keenly: "Wasn't Stanhope's daughter at his plantation during the fighting there?"

"She may have been," David shrugged.

Baker sensed he was dissembling and persisted: "I've reliable reports she was present and is now with Shelby's cavalry disguised as a man."

"That may be. She wouldn't be the first woman to do something like that, would she?" David evaded. "Weren't a wife and husband found dead in uniform, side by side, on the battlefield at Gettysburg?"

"Yes," conceded Baker, "there are women in uniform on both sides, probably more than we imagine. But back to Victoria Stanhope . . . will you let me know anything you hear about her? Her whereabouts may bear on her father's. I need all the information I can get, Venable. Stanton and the President depend on me. Mornay and Mary Louise Jackson do a great job for me, as does their protégée, Eve Radovich, in Los Angeles. They keep me informed what the likes of Eliot Sedley and Earl Newcomb are up to."

"And what are they up to?"

"Selfish interest. If Lincoln wins reëlection in November, they'll fall into line like good patriots, knowing a negotiated peace out of the question and the North bound to win. Meanwhile, my biggest problem is the President himself. He has no regard for his own safety. Somebody shot the hat off his head one evening not long ago as he rode alone out to see the sick and wounded at the Soldier's Home. I've tried to convince him to take more precautions. But he jokes . . . 'Baker, they're lousy shots. If they can't hit a target as tall as I, there's not much hope for 'em.' And that brings me back to Stanhope. Guess who he's using in his scheme to kidnap or kill Lincoln?" Baker paused with a gleam of satisfaction at knowing things his visitor did not.

"I can't imagine."

"Remember that actor Junius Booth, Junior, out in San Francisco?"

"Who played Brutus in Shakespeare's 'Julius Cæsar' at the Jenny Lind Theater while you and I watched?"

"Yes, well, he has a young actor brother, John Wilkes Booth, a romantic hothead from Maryland who thinks he embodies Southern honor and glory. Stanhope's using young Booth as catspaw. But we've got Tom Bowls watching Booth. Remember Tom?"

David recalled a ferret-faced fellow rather like Baker, with similar fearlessness and a similar nose for criminal activity. "Who used to drink with us at the Bank Exchange Saloon?"

"That's Tom. I've got more than a few like him from those old days, fellows I can trust." Then Baker congratulated David on his new assignment, but cautioned: "Sherman will be difficult to deal with. He and I were on opposite sides during the vigilante troubles in 'Frisco. He accused me of taking the law into my own hands. He don't seem to realize that sometimes you have to. Much will depend on how his invasion of Georgia goes. If he succeeds, we win the war. If he suffers disastrous defeat, we may lose it. But I'll bet you he takes the law into his own hands before it's over. Send me anything you think I should know."

They shook hands, and David went on his way, as his life took on ever new and surprising dimensions. God's plan for him and the nation seemed increasingly complex, increasingly unforeseeable, but he looked forward to meeting Sherman again.

Chapter Forty

Goodly's and Stubby's journey back to California on Mexican soil had been rudely interrupted by the Chiricahua Apaches who were roasting little Stubby alive over a slow fire. Stark naked, he hung suspended by both ankles from the limb of the cottonwood. His outstretched arms were picketed to the ground at either side of the fire. His head was a foot above the flames that were slowly killing him, and, from time to time, he jerked his head away from them spasmodically, and, as he jerked, he screamed.

"We cook the little fish first," Chief Cochise said quietly to Goodly.

Goodly Jenkins stood beside Cochise, numb with terror, hands lashed behind his back, compelled to witness agonies that would soon be his.

"Until the moment of my betrayal my people were at peace with you White Eyes," Cochise continued in fluent Spanish, contrasting the pale eyes of whites to the dark ones of Indians, "but after the soldiers invited me to eat a meal with them, and then tried to murder me, I decided to kill every White Eye I could. I want you to think of these things as you die."

The leader of the Chiricahuas was nearly six feet tall, naked to the waist, every visible muscle rounded and firm, and his black hair was cut off level with his chin. He had a beaked nose, a face of unusual intelligence and dignity — and now of implacable hatred.

After fleeing across the Río Grande from Benito Ferrer and his scouts, Goodly and Stubby had been taken by partisans to the headquarters of Mexico's embattled president, Benito Juárez, in the rugged Sierra Blanca, where Juárez led the struggle against his imperialist enemies and their French allies who had placed the Austrian prince, Maximilian, on the throne of Mexico. Eager for first-hand information about the great war north of the border, Juárez, stocky, dark-skinned, the first and to this day the only full-blooded Indian to be president of Mexico, had interrogated the two fugitives himself. Goodly had given him an eloquent description of the defeat of Sibley's Confederate Army of New Mexico and the advance of the victorious California Column into Texas. "We are fugitives from both sides. We want to join you," he had added with inspiration born of desperation, "and fight for democracy."

A faint smile of approval had touched the face of the usually impassive Juárez, and he had replied: "We have Americans already with us. Indeed, my bodyguard is composed entirely of them."

"It sure as heck is," a familiar voice had drawled from behind Goodly and Stubby, and they had turned and seen wizened little Copus, their former mentor, dressed in blue jeans and red flannel shirt like a Texas volunteer. "It's our uniform," he had explained after he had embraced them. "We're all Texans or Californians, all Rebels. All of us has drifted across the border, like you boys, in search of better days, and thanks to Mister President, here, we've found 'em."

Copus had vouched for them, and they had become members of Juárez's trusted bodyguard. "Juárez trusts us," Copus had explained, "where he can't trust his own people without risking a knife in his back." Thus there was civil war south of the border, too, and thus Goodly and Stubby had become part of it. With Juárez and his rag-tag guerrilla army, they had been forced back and back toward the U. S. border until this valiant champion of Mexican liberty had faced almost certain defeat, and had said to his loyal bodyguard: "I'll not ask you fellows to sacrifice yourselves for my sake. Go or stay as you may decide." Copus had decided to stay. Goodly and Stubby had opted for home and the prospect of finding gold as they went. In the wilds of the Sierra Madre they had found enough to fill partially a small leather pouch. It now stood upright on the ground, just beyond reach of Stubby's outstretched right hand, as part of the tableau Cochise had arranged.

"Have mercy," Goodly bleated, gibbering with terror.

"Mercy?" laughed Cochise. "What mercy have you White Eyes had on me? Mexicans killed my father and tried to kill me. Americans have captured my wife and child and tried to kill me. They're after me now. Why should I have mercy?"

Stubby never stopped screaming and jerking. A warrior stepped forward, knife in hand, and cut off his penis and jammed it in his mouth to shut him up. As Stubby choked and gagged, the warrior laughed and wiped his knife across Stubby's face.

But Stubby's death screams had attracted the attention of Lieutenant Benito Ferrer and his scouting party from Fort Bowie and their Papago and Pima guides. The California Column, under command of Brigadier General James Henry Carleton, then headquartered in Santa Fé, had been standing watch on the Río Grande to repel any further invasion from Confederate Texas but had also become engaged in a war within a war as it tried to quell the Chiricahuas and other bands who resisted encroachment on Apache homeland. In a recent fight Benito had lost two of his best men to Cochise, one of them Sergeant Pat Michaels. Horrified and infuriated by what he saw now, Benito gave the signal, and his men opened fire on the unsuspecting Apaches.

The warrior who had just mutilated Stubby fell forward into the fire, still with knife in hand. Cochise and the others dissolved into the surrounding countryside. Goodly, who had sunk to his knees, was left blubbering with relief, saved by the man he hated most. When Benito saw whom he had rescued, he couldn't quite believe it was the man he least wanted to save. Without a word he took out his knife and cut the thongs that bound Goodly's hands.

Goodly seized Benito's hands, sobbing and blubbering like an idiot: "You've saved my life. You've saved my life!"

"Don't thank me. Thank Stubby's screams."

They buried Stubby by the fire that had killed him. They covered the mound with heavy stones to protect the body from wolves and coyotes. They left the dead Apache untouched. Surely Cochise and his men would return and claim it. And then they turned back toward Fort Bowie with Goodly, not as prisoner, not as Confederate deserter, but as a lucky man who had miraculously escaped a horrible death after many adventures in the Sierra Madre and earlier with Juárez, for Goodly spared no words in telling of his recent history, including how he and Stubby had discovered gold near the old Toyopa mine. "And there's my sack to prove it."

Benito had decided he would say nothing to anyone about Goodly's part in the ambush at Stanwick's Station and his desertion from the Confederate Army of New Mexico. The poor bastard had suffered enough, he thought, with reluctant compassion. But Goodly knew what Benito wasn't saying, and it added to his gradually rekindling hatred, now that the moment of crisis had passed.

At dawn next morning the Apaches attacked, and in the twilight bullets flew back and forth. One struck down the trooper crouched next to Goodly. Goodly grabbed up the man's new Spencer seven-shot repeater and returned the enemy fire, and, as he did so, he caught Benito in his sights, and his bullet found Benito's right temple and ended his life, but no one on earth except Goodly knew this. Everyone else thought it the work of the murderous Chiricahuas.

After the attack was beaten off, the Californians proceeded, carrying Benito's body with them to Fort Bowie near the entrance to Apache Pass, and there Goodly was hailed as a hero and Benito mourned as a victim. After Goodly stood bareheaded with the others at Benito's grave, he proceeded homeward, spending his gold in Tucson and Yuma City as he went, and the very last of it at Bill Traven's Dixieland Saloon in Los Angeles where he and Stubby had first met Copus, and where Rosita Díaz was still the dazzling attraction. When he arrived home, at last, he was welcomed joyously as a hero by Buck and Iphy and even old Abe, if not by Elmer and Opal, and thus Goodly became an integral part of the final tragedy that was to be enacted in the Valley of Santa Lucia.

When news of the death of their elder son reached Ruth and Santiago Ferrer, they were devastated and took the menorah, the seven-branched candlestick, from the closet where it was kept concealed from prying Gentile eyes and — there being no rabbi within three hundred miles — Santiago led the family in recitation of the Kaddish, the prayer for the dead. Benito was the favorite son. Named for his *conquistador* grandfather who had ridden into the valley as a soldier of Spain, Benito seemed the one who would carry forward the flame most brightly. Now it fell to the hands of unlikely, even backward, Mark and studious Bernardina to carry on. Santiago blamed himself.

"I got him into the Army, Koenig and I did, after he'd been refused."

"But that was what he wanted," Ruth pointed out patiently. "He wanted to be accepted as a regular, and he was. He died knowing that."

"If he'd stayed home, he'd still be alive."

"He wasn't born to stay home."

Clara was heartbroken, too, when she heard the news, and so was Sally, and so outwardly was Pacifico, but inwardly he felt survivor's pride. He was alive. Benito was dead. And the jealousy of his friend, that had been steadily developing, now turned into a sense of triumph.

Chapter Forty-One

Immediately in front of David, under the Georgia hickory tree, General William Tecumseh Sherman sat on an upturned cracker box, a half-eaten hardtack biscuit in one hand and David's orders from Stanton in his other hand, as he quoted from them derisively: "Special observer!" The commander of a hundred thousand men was bareheaded, his hair disheveled as when David had last seen him at Shiloh. But Sherman's face was more lean and bronzed and deeply lined and his body was leaner, too, and his uniform was faded and rumpled as if he didn't care how he looked. The staff officers and enlisted men sitting or standing informally around them at this lunch hour in the field looked much as he did. "So Stanton wants you to look over my shoulder to see how I treat black people?" Sherman snapped with withering disapproval.

"No, sir, I'll be doing my duty following Secretary Stanton's orders, and yours."

Sherman glared at him a bit less witheringly. Obedience to duty — including what he perceived his duty to punish the South for its transgressions against the Union — was a driving force in Sherman, driving him toward Atlanta that lay over the horizon ahead. Though he disagreed with their policy of enlisting black soldiers, he didn't want to antagonize Stanton and Lincoln by rejecting their observer, yet wanted to make his position clear. "I'm like President Lincoln was, or said he was, Major," he snorted on, gesticulating toward Washington with his half-eaten biscuit. "I wouldn't free one Negro, if it wouldn't preserve the Union. I'd free 'em all, if it would. Meantime, I treat 'em like human beings, not angels. I hire 'em and pay 'em well. What more does Stanton want, eh? The moon? No,

I say blacks can help most now by staying put, taking care of themselves and their families, not flocking to my army to enlist or to be fed and protected. Speak up, sir! Weren't you at dinner with me one night at Caleb Wright's house in San Francisco?"

"Yes, sir." David remembered that sumptuous occasion at the mansion on Rincon Hill: Sherman and his lovely Ellen there at the candle-lit table, Sherman, the successful banker of Gold Rush days, interrogating him about his Iowa roots and California ambitions as gold clerk in Wright's great shipping firm.

"Wright was a good man, but misguided. Misguided like Stanton. Like all Abolitionists. You one?"

"Yes, sir."

"Well, don't proselytize around here. My men are busy fighting a war." Musketry broke out just ahead. Paying it no attention, Sherman read on through the orders. "Shiloh, eh? The sunken road and the peach orchard, eh? So you were there?"

"I'd rather not have been."

"And you were wounded?"

"On the second day while with your division."

"Humph." Sherman scrutinized him sharply as if for signs of fraud. "And Stanhope's Bend? Your blacks fought pretty well, did they?"

"Superbly."

Sherman grunted. "So I heard. But if I was to enlist 'em, half my men would quit. They're not fighting to free slaves. They're fighting to save the Union and their homes and families. And I've got to win a war with the men I have, not some ideal breed Stanton imagines. Understand?"

"I understand what you say, sir, though I happen to disagree."

"I see you've been awarded the Medal of Honor for gallantry," Sherman sniffed again, "but that don't mean much. They're passing out medals like candy these days. The whole thing's turned into a political circus. With Stanton as ringmaster. Well, you can stick around," he added gruffly, as he handed David's orders back to him, "but don't proselytize for Abolition!"

As Sherman turned away, a young staff officer, a major like himself, deliberately winked at David. Smiles went around the informal circle of officers and enlisted men who had heard this entertaining and informative dialogue. Those smiles and the informality of that circle and of Sherman struck David as perhaps more revealing that anything Sherman had said, as musketry broke out again a few hundred yards ahead, and a stray ball whistled through the leaves above them.

As he rode the front line with Sherman and his staff next day, David was struck again by the democratic informality of this Western army. "Hello, Uncle Billy!" his men greeted Sherman. "Have you got enough to eat?" he asked them. "Are you getting your mail? What do you think of our tactics?" And when they had expressed themselves frankly, he turned to David: "Any of 'em could command this army as well as I. Tell that to Mister Stanton, will you?"

He took David with him on grueling nighttime reconnaissances to explore the terrain over which the army would attack next day. They crawled on their bellies so that they could know the ground as their men would encounter it. "And so that you can tell Stanton how it's done!" Sherman had snapped afterward. David wrote Stanton that Sherman had shown him Negro laborers rebuilding a railroad the retreating Confederates had torn up. **"Go ahead, talk to them," he told me. I found he pays ten dollars a month and their food, which is more than most could earn in civilian life, or even in the Army, and they seem well-content to be where they are.**

Fugitive slaves, sometimes alone, sometimes with their families, continually flock to us for protection, but Sherman does not encourage them and does not claim to be their liberator. I cannot so far find any abuse of human rights. Yet I tell him frankly I don't agree with his attitude toward blacks as soldiers. And he tells me frankly he don't agree with mine.

In the days that followed, Uncle Billy and his democratic army slowly approached Atlanta, fighting, outflanking, outgeneraling their out-numbered Confederate adversaries and steadily forcing them back.

Fear of failure still drove Sherman, fear of relapsing into his old pre-Shiloh self when he had failed as civilian and as soldier, was dependent on a powerful and wealthy father-in-law for support for his wife and children. Some of this had come out during late-night conversations with David by the campfire when Sherman, who slept little, liked to prowl and talk. "Blood," he muttered one midnight when they are alone. "Three hundred thousand of their bravest must be killed before the South will think of peace, and we must lose an equal or greater number since we will be the attacking party. You were at Shiloh. You saw what happened. It baptized you, too, eh?" And David told of his moral death and resurrection there, and Sherman told of his similar rebirth, and then raged on. "A new nation of millionaires will arise from this bloody slaughter, arise on our blood and bones, and frolic and glitter as if they were newborn out of the head of God Almighty, rather than from suffering and death."

David saw Sherman as a great but flawed leader, sprung from the people, sprung out of the heart of the Midwest like himself, like Grant, like Lincoln, to lead the nation to victory and glory. David wrote Martha and Mornay: **For all his** faults, **Sherman has a fierce honesty we need. And he is a great general. While Grant hammers headlong toward Richmond and loses tens of thousands, Sherman avoids frontal attacks and loses a few hundred. He will capture Atlanta.** Atlanta was the backbone of the Confederacy, David explained. **It's not only a strategic rail center but also a center of munitions-making and other manufacturing vital to the South's war effort. Capturing it will break the South's backbone.**

And Martha wrote in return: **I no longer go to the post office to receive your letters. They are delivered to our door. Isn't that wonderful?** Home delivery had been instituted because the sight of so many people breaking into tears at post offices as they read of the deaths of their loved ones had become so painful for others to see, and so damaging politically to the Lincoln administration, that the President had approved home delivery. Martha added: **The terrible casualties Grant is suffering are causing such dissatisfaction that Papa and Gillem feel Lincoln may not be reëlected. I pray that you won't risk yourself unduly. Isn't it time you rested on your laurels and let others lead the attack?**

But David and Sherman didn't rest on their laurels and were continually under fire as they rode the front line. Then one night in late August, Atlanta all but surrounded, everything seeming to hang in the balance, the two of them, alone by the embering fire, Sherman opened up as never before. He had just received word of the death of his eight-year-old son, Willy, from typhoid. "The Lord giveth and the Lord taketh away, David," Sherman said grimly. "He may give us Atlanta. But he's taken my Willy." Sherman and his beloved Ellen had three other children, but Willy was their favorite. "I wish Willy were alive and I were dead. I may win the election for Lincoln by capturing Atlanta. But that won't give me back Willy."

Then, reminiscing to surmount his pain, Sherman went on: "You never knew California before the Gold Rush as I did." As a young lieutenant, Sherman had lived in Monterey by the sea, amid whitewashed walls and red-tile roofs, the music of guitars, the fragrance of honeysuckle. "Until the year before, it was the Mexican capital and before that the Spanish one. Horsemen in colorful dress dashed to and fro. *Señoritas* smiled. Everywhere there was kindness. The Californians liked us Americans, and we liked them. It could have been a happy marriage. Then came the discovery of gold." Sherman had carried official word of the discovery, along with sample nuggets packed in a tea caddy, to President Polk in Washington City, and Polk had announced to the world that gold had been discovered in California. "That was the point of no return. After that, the world rushed in, and we lost our Eden. Now California is everybody's dream place," Sherman growled, "but the more people flock there, the more they'll ruin her. If we'd married her, instead of raping her for her gold, we could have created a society such as the world has never seen, such as young people need to know, such as I wish my Willy could have experienced like I did."

David felt that, through Sherman, he was glimpsing something very precious, now lost like a golden nugget misplaced. "I understand, sir," he replied, wishing Sherman could tell him more about himself and his far-ranging, desperately driven life. Sherman hadn't mentioned lovely María Ignacia, the belle of Monterey, with whom he had fallen deeply in love. "I'm sorry about your son."

"Hark, what's that?" Sherman's keen hearing had detected an unusual sound, magnified by the late-night air. Then David heard it, too — a distant, constant, rumbling.

"That's not artillery," Sherman barked, "it's wheels. It's wagon wheels, David. They're evacuating Atlanta!"

Chapter Forty-Two

"Kiss me," Eve commanded unabashedly, "you'll be elected."

"Wait till the votes are counted," Pedro retorted. "What Lincoln and I need now is votes, not kisses."

Because he was so young, because he was a *californiano*, because of his advocacy of Wing Fat against Hortensia de la Vega, the Republicans hadn't backed Pedro for county attorney in the fall elections of 1864. So he was running on his own as a Progressive Independent, a label he and Eve had concocted with the approval of Ambrose and Ethel Curtis and Simon and Deborah Koenig. They all had agreed it was catchy and prophetic. "Even if you lose, you'll win," Ethel Curtis assured him now as they planned strategy in her living room after supper. Deborah Koenig concurred and added: "You'll have established who you are and paved the way to the future." But Simon cautioned: "You must expect to be defeated." And Ambrose warned: "And you'll be laughed at and slandered." Eve rejoined proudly: "But he'll not have let down Wing Fat and others who look to him for leadership in the struggle for human rights. Oh, if only women could vote!"

Having already thought of everything they had said except Eve's demand for a kiss, Pedro told them: "Anyhow, it's something I feel I've got to do. Your support will be essential."

At first, it seemed he would need a bodyguard, too, because there was so much anti-Lincoln, anti-war, anti-human rights feeling in Southern-sympathizing, bigoted Los Angeles, where "Peace" Democrats and other Southern sympathizers plus others simply sick and tired of the war saw a vote against Lincoln — and a vote against all those like Pedro who stood with Lincoln — as a vote for peace. Feelings ran so high that, before a pro-Lincoln rally could be held in the old plaza, troops had to be brought in from Camp Latham near San Pedro and Camp Drum near the adjacent port of Wilmington to keep peace in the streets.

Nevertheless, when his turn came to address the rally, where the bandstand now stands, Pedro declared: "I'm with Lincoln. But I go further. I stand for emancipation and full civil rights for everyone, black, yellow, brown, or white, male or female." There was a stunned silence, then one or two cheers for these extraordinary, even revolutionary, sentiments, while Pedro went on to remind his hearers: "I defended the rights of Wing Fat against Hortensia de la Vega because I thought Wing's cause was just, not because I had anything against Hortensia. I'll gladly defend her, too, if need be. I'm looking forward to the new day that is dawning, the day we can establish a new society here in this beautiful land," unknowingly echoing what Sherman and David were saying three thousand miles away, "that can put to shame for fairness everything that has gone before it. Elect me and your rights will be defended as I defended Wing Fat's, regardless of the color of your skin, regardless of whether you're a man or a woman."

Laughter broke out at such a fantastic, impractical vision, and there were derisive shouts of "Chink lover!"

Undeterred, Pedro campaigned on street corners, even went door to door. Most people thought he was crazy. Some said he was a stalking horse, dividing the votes of his Republican and Democratic opponents. His family told him he was out of his mind. Except for his still adored Rosita, they sided with Doña Hortensia and the *grandees* who had ruled them so long. Rosita declared: "I'm for Pedro. He has as much right to go his own way as I have to go mine!" and thus she infuriated family and friends but intrigued patrons of the Dixieland Saloon where she attracted more attention than ever among its mainly Southern-sympathizing anti-Pedro clientele.

Earl Newcomb advised Don Porfirio to pay no attention to Pedro's candidacy. "He'll harm himself and Lincoln more if we ignore him," Newcomb declared. "Let's focus on discrediting Lincoln." Former Union General George B. McClellan was the Democratic nominee for President. Lincoln had made cocky little McClellan commander of the Army of the Potomac, then had removed him because of McClellan's reluctance to fight. Newcomb and Porfirio followed the accepted Democratic line: "Lincoln is jealous of McClellan. If he'd left him in command, the war would have been over long ago. Now McClellan will end it by making peace and stopping the bloodshed."

As for the drought and hard times currently plaguing Southern California, they blamed them on Lincoln, too, while buying up downtown lots for as little as $2.50 each. Using mainly Sedley's money, they bought once glorious ranch lands, now littered with bones of sheep and cattle killed by the drought, for as little as fifty cents an acre, as they looked to the day when the railroad would reach Los Angeles and create a boom.

On the eve of the election, as feelings reached fever pitch, Pedro was walking homeward across the plaza when he came face to face with Don Porfirio mounted on his golden palomino. Don Porfirio couldn't resist taunting him. "*Californiano*, you'll get your come-uppance tomorrow!"

"And you'll get yours day after tomorrow," forecasted Pedro tartly, "because the future is on my side, Don Porfirio, not yours."

Pedro's tartness reminded the *grandee* of his abiding intention to horsewhip this rebellious youngster, and he suddenly exploded: "Hold your tongue, *cholo!* Your tongue has besmirched the name of my Hortensia and has thereby dragged my honor in the dust, and you shall pay!" And taking the quirt from his saddle horn, he leaned forward to whip Pedro, but Pedro deftly snatched the quirt from his hand, cracked the palomino over the rump with it. The horse gave a great leap forward, and Don Porfirio toppled into the dust of the plaza as many witnesses stared in astonishment and disbelief. Pedro tossed the quirt in the direction of the prostrate *grandee* and walked on home.

No plaque marks the spot today, yet it would be remembered as the site of the first overt confrontation between ordinary *californianos* and the overlords who had intimidated and dominated them for nearly a hundred years.

Don Porfirio stalked home in a rage and began loading his old flintlock pistol to go and shoot Pedro, but Hortensia hastily summoned Newcomb, and Newcomb persuaded him that murder was a serious business and that witnesses had seen Porfirio initiate the hostilities. "It's just not worth risking your neck, Don Porfirio. We'll win tomorrow. Let that be your satisfaction. That and our plans for the future."

When Father O'Hara intimated to Clara that he intended to vote for Lincoln, Clara burst out: "The day Lincoln's Supreme Court gives me title to my ranch is the day I'll vote for Lincoln!" And when O'Hara gently reminded her that the Supreme Court was not controlled by the President, she railed on: "But his General Halleck is my lawyer! So is Lincoln a lawyer! Don't tell me war and politics is all two lawyers talk about when they get together! No, let them talk about my ranch, and tell their lazy old court to get busy and rule on my case."

Being an Indian as well as a woman, she was doubly ineligible to vote, but O'Hara liked to pretend otherwise and so nodded sagaciously.

Clara was preoccupied, anyway, by the drought which was

starving her cattle, too, but she refused to cut down trees as the Jenkinses and other squatters and many ranchers were doing, so that the cattle could eat their leaves. "It is sacrilege!" she declared with furious disapproval, and, instead, she drove the remnants of her once great herds deep into the wilderness, hoping they would survive there by browsing on trees and chaparral and nibbling the tough native grasses that had endured in the back country long after the lush lowlands had been denuded. As she drove them in company with Sally, Pacifico, Isidro, and her *vaqueros*, she wondered with an aching heart if Francisco and Helek were still alive and perhaps watching. Word of the deaths of Ta-ahi and Letke had spread all over the valley. She couldn't bear to think of it. Were Francisco and Helek dead, too? She knew Buck and his Rangers had searched high and low for them. But they were keeping to the remote heart of the wilderness, warier than ever, trying to devise a way of avenging the deaths of Ta-ahi and Letke and a new way of resistance.

At the saloon in Santa Lucia, Buck Jenkins, following the anti-Lincoln line, spoke openly of the need for an end to the war "that's led to the deaths of Stubby and Benito and to all that my brave Goodly suffered." Goodly, too, argued for peace, but, secretly, he and Buck and the Rangers were ready to rise and welcome that fantasy army of Confederates who might yet come to liberate California from Northern rule, once Lincoln was defeated at the polls. Goodly's murder of Benito ate at his conscience now and then, but not enough to bother him much. He had told the lie about the Apaches' killing Benito so often that it was beginning to sound like the truth. He still had to get even with Pacifico, though. But Buck told him: "Forget that hen-pecked cripple. It's his dad we want. He hates his dad. And he might help us catch him."

★ ★ ★ ★ ★

Up in San Francisco, Sedley remained publicly uncommitted while secretly contributing to both parties, and Mary Louise and Mornay reported to Lafayette Baker in Washington that only a great Union victory would swing the war-weary state and Sedley into the Republican camp. Sedley seldom slept in his mansion on fashionable Rincon Hill south of the heart of town. Occasionally he gave a supper there for close friends, Mary Louise supervising its preparation but not mingling with his guests. When the guests brought up the subject of his wife, Sedley smiled ironically and said: "You've heard the same rumors I have. She's a spirited girl, is Vicky, and, when she commits herself to something like the Southern cause, she may go all the way, especially after the death of her brother and the loss of their plantation home."

Meanwhile, a new Pacific Railway Act had passed Congress, thanks largely to Sedley's influence. It granted even larger subsidies in federal lands and federal bonds and reduced those bonds to second mortgage status, enabling the Central Pacific to sell its own bonds as first mortgages, and thus to raise immediate cash for construction. Rails had been shipped around Cape Horn in the hold of Sedley's *Great Western* and put in place; and the company's first locomotive, *Governor Stanford*, similarly shipped, had begun shuttling supplies, work crews, and dignitaries back and forth from Sacramento to the construction front in the foothills. But in the high Sierra ahead, construction would cost a million dollars a mile, and money was still the name of the game. Sedley was planning to go to Washington after the election to meet with Lincoln or McClellan, whichever was President.

On September 2, 1864, just when it seemed even to Lincoln that McClellan must win, the President received a telegram from Sherman: **Atlanta is ours and fairly won.**

Handing the telegram to Stanton, Lincoln said: "By Jove, Mars, this changes the picture a little, don't it? Maybe I'll be elected, after all."

Jubilation ran through the North. **I'm so proud of you and Sherman,** Martha wrote David as if he and Sherman alone had achieved this crucial victory. **Papa says it may be the turning point.**

Crucial it proved. When the results of the November election were in, Lincoln had carried Los Angeles County by two hundred and seventy-nine votes and California by over twenty thousand and the nation by over four hundred thousand. "Now kiss me," Eve commanded Pedro. He had received nineteen votes. "You've won by losing. You've made your points and established yourself as the champion of ordinary people and their aspirations, and of women and other oppressed minorities."

"Next time will be different," Pedro agreed, "and, meanwhile, Don Porfirio will spend his life trying to get even with me." But that night he and Eve celebrated their victorious defeat in ways that give them great satisfaction.

Meeting with George Stanhope at Niagara Falls, Canada, just across the U. S. border, John Wilkes Booth told him: "This is our last chance. It's now or never." And Stanhope agreed. "Kidnap Lincoln, but don't kill him. We can do that later if need be."

As David sat horseback with Sherman and his staff on a knoll eastward of the captured city and watched the army move past them, Atlanta lay in smoldering ruins behind them. Sixty-thousand strong, the army would live off the countryside and lay waste that countryside as it advanced toward Savannah and the sea, and thousands of former slaves would continue to flock to it and greet it as the hand of God, and David would continue to feel himself part of a divine purpose, part of a mighty convergence, wonderful and terrible as it unfolded.

Reuben's black regiment was moving by train to Virginia to reinforce the Army of the Potomac, which was bleeding nearly to death as it struggled to capture Richmond and end the war.

Chapter Forty-Three

Four months later Christ's blood was on his mind as David sat in Ford's Theater in Washington on Good Friday, April 14, 1865, and so were the thirty pieces of silver Judas had been paid for it. Jesus's crucifixion, the money involved, the resurrection that followed seemed a metaphor for all that had happened during the past four years to bring David Venable and the nation to peace at last, and David, here, to John Ford's popular theater on 10th Street with the performance about to begin. Five days earlier Lee had surrendered to Grant at Appomattox. The war was all but over.

After capturing Savannah, Sherman's brilliantly victorious army had advanced northward to Goldsboro in North Carolina, where David had left it to come here to Washington to make a final report to Stanton. While still not enlisting blacks as soldiers, Sherman had encouraged black refugees to cultivate unoccupied land to support themselves and their families. But the Secretary of War remained skeptical. "Ain't it mainly window dressing?" Stanton's ardent Abolitionism demanded absolute proofs to match his ideals for the future of the "Negro race," as he called it.

"Sir, Sherman is difficult," David conceded, "but I believe his intentions are good. He wants refugees to become self-sufficient as soon as possible, and he meets from time to time with black leaders to bring this about, and they continue to express approval of what he proposes. True, he still refuses to accept blacks as soldiers. Claims it would impair the efficiency of his army. I continue to tell him he's wrong. But he won't listen."

Stanton sniffed. "I want you to stay with him and keep me informed."

David hoped to visit Richmond on his journey back to Sherman. The Confederate capital had been occupied by Negro troops, Reuben Stapp among them. It seemed an ideal place for him and Reuben to be reunited. And tonight he had hoped to attend the theater with Lafayette Baker as a commemoration of old days at the Jenny Lind Theater in San Francisco. But on calling at the headquarters of the Secret Service, following his meeting with Stanton, he had learned that Baker had been called to New York to investigate an important case of fraud against the federal government by a ring of bogus recruiting agents. Baker had left a note saying he was sorry to miss their evening together and enclosed the ticket he had purchased at David's request.

David had no inkling the President and Mrs. Lincoln would be attending tonight's performance until he entered the crowded theater and saw that the front of the box immediately overlooking the stage was draped with flags and red, white, and blue bunting.

Even so, the play, "Our American Cousin," a vapid comedy about a bumpkin who goes to England to inherit a fortune, had already begun when there was a stir around him, and he looked up from his third-row seat to see the President and Mrs. Lincoln entering their box almost above his head. With them was a handsome young couple, Major Henry Rathbone and his fiancée, Clara Harris, favorites of the Lincolns'. The actors stopped speaking and turned toward the Presidential party as the audience rose to its feet, David among them, and applauded and cheered the leader who had brought the nation through the agonies of war to peace at last.

Lincoln advanced to the railing and acknowledged this spontaneous welcome with a bow, and then another. He looked shockingly thin and care-worn to David, but his face was radiant with a smile of benign joy. Peace at last. It was the end of a busy day for Lincoln. Rising early, he had gone to his upstairs office a few doors from his bedroom. There he had worked at his desk until eight o'clock when he breakfasted in the family dining room on the first floor with Mary Lincoln and their son, Robert, a captain on Grant's staff. Robert had been at Appomattox Court House five days earlier when Lee had surrendered. Now he described the occasion to his parents, dwelling on Grant's homey simplicity, Lee's courtly grace. "There they were, Shovelry and Chivalry, summing up in their persons the two opposing sides, just as you do, Dad, when compared to Jefferson Davis."

After breakfast Lincoln had returned to his office for a series of interviews with prominent persons, including Sedley who had come from California when a Union victory appeared certain, for he wanted a share of the spoils and a hand in shaping the new policies that must now emerge. Lincoln had welcomed him warmly. "We couldn't have won without your help, Eliot. Your gold helped sustain our credit from first to last. Money and blood. They're at the heart of all that's been happening, and California has been extraordinarily generous with both. Over sixteen thousand of your boys volunteered, Stanton tells me, and California contributed over a million dollars to our sanitary fund to help needy soldiers. That's more than any other state."

"It's thanks to your leadership, Mister President."

Lincoln had waved away the compliment. "Let's talk about the future. How is your railroad progressing?"

"Crocker's pushing through snow twenty-five feet deep in the Sierra, blasting through solid rock. He's begun employing Chinese. We can't find anyone else willing to do that kind of work."

"How are the Chinese performing?"

"Splendidly. They work harder and live on less than a white

man. Even so, Mister President, construction costs will soon be running a million dollars a mile. We'll need your continued support and Congress' to complete our end of the line."

"And the Union Pacific pushing westward from Omaha will meet you where?"

"Somewhere near Great Salt Lake, I'd guess."

"A tremendous enterprise," Lincoln had commented, "one of which our nation can be justly proud. But let me ask a question. Do you think the Chinese are entitled to full citizenship some day, just as Negroes are entitled to it, and just as your Spanish Californians already have it?"

"Yes, I speak from experience. All races can help this country prosper and be proud of itself." Sedley's views on race were entirely pragmatic. For him, anything that worked, worked, and that was the end of the matter. Whether people were white, black, brown, or yellow was beside the point.

Lincoln had nodded agreement. "I appreciate your frankness. How are things out there generally?"

"Booming. May I invite you and Missus Lincoln to come and see for yourselves, now the war is over?"

"Thank you, we intend to. We may even settle and spend our declining years out there. I hear the Carmel Valley is an especially nice place."

"Yes, but there's another valley I shall want you to see. It is the Valley of Santa Lucia. It is the most beautiful in all California."

"Then we shall certainly make a point to visit it. We'll also want to see your big trees and Golden Gate. And I want especially to see that Yosemite Park I created with the help of you folks out there, and, of course, Congress'. But I signed the bill. Does that entitle me to a look?"

"It sure does," Sedley had agreed, "and on the way we can visit my El Dorado Gold Mine that has contributed so much, as you say, to a Union victory."

"Halleck was telling me of a famous old Indian woman, a client of his, who lives on a *rancho* called Olomosoug, if I pronounce it correctly. Know anything about her?"

"I know her very well. She and her ranch are in that special valley I want you to see."

"Is she really an Indian?"

"She's an Indian princess."

"Then I certainly want to see her. And so will Missus Lincoln. Mary and I see California as the culmination of this nation's destiny, Eliot. It's a land of extraordinary promise. I hope our brave soldier boys, who've served so well so long, may find homes there. We're a westering people, and California is at the end of our quest for a better life."

"I couldn't agree more." And then Sedley had turned to the subject of money and the opportunities that existed for making it in California. "For example, I'm forming a syndicate to purchase land in the southern part of the state, Mister President. A modest investment now will yield great profit in the not too distant future." And he had outlined the plan he and Newcomb and Don Porfirio had developed for converting the Los Angeles area into a vast complex of towns and farms. Sedley knew Lincoln needed money. Mary Lincoln had put her husband deeply in debt with her lavish expenditures on clothes and for White House furnishings. Sedley had seen an opening whereby the President could become his man. Lincoln could be enormously useful to him whether in Washington or California.

"I don't have any money I can invest at the moment," Lincoln had said frankly, "but keep me in mind, and I'll appreciate it. Let's talk further before you go home."

At mid-afternoon Lincoln and Mary Lincoln had gone for their usual carriage ride. That Good Friday had begun warm and bright but had become overcast. At first Lincoln had felt a return of foreboding thoughts. Last night he had dreamed he was on water in a peculiar, indescribable vessel moving with great rapidity toward an indefinite shore. But, then, as they had talked, he had managed to shake off his foreboding feeling, and had said to Mary: "Mother, I was speaking with Eliot Sedley this morning, and he was urging me to come and settle in California. What do you think?"

"I think it might offer better opportunity for our two boys. I'd certainly like to go and take a look, though first I'd like to visit England and Europe."

"Well, let's think about it. I could practice law. Halleck has offered me a place in his old firm. Sedley says he can steer business my way and offers me investment opportunities." The thought had crossed Lincoln's mind that he might become a California millionaire like Sedley and live on a ranch such as Sedley and Halleck had described. But more likely it would be a farm such as he had been familiar with in his Illinois days — a simple homestead with fruit trees and a corn patch and a hay field and cows and horses, where the sun would always shine and the air never grow cold.

Lincoln hadn't wanted to go to the theater that evening. But it been announced that he would attend, and he had felt he must. People would be expecting him. He could not let them down.

Now the actors delivered lines that evoked laughter, and David saw Lincoln and Mary Lincoln laugh, too. From time to time the President leaned forward and put his arm on the railing of the box as if following the play with enjoyment. Midway through the third act, during another outburst of laughter, David heard a sound like a shot. He looked up and saw that Lincoln had slumped forward against the railing, and that a man with a dagger in his right hand was leaping from the box toward the stage below. The man was young, dark haired, good-looking. As he was in the act of leaping, one of his spurs caught in the American flag that decorated the front of the box, and he landed awkwardly on the stage, nearly falling, but, straightening up, brandished his dagger and cried in a theatrical voice: *"Sic semper tyrannis."* Thus always to tyrants. David thought it must part of the play.

John Wilkes Booth had escaped the surveillance of Tom Bowls, Lafayette Baker's ace detective and David's acquaintance from San Francisco days. Bowls had been looking for Booth in the Niagara Falls area where Booth had made contact with Stanhope earlier and had received the money he was living on now and using to involve others in their conspiracy. Booth was twenty-six, a native of Maryland, a noted actor from a family of noted actors. His father had been a leading performer of Shakespeare. His brother, Junius, had produced and acted in plays in San Francisco for years and had, indeed, recently returned from California but had been unable to talk his younger brother out of his almost rabid Southern allegiances. John Wilkes Booth liked to think of himself as a member of the Southern gentry. He believed in aristocracy and in slavery. And he had a penchant for the role of Brutus who struck down Julius Cæsar in Shakespeare's play. Booth believed that in striking down Lincoln he might be striking a blow that would save an almost lost cause by throwing the North into turmoil and thus, by some miracle, give the South a chance yet to win.

Until tonight he had thought mainly of kidnapping Lincoln, as he and Stanhope had originally planned. But news that Jefferson Davis was still at large after fleeing Richmond and that the Confederates facing Sherman hadn't surrendered, plus his rage at thought of the President's enjoying the adulation of this theater audience and of millions more throughout the

North, had triggered him to this desperate act.

David heard Mary Lincoln's hysterical shriek: "They've shot the President!"

Booth limped off stage and disappeared. The blood on his dagger was not Lincoln's. It was the blood of young Major Rathbone who had leapt from beside his fiancée and grappled valiantly with Booth. But the blood on Mary Lincoln's hands came from the bullet hole at the back of the President's head.

Unaware of what had happened in Ford's Theater, Mornay was writing David joyfully: **Reverend Ardmore plans to retire on the first of September. I am submitting your name to the St. Giles vestry as a candidate to succeed him. Do you hear California calling?** Martha added a postscript: **You've escaped me too long, my dear volunteer. Will you now volunteer to come my way? There is a new world waiting for us in which I pray we shall never have to write letters to each other again.**

Chapter Forty-Four

Keeping to the high ridges, moving from place to place as silent as shadows, Francisco and Helek left no trace as they sought revenge for the deaths of Ta-ahi and Letke, yet sought also to survive and to keep the resistance alive. Buck and his Rangers came after them with dogs, but they left no tracks, and each morning they rubbed themselves with bay leaves or the leaves of the pungent sumac to conceal their body odors. They killed no game, lit no telltale fires, but subsisted entirely on nuts, seeds, berries. They still grieved for their loved ones, but Helek had begun to think more and more about Sally, his half-brother's wife. Someday he would have to leave the wilderness, and a girl like Sally would be his wife. Francisco sensed his son's growing needs. Yes, someday Helek would have to enter the world. But how, where?

And then one day when they were foraging separately as they often did — as a precaution against both of them being surprised and captured by the A-alowow — and then reuniting later at the cave or a thicket they had designated as that night's resting place, Francisco heard the old familiar call of the mountain quail repeated three times, the call of the resistance. He answered, and soon a familiar figure emerged from a clump of gray pines on the ridge not far ahead, and he recognized white-haired Halashu, whom he had last seen plowing his meager plot on the reservation. Before he heard Halashu's words, Francisco guessed what they would be.

"Lead us again, Francisco, lead us again. We want to be free. We heard your call. We have not forgotten." A litany of injustices perpetrated upon the reservation people by their dishonest government agent followed. "He's cheated us of food

304

and clothing that was rightfully ours, of implements and seed for our crops, even of our land which he gives to cronies or allows them to use." Other whites had encroached constantly, too, grazing cattle on their hunting and gathering grounds and crying — "Indian uprising!" — if they objected or resisted, "or shooting us dead!" Only soldiers from the nearby fort were sometimes helpful. "They intervened on our behalf, Francisco, even blamed the settlers for causing trouble. But the agent won't heed them. No one in authority over us will. It all comes down to greed, dishonesty, corruption," the old man wailed. "And we who went there freely in good faith are treated little better than troublesome animals."

"But is this not as I predicted long ago?" Francisco interposed wearily, "at the time of the dispersal, when you chose the reservation?"

"It is. But we can bear it no longer. My people, your people, have sent me to find you, to beg your help."

"But I have not only my own safety but that of my son to think about." And Francisco told how Buck and his Rangers pursued him and Helek and of the deaths of Ta-ahi and Letke.

"Ah, what a tragedy, what a tragedy!" deplored old Halashu. "But it is what we can expect. It is what makes me desperate and brings me here."

"You made your choice. Why do you come back upon me now?" Francisco demanded sternly.

"We were wrong. Be merciful. We ask your forgiveness. Help us now in our hour of need."

"And what is it you want me to do?"

"Lead us to your mother's Indianada. Her village welcomes all comers. It respects old customs and new. There we can be safe from the A-alowow. They dare not meddle there."

"I would not be too sure of that."

"Besides, you and your son can't remain in the wilderness

forever, can you?" old Halashu persisted. "With only yourselves for company? You must emerge sometime. Why not in this way . . . a way that may not only preserve you both but your people as well? Now that the great war among the A-alowow is over and peace is in the air and slaves are flocking to freedom, perhaps we shall be seen as doing likewise!"

Francisco remained unconvinced. "Why will it not be as before? When you behaved against my advice?" All along he had sensed it might come to this, that it might be an inevitable part of a tragic if glorious scheme in which he was to play a leading rôle. He felt it in his bones. But still he held back. "Soldiers will follow you if you leave the reservation. So will settlers. They will cry 'Indian uprising,' as you say. You will bring ruin not only on yourselves, but on me and mine."

Halashu took both his hands in his. "My son" — for Francisco was enough younger to be his son — "I've heard you say that the very act of resistance has merit, and that one path to survival and recovery of our rights may be to attract so much attention to our plight that changes might be made. Do not rule out this peaceful method. We shall not use force. There will be no violence on our part, I promise. We shall be the justly deserving . . . the wronged, the persecuted . . . trying to return home to our rightful place. As Kakunupmawa rules, listen . . . listen for the sake of your people, for the mother who bore you and who fights for you in her own way."

Francisco was moved by what the old man said. After all the slaughters, after all the other wrongs, this just might catch the public's attention and lead toward justice. It was a vision of such fantastic dimension, such grandeur, that it captivated Francisco's imagination. But reason told him it might never work, that such a procession of fugitives through the wilderness might never succeed in reality. Yet, in his imagination it already had, as it had in the imagination of noble old Halashu. And thus Francisco was won over. The thought of Helek helped and hindered. He feared for the boy's safety. Yet, here might be the way for Helek to enter the world. Buck and his Rangers might not dare resist such a peaceful and unexpected challenge in such a public context, for the world would surely be watching. Yes, this just might be the way to lift the darkness that had settled upon his soul since the death of his loved ones, a way to bring himself and Helek into the world and to create a new kind of resistance.

"Go back and talk to your people, Halashu. Talk especially to your young men who must be firmly controlled, if this scheme is to succeed without violence. Indeed, all your people, including women and children, must be whole-heartedly committed to it, or it will never work. Secrecy will be essential, too. Meanwhile, I shall go and talk with my mother and see if she is willing to receive us."

"Blessings be upon you!" old Halashu cried. "You are, indeed, the leader of your people. It shall be as you say," he reassured Francisco. "And when shall we meet again?"

"Here at this same spot when the moon is full again."

Francisco discussed it with Helek, and Helek agreed it must be done.

"It may end in bloodshed," Francisco warned.

"If so, I am ready," his son replied, "aren't you?"

"I am. But it may avenge Mother and Sister not by blood, not by death, but by life, a kind of life they would have joined in gladly, I think, don't you?"

And Helek agreed with that, too. "I am ready," he said simply, feeling closer to his father than ever before.

Old Clara, lying awake in the darkness, wondering if she would ever see son and grandson again, heard an owl call three

307

times from the hillside, then four times more. Some instinct lifted her from her bed and moved her to the open window. There she waited, and there was where Francisco found her. For a long moment they clung to each other in silence.

"After so long . . . at last you have come!" she gasped finally, holding him at arm's length to see him better in the starlight.

"I have come home, *Mamacita*."

She could no longer restrain the tears. They flowed in a gush of remorse and joy. He held her tenderly, while she wiped them away. "After all these years," she whispered, "after all these painful years!" And then practicalities asserted themselves, and she became her usual self once more. "Naked as a baby! Come in!" She pushed back the shutters. "You must be cold!"

He chuckled. "I go this way all the time. As did your father, as did all those men of old time. You saw my son and me. This is how we go, always."

"In resistance," she murmured to complete his point, "with a stone knife through the topknot of your hair!" She helped him over the sill into the room. "Clothing always was nonsense. So is everything but this." They sat side by side on her bed in the dark. "Tell me what it is you want?"

"I want your help, *Mamacita*."

He told her of the scheme he and Halashu had conceived. "It will be a peaceful migration from the reservation to your Indianada, the kind of thing you and my father dreamed of. Helek and I will lead it, and so come back to you, and so reënter the world. It will bring old ways and new together as never before in harmony and peace."

She was silent for a thoughtful moment. As if he were a child again, he found himself waiting her opinion. "It is madness," she said softly, tenderly. "It is magnificent madness." But her words vibrated with quiet joy.

"I knew you would approve."

"I don't approve," she said, fiercely bridling. "It is fool-hardy, crazy, just like you. Halashu is unreliable. I would never count on him. But," she hesitated, "I hope with all my heart and soul you will succeed. When will you come? I want to see your son. My heart breaks for what happened to your wife and daughter. How will you deal with the soldiers if they try to stop you? Or with the squatters if they intercept you?"

"Moving swiftly and secretly, we plan to arrive before that happens. Should it happen, we shall say we are coming peacefully to join your Indianada."

"What utter nonsense. The worst always happens. It is a beautiful idea. But it is madness. It will never work. You may be killed. So may Helek."

"But will you receive us, if we succeed?"

"Of course. With open arms. But do not attempt it, I beg you, for madness is what it is."

"Would you have me turn my back on our people?"

That silenced her.

"No," she resumed after a moment, "but I would have you alive. And my Helek alive. And both of you here under my roof."

"Then let us dream of that outcome while we work to implement it."

"And pray God to help!" she muttered.

"And pray God to help," he concurred in the old way she had taught him as a child, long neglected, now used again as he grasped for clearer, fuller understanding of what must lie ahead.

"Is my Helek with you?"

"He waits atop the bluff."

"Tell him his grandmother loves him. When shall I see you again?"

"When another moon has passed, if all goes well."

"Go quietly," she commanded. "Someone may be listening."

Wakened by the owl call, Sally roused Pacifico, who had been snoring beside her. "Go see if your grandmother's all right. I think I heard a noise in her room." She would have gone herself, but impatience with her husband's indolence and fecklessness was growing. Was she stuck for the rest of her life with this good-for-nothing who never did his share? She poked him again with her elbow. At last Pacifico got up and did as he was told.

But, as he approached Clara's door, he heard the soft voices behind it, took his hand from the latch, listened closely, heard much that passed between her and Francisco. It filled him first with astonishment, then anger, then a renewed desire to revenge himself for his father's neglect and his grandmother's scornful treatment of him. As he realized he had them both in his power, what seemed a brilliant idea came to him, an idea so daring he hesitated before lifting the latch until he felt sure Francisco was gone. Then he entered and found Clara still standing at the window, gazing into the darkness. "Excuse me, *Mama Grande*. I thought I heard someone."

She whirled on him indignantly. "Don't be ridiculous! It is such a warm night I opened the window."

"I thought I heard my father's voice," he persisted.

"Your father's voice?" she retorted. "How could that be?" But he sensed her underlying pretense, and it increased his confidence.

"I think you know more about that than I."

She faced him indignantly, in white nightgown and white nightcap, then abruptly she gave way, feeling he already knew, thinking it best to have him on her side. "Swear you won't tell anyone?" she commanded.

"I swear."

"Swear it by the silver buckle I gave you when I made you head of this household?" she insisted.

"Mama Grande," he feigned puzzled surprise, "why take on so? What's this all about? Of course, I swear by the buckle or by anything else you may require."

She snapped fiercely, unable to keep the annoyance out of her voice: "It's all about something very important, something very important, indeed!" As she told him of Francisco's visit and its purpose, he felt grimly exultant, supremely triumphant as never before, knowing that now he truly had them both at his mercy, these two who did not like him, even held him in contempt. "Why, whom should I tell, *Mama Grande?*" he persisted again when she pressed. "I won't even tell Sally."

She clasped both his hands in hers, suddenly intimate, suddenly sentimental. "You are my dearly beloved grandson! This can be the culmination of my fondest dream, of your grandfather's, too. Do you understand?" She beseeched him with all her strength, praying silently that he would understand, would join in her great hope.

"I understand, *Mama Grande*. Never fear. I understand thoroughly. You must go to bed now. You must trust me."

When he returned to his own bed, Sally asked sharply: "You were gone a long time. What was it?"

"Oh, some old owl waked her, and she wanted to tell me of her and my grandfather's dream for this valley . . . you know, the old story."

Sally was not quite convinced but accepted his explanation. He felt that now he had her in his power, too. Through Clara, whom she adored, he could strike at her. Pacifico lay awake most of the rest of the night, nursing his new-found sense of triumph. The future of Clara, of Sally, of his father, of the ranch itself, was in his hands if he chose to reveal what he knew.

Even so he might have done nothing. At such crucial moments Pacifico was apt to procrastinate and remember his crippled hand, and it seemed to ache more — "injured in the New Mexico Campaign where poor Benito lost his life," as he liked to say. So he let a month go by and might not have acted at all had he not encountered Buck Jenkins by chance at the river crossing midway between the hacienda and the cabins. Suddenly it seemed the moment he'd been waiting for. Both he and Buck were on horseback. They watched each other warily as they exchanged perfunctory greetings. After commenting on the hot weather, Pacifico ventured a casual: "Guess you heard the news?"

Buck replied with similar casualness. "About what?"

"The Indian uprising."

"Cain't say that I have," Buck drawled with even greater casualness, keenly alert for almost anything except what followed, as Pacifico told what Clara had told him. It flabbergasted Buck, but he acted as if it were nothing, crooked his right leg around his saddle horn, and began rolling a cigarette, offering Pacifico the makings. "You don't say? Now, ain't that somethin'?" And after Pacifico had rolled his smoke and they had both lit up and the dead match had floated away down the stream, Buck casually inquired: "When did you say all this was scheduled to transpire?"

"At the next full moon, likely."

Buck considered the tip of his cigarette and carefully shook a bit of ash from it and continued matter-of-factly: "That's right about now, ain't it?"

"Right about now."

Buck had long sought an ally in the enemy camp. Now he

312

thought he had found one. "Too bad about Sally," he said, as if unburdening himself to a bosom friend, repaying one confidence with another.

"Too bad?"

"I hate to say it. I hate to say such a thing about my own niece, about your own wife. But that's how it is. We're talking right frank, ain't we? Man to man, ain't we? Like neighbors should?"

Pacifico assured him they were.

"Well, then, too bad she's rotten at heart. Turned her back on us. She'll do it on you, I warn you, my friend. Once a turncoat, allus a turncoat, I say. She's after your land, your name. You know how women are. Twice as greedy as men when it comes to matters of property. Stop at nothing."

Pacifico crooked a reciprocal leg over his saddle horn and rested it casually on his horse's neck. The interest ignited in him by Buck's words burned deeply. The river was sole witness to their extraordinary understanding as Pacifico worked the conversation back to Francisco and the planned flight of Halashu's people from the reservation across the wilderness to Clara's Indianada. "They'll bring trouble with 'em, as I see it. I don't want 'em to march here with a lot of commotion and settle on this valley, crowd us out, and I don't guess you do, either, Buck. But," he shrugged, voice dropping away, "I don't suppose there's anything can be done about it. Just thought I'd let you know."

Buck seemed to meditate, inhaling and exhaling, while the water flowed at their feet and a mourning dove cooed in an alder nearby. The crossing was tree shaded, out of sight until you were almost there. At last he flicked his second cigarette butt into the stream and held out a brawny hand. "Pardner, I appreciate your frankness. You can count on me. That's the kind of man Buck Jenkins is. But I sure do agree with you."

313

His right eye narrowed ever so slightly. "It would be a pity for all them redskins to descend on this valley, make a big pow-wow here, crowd us out of house and home, spoil our peace and quiet. And it's a pity, a crying-out-loud shame, no one cain't do nothing about it."

When Sally asked Pacifico where he'd been, he replied coolly — "What business is it of yours?" — so that she looked at him sharply, as if at the sound of a new voice. He felt himself beginning to have his revenge, and it tasted sweet.

As for his meeting with Buck, Pacifico could foresee what would flow from it as clearly as if he were going to be there himself, and that foresight gave him profound satisfaction.

Chapter Forty-Five

The great war among the A-alowow, the Civil War, the War of the Rebellion, the War Between the States, was, indeed, over, and David was sitting his horse behind Sherman as they waited beside the national capitol with other staff officers to lead the army down Pennsylvania Avenue toward the White House. Sherman had declared: "By God, we'll out-march those Easterners, or I'll know the reason why!" It was now or never. The Eastern army, the Army of the Potomac, marched yesterday. Today it was the Western army's turn. It was Wednesday, May 24, 1865.

A signal cannon boomed; the bands struck up. Sherman leading the way on big bay Sam, the army began to move around the corner of the capitol building and down toward the President's House, and David felt this was the supreme moment of his life.

The avenue before him was like a river running between solid banks of people, solid walls of sound. Scores of thousands had come to see the Grand Review, especially to see Sherman's army, unseen by Easterners before. The much defeated Army of the Potomac was a familiar sight in and around Washington. Sherman's undefeated army had attained almost mythic status. It was the embodiment of victory.

People were in trees, on rooftops, at doors and windows, some cheering, some sobbing, some waving flags, some waving handkerchiefs, some were throwing flowers, some were holding children up to see. They knew this moment wouldn't come again; David's eyes met theirs. Theirs met his, and an understanding passed. This bright spring day was the culmination of four terrible years of national agony.

The cheers were louder than yesterday, louder than David had ever heard, and, when Sherman doffed his hat to acknowledge them, his dark red hair shone in the morning sun. This was his moment of vindication, his Biblical coming into the city, his and David's, his and the entire army's. Yesterday for six hours David had watched the Army of the Potomac march by, hoping he would see Reuben and the 191st Colored. Having missed them in Richmond, he had felt sure he'd find them here, marching among their fellow white soldiers of the Eastern army. But, no, he had not see them. Full of misgiving and rising anger, he had gone looking for them and had found them at a camp in some woods back across the Potomac where they had been literally segregated and left behind. "What happened?" he had asked Reuben after they had embraced. Reuben, now a captain, now commanding the company, left arm missing, left sleeve pinned to his chest below his Medal of Honor, had replied: "We don't know. We were supposed to march. I guess they forgot about us." But David hadn't thought they'd forgotten. He had thought the oversight deliberate. "Reuben, I'll look into this. First, tell me what happened to your arm?"

The Minié ball had shattered his wrist. Gangrene had set in. They had amputated the hand. Gangrene again. They had amputated the arm at the elbow. More gangrene. They had cut his arm off at the shoulder. "At least it was my left one."

"But you got your Medal of Honor."

"I thank you for recommending me." Reuben was among some twenty blacks to receive the nation's highest award for valor.

"And you're a captain now! Congratulations!" Reuben was one of the few blacks promoted from the ranks to the officer corps. "But, again, why weren't you and your men in the Grand Review?"

"I guess they decided they didn't want us," Reuben had joked wearily, bitterly.

"Damnation!" David had exploded in most un-Christian wrath as others of his old company gathered around him. "Cap'n David!" they had greeted him affectionately, had seized his hand, had embraced him, had laughed and delighted in him; and he had been swept up again in their comradeship and love, and his love for them, and then his bitter disappointment at their exclusion from the parade.

Later that evening he had found Stanton in his office as usual and had asked the Secretary about it. Stanton had thrown up his hands in disgust. "They were supposed to march. Then the order was countermanded. I objected. But President Johnson was afraid fighting might break out between white and black troops, prejudice remains so high. It's already broken out between white soldiers of the two armies. Also he feared that to include blacks might alienate some people at a moment of national healing."

"But what about the feelings of the blacks?"

"That's what I told him, but I was overruled." Thus two hundred thousand blacks who had served in uniform during the war were not represented in the Grand Review. "Nor will they be tomorrow," Stanton continued, "for Sherman's army will march without Negroes in uniform, as it has always marched."

"I think it a shame and a disgrace."

"So do I. At least we got the Medal of Honor for your friend, Stapp, and we equalized black soldiers' pay. The question of Sherman including them as volunteers in his army is moot, now, since both armies will soon be disbanded. In future our regular forces will be open to Negroes, and they will enlist there and do well, I predict."

"I agree, sir. I hope we can keep in touch about all of this."

"You'll be heading for California soon, I suppose?"

"As soon as possible."

"Speaking of California, reminds me of that New Almaden Quicksilver Mine scandal. We had solid evidence of fraud against Sedley and his crowd. But Lincoln insisted we drop the matter because so many gold miners felt their claims threatened by our move against New Almaden. War is a matter of money, you know, Major, as well as of blood." David would never forget those words. "The war was costing us three million a day, and the President didn't dare risk alienating California's gold, or Mister Sedley. You've done a good job. If hostilities weren't over, I'd promote you. Give Mornay my regards. He's been a great help, a very great help."

Behind David, now, Sherman's army stretched for twenty miles, back across the Potomac into Virginia. Sherman had ordered: "Don't gawk like country bumpkins. Keep eyes fixed fifteen feet ahead and march naturally, march like you marched through Georgia." Turning his head, David saw the army was doing so. A pretty girl ran out and handed Sherman a wreath of red roses. Sherman bowed and smiled. The cheers grew louder, the laughter happier. *Yes*, David thought, *this was a supreme moment of coming together, of peace at last, except for the excluded, like Reuben and his men. And what about Mutt Howell? And what about Beau?* A sharp pang of survivor's guilt, of sorrow, pity, surged through David. Still, the absent were there in spirit. They were marching in him and the others. This was their moment, too, this mighty convergence. It was as if the entire nation were here in one body and soul for this moment of epiphany and discovery of a new truth, a new self.

A girl with dark black hair and bold eyes like Vicky's ran out and handed him a spray of yellow daisies. Where was Vicky? And what was happening to Martha and Mornay and Gillem and Mary Louise and Eve and the others out there where the sun was just rising? Gillem had written from San Francisco: **Young fellow named Sam Clemens came in the other day and asked me for a job. Been working for the _Territorial Enterprise_ at Virginia City, Nevada, smack dab atop the Comstock Lode. "Walking on a hundred million dollars every day," as he put it. I couldn't use him, so he went on down the street to the _Morning Call_. Writes under the pen name "Mark Twain." Used to be a pilot on the Mississippi and says it's a steamboating term for "two fathoms." He's quite a humorist. I think you'd like him.**

The reviewing stand opposite the White House was roofed but open-sided, draped with flags and red, white, and blue bunting, and David could clearly see the President and Grant standing, side by side, to review them, and he reflected on President Andrew Johnson and Lieutenant General Ulysses S. Grant — Grant, once a bankrupt, young captain looking despairingly down that black hole in a San Francisco waterfront street, the dark hole of failure, whiskey on his breath — Grant had become now General in Chief of the Armies of the United States. David hadn't seen Johnson before but knew of his long fight against the powerful slaveholders who tried to control his native Tennessee. Gnarled, homey, earthy, Johnson was the only President who had never gone to school. A poor tailor's son, he had worked every inch of his way up the ladder of life. His young wife had read to him, had taught him to read. He had taught himself how to be political and battle the slave-owning oligarchy. Johnson might lack humor, tact, grace, as his critics said, but he had courage, honesty, strength. By the end of this day he would have reviewed one hundred and fifty thousand armed men of the United States in forty-eight hours, more than any other President before or since.

Sherman raised his sword in salute as he passed the stand, then turned aside into the White House grounds and dismounted and left his horse, and David did likewise and followed Sherman into the stand, Sherman snapping irritably over his shoulder: "Here's my chance to get even with your boss!"

As David reached the section reserved for aides and foreign observers, he saw Johnson extending his hand to Sherman.

Then Sherman was shaking hands with Grant. The two failures were now the two heroes. Like David, both had dreamed of wealth and happiness in a golden state. Both had failed. All three had since descended to the depths of near despair. Now they were united in victory, personal and national. And for Julia Grant and Ellen Sherman, sitting there, smiling, as they watched their husbands, this had to be also a vindication of the deepest kind.

And then Stanton was holding out his hand to Sherman, and Sherman was ignoring it. He was publicly snubbing the Secretary of War, not forgiving him for sending David to "look over my shoulder," not forgiving him for rejecting the lenient surrender terms Sherman had negotiated with the Confederate army in North Carolina, terms that might have brought peace from the Atlantic to the Río Grande along lines Sherman knew Lincoln had publicly announced. But Stanton had rejected them. Stanton had gone over to the hard-line Radicals. Stanton flushed at Sherman's snub and let his hand drop. Sherman moved on and took his seat.

Amused, yet saddened, by the enmity between two great, if flawed, leaders at this moment of peace and reconciliation, wondering if it was indicative of divisiveness and recrimination in the postwar nation, David watched the army passing in review in the long, swinging stride he knew so well. It had carried these lean, bronzed figures over so many undefeated miles — how many? a thousand? fifteen hundred? — from Donelson and Shiloh roundabout to Vicksburg to Chattanooga to Atlanta and Savannah and up through the Carolinas to this moment. Some were barefoot. Many wore beards. They wore the same tattered, faded clothes they had worn for months. Sherman wanted them to look exactly as they had on campaign, so all the world could know. Moving confidently with a self-reliant step, they seemed like heroes hallowed by hardship, peril, seemed pared to an essence of flesh and spirit, under their tattered battle flags. Many of the flags had been reduced to rags by weather and bullets. In their careless informality they were a striking contrast to the military precision, the spit and polish, of the Army of the Potomac David had seen yesterday.

As they passed the stand, they tore their hats from their heads and spontaneously cheered the President, Grant, Sherman. But where were those half million others who had died when you added up both sides? They, too, were part of the atonement, the purgation, the glory. And David felt his breath leave his body with the awe of it, the sorrow of it, the wonder of it, the terror and beauty of it, the mystical unity and brotherhood, as he heard a foreign diplomat behind him say to another: "An army like that could whip all Europe," and the other reply: "An army like that could whip the world!" He closed his eyes. His flesh and blood were part of this personal and national fulfillment, part of this atonement of the profoundest kind. A nation purged by blood, North and South. He likewise. Today, this moment, a new beginning. Ahead stretched vistas of unimaginable joy, out toward the Golden Gate, Martha, Mornay, a better world.

Then came the Negroes of Sherman's labor force. They carried picks, shovels, axes over their shoulders. They wore the ragged faded clothes in which they had fled to freedom and had labored for victory. They swung along, proudly in rhythm, grinning with happiness, irrepressibly singing and laughing in keeping with the beat of their feet and the band music. David thought how ironic it was that Sherman, often criticized for being anti-Negro, should be the general to have Negroes with his army in this Grand Review.

Then came more soldiers. Then came a dozen patient mules wearing Western-style pack saddles, carrying camp gear on one side and boxes of hardtack on the other, exactly as during the campaign, while others carried gamecocks and dogs and cats and even a pair of small black boys, all together eliciting uproarious cheers and laughter. Then came more blacks, men, women, children, dozens of them, some afoot, some on donkeys, some in wagons with pots, pans, bedding, all their worldly belongings around them. Among them were the army's black sweethearts, some in smocks, some in finery, also among them the shameless white "bummers," rascally foragers and looters, some in uniforms, some in rags, all there, all part of the whole. Sherman wanted the world to see his army as it truly was, and the world was seeing. It said so much about Sherman's rugged, if flawed, common sense, common humanity, that tears of emotion rose in David's eyes. He wished Lincoln might have lived to see this people's army, this victory, this reconciliation. Yes, there will be a new world.

The cheers were far louder than yesterday's. Perhaps because these were the almost mythic men from the West who had never been defeated. Perhaps because marching with them were the blacks who represented so much of what the nation had bled and died and hoped for, and was reborn into now. Perhaps because they all seemed to come from that region toward the setting sun that had captured the nation's imagination, from that frontier edge of the American people as they advanced westward into the future. Black and white, they were more than they knew or would ever know. Tears filled his eyes at sight of them, marching off so gallantly, so good-humoredly into history, never to pass here again, never to raise the battle cry of freedom again — at least not in the old way. But there would be other ways.

Collecting himself, David looked around and saw Sedley watching him with an ironic smile. His first reaction was total astonishment, total disgust. Why, how, by what quirk of fate, should this creature, so apparently antithetical to all he most deeply believed and cherished and had just experienced so profoundly, be here?

In fact, Sedley had stayed on in Washington after Lincoln's death for good business reasons. Sensing uncertain political weather ahead, he had wished to ingratiate himself with the new President. Next Monday he would meet with Johnson and his cabinet to discuss retirement of the war debt and repeal of the income tax, first in the nation's history, that had helped pay for the war. Sedley also had wanted to renew acquaintance with Grant and Sherman, the two most powerful men in the nation after Johnson, both of whom he knew as needy men in California, both of whom might need money again. There was much talk of them being future Presidents. Sedley also had wanted to speak further with Halleck about expediting Clara's appeal to the Supreme Court, now that Chief Justice Taney had died.

He wasn't surprised at sight of David. The newspapers had informed him of his old adversary's new status as war hero and close associate of Sherman and Stanton. Here or wherever, in uniform or out, David was simply one of those arrayed against him in the natural struggle between the haves and have-nots. Sedley accepted that conflict as part of life, while

323

ironically noting David's evidently emotional response to the spectacle now before them both. For Sedley the Grand Review was simply the business of the moment, nothing to get excited about.

War that exchanges blood for gold, David thought with disgust as their eyes met. *Your gold, my blood.* His anger rose as he thought of Shiloh and Stanhope's Bend, and with a mighty resolve he swore again never to rest until humankind was changed for the better and a New Jerusalem created on this suffering, misguided earth. But then he collected himself to dissemble and play the game of appearances, and he smiled back affably at Sedley, wondering where Vicky was.

Vicky was at that moment in the wilds of western Texas, riding toward the Río Grande with General J. O. Shelby and a remnant of his famous Iron Brigade, eight hundred strong, their red battle flag still flying, still undefeated, Union cavalry hot on their trail. Dick Taylor had been killed at the battle of Pilot Knob. Vicky had shot down the blue trooper who had killed him. Now she was Shelby's lover. Stanhope had sent word to her. **Ride for Mexico. I'll meet you there.**

After the review was over, David met Reuben on the steps of the capitol as planned. Twilight had come, and the lights were being lit, but people still thronged in and out of the great building under its mighty dome atop which stood the Statue of Liberty — later called the Statue of Freedom — a female figure with sword in one hand representing war, flowers in the other representing peace. David told Reuben how he had first seen the statue lying on the ground at the time of Lincoln's first inaugural address when moved by compulsion he, David, had walked out of his church in Philadelphia and had come down and stood in the crowd before the unfinished capitol, the unerected Statue of Liberty "while Lincoln spoke of the threat of disunion, of war, but of the mystic cords that hold our nation together." Now the dome was finished, the union saved, the statue in place, up there in the dusk, brooding in the twilight over this day and the unfinished business of freedom.

David gripped Reuben's arm, almost too full of emotion to speak further, and then with sudden impulse: "Reuben, let's stage our own Grand Review. Will you walk with me down Pennsylvania Avenue to the White House?"

"Why, of course, I will!" Reuben declared, catching the spirit of the occasion, "but won't it be a long walk for your game leg?"

"Not any longer than for your game arm."

People were staring at them, some admiringly, some just curiously. A black officer was a rare sight in Washington City, especially one with only one arm. "He dressed up in those clothes?" David heard a woman's voice ask suspiciously. Some people still couldn't believe there were bona-fide black soldiers in the Union Army, let alone black officers, let alone one wearing the blue ribbon and gilt-bronze star of the Medal of Honor that matched the one on David's breast.

"Come on, then, let's start!" David laughed aloud in delight at the prospect of what lay ahead for the two of them, as they descended the steps and began walking down the grand avenue into the future, into the darkness where there was yet so much light.

"Reuben, the armies will be disbanded soon. Shall we go West together?"

"Yes, let's go West together."

Chapter Forty-Six

On the day of the next full moon Francisco and Helek crouched in a clump of wild lilac at the crest of the ridge near the gray pines where Francisco had met old Halashu a month earlier and where they had planned to meet again. It was nearly noon, and Halashu had not appeared. Francisco was beginning to think the old man had proved unreliable, as Clara had warned, and that their plan for a peaceful exodus of the reservation people through the wilderness to Clara's Indianada was dead, when there was movement under the pines beyond the grassy opening and a procession of harried-looking women, children, and old men came into view. At the same time there were rifle shots in the distance beyond the ridge and then a distant shout. Then Francisco knew in what fashion Halashu had failed to keep his word to come secretly and in peace — in fact, seemed to have come prematurely with all his people and with violence — and Francisco's heart sank with disgust, and weariness rose in him, for this was almost exactly as he had feared.

The harried procession of fugitives stared with astonishment at sight of two nearly naked men emerging from a lilac thicket, and some of the girls and young women giggled, for Francisco and Helek wore only their waistnets and were barefooted and carried their flint knives thrust through their topknots. They stared back at these refugees of their own kind who wore clothes with a modesty which seemed false, deserving as these people might be in other ways. Helek could not take his eyes off the girls. He felt shy under their eyes, different from them, yet not unwelcome as they began to smile. They had never seen anything like him, a wild man so young, handsome, all but naked. Yet fear was driving them, and with the rest they came forward and gathered around the two, crying in breathless, frightened voices: "Save us! The soldiers are close behind!"

Many of the refugees carried their belongings on their backs in conical-shaped baskets. Some carried babies lashed upright in willow cradle frames. Other children toddled bravely alongside like frightened wild things. At sight of these harassed people of his own blood, compassion began to overcome Francisco's initial disgust, and he demanded: "The soldiers? What's happened? Where is Halashu?"

An old woman, withered, yet vigorous, tousled white hair nearly covered by a red bandanna, pushed forward. Francisco recognized Alaquta-ay, Halashu's wife, whom he had last seen hoeing in the corn patch beside Halashu's plowed field, raising her hand beside his to acknowledge the quail call of the resistance that Francisco made them that day. Now she burst out: "Halashu fights beside our young men."

"But why did he act so prematurely? Why did he not wait?"

"Because our young men would not wait. They were impatient for freedom. They were also inspired by our new medicine man."

"Medicine man?" Francisco recalled Halashu's mention of a new prophet, come from the north, and the high hopes he was raising.

"Yes, his magic will protect us from the white man's bullets and will make the white man go away and leave the land to us as it once was." Alaquta-ay's eyes shone with fanatical belief despite her evident exhaustion. It was a measure of these people's desperation, Francisco thought.

Even so, things had gone well at first. They'd slipped away in small groups from the reservation under cover of darkness, and after all night and all day of steady travel were climbing the slope of the great ridge toward this meeting place when the soldiers overtook them "and fierce words broke out between them and our young men, and shots were fired. We wounded one."

You'll wish you hadn't, Francisco predicted to himself. He could see it all clearly and hear the words that would soon be spreading far and wide and appearing in newspapers: "Indian uprising! Runaways from reservation take to warpath!" But he said aloud in a commanding tone: "My son and I have come to help you." He turned to Helek. "Lead them off along the ridge till you reach the sacred precinct of the House of the Sun. If we have not overtaken you meanwhile, wait for us there. I shall wait here for Halashu and the fighting men." And, as he watched the fugitives hurry off after Helek, he heard shots and shouts coming nearer from behind the ridge.

Soon old Halashu and a young fellow who must be the new medicine man appeared — Halashu looking weary and distraught, the young man trying to appear confident. He wore a long white shirt of bleached deerskin and a feathered headdress over long dark hair. He was emaciated, wild-eyed, apparently expressive of a new idea, but actually, as Francisco perceived with weariness and renewed disgust, embodying a futile and forlorn hope. The A-alowow would not go away no matter what color shirt he wore and how hard this melancholy yearling danced or exhorted. Life was inexorable. And time was running out. "I thought you were coming alone and in peace to speak further with me," he upbraided Halashu. "Instead you come with all your people and bring war."

The old man threw up his hands. "I could not help it. My young men are filled with impatience and desire for freedom. Hear how they fight back?" There was the sound of another shot.

"They will be filled with lead, some of them," Francisco retorted bitterly, "but that cannot be helped now. You failed to keep your promise, Halashu. But I shall keep mine. Who is this with you?"

"This is Tagich, the sacred messenger I told you of. He brings a powerful new magic."

"Well, we shall need it," said Francisco grimly, with a nod of restrained greeting.

Tagich gave him a similar nod.

Halashu asked: "You spoke to your mother?"

"I did. She will receive us gladly."

A shot sounded close at hand. But Tagich did not flinch, and Francisco decided he might have to respect him.

"The A-alowow are at our heels!" groaned Halashu.

"Of course!" Francisco quickly weighed up the factors. It was nearly mid-afternoon. Helek and the women and children should be nearing the House of the Sun. As he was thinking, harried grim-faced warriors began to slip silently into view. Halashu called, and they came toward him. Francisco greeted them in traditional fashion — "Ho!" — holding up his right hand, receiving their acknowledgments, sometimes merely a nod. They were in the thick of a life and death struggle, he realized, tough-looking fellows, most of them young, willing to take risks, already battle hardened, he could see. And somehow, secretly over the months and years, they had contrived to equip themselves with weapons and learned how to use them despite regulations to the contrary. His heart went out to them. They seemed ready to risk all, as he had done.

"Let us fight together," he said to them. Explaining where the women and children had gone, he added: "We must delay our enemies to gain time, so let us set fire in this dry grass and let West Wind help us!" He knelt with his fire stick to set the first blaze. Soon a dozen were flaring, and the wind, which reached briskly into the high country almost every afternoon in summer, was catching up the fire and running with it to throw it in the face of the A-alowow, as Francisco led the way off along the ridge to overtake Helek and his party.

Chapter Forty-Seven

Buck was sliding shiny new cartridges into his Henry rifle. His loaded Remington was already in its holster at his belt. "What's up? Why this cat-that-swallowed-the-canary look?" Iphy demanded. Buck paid her no heed.

"Shut up, Ma!" Goodly was loading his Spencer carbine. Like Buck he seemed preoccupied.

Old Abe said: "Injuns don't scalp easy these days, boys. Not like old days. Better remember that!"

"An' they don't sell for what they used to bring, the women and kids don't," Opal put in, encouraged to intervene by Iphy's example. She and Elmer had no sympathy with Buck's and Goodly's sometimes secret, sometimes merely questionable, doings.

" 'Sides, it's ag'in' the law now," Elmer pointed out. He had just come in from work, shirt stuck to his body with sweat. It was August, and the last of the hay had to be stacked. Elmer spoke with the sullen resentment of the farmer, the footman, for the horseman. "There's aplenty to do out there!" he added significantly.

Little Opaline and Abraham, Junior, had followed him in. They all stood silently just inside the open door of the cabin, forming with the others a kind of jury, sitting and standing in judgment on Buck and Goodly.

Buck addressed his father grudgingly. He thought the old man far gone in senility. "Let me give it to you straight from the shoulder, Dad. There's a Indian uprisin' a-brewin'. I got word on the q. t. You and that daughter-in-law o' yours" — meaning Iphy — "don't want to lose your scalps, do you?"

Abe's eyes narrowed with gravity. "You sure you know

where you're headed?"

Buck met his look. The generational differences between father and son, old and new, the then and the now, rose between them. "I'm sure."

But Abe declined to abdicate his position as patriarch and leader of his people in their destined search for the promised land, a new home in a golden state. He shook his head skeptically. For emphasis he spit into the coffee can on the floor by the near leg of the puncheon table where he sat, wearing frayed and faded buckskins as usual. "Seems late in the day for an Injun uprisin'. If I was a Injun, I would of uprose before now. Don't make sense now. I'd have to be crazy to try it now."

"Maybe they are crazy" — Goodly snapped the last cartridges into his carbine — "but they can still put an arrow between your shoulder blades."

Iphy placed her hands on hips and guffawed. "You make me sick, you two. Forever seein' red men behind every danged tree in the forest. Who you think you are, Daniel Boone? This here's modern times, like Granpa says. The war's over. You two ought to act like you've growed up at last, but I reckon" — she sighed sarcastically — "that's a-askin' too much. That'll take another hundred years. Granpa," she turned to Abe for support, "give 'em some of that asafetida o' yours. It might bring 'em 'round!" She referred to the little leather bag of beneficial herbs Abe carried for health and good luck, slung from a deerskin string around his neck, hidden by shirt and snow-white beard. Like a family secret it was rarely mentioned. He shook his head.

"Asafetida'll not do it, daughter-in-law. Some things is curable by medicine, some ain't. This here ain't. Boys," he turned sternly on his two descendants, "listen to me. We got plenty on our plate here. We got a decision of the court about our

331

claims to this land being good, if hers ain't." He waved a hand toward the hacienda. "We got a crop to harvest. And we got a cow with colic, and a horse with the blind staggers, and a cat that's lost her meow, and I got a achin' back . . . and I got a achin' mind the more I think 'bout where you're headed. We don't need scalps. We need peace, quiet. Right now strikes me as a mighty poor time to start another war."

"Dad, it's them who's started it." Buck was equally serious in his turn. He knew his old father was approaching the end. A bit longer, a year or two, and the family would have a new head, himself. Meanwhile, he must try to keep a failing mind in touch with reality.

"They?"

"Him. That greaser half-breed. He's behind the whole thing. He's fixin' to overrun the valley with Injuns. He hates our guts. I hate his. An' I'll get him, if it's the last thing I do!"

Abe spit a final time. "Don't talk about last things, Son. Somebody might be listenin'."

Turning their backs on the family jury, Buck and Goodly mounted up and rode away, without further word, to gather the Rangers and hurry into the wilderness to intercept Francisco and Halashu and their people.

Iphy cried out with sudden foreboding as she watched them go. "You spoke it true, Granpa. They don't know where they're headed. . . . They don't, they don't!" Her eyes went wild as if she'd seen something frightful, as she ran to the door and shouted after them: "Come back, you crazy fools! Come back, come back!" But they rode on unheeding.

From the hacienda Pacifico watched them go with quiet satisfaction.

The fires served to delay the soldiers as Francisco and Halashu and their fighting men hurried on toward the House of the Sun. There they overtook Helek and the women and children and older men, and all moved on toward the ancient trail up which Francisco and Helek had once climbed, that led down to the river and the lowlands and Rancho Olomosoug. But as they started to descend, they saw, far below, Buck and Goodly and the Rangers, twenty or more, coming toward them, and the Rangers saw them and sent up an exultant shout. When the fugitives turned back, they saw the blue dragoons in the distance coming toward them along the ridge. So they hastened to take refuge in the only place left them, the sacred precinct at the House of the Sun where the First People, turned to stone, arose from the earth in the form of those great, rocky outcroppings that formed a rough circle around the largest rock of all containing the sacred cave.

"Let us fight here where Kakunupmawa and the First People will fight beside us," Francisco proposed, and the other leaders agreed, and the fighting men took up strong positions among the rocks that enclosed the hallowed precinct with its perennial spring, while the women and children and older men took shelter in the hollow below the cave rock, screened from all directions, just as the troopers approached from the one hand and the settlers from the other. "Fire shots to warn, not to kill," Francisco commanded. He saw negotiation as the best way out of their dire predicament.

The shots were fired, and the dragoons drew back and took cover, uncertain of what lay ahead, as did the settlers, while Buck shouted in triumph: "We've run 'em to cover, boys. Just take your time, now!"

As twilight fell and they sat in council and prayer in the great Cave of the Sun, the House of Kakunupmawa, the image of Kakunupmawa almost invisible on the wall behind them, Helek on guard at the side window entrance, Francisco and Halashu and Tagich discussing strategy. "In the morning they will either attack or ask us to surrender. If it is surrender, the decision will be ours," Francisco said. He felt this was the final round, the culmination, here at the House of the Sun, an appropriate place at the deepest heart of his people's world, the world Buck and the soldiers wished to take from them forever.

"We shall never surrender," Halashu vowed. "Not now! Not after all that's happened!"

Francisco upbraided him. "How can I trust you?"

"Because we have already fought side by side."

It was a good answer. Francisco clasped the old man's hand. "Then let us persevere, old warrior, and know that Kakunupmawa will stand beside us, here at his house, and that what we do here will not be forgotten, but will be remembered as a credit to ourselves and our people, and may even cry out for us to the world. Do you agree?"

"I agree!"

"We must at all costs keep them from getting inside our circle of rocks, while husbanding our scarce ammunition and arrows," Francisco asserted further. "We must shoot only to kill or only when certain we can wound, while exposing ourselves very little, so that they do not know where we are. We must make them pay as dearly as possible. It may cause them to pause and consider."

"And if they propose a truce?"

"We must be wary of that. It is a method they treacherously use to destroy others. Yet it is perhaps our best hope." Francisco spoke realistically of the heavy odds, their shortage of food and ammunition, the unlimited numbers and resources of the enemy. "But the longer we hold out, the more the world . . . the more Kakunupmawa and all the Sky People . . . will rally to the justice of our cause."

Helek felt pride and admiration surge even higher as he

listened, realizing his father was truly a leader of their people.

But their predicament opened the way for Tagich to intervene, and the young shaman said in a voice weighty with surprising authority, coming from one so youthful and frail-looking, that this trouble would never have occurred had old Halashu and Francisco listened more closely to him. The solution, he insisted, now lay in his supernatural power. "Negotiations are foolishness. Let us have a dance, and afterward I shall scatter a magical powder around our camp, so that white man's bullets will never touch us. And if they try to enter the circle I shall draw, they will drop dead!" It was what many wanted to hear, including Halashu, and Francisco was obliged to accept it in the interests of unity.

Therefore, a weird chanting soon came to the ears of the whites, as they waited in various stages of alertness and apprehension out beyond the mysterious enclave of contorted rocks. Concealed in the hollow at the base of the cave rock, the People of the Land and the Sea were dancing by the light of a full moon, faces painted red, women and men intermingling around Tagich who danced as they did, chanting in unison as their left feet moved forward together, and their right feet were drawn up beside their left, and all swayed together, slowly, emphatically, around and around; while Moon, the great eye of the night sky, rose higher, and the smaller, but always unmoving, forever unchanging eye of Sky Coyote, the North Star, regarded them unblinkingly.

They danced and sang, and the white men, lying in their blankets or standing at their posts, felt superstitious shudders and uncertainties as to their future, as they recalled stories of ferocious Indian warriors, scalpings, tortures, magical dances. Buck grunted to Goodly: "Hear them damned savages? Tomorrow we'll make 'em sing a different tune, eh?"

Afterward Tagich went out ceremoniously alone with his

pouch of red ochre powder and scattered it in a circle around the defensive perimeter.

"The fellow's a fool and will in the end do more harm than good!" Francisco muttered.

"But many believe in him!" Halashu cautioned.

Toward morning Helek heard the mournful cry of the poor-will, so lonely, so melancholy, like a dirge, heralding what was to come. Yet he felt keen anticipation, too, as he thought of Kakunupmawa, in whose house they had taken refuge, who would rise with the dawn and bestride the world with his great torch in hand. And perhaps his thumb would slip a little and his fire would burn the murderous A-alowow who intruded on his domain and threatened his people with death.

Next day broke hot and still. "If they rush us, lie low, cling to the rocks, our friends and allies," Francisco advised the defenders as he made final round of the perimeter, the knife in his hair his emblem of resistance. "Let them eddy in among our rocks if they dare. Shoot to kill from above and below. From behind and in front. From every unexpected direction. So that they do not know which way to turn to find us."

At sunrise the voice of Captain Luther Lindsay broke the portentous silence. Lindsay called on Halashu and his band "and all others who might have joined you" to surrender and "thus avoid further bloodshed. I promise you a safe return to the reservation and no reprisals." Lindsay did this despite Buck's earlier objections: "They're killers. They don't want peace. Blood is what they want. Blood is what we oughta give 'em."

Homer Gatlin put in: "Injuns done for my boy Stubby. I'd like to do for them." He didn't say which Indians had killed Stubby.

Nearly as many settlers as soldiers had congregated at the

scene, and many like Buck and Homer were urging bloodshed.

There was no reply to Lindsay's offer. The rocks remained ominously silent. "I give you one last chance!" he shouted through cupped hands. Lindsay was short, and thickset, dark, well intentioned, and here he was, out in this god-forsaken wilderness ingloriously chasing people who wanted only to be let alone and return to their homes. It made him sick. But it had to be done.

When his voice echoed off the silent stone and there was no answer, he ordered his dismounted troopers to edge forward in a skirmish line.

Buck and the settlers waited under cover on the opposite side of the perimeter "to intercept 'em if they run," as Buck had explained to Lindsay, since to advance on the circle of rocks from every side might mean shooting each other. Lindsay saw through this excuse for keeping out of harm's way, although it made sense under the circumstances.

The defenders, thirty-one fighting men, did as Francisco advised. And as Kakunupmawa climbed higher, torch in hand, till he reached the summit of the sky, it seemed to Helek — on guard at the cave by his father's orders, fuming at missing the fight — that Kakunupmawa's thumb deliberately slipped and let unmerciful heat fall upon the A-alowow, while the People remained hidden in shady places, using their weapons with deadly effect.

By nightfall three troopers had been killed, five wounded. Lindsay realized he had failed. "Wonder where in hell they got their repeating rifles?" he speculated gloomily to Buck. Several of the People were using new Henrys and Spencers, while Lindsay's men carried outmoded Sharps single-shot carbines. "They're clever, Lindsay, devilish clever." Then Buck adopted his most sagacious tone. "They got water at their spring, I reckon, but not much food. Why not starve 'em out?"

But that seemed too slow. For all his good intentions, Lindsay wanted honor, glory, promotion. So Lindsay ordered another attack next morning. But his men were more reluctant than ever to press against the prickly perimeter of rocks, bullets, arrows, plus adversaries they couldn't see, and they fell back with two additional wounded, while the People escaped injury.

Inside the perimeter Tagich exulted: "They dare not cross my magic red line, while we remain unharmed!"

That night there was a victory dance, the People joining hands, faces painted red with two horizontal black lines on each cheek and Tagich wearing his white deerskin shirt, predicting in guttural sing-song as they all moved in unison that this was the beginning of the end, their ancestors would return from the dead, the white men would disappear, and the land be again as it was, "our land, teeming with game and seeds and bulbs and berries, and peace!"

Francisco's eyes moistened despite himself at the tragedy of it all, the unutterable, pitiful tragedy.

The girls and young women looked around inquiringly for Helek, but, though attracted, he was shy and didn't join in the dance, having his mind also on that image of a girl with white skin and yellow hair who would be his mate some day.

Chapter Forty-Eight

"Battle?" Clara demanded with dread. "What battle?"

Pacifico had returned from town with news of the fighting at the House of the Sun. With well-feigned concern he gave particulars to Clara who sat on the verandah, sunning herself. She felt less energy these days. "Francisco is leading the runaways. But soldiers and settlers have surrounded them." While he spoke, as if deeply deploring the whole matter, he saw with satisfaction how the news upset her.

"Saddle me a horse!" she commanded, heart beginning to pound. "I shall go and see for myself!"

"*Mama Grande,*" Sally remonstrated, "it might only worsen matters. And it's a very long way." She turned on Pacifico. "Why don't *you* go and help your father? That's where Buck and them were headed, I bet!" she cried with sudden prescience and added: "And I bet you knew! That's what Isidro meant when he said he saw you two, you and Buck, talking at the crossing!" Pacifico tried to bluff it through, but she was on him fiercely. "You *did* know! I can see you did!"

Abruptly Clara intervened. Laying her eyes on Pacifico, suddenly she knew. "You knew where Buck was going?" And as the whole truth dawned, her fury rose. "You told him! You told him where to go! You told him all!" She saw the guilt in his face, and it nearly killed her with anguish and despair, while enraging her even further. "You are a coward and a sneak," she shouted, "as well as a traitor. You've betrayed your own flesh and blood and mine!" she stormed. "Give me back that belt. Give me back the belt with the silver buckle I gave you when I made you head of this household. You're no longer fit to wear it!"

339

With a furious burst of energy she rose from her chair and stripped it from him as he stood shamed and unresisting. Turning to Sally, she held it out: "Here, you take it. You wear it. You're the head, the *Señora* to be." The words glowed as they poured from her. "Daughter of my spirit, if not of my flesh, I entrust this house, this land, this life, to you. You wear this belt. You carry on!"

Horrified, infuriated, and dismayed by what Pacifico had said and by what Clara had just done, Sally was now also filled by a rush of profound joy and determination as she accepted the ancient symbol of authority that Clara had handed out to her — which called on her to assume responsibility, to be great. "I thank you, *Mama Grand*e," she murmured, as the old eyes looked unwaveringly into hers, and hers responded with similar spirit. "It is a great honor. I shall try to wear it well." And she took it and buckled it around her waist, noting that it fit perfectly.

Pacifico had slunk away. The two women stood there alone, facing one another.

"I shall go to San Francisco and speak to Eliot Sedley. He will speak to the governor." Clara was imagining now, more than affirming, as her strength ebbed away. "This war must be stopped!" But her heart still beat like a hammer, beating into her consciousness the growing frailty she never admitted even to herself. The verandah, the landscape beyond, reeled a little, and she abruptly sat down again. A dark feeling of impotency and despair settled upon her.

"It would be a long and tiring trip," Sally suggested tactfully, seeing how matters stood. "Why not wait till we hear more, till we are sure?"

"We might hear too much!" But Clara made no move to leave her chair.

Father O'Hara appeared from the doorway behind them.

"Ah, here you are!" Unaware that Pacifico had preceded him, he, too, had come with news of the battle.

"Will it end peacefully?" Clara beseeched him.

O'Hara settled into his usual chair. "I hope and believe!"

"But is that enough, Father?" Clara cried. "I've hoped and prayed and believed all my life, and look at me! Bereft of husband, as good as bereft of son and grandson . . . ," she trailed off, thinking of Francisco and Helek, then grimly of Pacifico.

"What grandson?" O'Hara was puzzled. "Has something happened to Pacifico?"

Indeed something had, she thought, but shook her head and decided, instead, to tell him and Sally of that encounter with Francisco and Pacifico on the bluff above the house years ago and of her plan and Francisco's and Halashu's for them to lead the reservation people to her Indianada "and now they must be surrounded by soldiers and that execrable Buck Jenkins and his men!"

Sally was speechless with wonder. O'Hara took a deep breath, put hands on knees, surveyed Clara with wonder and admiration. Of all their intimacies this was perhaps the most revealing. "And you hoped they could come here and take refuge and implement that dream you and your husband shared, and I share, too! Magnificent!" He smiled gravely. "I thought I was bringing you news. But here's news, indeed." Then still more gravely: "It places a heavy burden on you, doesn't it?"

"Yes."

"But doesn't it make you justly proud and grateful . . . that such a burden, such a blessing, has been entrusted to you?"

"But, Father, I don't want such blessings!"

He continued gently: "Maybe God knows that, as I do. Maybe He's just testing you . . . testing you so that you can show your greatness, your worthiness . . . so that you can be an example to others."

She grew still and small inside. "Father, isn't that asking too much?"

He shrugged. "Does God ever ask too much? Hasn't He given you a son, and a new-found grandson, life, this moment? And this magnificent ranch?" He waved a hand at it. "How can you fail to be grateful, to accept whatever else He may give you?"

She was silenced, feeling him right, yet not sure she had the strength to measure up to the challenge he held out.

Chapter Forty-Nine

Captain Lindsay's third attack had been repulsed with more
casualties when Major Billings, agent at Conejo Indian Reservation, arrived at the House of the Sun and explained to Lindsay
and to newly arrived news reporters that Halashu and his fugitives, while on the reservation, were so infected by the words
of their new shaman "that they refused to plow or plant or do
any other kind of productive work, but insisted on living in
their old barbaric way on wild plants, berries, fish, and game
while disregarding all efforts to civilize them and all prohibition
against dancing and the practice of their old pagan religion.
They've become unmanageable," Billings averred, sorrowfully
shaking his head as if in commiseration with the unfortunate
runaways, though actually busily engaged in feathering his nest
at the expense of both Indians and the federal government.
Billings was not a military man. He had been given the name
Major by an ambitious mother who had hoped he would succeed accordingly. And in his own view he had. "Before returning they should be made to renounce all wild ways, including
their pernicious dancing and superstitious religion."

"Let's get them to surrender first, sir," the harassed Lindsay
replied shortly. "Will you help? Perhaps they'll listen to you
and come with us peacefully."

But when Billings addressed the rocky stronghold, promising its defenders good treatment and no reprisals, if they returned with him to their former home — "Where I guarantee
that you will receive blankets, food, clothing, cloth for dresses,
needles and thread and buttons." — there was no answer. And
Billings went away with a sorrowful face, telling Lindsay these
savages were incorrigible.

A nighttime sortie by the defenders at the House of the Sun wounded two troopers and netted the People a Colt revolver and a Sharps carbine.

A retaliatory attempt by Lindsay to burn the People out failed when a change of wind drove the flames back upon the attackers. Again Tagich claimed credit. But Francisco's original strategy of lying low amid the great rocks and outcroppings was actually what prevailed. And, as if Kakunupmawa was helping them, the defenders discovered much needed food in the innumerable caches of acorns, nuts, seeds, made by squirrels, rats, and mice in the many holes, nooks, and crannies of the rocks of his sacred precinct. Kakunupmawa seemed to fight on their side, too, thought Helek, as day after day the sun beat mercilessly upon the attackers as if bent on destroying them, while the defenders rested in their cool caves and crevices. Again Tagich claimed credit, implying his power was greater than Francisco's. But when two warriors were hit by bullets, despite his assurances of invulnerability, and one of them died, his reputation suffered. Even old Halashu's face showed doubts, and old Alaquta-ay and the other women wailed the death song, wondering how much longer they themselves might survive.

"Hear the damn witches!" raged Buck. "I tell you, Lindsay, they're savages." Buck was constantly at Lindsay's elbow, shouldering his way through reporters or giving them interviews as "leader of the Volunteer Rangers and the Settlers' League, co-ordinating our activities with those of the United States Army."

Lindsay realized Buck and the settlers were using him, and that his men bled while others talked, but then Buck took a new tack. "Let me parley with 'em, Lindsay. I'm a old hand at it. They're scairt of you soldiers, anyway. I'll make a treaty with 'em that'll last!" he promised grimly.

Lindsay demurred. "This is my scrap, Jenkins. I'm into it, and I want to finish it. But why don't you fellows take a little of the heat off my boys for a change?"

"That's just what I'm aimin' to do," replied Buck grandly, "but you won't listen!"

Some of the more sensible settlers took exception to Buck's views and style, but his established position made it difficult for them to be heard.

As the Santa Lucia War, as some were calling it, dragged on, it became a celebrated cause. Most people, on learning of it, adhered to the accepted view that the only good Indian was a dead one. But up in San Francisco, Mornay and his group decried what was happening at the House of the Sun, and down in Los Angeles Eve and hers did likewise, as did Reuben and David meeting in St. Louis to come West together. A nationwide sympathy for Indian rights was slowly developing. Eve decided to go and report the situation for Gillem. Overcoming all obstacles as usual, she arrived at the House of the Sun, observed the stalemate, learned that the fugitives claimed to have been on a peaceful march to take refuge with old Clara, decided she must interview Clara, made her way roundabout on foot, by wagon, by stagecoach, and buggy to Rancho Olomosoug, and there Clara confirmed the fugitives' claim, adding proudly: "My son is among them. He will lead them to me, if he's allowed to. I hope what's happening will bring the government to its senses."

Eve's impassioned report was widely circulated and aroused much sympathy for the People, and for a moment it seemed that a peaceful settlement might be possible.

But, instead, two companies of infantry plus a battery of mountain howitzers and two brass 24-pounder Coehorn mortars arrived at the House of the Sun under command of Colonel

Armstrong Embree who relieved Lindsay. Embree, burly, blond, egotistical, a veteran of Gettysburg and the Grand Review down Pennsylvania Avenue, was looking for his brigadier-general's star as he turned this embarrassing situation into victory before the eyes of all the world and his superiors. "We'll parley with 'em first," he advised Lindsay and Buck. "That's my orders from General McDowell in San Francisco. And from Washington City, I might add. Grant and the President are much concerned." Though he had had no experience fighting Indians, Embree wore his curly yellow hair down to his shoulders as though he were a Western mountain man. He secretly believed that his mere appearance in uniform would strike terror in the hearts of the savages, and they would submit.

"You can't trust 'em, Colonel," Buck protested. "They'll lift your scalp like pickin' a plum, if they have a chance."

"I wasn't born yesterday, Jenkins," Embree assured him.

Buck persisted. "They're wearin' thin, Colonel. They got water from a spring, true, but not much food. 'Long about now they'll be disagreein' and thinkin' of ways to surrender. Let me treat with 'em. I'm an old hand with Injuns. Besides," he added as clincher, "I know their real leader. It ain't that old man from the reservation. It's that renegade, Francisco Boneu, whose mother owns a big ranch down in our valley. He's been causing us trouble for years. I've been after him for years, and I've got him now. Let me come along and bring my boy, here," introducing Goodly. "He knows Injuns like his catechism. Speaks Spanish like they do. An' he's a vet'ran of the service, too." Buck didn't specify which service. "Licked the Apaches in New Mexico Territory like I done the greasers in ol' Mexico herself. With us present, the savages will know we settlers are in on this final settlement, same as you are."

Embree was favorably impressed with this wisdom. "Come along, then. Let's go."

The three marched out into open ground between the two lines, an aide holding a white flag of truce on a pole beside them, and Embree spoke through the speaking trumpet he had brought for this purpose. "Francisco Boneu and Chief Halashu, I am Colonel Embree. I invite you to a peace parley when the sun is at high noon tomorrow, here, where I'm standing. Three of us will come unarmed. Three of you will come unarmed. We will meet under a flag of truce and will make peace, and you will go home unharmed, with no reprisals, no more bloodshed. Food, blankets, and gifts and security will be waiting for you at the reservation. If you do not accept my offer, I am prepared to cannonade your positions. Therefore, it is in your best interest to make peace while you are still alive. Boneu, I speak especially to you, since I'm told you understand English perfectly."

His voice echoed arrogantly among the silent rocks of the stronghold, and again there was no answer.

Then Embree let Goodly repeat his offer in Spanish. Still no answer.

Buck congratulated Embree afterward. "You were dead right to threaten 'em with cannonballs, Colonel. If there's one thing Injuns fear, it's a cannon. They'll come to parley tomorrow. You watch!"

That night the debate in the stronghold was heated. Tagich and his supporters wanted to fight on. Francisco wanted to negotiate. "Painful as it may be, it is our best choice."

Halashu wavered. "We have our women and children to think about."

Francisco agreed, but argued further. "All the good will, all public support we may have created among the A-alowow by being deserving of justice, may disappear, if we fight on. We have made our point. We can submit with good grace. All but myself."

"And why not you?" Halashu cried.

"Because it is too late for me. But not for you. And not for my son."

"But how can I submit and not you?" cried the valiant old warrior. While Halashu wavered, Tagich and his supporters executed a clever maneuver. Two of them suddenly seized and held old Halashu while a third draped women's clothing over him, crying in front of all the council: "We need a man to lead us, not a woman!" While Halashu struggled, smarting under this trick, others joined in heaping derision. At last, despite Francisco's vehement protests, shaking himself free, he declared: "I agree. Let us fight on."

"You've made a fatal mistake," Francisco told them all, "and I will have none of it." He knew he would be blamed for whatever happened, that final responsibility would be his, as Embree had indicated. He felt fate moving inexorably forward, taking him and Helek with it.

Next day, after no one appeared to parley with him and Buck and Goodly, Embree grimly ordered the cannonade to begin and to be followed by an all-out attack by infantry and Lindsay's dismounted dragoons. But his solid shot bounced off the rocks, and his shells burst harmlessly among them, doing the People almost no harm while frightening them half to death and killing Tagich who foolishly walked out among the bursting shells to show that his power was greater than theirs and they could not hurt him. When the bombardment ceased and Embree called one last time for a surrender, old Halashu led a straggling procession out of the stronghold.

From the mouth of the cave of the House of the Sun, Francisco and Helek watched them go, for, despite his father's pleas, Helek had refused to join in the surrender. "My place is by your side," he insisted. The others tried to go proudly, but Francisco knew their spirits were broken. They had en-

sion wedged Helek into that pitch-dark niche behind the painting of Kakunupmawa, that secret hiding place his father had shown him years ago.

There, all but sealed up in darkness and débris, he regained consciousness gradually as if from a horrible dream, to smell the acrid powder, the dusty fallen rock, and sense the death.

Peering out, he saw Buck's head and shoulders appear at the entrance hole. Buck was chuckling for the benefit of someone behind him as well as himself. "We got 'im at last, Goodly!" He crawled into the cave, pistol in hand, watching carefully for any sign of life. When there was none, he began to probe the débris with his foot.

"Dead?" Goodly was at the entrance now, his evil face and gloating tone an obscenity to Helek.

"I reckon!" Buck put his pistol in his holster, but probed on with booted foot. "I reckon this here's the end."

Then Helek saw something appalling — a mutilated figure rising from the ruin, one arm hanging useless, taking a flint knife from his hair and grappling with Buck and stabbing him and stabbing again with that long-pointed stone blade. Buck cried out, and the two fell together, locked in each other's embrace.

Helek was about to struggle out to help his father, when, with a cry, Goodly, followed by soldiers, forced his way through the entrance and knelt above the two bodies. "They've done for each other at last!" he heard Goodly mutter gloomily.

Trembling all over with rage and horror, Helek decided to remain quietly where he was, hidden behind the great figure of Kakunupmawa, and, if he lived, he would take his vengeance as best he could.

He didn't know that in the moment of his death Francisco understood that he had struck home and that Ta-ahi and Letke were avenged at last.

But Helek did sense that the ancient web was broken, once and for all time. After long hours of hiding, stretching into days and nights which only one of his fortitude and conditioning could have endured, he emerged when all whites had left the great ridge top in silence and loneliness again, emerged from the rubble and slipped away into the wilderness to begin his solitary search for survival, for freedom, and a new identity.

Chapter Fifty

Dismounting from his white mule that same day, O'Hara handed Clara the letter. She saw it was from Sedley. "More bad news? That's all I hear these days."

"Each day is a work of God, *Tía* Clara."

"But sometimes I wish He would quit work!"

The letter felt heavy. Opening it, Clara read the first line and burst out joyfully: "My title to the ranch has been confirmed at last!" She read rapidly, excitedly, until the final lines. There her eyes stopped.

It is better protection for your interests, *Tía* Clara, as well as for legal and tax purposes, that you now transfer title to my name. There's no need for you to be troubled by all the fuss and expense attendant upon an official survey, now that your title has been confirmed — likewise all the bother and costs of a suit of ejectment against the squatters, who now have no further rights. I will see to everything. There is much cause for rejoicing. The moral title will, of course, remain in your hands.

Devotedly,

Eliot

She read those last lines again with sinking feelings of horror and despair. They seemed a final blow. The ranch that was dearer to her than life seemed to be slipping from under her as if the ground were caving in. **Moral title will, of course, remain in your hands.** She had suspected it. Now it had actually happened. A great sob of despair broke from her.

Her life's work seemed ended.

"What is it, my dear?" asked O'Hara with concern.

She handed him the letter. When O'Hara finished reading, he looked away at the hills across the river, then back at her. "I did not think he would do this." His tone said more than his words.

"I did. He's a monster, Father, a clever, rapacious monster, a true representative of the white men who've flocked into our land and devoured it . . . devoured me and mine as they've devoured so many others. Let me pronounce a curse upon them!"

O'Hara held up a cautionary hand. He could see Clara was on the verge of becoming hysterical. But she waved his hand aside. "Let me pronounce a curse with you as witness. Let me prophesy this land they've raped and devoured will one day rise in revolt against the white men!"

She took back the letter and slapped it with the tips of the fingers of her other hand, as if it might be Sedley. She was shaking all over with something beyond ordinary emotion, something almost epiphanic, from another state of consciousness, O'Hara thought, so that her old body vibrated with strength and truth and seemed young again. "Come, let us sit down and discuss this matter," he proposed. But she seized his hand in both of hers and, appealing with her face, her heart, she asked: "Why is there evil?"

He shook his head gently while pressing her hands in return. "The devil is as deathless as God. Aren't they both central to the great drama of our existence?"

"But I'm weary of such drama!" she almost shrieked.

"No," he said quietly, "I don't think you are. Come, let's sit down and reason together."

She shook her head. "I've reasoned enough. I think it's time for me to go. I feel like an old leaf ready to drop." She tore up the letter and let it fall to the courtyard in shreds like leaves. "I feel it's time for me to go, and make way for something new." She spoke despairingly, wondering how Sally might carry on the ranch without her as its "moral owner." Sedley's use of the word moral seemed particularly despicable.

"That's doesn't sound like you," O'Hara soothed, increasingly concerned at her agitated state. "Where is that faith I know so well, that patience which is like Job's?"

"Gone, Father!" She spoke with bitter disillusion. "Gone like my ranch, like the flesh and blood of my people . . . gone like my husband, my son, my grandson Helek, gone into the earth, into the air. And now I must go, too!"

"Wait a little. Your son is still alive. So is his son. This terrible war may end any day."

"Do you realize they were coming to see me?" she almost shouted at him as the pent-up thought burst out. "Coming in peace with a remaining fragment of my people, to take refuge with me, here in my Indianada, when this murderous business overtook them and began devouring them . . . there at our sacred shrine at the House of the Sun? Imagine," she demanded of him, "imagine them to be in one of your churches, your cathedrals . . . yes, even in Holy Jerusalem at a most sacred shrine, and beset there by these voracious A-alowow . . . these Sedleys . . . they are all Sedleys no matter what their names . . . beset and finally devoured. No, I am done praying," she went on, "done believing!" She flung up both hands, as if throwing off a great weight, then she rested them gently on O'Hara's shoulders, for she truly loved him and did not want to hurt him. "Now leave me, Father. Please leave me. I wish to be alone with my sorrow."

Seeing she was deeply in earnest, he thought it best to shrug as if it was no great matter. Taking her hand, lifting it to his lips, he kissed it, then, turning, went to his mule, remounted, and rode back down the valley, passing old Abe who was coming up the road slowly on foot from the cabins.

They greeted each other politely yet warily. There was still no great trust between them and their opposing faiths. Then Abe continued toward the hacienda, preoccupied with his thoughts.

Moments later two ancient adversaries faced each other at the courtyard gate. Abe held his battered leather hat in his hand. His face was somber. "Lady Clara, prepare yourself. I bring bad news."

She met the gravity of his look. "It can't be worse than I've just heard. Go on."

But when he told her what had finally happened at the House of the Sun, she gave a piercing cry as if mortally wounded. "My son killed your son?"

He echoed less stridently, but no less piercingly: "My son killed your son," and added: "Do you reckon it's enough, reckon it makes us even? I do."

But this blow, coming after the one O'Hara had just delivered, left Clara almost without breath, almost without life. In a strange voice he hardly recognized, Abe heard her whisper, as tears clouded her eyes: "And my son's son?" Not quite understanding, Abe nodded in agreement with her grief rather than her words, and she surmised the worst.

"So they killed each other!" She whispered the words to herself as if in reverie, sounding remote, detached. "It was fated. Perhaps since that day you first arrived here so long ago, my old friend, it was fated."

He spit and twisted his hat and replied thoughtfully, contemplating the distance. "I reckon mebbe so. Mebbe I felt it in my bones. But never in my heart, lady. Never in my heart! I reckon it was a great pity, ma'am. I'd give a lot for it not to have happened. I reckon you know that?"

356

She put out a hand and touched him, for the first time realizing he, too, had been terribly bereaved, terribly pained, but was standing there bravely. "Old friend, old enemy, I know . . . I know. We've done the best we could. Now let's step aside, leaving the way open for others."

A tear appeared in each of his rheumy old eyes. Keeping them both on hers, he said simply: "Lady, you're hard to beat. I always said you was. I always will say it."

He took her hands in his, squeezed them, turned silently away.

Clara watched him disappear. Then she lifted her eyes to the promontory above her, site of the sacred shrine which had overlooked her and her home all her life. That shrine where she once saw Francisco and Helek, had overseen her dreams, her sorrows, her joys, this moment. "It's time," she said softly to herself. "It is time." Instinctively she turned and looked across the valley to the rounded hilltop with the solitary oak at its summit under which Antonio lay buried. "It is time, my husband. It is time."

Sally, attracted by her piercing cry, came out while she was still talking to Abe, but remained at a distance. Now, as Clara started up the hillside toward the shrine on the top of the bluff, up the ancient trail where Tilhini and others before him had led their people each December at the time of the winter solstice to worship at the shrine, Sally sensed something profoundly momentous and ran forward and said with concern: "*Mama Grande*, let me go with you!"

Clara shook her head without looking aside. She was afraid that, if she looked, her resolution would break. "No, daughter. This is a walk I must take alone. But remember, you are my daughter," she rasped in a hoarse whisper, "in every way!"

Hearing the desperation and grief in her words, Sally decided to respect them.

Slowly Clara climbed the hillside alone. Its fragrance came to her like life's breath: the cool damp mothering earth, the sage, the tree leaves, flowers here and there — last farewells to spring, golden yarrow, and delicate maidenhair fern. *All are witnesses*, she thought. *All are witnesses like I am.* She seemed to be ascending through all life to a culmination.

The sun beat down directly on the promontory with its sacred ring of stones, red-tipped pole in the middle with tuft of condor feathers hanging from it, frayed and weathered like herself. She lifted her face to the sun, opened her arms wide, embraced it all — all life, all experience, past and future, and so stood for some time in silence.

Then she sat down and prepared to wait. As the sun descended toward the sea and the day began to die, she would let her life go, too, and, while waiting, she thought of Antonio and that moment they had first met, the valley shining with summer beauty, opening its arms toward the sea, and the newly arrived white men camped there at its shore, and all the People marching toward them singing as one person, to welcome these strangers as benefactors and brothers. A sob caught at her throat as she remembered Antonio with his yellow hair, astride his great brown four-legged animal such as she'd never seen before, she thinking horse and man one creature, she nevertheless stepping forward boldly from among the others and presenting him her most precious possession — that battered silver buckle her father obtained in trade from a Mojave and gave to her; and Antonio looking down at her in amusement and delight, she just a slip of a thing, he so handsome. She remembered their first love making, after swimming together naked, on the warm sandy bank beside the river that was and remained the Tears of the Sun, shed for their benefit and for all humankind. She remembered the miracle of their shared flesh, so filled with joy, and their shared spirit with its dream, present there already like a tiny unborn child, of the union of races and cultures they embodied — a dream they would spread through all their valley, all their world. And she remembered them, later, taking possession of this land, their ranch, with such high hope, walking around over it, picking up handfuls of soil and stones, and letting them fall back upon the earth in the traditional way, while breaking twigs and declaring to the surrounding air and to high heaven that this place was theirs — this place now stolen from her.

The sorrow and pity of it almost overwhelmed her, as she thought of the birth of their only child after her long years of barrenness and many prayers; the high hopes they'd had for Francisco — his rebellious, prodigal, unhappy self and now tragic end; and with him that remnant of their people, including the lovely bright lad, his son — her last remaining seed for she thought of Pacifico as already dead. She burst out aloud in despair: "That's what life is . . . an inevitable killing, on and on and on!" — and she thought of how she herself shot her own brother to death those long years ago at the moment he killed Antonio with his arrow. More blood. More death. And aloud wearily: "So go all my dreams, all my efforts, all my strengths!"

The sun was nearly down. She felt her life ebbing. She willed it to go, dying with the day, down with the sun over the edge of the world toward something else, yes, toward something else. Her last look was across at the hilltop where Antonio lay buried.

She would lie beside him there, as Sally had promised.

At first Sally thought it best for Clara to be alone with her sorrow, but, at dusk, growing worried when the old woman did not return, she climbed to the top of the bluff and found her. She was lying inside the ring of stones, face down upon the earth, arms outstretched as if to embrace it.

Sally knelt in the half light and tears fell on Clara and the earth. "You were my mother," she whispered, "my true mother."

Chapter Fifty-One

"Morally questionable? Why was it morally questionable?" Sedley had come down for the funeral service, and afterwards was discussing right and wrong, life and death, with O'Hara as matter-of-factly as if they were merely details of a business transaction. "It was all in her best interests," Sedley continued. "She could never have kept possession of the ranch without my help. Look around. How many native Californians, Indian or otherwise, male or female, have held onto their *ranchos?* You can count them on your fingers. No" — he smiled with genial persuasiveness — "it could never have happened without my help. She had the use, the enjoyment of this beautiful place until the end . . . and now Sally and Pacifico can do likewise as long as they live, so far as I'm concerned. Why is that morally questionable?"

They were sitting on the verandah where Clara and O'Hara so often had sat, overlooking the garden that she had loved. Across the valley on the hilltop she was lying in peace, at last beside her beloved Antonio.

O'Hara marveled at the effrontery, the unscrupulousness — or was it merely the unabashed pragmatism? — of this man beside him. "Have you discussed the matter with Sally and Pacifico?"

"No, but I intend to. The ranch will be theirs in all but name. I want it to continue as I first knew it. I want it preserved unspoiled. To that end I engaged in necessary subterfuge because I knew Clara would never accept outright largesse. Yet she never could have afforded . . . never could have managed alone . . . an outcome both she and I very much wanted. So, you see, in a roundabout way, her desire has been achieved."

Roundabout way. To Sedley it had been, O'Hara realized, no great moral issue, simply an intricate business deal. He was both amazed and dismayed, not quite convinced, not quite doubting. "Why do you keep it in your name?"

"You know Pacifico as well as I." Sedley lowered his voice confidentially. "He'd lose it in five minutes, maybe ten. As for her alleged other grandson, even if he's alive, what chance would he have, owning a property like this?"

O'Hara knew Sedley was right.

"Do you agree, then?" Sedley pressed gently.

O'Hara was about to when Sally and Pacifico joined them, somber-faced. From inside the house behind them came sounds of women weeping and from the Indianada below rose the poignant death wail. Clara was being mourned in two ways, by two faiths, two cultures. It would have pleased her, O'Hara thought. Deeming it best to put the best face on what was inevitable, he said: "Sit down, you two, and hear what your Uncle Eliot has just told me."

As Sedley told them, their minds' eyes were opened wide as O'Hara's had been. Sally was first to react, bridling: "You mean we'll be living here as your guests, at your pleasure? I don't like it!"

"Would you prefer not to live here, then?" Sedley inquired mildly. "Would you prefer to leave the ranch? I thought Clara wanted you and Pacifico to have it and love it as she did?"

Sally saw the dilemma and was silent, but to Pacifico there was no dilemma. "Of course, Uncle Eliot, we accept with gratitude. We know she would want us to remain. What would she . . . what would we . . . have done without you? Your solicitude, your generosity, have been boundless!"

Sally sickened at such groveling. "There must be some catch to it. It don't feel right." She was torn between the humiliation of Sedley's proposal and the thought that, indeed, Clara would want her, want them, to continue — at least to play for time and see what developed. *You are my true daughter.* The words came back and sank home. "But I'll do it," she said at last. "I'll do it for Clara's sake."

She could hardly bear the thought of spending the rest of her days with Pacifico, but resolved, there and then, to try and do so for the sake of the woman she had loved and admired more than any other in the world, and for the sake of the ranch which she loved almost as much as Clara had. She proudly wore the belt with the silver buckle Clara had given her. Pacifico had never asked for it back. O'Hara and Sedley and others had accepted without comment Sally's wearing of the belt as part of a general transition, part of Clara's legacy, part of an intimate relationship that was none of their business.

Sedley smiled his approving smile that meant a deal was satisfactorily concluded. "It's agreed, then?" He looked from one to the other. "And Father O'Hara is witness? I wish Victoria were here. When she comes home, we'll avail ourselves of the extra bedroom from time to time as we have in the past. But operations will be entirely in the hands of you two." He turned to O'Hara. "Will you put your blessing on it, Father Michael? I'm sure Clara would like that."

Somewhat reluctantly, yet for Clara's sake, too, O'Hara put his blessing on this sublime fraud, this masterfully immoral, yet apparently highly moral, hoax, this grand charade which was so typically Sedley's.

Chapter Fifty-Two

"May the sky fall on that son-of-a-bitch!" Iphy declared about Sedley. But she held steady as Elmer and Opal set fire to the cabins. All their belongings were loaded on the two waiting wagons. All their right and title to their claims, their years of work and hope, vanished with the court's decision, confirming title in the ranch to Clara and, thus, to Sedley. And thus the Jenkins family was on the move again, headed for a new home somewhere, all their possessions, all their dreams, all their hatreds, going along.

In the foggy early morning darkness — for the sea fog was deep inland this morning, casting a shroud of additional gloominess over all that was happening — they moved out slowly, heading up the valley toward the wilderness, not looking back, not wanting to see what was happening behind them, keeping eyes toward the future.

Sally saw the strange procession coming through the mist, saw the strange glow made by the burning cabins in the darkness behind, ran out to discover what was happening. After all, these were her people, her flesh and blood. During all the years of conflict, overt and covert, that bond of blood and flesh was one she never could break, even if — with the exception of Abe and Iphy — they never could quite forgive her defection to the hacienda.

"Where you going? What's happening?" she cried as she approached the old wagons, their frayed and faded canvas hoods up once again as if crossing the plains, livestock following, horses, cattle, sheep. There were pigs and chickens in crates on the wagons. Iphy drove the first one, Opal the second. Elmer and the children herded the stock behind. Abe was seated beside Iphy. "Granpa, what's up," Sally cried in consternation, seizing the old man's hand, while Iphy drew rein but kept her face straight ahead. It was hard for her to look aside for even a moment, now that their mind was made up, their purpose set, and the fire was blazing behind them. Sally sensed this as she persisted. "Where are you headed, Gramps?"

"Into the hills, Granddaughter."

"Why so?"

"To find us a new home."

"There ain't no road."

"We'll make one."

"You crazy?" she cried in disbelief.

"No, this here's just one more bend in the trail, Granddaughter. We ain't got to the end yet. There's land in them hills ain't nobody claimed." He motioned ahead. "Land no man, no court, nobody on earth can take from us, I reckon. Yeap, we'll find us a place an' put down roots where there ain't no Mister Sedley, no *Señora* Sally" — he spoke kindly, yet frankly, from a certain distance — "to hinder us." There was a space between them, a whole chasm opening, she realized. She felt almost as if he had struck her.

The cabins were flaming and crackling, shedding an eerie light on the valley. From hacienda and Indianada came cries of alarm.

"Get a move on, up there!" Elmer shouted from the rear of the stalled procession. Since Buck's death, followed by Goodly's, Elmer had taken charge.

Goodly's body had been found at the river crossing midway between cabins and hacienda, a stab wound through the heart, the print of a bare human foot in the sand beside it, left there like a kind of signature. No one knew who had killed Goodly, but many, including Elmer, thought it was that wild Indian son of Francisco's, now widely known to have been with his father in that last battle at the House of the Sun and to have disappeared, where no one knew.

Abe looked down at his beloved Sally. He had always cared, always supported her. "So long, Granddaughter!"

But she caught at his hands and at Iphy's which held the reins of the mules. "Speak to me, Iphy. Why did you let 'em do it? You could have stayed on forever, far as I'm concerned!"

"We're not like some," Iphy sniffed, head in air. "We got our pride." She knew that Sally had had to give up some of hers in order to submit to Sedley's will. "We ain't willing to accept charity. And now, Granpa," she added with regal dignity, "if you're through speech-i-fyin', we'll move along."

They would be going through the ranch. Sally had the right to stop them, but she would not exercise it. They had some inalienable right to go where they were going, to try and find a new place to live.

She stood back. "Good luck," she murmured. And that was all. But she meant it, profoundly sensing all she was losing as well as what they were losing, sensing herself left behind, sensing the distance between them and her henceforward, realizing how alone she was now.

Behind her, scores of others had come to watch in silence or with excited outcries, her people, now that she was *Señora* Boneu, mistress of the hacienda.

She heard Pacifico's whining voice asking her what was happening, as if he couldn't figure it out, but she could, and she snapped — "You wouldn't understand!" — and turned away, tears in her eyes, but admiration mixed with longing and sorrow in her heart.

The two heavily loaded wagons came to a halt at the crest of a promontory above the river. Ahead the cañon opened, golden hills of grass appeared, the land seemed bright.

366

"This here the place, Granpa?" Iphy asked.

The others listened to hear what Abe would say. From time to time over the past miles, they had asked the frail old man that same question. Each time he had looked around, sniffed the air, shaken his head. "No, 't ain't wild enough. Not yet." He wanted to be sure they were beyond the reach of law courts, beyond Sedley's, beyond all boundaries. This time he was silent a long while, looking, feeling. Then he nodded. "Feels right. Feels wild and good. And look ahead!" He pointed. It did look like a promised land, golden with afternoon sunlight, locked away at the heart of the wilderness, nobody apparently claiming it. They did not think of it as Indian heartland, the core of Clara's people's physical and spiritual world, Helek its only remaining occupant. They saw no tracks, no sign. The land seemed wholly empty, wholly lost and waiting to be found.

"Go to it!" Abe's voice rang out with conviction. "Go find us a way. This'll be our place. Yeap," he added, looking around again, smelling the wildness, the sense of newness that came from the first red-barked manzanita, the first thorny back-country chaparral and spiny yucca, the more pungent grass and the first pines. "This here's the place."

Elmer took his axe and went ahead on foot to cut a way toward it, while young Abe and Opaline, horseback, helped by the two dogs, held the livestock in place behind the wagons. Iphy and Abe in their driver's seat, and Opal behind them on hers, kept wagons and mules where they were.

"I'm gettin' stiff," Abe announced after a bit, "gonna stretch." Iphy looked at him with sudden concern. Something in his voice, his manner, didn't seem right. "You take your asafetida yet?"

"You saw me."

"You feel sick?"

"Feel fine, jus' stiff. Jus' stiff in my back an' legs." He didn't mention the breathlessness, the pain in his chest.

She wasn't quite convinced but watched him get down and go off, tottering once, toward a patch of tall, green, rod-like, water-loving arrowweed that grew strangely alone on this slope high above the rushing river. The idea crossed her mind that she had never married Buck but this old man himself, they were so close in spirit. Sometimes it seemed that Buck, dead so recently, had really been dead to her for years. And in a way, she admitted to herself much as she hated to, this was true of Goodly, too. She had deplored them in life as she deplored them in death. She could hear the water rushing in the gorge below. From ahead came the ring of an axe. A primordial thrill of satisfaction ran through Iphy. Her son was cutting a trail for her. She was again the matriarch, mother of pioneers. Her spirit swelled as it hadn't in years. She felt young, ready again.

When she looked around for Abe, he was standing breast deep among the rod-like arrowweed, gazing toward that promised land ahead. He, too, must have felt it speaking to him, even if he was just taking a pee. Yes, he too must be feeling young again. That really was why he'd gotten down from the wagon. To go and get a better look. But as she looked again, something about the way he was standing slumped in the weeds alarmed her. Tying the reins firmly to the seat, calling back to Opal to watch things, she dismounted and went to see.

As she drew near, she said softly: "Granpa?" But he didn't answer.

She knew he was dead before she touched him, dead, standing braced upright by the stiff weeds, dead with eyes fixed like Moses's on a promised land he'd found but was never destined to enter, dead at last — she could hardly think of it all, it was so much, so vast an expanse, so big with meaning, too, from his initial trip into the West as a youth with Lewis

368

and Clark to the mouth of the Columbia, deserting, solitary pathfinding against all odds and obstacles down to California, penetrating this very wilderness, discovering the Valley of Santa Lucia. "Why, he must have passed right through here," she said aloud. "He must have known where he was a-taking us all the time! Didn't you, Granpa?" she asked through tears, speaking as if he were alive, propped there in the stiff arrow-weed. She took the old body in her arms and cuddled it tenderly one last time, and spoke to it again. "You was great, Granpa. You inspired us all, give us strength when we was lowly, knocked us down when we was uppity, counseled us wisely when we was crazy. And you led us here. You led us home at last."

Opal was calling from the wagons. "What's happened, Mama?"

"Nothing much," Iphy replied stoutly. "Granpa's just died, that's all. Come help me. We'll start diggin' his grave. He always said, bury me standin' up. An' I promised I would. Said he never in his life" — Iphy was talking to the sky, the hills, the world, her eyes blinded by tears — "looked up to any man, and didn't want to start after he was dead."

Elmer was coming back to them through the trees, calling that he'd found a way. The going would be tough, but they could make it.

Author's Note

I could not have written this book without the help of Sandy McDonald, Jackie Collier, Mariette Risley, Clinton Cox, Vicki Piekarski, and Jon Tuska among many others including librarians at the Huntington Library, the Bancroft Library, the California State Library, and the Santa Barbara Public Library.

Among many sources consulted for background material for my fictional narrative, particularly helpful were THE ELUSIVE EDEN by Richard B. Rice, William A. Bullough, and Richard J. Orsi; AMERICANS AND THE CALIFORNIA DREAM: 1850-1915 by Kevin Starr; ARMY LIFE IN A BLACK REGIMENT by Thomas Wentworth Higginson; also William Preston Johnston's LIFE OF GEN. ALBERT SIDNEY JOHNSTON, Lloyd Lewis's SHERMAN: FIGHTING PROPHET, Alfred Bigelow Paine's MARK TWAIN: A BIOGRAPHY, and Carl Sandburg's ABRAHAM LINCOLN: THE WAR YEARS.

But nowhere have I found the answer to a perplexing question that today would make headlines and be featured on prime-time television news: why were black soldiers excluded from the Grand Review of Union armies in Washington, D. C. on May 23-24, 1865? Historians who've researched it for years tell me they've found no answer to this question loaded with racial overtones. Since the decision to exclude blacks from what amounted to a national victory celebration must have been made at the highest level, given the momentousness of the occasion, I have attributed it fictively to President Andrew Johnson. If I do Johnson an injustice, I hereby apologize to him and his descendants. As for the more than two hundred thousand blacks then serving in uniform, perhaps an apology of another sort is due.

R. E.

About the Author

Robert Easton was born in San Francisco, California. In one way or another all of his work has been centered on the history and people of the American West. His first great critical and popular success was THE HAPPY MAN (1943), a portrait of California ranch life in the late 1930s. *The New York Times Book Review* said of it, "Good writing of a kind that is difficult and rare," and *The New Yorker* stated that it has "a clear narrative style and a sure sense of authenticity." Easton went on to write MAX BRAND: THE BIG "WESTERNER" (1970), a biography of Frederick Faust, and recently with his wife, Jane Faust Easton, edited THE COLLECTED STORIES OF MAX BRAND (1994). After three decades of research, his epic Saga of California began with THIS PROMISED LAND (1982), spanning the years 1769-1850, and is continued in POWER AND GLORY (1989). Since THE HAPPY MAN there can be no doubt of Robert Easton's commitment to the American West as both an idea and as a definite and distinct place. Beyond this, in all of his work he has been guided by his belief in what he once described as a writer's concern for "the living word — the one that captures the essential truth of what he is trying to say — and that is what I have tried to put down." Robert Easton's next **Five Star Western** will continue his Saga of California in DEATH AND RESURRECTION.